DERAILED

ALSO BY LEENA LEHTOLAINEN

DERAILED

A MARIA KALLIO MYSTERY
LEENA LEHTOLAINEN

Translated by Owen F. Witesman

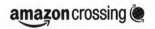

Text copyright © 2008 by Leena Lehtolainen
Translation copyright © 2018 by Owen F. Witesman
All rights reserved.

Previously published as *Väärän jäljillä* by Tammi in Finland in 2008. Translated from Finnish by Owen F. Witesman. First published in English by AmazonCrossing in 2018.

Published by AmazonCrossing, Seattle

www.apub.com

Amazon, the Amazon logo, and AmazonCrossing are trademarks of Amazon.com, Inc., or its affiliates.

ISBN-13: 9781503904491
ISBN-10: 1503904490

Cover design by Ray Lundgren

Printed in the United States of America

For Otso

CAST OF CHARACTERS

THE LAW

Akkila: .... Patrol officer, Espoo PD

Autio, Gideon: .... Detective, Espoo Violent Crime Unit

Grotenfelt, Kirsti: .... Forensic pathologist

Honkanen, Ursula: .... Detective, Espoo VCU

Jarkko: .... Criminologist, Ministry of the Interior

Kaartamo: .... Assistant chief of police, Espoo PD

Kallio, Maria: .... Criminologist, Ministry of the
Interior; Detective Lieutenant, Espoo VCU

Koivu, Pekka: .... Detective, Espoo VCU, Wang's husband

Kuusimäki, Anni: .... Commander, Espoo VCU

Montonen: .... Patrol officer, Helsinki PD

Outi: .... Criminologist, Ministry of the Interior

Perävaara: .... Commander, Helsinki VCU

Puupponen, Ville: .... Detective, Espoo VCU

Puustjärvi, Petri: .... Detective, Espoo VCU

Rajakoski, Mikko: .... Senior inspector, Ministry of the Interior

Rasilainen, Liisa: .... Patrol officer, Espoo PD

Reponen, Katri: .... District prosecutor

Söderholm, Kaide: .... Ballistics expert

Ström, Pertti: .... Detective, Espoo VCU, deceased

Taskinen, Jyrki: .... Director, Espoo Criminal Division

Wang-Koivu, Anu: .... Juvenile Unit, Koivu's wife

THE SPORTS WORLD

Harju, Miikka: .... Office assistant, Adaptive Sports Association

Häkkinen, Satu: .... Secretary, MobAbility

Koskelo, Ilpo: .... Toni Väärä's coach

Litmanen, Hillevi: .... Secretary, Adaptive Sports Association

Ristiluoma, Tapani: .... CEO, MobAbility

Salo, Eero: .... Discus thrower

Särkikoski, Jutta: .... Freelance sports journalist

Terävä, Sami: .... Discus thrower

Väärä, Toni: .... Middle-distance runner

Vainikainen, Merja: .... Director, Adaptive Sports Association

Vainikainen, Pentti: .... Head of Social
Affairs, Finnish Athletics Federation

Vainio, Anneli: .... Accountant, MobAbility

SUPPORTING CAST

Eeva: .... Maria's sister

The Groke: .... Tove Jansson character,
used here as a pseudonym for an abuser

Heikkinen, Eija: .... Tapani Ristiluoma's ex-girlfriend

Hemulen: .... Tove Jansson character,
used here as a pseudonym for an abuser's partner

Juice (Juhani Leskinen): .... Finnish singer-songwriter

Leonardo: .... An anonymous abuse victim

Linnakangas, Jari: .... Mona's father,
Merja's ex-husband

Linnakangas, Mona: .... Merja Vainikainen's daughter

Litmanen, Jouni: .... Hillevi's ex-husband

Ljungberg, Kristian: .... Attorney, Ursula's boyfriend

Marita: .... Antti's sister

Sarkela, Antti: .... Maria's husband

Sarkela, Iida: .... Maria's daughter

Sarkela, Taneli: .... Maria's son

Siudek, Przemyslaw: .... Building cleaner

The Snork Maiden: .... Tove Jansson character,
used here as a pseudonym for an abuse victim

Virtanen-Ruotsi, Leena: .... Maria's friend

Väinölä, Jani: .... Convict

PROLOGUE

The road from Salo to Inkoo was dark, and "Moose Crossing" signs flashed ominously along the shoulder. Freelance sports reporter Jutta Särkikoski drove as slowly as she dared, given the man sitting next to her was in a hurry to get to Helsinki. Jutta had already dropped off the freelance photographer at his home in Kisko, which was why they were taking this route, instead of the freeway, from Turku to Helsinki.

Jutta had been in Turku interviewing the middle-distance runner Toni Väärä and his coach, Ilpo Koskelo, about the young man's incredible breakthrough that summer. Väärä's most successful season to date had just concluded with a win in the 800 meter at an international meet between Sweden and Finland. With a finish time of 1:44:13, he'd launched himself to fifteenth in the world, which had caused quite a sensation.

Everyone wanted to know the secrets behind his sudden success, and so Jutta Särkikoski had successfully pitched an in-depth profile of Väärä to a general-interest magazine. The meeting in Turku, where Väärä currently lived and trained, was just the beginning of her research.

Rain began to beat more violently on the car windows. Jutta didn't waste any time trying to chitchat with Toni Väärä. He was known for being taciturn, like the athletes of bygone eras who responded to reporters' questions humorlessly and as briefly as possible. Landing the interview with Väärä had taken a good deal of effort. Since he had yet to hire a manager, Jutta had been forced to call the Athletics Federation over and over to get his contact information. Jutta would have preferred to interview the runner one-on-one, but Coach Koskelo wouldn't allow it. Then, after all that, they'd canceled and rescheduled several times before meeting.

As luck would have it, Väärä needed a ride to an event one of his sponsors was hosting in Helsinki, and so Jutta volunteered to drive him. Once they dropped off the photographer in Kisko, Jutta hoped that she and Väärä might finally be able to have a private conversation.

In the sporting world, attitudes toward Jutta Särkikoski were mixed. The previous winter, she'd received a hot tip about two promising national-level discus throwers employing fitness-enhancing methods not approved by the antidoping regime. Rumor had it that not only were they using anabolic steroids, they were also dealing. Jutta had checked and rechecked her facts before selling her exposé to one of the tabloids. Despite not revealing her sources, her article was taken seriously. The discus throwers in question—Eero Salo and Sami Terävä— were subsequently caught by a surprise drug test. Their B-samples confirmed the use of banned steroids, and a police raid uncovered a quantity of drugs that indicated an intent to distribute. In addition to being barred from competing, the two athletes were charged with possession of illegal substances and trafficking, though the trafficking indictment was eventually dropped for lack of witnesses.

Jutta received more than just praise for her revelations. Promising track-and-field athletes were few and far between in Finland, and to many, Jutta was a traitor who had cut short two bright careers. The athletes' supporters claimed that everyone was doping—some just had money for drugs that didn't show up in tests. Those who'd heard about the Väärä interview beforehand took it as a sign that his success might be attributed to illegal doping, and his coach's protectiveness did nothing to dispel their doubts.

Suddenly a dark figure appeared in the gloom. A moose? Jutta flinched, and the car made a small swerve. But it was just a person, some fanatic out for a run in the rain. Presumably a kindred spirit of Toni Väärä, who claimed that his success was merely a result of hard training. He hadn't missed a single session in years, regardless of what was falling from the sky. Jutta gave the runner as wide a berth as possible, almost pulling into the left shoulder. The glow of a headlight flashed in the rearview mirror. At the top of the next hill was another "Moose Crossing" sign. Jutta preferred to drive these kinds of roads in the slipstream of a semi, close enough that a moose couldn't get between her car and the truck. Now the road was empty.

Another light appeared in Jutta's rearview mirror, flickering through the rain. As it got closer, Jutta could make out a van approaching at incredible speed. It swerved once, but then the driver regained control. *Just let them pass,* Jutta thought, slowing down to make it as easy as possible for the reckless driver to get by. Only a trace of the solid yellow centerline was visible, but the van stayed to the right of it, slowing down behind Jutta's Renault.

Bam! The van barely tapped the car, but Jutta nearly lost control.

"Oh my God!" she screamed. Toni Väärä turned to look back, but he couldn't see anything beyond the dark-colored vehicle riding their tail. Jutta tried to speed up, but the van kept pace. Then it sped up, pulling up next to them but not passing. Instead, its right-front corner crashed into the left side of the Renault.

"What is this maniac doing?" Jutta screamed, and Toni yelled something too, but they couldn't hear each other because the van had hit them again, sending them careening toward the guardrail. Jutta's attempts to brake were in vain.

Just before losing consciousness, she saw her blood mixing with the gout spurting from Toni's femoral artery.

1

Over the past few months, I'd been having a lot of nightmares. I saw everything I'd experienced in my life: the muzzle of a moose rifle points at my chest, and when it disappears, a mailbox explodes, launching my daughter, Iida, into the air. In some of the dreams it's dark, and I'm climbing a ladder away from the explosion that's about to happen in the mine shaft below. The worst nightmare is the one where a syringe full of cyanide is about to be thrust into my carotid artery, and I can't breathe . . .

That was usually when I woke up, but it took a while before I realized it was only a dream, just memories from my old job, embellished by my imagination. Sometimes I wondered why the nightmares hadn't started until after I'd left policing. Was my psyche not ready to face what could still happen on any given day? It was only in hindsight that I realized I'd been far too deep inside the cases I investigated. As a lead investigator, I should have kept my distance from suspects and instead focused on the big picture. But I'd liked doing interviews and working with people. Maybe the lieutenant and unit commander jobs had been wrong for me from the start. Or maybe I'd been the wrong person for the jobs. Now I felt like I was where I belonged.

The early fall morning I woke up to was sunny. It was ten past six, and the alarm wasn't set to go off until seven thirty. I closed my eyes and tried to relax, but images from the dream continued to flash through my mind. *That's all behind me,* I repeated to myself. *I don't have to do that anymore.*

A few years had passed since I'd resigned from my position in the Espoo Police Department Violent Crime Unit. At the time, my plans for the future had been clear: my friend from law school Leena Virtanen-Ruotsi had received an inheritance from her aunt, and we intended to start a law firm specializing in assisting people with limited means. Leena was a member of the bar, and so I planned to handle all the jobs that didn't require membership. I was slowly recovering from an assault I'd experienced during a murder investigation—I hadn't quite realized what poor shape I was in until after I resigned.

A change of professions seemed like the best possible solution. Once we'd made our decision, Leena and I had been over the moon, and we spent the whole spring and early summer making plans. That all came to a sudden halt when life presented yet another unpleasant surprise.

On the weekend after the Midsummer holiday, Leena was driving to her brother's cabin south of Turku. The rest of the family had gone ahead by bus, but Leena and I had been at a concert, and so she didn't leave Helsinki until nearly midnight. A man who had drained most of a bottle of Koskenkorva vodka before getting behind the wheel had happened to be coming from the opposite direction. Even though Leena tried to swerve, the cars collided. The drunk driver was killed instantly, but Leena lived. That was cold comfort, however. The lower half of my friend's body was paralyzed, necessitating a years-long course of surgeries. From the beginning, she begged me not to build my life around the uncertainty of her recovery. So I was out of a job.

Because I'd left my position voluntarily, I had to wait for my unemployment benefits to kick in, but I had no intention of remaining idle. Soon after the accident, my former boss, Jyrki Taskinen, contacted me. Could he lure me back to the Espoo Police Department, he wanted to know? There was a position open in White-Collar Crime. I laughed at him, good-naturedly of course. I didn't have the qualifications for that kind of investigative work, though I'd gone to law school. And Jyrki should have known that.

Word of our misfortune reached other law school classmates. Expressions of sympathy streamed in for Leena, and I received a call from Mikko Rajakoski, a senior inspector in the Ministry of the Interior, who had started law school the same time we had.

"Hi, Maria. I was just playing squash with Lasse and Kristian."

"Getting the old gang back together, eh?" Lasse Nordström and Kristian Ljungberg had also been my classmates, and I'd even dated Kristian for a while.

"Yep. I hear you're a free woman at the moment. Not working, I mean."

"Yes. Not everyone has the career-ladder climbing skills of Kristian."

"Or Kristian's connections. But it's connections I'm calling you about, because you're exactly the person I need. You worked a lot of domestic violence cases in Espoo, right?"

"Unfortunately."

"Well, the ministry is starting a domestic violence research project. The idea is to study its different forms and then look for effective prevention measures," Mikko said, and then went on for fifteen minutes about how openly talking about violence against children, especially when it is perpetrated by mothers, is socially taboo. Unfortunately, I knew he was right. The investigation of domestic violence had become politicized, sometimes being used by feminist organizations or, alternately, the men's rights activists, specifically when women were the ones who carried it out.

I was well aware of all of this, but I let Mikko talk. For a while I'd been thinking about going back to school for a licentiate degree, and this could provide me with the research data I would need. I asked Mikko if I'd be able to use the results academically, and he didn't see any reason why not. Doing this sort of study now seemed sensible, since domestic violence prevention efforts had only started to gain traction in the late nineties.

So, after being unemployed for just a little while, I went back into service at the Ministry of the Interior, this time as a scientific researcher. I'd be collaborating with a social worker and a psychologist, and we'd be working with the Police University College, the most recent iteration of the old police academy. At the PUC, I was assigned to teach courses on recognizing intimate-partner violence, some for recently graduated cops and some as in-service training for officers further along in their careers. Though the school had changed since my time at the academy, the cafeteria still employed the world's most pleasant cashier, who remembered me too, even after twenty years. To hear others tell it, she remembered all the academy's past students and knew where each had been assigned after graduating.

"I understand you've spent time pursuing other opportunities," she said as she handed me my plate of veggie pasta. "In police work, you shouldn't worry too much. You just have to solve the crimes. It seems you let the stress get to you."

When I gave a confused smile, the cashier said she'd followed my career carefully. As I ate my pasta, I thought about what she'd said. She was probably right. A police detective couldn't stay entirely unemotional, but she had to be impartial, and that was where I'd slipped up far too often. But now my task was to search for patterns in human behavior like any other rigorous scientist. I wouldn't need to interfere in my research subjects' lives; I just had to listen calmly and record data. Still, my old life continued to return to me through nightmares, as if to remind me that I would carry the weight of everything I had experienced for the rest of my life.

My husband, Antti, was still working as a mathematics researcher, having received a three-year fellowship from the Academy of Finland. His current project continued in the same vein of mathematical utopianism he'd pursued in his globalization project at the University of

Vaasa. For the academy, he was working on a multidisciplinary project examining how shifting focus from income taxes to environmental and consumption taxes would affect the Finnish economy. Antti was excited about it.

"I've always thought of mathematics as a political science. Two plus two is always four, but numbers aren't neutral. You can ask who those two and two belong to. Was one of the twos taken from someone with six and the other from someone with only three?" he'd said one day recently as he updated me about the project.

So we both enjoyed our work, and our kids liked that we were both at home nights and weekends. Antti had spent a few years commuting between Vaasa and Espoo while I'd tried to handle my erratic police schedule and childcare. Without my mother-in-law's help, we never would have survived. She had been indispensable in more ways than one: she had also forced Antti and his sister, Marita, to use the inheritance from their father sensibly. With it Antti and I had bought a house. We didn't have a prenup, since when we married it never occurred to us that we'd ever have any assets to fight over. The inheritance had covered half of the purchase, and the rest we financed with savings and a mortgage.

The past two years had been the best time of my life. Maybe a house in a densely populated neighborhood in Espoo, Finland, wasn't paradise, but we had good public transportation to both of our jobs and the elementary school. A few weeks ago Taneli had started first grade, which met for half the day, and Antti and I had been taking turns coming home early from work. Iida was in fifth grade, and the early symptoms of puberty were already appearing. Maybe this would be our last peaceful winter.

September had been warm so far. The forests were full of mushrooms, and violets still bloomed in the yard. And nightmares were just nightmares, memories of a past life.

Though I had over an hour before the alarm went off, I realized that I was wide awake. Our cat, Venjamin, had also sensed this. Soon he would crawl off my feet and pad into the kitchen to meow for food. I decided to get up and go for a run.

The thermometer outside the kitchen window read eight degrees Celsius. A few leaves had already turned red on the maple tree in the yard, even though September was only half over. I made and drank a cup of white coffee, fed the cat, stretched a bit, and then went outside to the brisk morning. I started to jog at an easy pace.

Leena still wasn't walking, but she hadn't completely given up hope. I thought of her almost every time I went out for a run. My own steps weren't as light as they had been when I was twenty, but a three-and-a-half-mile wake-up jog still only took me a little more than half an hour. I didn't even try to keep pace with the two men in front of me, who were a couple of decades younger and nearly a foot taller than me.

When I got home, Taneli was already out of bed. He had morning ice skating twice a week, and he tended to wake up early on days he didn't have practice too. Even though Iida grumbled about having to be seen with her little brother, she walked with Taneli to school. I ate a hearty breakfast with the kids, and then we all left together. Antti jumped on the bus to Otaniemi, and I headed for downtown Helsinki. The ministry had rented us offices on the main railway station square, which felt luxurious for a person whose view at her previous workplace was the Turku Highway.

I loped up the stairs to the fourth floor. Inside I caught the scent of coffee: my colleagues, Outi and Jarkko, had already arrived. I shouted good morning and went into my own office. A silly picture of Iida and Taneli stared at me from the desk. It had been taken in Vimmerby, Sweden, at a theme park celebrating Astrid Lindgren's stories. I'd passed along my love of Pippi Longstocking to my kids. They'd posed as Ida and Emil, the prankster brother and well-behaved sister from another of the famous Swedish author's series. When I took the picture, Taneli had still been a towhead, but now his hair was starting to darken.

My own hair was longer than it had been at any other time in my adult life, flowing down well past my shoulder blades. I only did it up when I was going for extra credibility, which I didn't need to do every day in my current job. A researcher could look bohemian, but a detective lieutenant had to hide behind formality. The previous week I'd visited the hairdresser, and the gray strands that had appeared in the red were hidden again for the time being. The laugh lines around my eyes had deepened, and I still had freckles from the summer sun. Every year my nose seemed to turn up a little more. Good: at least one part of my body was defying gravity.

I put the *salmiakki* licorice I'd bought at a newsstand to keep my spirits up in a drawer and opened my e-mail. As usual, messages were waiting from two of our research subjects, who called themselves Leonardo and the Snork Maiden to maintain their anonymity. Early on in the project, we'd fished for material and subjects every way possible. Some of our contacts came through the police and social services, and others managed to find us on their own. Because the research was confidential, we didn't try to discover the real identities of the people sending the messages. Some people told us their real names, some didn't—we left the choice up to them. At first that had been hard for me, because as a police detective, I'd been used to intervening, but gradually I'd learned to accept that I wasn't responsible for my research subjects.

Outi, Jarkko, and I had engaged in lengthy discussions about whether we could trust anonymous sources, ultimately deciding to separate material from them in its own section of the study. We were interested in why people wanted to remain anonymous, since it was precisely the invisibility of domestic violence that we hoped to examine. Jarkko, ever the realist, ensured that we never developed any illusions about our ability to put an end to such an intractable evil, but every little increase in our understanding could make the world a better place.

I'd deduced that the Snork Maiden was a teenage girl who had been abused repeatedly. She told me that she'd found the project through a brochure distributed at her school. I'd tried to get her to talk to the school welfare officer about her experiences, but she didn't want to.

The e-mail began, as the Snork Maiden's messages usually did, with a description of what she'd last read. The Snork Maiden liked violent books, especially ones based on real life. They were probably a kind of therapy for her, because the people in them were having an even worse time than she was. Then she came to the point, which was what her family member she called the Groke had done this time. Along with the Snork Maiden and the Groke, a person nicknamed Hemulen also lived in the home but was frequently away. Sometimes it seemed that the Groke was the Snork Maiden's father and Hemulen a stepmother, but sometimes I suspected that Hemulen was an adult sibling or the mother's boyfriend, and that the mother was the Groke. I wasn't even entirely sure of the Snork Maiden's gender. Based on the name, I'd assumed she was female, but there was no way to know for sure.

> I was home alone with the Groke. I tried to stay quiet in my room and write my history paper. Hemulen hasn't been around for a couple of days. He's probably out of the country for work. The Groke is always in a better mood then. That's why she surprised me.
>
> I'd just done the wash and was ironing the Groke's and Hemulen's pillowcases when the Groke came into the laundry room. The Groke hates wrinkled sheets, and you have to iron the pillowcases because she doesn't think the wringer makes them straight enough or something. She always has a reason. I'm afraid of the wringer. When I was a little

kid, the Groke said that it would suck my fingers in if I wasn't careful with it. I imagined my fingers getting squashed like a pancake and coming out all stretched. In one of our schoolbooks there was a picture of a painting with clocks that were sort of melted, and I thought they'd been through the wringer.

The Groke seemed to be in a bad mood, and the Groke and a hot iron in the same room is a bad thing. Extremely bad. Of course, she found a reason to complain: I'd washed her hundred-euro green shirt with the whites too hot, and now it was all fuzzy and linty. I didn't see any lint. She was making shit up again. I realized that I had to unplug the iron fast, but I wasn't fast enough. Even though I'm bigger than the Groke, she's stronger. She grabbed my wrist and started pushing the hot iron toward my face. It was so close to my skin I could feel its heat, and then suddenly I let go of it and pivoted, pushing the Groke. She was surprised enough that I got away. I locked myself in Hemulen's office, because the Groke won't dare break that door. She says that Hemulen won't believe me if I tell, and that it wasn't Hemulen's business anyway.

I'd received a couple of dozen e-mails from the Snork Maiden, each more chilling than the last. Sometimes I thought I'd have to figure out who she really was. It was irresponsible to leave her alone with the Groke—judging by her e-mails, the Snork Maiden was in mortal danger.

The first message had come just after Christmas. The Snork Maiden must have been looking for somewhere to talk about what she was experiencing, because our project hadn't done any advertising since early the previous fall. We already had plenty of material by that point.

In some of her e-mails, the Snork Maiden said the Groke and sometimes Hemulen had threatened to send her away because they thought she was crazy. I wasn't a psychiatric professional, so I couldn't make a diagnosis, but it seemed likely that the Snork Maiden's neuroses were a reaction to her environment. She talked about her compulsion to always sit with her back toward the wall and how she detested anything with holes in it. She couldn't eat Swiss cheese or watch porridge bubbling. Each time I replied, I asked her to contact me using her real name if she wanted help. She hadn't yet done so, and I had to remind myself that my job in this project wasn't to do police work.

The message from Leonardo wasn't any more comforting. Like Snork Maiden, he sent his message from a server that didn't allow me to trace his identity. I wasn't completely sure of his gender either, or his age, though he was clearly a young person. Leonardo's latest stepfather—he seemed to be the third so far—abused him sexually. Leonardo wrote that when he had told his mother, she accused him of lying. Yesterday the stepfather had come into Leonardo's room and forced him to perform oral sex.

I felt like retching as I read Leonardo's e-mail. I wondered for a moment whether it would be unprofessional to tell a research subject that I knew exactly how horrible it feels to be raped. I decided it would be. I tried to craft my words to encourage Leonardo to contact either me or the police.

> No one has the right to treat you that way or to call you a liar. You are a valuable human being. I know a lot of police officers, so if you tell me where you live, I can find the right person for you to contact.

> And you can contact me between nine and five at this e-mail or the phone number below. We can help you, Leonardo, and your stepfather will get the punishment he deserves.

I considered that last line for a long time, because sex offenders often received outrageously light sentences.

I also knew how difficult it was to recount being victimized like that. Every interview and court proceeding requires reliving the attack again and again. With that thought a bitter, salty taste rose to the roof of my mouth. Sometimes my memory for tastes and smells was *too* good. I tossed a salmiakki skull in my mouth and savored the licorice flavor, trying to think about something else. I read a couple of other e-mails and called a phone number provided by another contact. That ended up taking the rest of the morning.

I'd arranged to meet Leena for lunch. For the first two years after the accident, she'd only traveled from home to the rehabilitation center and back. I visited her whenever I had time. During the last year, she'd started venturing out into the city again, even though getting around Helsinki in a wheelchair was difficult to say the least. Fortunately, the Ateneum Art Museum had an elevator, and her wheelchair fit at the tables in the restaurant with a minimum of rearranging.

After we got settled, I went to assemble a salad for her at the buffet. Leena was in a better mood than she had been in ages, and I quickly learned why.

"I got a job," she announced. "I've had enough of disability leave."

"Wow! Where?"

"At the Adaptive Sports Association!" Leena said, grinning widely. "I'm going to be their part-time lawyer. Mostly I'll get to work from home. Jutta tipped me off about the open position. Have I mentioned Jutta? I met her at the physical therapy center."

I realized immediately whom Leena meant. That name had been in all the papers after Jutta Särkikoski had been disabled in a car accident the year before. Apparently, Jutta believed that the collision wasn't really an accident and that someone had wanted to intimidate her, maybe even silence her altogether. I remembered that one of Finland's best hopes for the Beijing Olympics, the middle-distance runner Toni Väärä, had also been injured in the accident. According to reports, he didn't remember anything about it or the preceding car ride. Some maliciously speculated that Särkikoski was taking the opportunity granted by Väärä's amnesia to claim that she was forced off the road when in reality she simply lost control. The fact that the other vehicle was never found confirmed these rumors in the minds of many. However, Särkikoski's car bore dents and traces of dark-gray paint on its left side. A man who'd been out jogging on the Inkoo-Salo road had also reported a dark-colored van nearly running him down as it sped toward Inkoo.

Surgeons had operated on both of Särkikoski's legs several times. Väärä's worst injuries were to the lumbar spine, and at first it was uncertain whether he would ever run again. A few weeks ago, I'd noticed a blurb on the sports pages saying that he was training again, shooting for the 2009 World Championships. No one was writing stories about Jutta Särkikoski's condition, however. I'd gotten the impression that she wasn't very popular among her colleagues.

"When do you start?" I asked Leena before taking a bite of my shrimp salad.

"In a couple of weeks. Who knows, maybe I'll take up wheelchair racing or chair dancing," Leena said with a grin. Even though Leena detested competitive sports, she had always been active, and forced idleness obviously got her down. I doubted I would handle a permanent disability as well as she had. Getting the services that people with disabilities deserved required determination, and Leena's legal training had been a help not just for her but also for others who hadn't known to demand the service contracts or the free rides they were legally entitled to from the city of Espoo. Out of necessity, my friend had become an advocate for disability rights. Even though we hadn't been able to start our law firm, we were each still working to save the world, what we'd dreamed of doing when we were in school.

That afternoon I had a meeting with a social worker from Joensuu, which was located to the east, near my own hometown. He was an expert in domestic violence; he could have written a book on the subject. However, he preferred client work over research. In the world of social services, every man was valuable, since they were rare and off-set the possible bias that some people claimed female social workers had that favored their female clients. As I walked to the bus station, I noticed a woman with a blond ponytail rushing ahead of me, which was an accomplishment since she was using forearm crutches. She turned her head a little, and I got a glimpse of the side of her face. I realized again what a small place Helsinki was—it was Jutta Särkikoski. I caught up to her, and she cast me a quick glance as if startled, but her expression relaxed when she saw that I was no one she knew, just a harmless stranger.

I almost tried to talk to her, but what would I have said? Instead, I continued to the bus stop. Once on board, I answered a text message from my mother, then pulled out a book about a detective in Tampere, whom I would have loved to have as a colleague. At home the usual chaos awaited me, and I fed my family before heading off to band practice.

Over the years, the Flatfeet had almost learned to play. We were just buddies from the force who liked to perform but didn't have any great musical ambitions. Even though I wasn't a cop anymore, they'd let me stay in the band.

As I dropped the drummer off at home after our intensive two-hour rehearsal, I felt like I really didn't have anything to complain about. All I had on the horizon was the same old, same old, and that was just fine with me.

2

Leena called me two days later. I guessed from her tone that she was about to ask me for a favor, like giving her a ride somewhere or going with her to a movie or concert. Dependence on others and using accessible transport was still hard for her, but she could travel in a normal car as long as her wheelchair fit and someone was there to help her in and out. At first, I'd let her buy my tickets to whatever we were seeing, but then I realized that was unfair. I enjoyed our outings just as much as she did. And I didn't want her to feel like she always had to pay extra, at least not with me.

This time the call wasn't about getting a ride or attending a cultural event. Rather, Leena wanted me to meet her friend Jutta Särkikoski. "Would Friday night after Iida's synchronized-skating practice work?" she asked.

After quickly conferring with Antti, I agreed. For the rest of the week, whenever I found a quiet moment at work, I googled Jutta Särkikoski and the details of the doping scandal. After ending up on a discussion board, my stomach turned: the majority of people writing comments considered Jutta a traitor to her country, even though she had just been doing her job in accordance with journalistic standards. Many of the posts questioned her professionalism, because a mere "girl" couldn't understand the rules of the sporting world. Even if that girl

Derailed

was an established journalist with a degree in sports science from the University of Jyväskylä.

The doping article was relatively easy to find after a little searching through the archives of the tabloid newspaper that had published it. The headline said it all:

DISCUS THROWERS SALO AND TERÄVÄ DOPING

Jutta Särkikoski, Vantaa/Nokia

Two of Finland's greatest hopes for the future of discus throwing, Eero Salo, 21, and Sami Terävä, 23, are suspected of using illegal doping substances, including anabolic steroids. According to information received by our newspaper, near the end of July Salo and Terävä visited Estonia by helicopter and brought back hundreds of anabolic steroid tablets. The men then sold the drug at gyms in their hometown of Vantaa and in Nokia. Through interviews with several people who purchased doping drugs and received instructions for their use from Salo and Terävä, it has been established that buyers included both professional and amateur athletes. To date, no criminal reports have been filed.

Salo and Terävä are members of the Finnish Athletics Federation B team, and Sami Terävä received EUR 3,000 in training funds from the Finnish Olympic Committee. Both were last tested in the spring before the international competition season, and at that time all results were clean. According to information received by our newspaper, following this, Eero Salo failed to appear for one scheduled doping test.

Jutta wouldn't have risked a charge of libel and the possibility of demands for compensation, so she must have substantiated the information about Salo and Terävä's activities. After the article, Salo and Terävä weren't able to avoid doping tests for long, and both tested positive across their A and B samples. Apparently, one of the men's clients had developed a conscience and decided to file a police report, and Salo and Terävä were either stupid or greedy, and they hadn't disposed of the drugs in time. The chain of events was actually a bit comical, but the case still aroused intense emotions in some track-and-field fans. Jutta was seen as having taken advantage of the athletes to advance her career. From other sources I learned that Jutta had received death threats following the publication of the article. That seemed excessive, especially since Jutta's reporting had been accurate.

Leonardo replied to me on Friday.

> Hi. I live in the city. I guess our police district is East Center. But the cops won't believe me. Who would want me? I'm ugly and fat. That's what my mom said when I tried to tell her what that shithead did.

If I worked in the Helsinki East Center Police District, I would have started sifting through our databases for women with multiple marriages and teenage children. But that probably wouldn't have helped find Leonardo, since I didn't know whether the mother's partners had been husbands or boyfriends. All I could do now was send Leonardo the contact information for his neighborhood police office and one of my colleagues who worked sex crimes in that area, whom I knew to be an approachable, sensible person. I just managed to finish the e-mail before Hillevi arrived for our final meeting.

My good friend and former colleague Pekka Koivu from the Espoo police had sent Hillevi our way. She provided a typical case study of how domestic violence escalated. The shouting and slapping while she and her now-ex-husband, Jouni, were dating turned into punching and hair pulling after their wedding. Hillevi hadn't told anyone about any of it. When Jouni stabbed Hillevi under her left collarbone, friends and relatives were shocked. They'd seemed like such a happy couple, who hadn't wanted for anything but a child.

"No one would have believed me if I'd told," Hillevi had said during our first meeting when I asked her why she'd kept quiet. "According to Jouni, I was just exaggerating. 'Everybody slaps their old lady around a little when they don't behave,' he'd say."

Koivu had handled most of the interviews following the stabbing, and according to him, Jouni Litmanen had been a self-confident, even charming man who dismissed the stabbing as an unfortunate accident— the knife had just slipped—and claimed that Hillevi's accusations of repeated attacks were nonsense. His wife's body bore evidence of previous beatings, however, including two broken and poorly healed ribs, as well as burn scars. Koivu had done careful work, ultimately convincing a couple of neighbors to admit that they had heard sounds of fighting and strange thumps from the Litmanen home. Hillevi's boss also testified to noticing bruises on her from time to time.

Usually people didn't want to intervene. Looking the other way was easier. Occasionally, in my work as a detective, I'd also run into a witness who felt she was above getting involved, or that he wasn't the kind of loser who had to deal with those issues. The country as a whole was more secular now than in the past, and few Finns still feared the wrath of God or hell. But whether people were religious or not, it seemed as though everyone thought they could find redemption on earth by feeling superior to everyone else. For some people, self-esteem required comparison. You were closer to paradise if you were thinner or looked younger than your neighbor, weren't on welfare like your cousin, or

21

weren't pissing yourself like that wino at the front of the tram. That was probably the allure of reality television. People got to watch someone getting booted off the island or being sent home without the trophy, whether the trophy was in the form of a fiancé or prize money. Then viewers could thank their lucky stars they weren't as unattractive or as bad at dancing as those idiots on TV. In the same vein, it was simply easier to treat domestic violence victims as if they were to blame for their troubles, and Hillevi would have received plenty of "no" votes if there were a show that judged people based on the problems in their life.

Hillevi was thirty-four but looked older. She had difficulty sitting through our forty-five-minute meetings without smoking. Her dark hair was cut short as if to ensure that no one would ever pull it again. Eyeglasses hid much of her face, and she tended to keep her small, narrow mouth shut. I had to squeeze every word out of her. In Hillevi's case, my job was to find out if the police had operated in a way that may have prevented or discouraged her from filing a criminal complaint. My initial assumption was proven wrong during our very first meeting: Hillevi hadn't been afraid of the police, only of her husband.

She still moved in a nervous, birdlike fashion, as if Jouni might burst into my office at any moment and stab her again. A sudden glance over her shoulder reminded me of Jutta Särkikoski. Sometimes I still had that same kind of vigilance while I was out jogging, at least when there weren't other people nearby. I knew the person who'd attacked me was serving a ten-year sentence, but sense rarely won out over emotion.

Hillevi's situation was much worse than mine. Jouni had received only two years and would be out in a year because it was a first offense. Seven months had already passed.

Hillevi had just returned to her secretary job. Work matters weren't part of our project unless they had something to do with the abuse. We did have a few workplace-violence cases to study, but they had all happened in family businesses, mostly in ethnic restaurants where a whole extended family worked together. If the crime was recorded as workplace related instead of domestic, it was taken more seriously in Finland and most other countries. Many still held the old belief that the workplace was a public space, while the home was inviolable.

The clients who participated in the project had agreed to allow officials to exchange information about them, which had been quite the bureaucratic can of worms. Most of our sources were victims, so we had access to their records. But information on perpetrators wasn't always available other than from court records. The most cooperative perpetrators were alcoholics in recovery, but mostly people completely denied what they'd done, people like Jouni Litmanen. I suspected that the Snork Maiden's Groke belonged to that group too.

"Make sure the restraining order is in effect as soon as Jouni goes free," I advised Hillevi at the end of our meeting and then sighed to myself. These were precisely the kinds of issues Leena and I had wanted to take care of in our law firm. Social services would arrange counseling for the prisoner rejoining society, and there was nothing wrong with that per se. But sometimes the victims got overlooked, and they weren't always informed of what their rights would be once the perpetrator was free.

"Where do I apply for it? I don't think I can," Hillevi replied, and her thin shoulders rose a good two inches in agitation.

"She was always so helpless. Of course I lost my temper sometimes," Jouni Litmanen had said to Koivu during his interrogation. Hillevi reminded me of a girl I knew in school. Anne was her name, and she would become paralyzed by fear and then pee her pants when the bigger boys started throwing snowballs. Once I'd tried to protect her, blocking her from them and shouting. The boys knew my reputation, so they stopped that time. But I don't know what happened to Anne after school, since to get home we walked in opposite directions.

As was my habit, I gave Hillevi my card at the end of our conversation and told her to contact me if she had anything new to report. The card only had my work cell phone number. The project didn't offer services twenty-four seven, just during regular working hours.

A giddy feeling of freedom came over me once again when I closed the office door behind me. I was more than ready for the weekend. My clients came from all over Finland, so I rarely ran into them during my free time. However, today two guys I knew from my days on the force in Espoo were sitting at the base of the Aleksis Kivi statue in the square, drinking beer. Jani Väinölä and Mape Hintikka seemed to be on furlough from prison, apparently legally, since they were hanging out in a public place. I said hi to them, but I didn't bother stopping to chat since they were already so far gone. We'd nailed Hintikka for a stabbing, but my history with Väinölä was complicated enough that I only wanted to interact with him when he was sober. I suspected the pair had enjoyed something more bracing than the twelve pack they'd gone halfway through.

Iida had arranged to sleep over at her friend Nea's house after skating practice, so I was able to leave for Leena's house earlier than planned. I picked up a bottle of wine at the Big Apple Mall on my way. Even though Leena was still on medication, she could have a glass every now and then.

Her home in southwest Espoo had undergone remodeling after she became wheelchair-bound. Why would she and the family architect have thought of accessibility when they'd originally planned the house? Who of us would have? Accidents only happened to other people. I asked if she needed any help around the house before Jutta arrived and ended up folding sheets with Leena's eldest daughter. She was already full-grown and heading out for the evening. I tried to ask Leena why she wanted me to meet Jutta, but Leena just said that Jutta could tell me herself. On Leena's desk I saw literature about sports, some of it in English, mostly focusing on athletes with disabilities and disability categorization. She was obviously boning up for her new job.

Jutta Särkikoski arrived in her own car, because despite her injury she was able to drive an automatic transmission. We greeted each other, curious like two dogs meeting for the first time, neither of us sure who was the leader of the pack. Jutta was young, thirty at most, thin, and about four inches taller than me. There was a sort of impatience about her, as if she was used to doing everything faster than she could at the moment. Her blond hair was pulled back in a ponytail, and her clothing was loose and relaxed, with an emphatic sexlessness. She wore very little makeup, and her face showed the tension that comes from having experienced severe pain.

Leena chased the rest of the family out of the living room so we could speak in private. I'd seen her do this a few times over the years and knew that Leena's family didn't mind. Her husband was a lawyer specializing in competition law, and the family's three children seemed to have absorbed a respect for confidentiality from their mother's milk. Leena opened the wine, and Jutta asked for a cup of tea. When Leena went to the kitchen to put the kettle on, Jutta began to speak.

"I know you're not a police officer anymore, but it's actually better that way. I don't trust the police anymore. They made horrible mistakes in that doping investigation and the car accident, as if they didn't trust me, or they were getting orders to bungle the job from higher up. I wanted to talk to you because the death threats have started again."

I had a hard time believing the police hadn't taken her death threats seriously. I asked her what she meant by "mistakes."

"For starters, they didn't try to find out where Salo and Terävä got the drugs, even though they were illegal. Of course, I didn't reveal my sources."

"But you knew where the drugs came from?"

"I knew. I'd received a tip from my source. But it wasn't my job to follow up—I'm not a police detective."

"I'm not either, not anymore. What was the result of the accident investigation?"

"I haven't heard anything in six months! I called the lead detective when the death threats started again, but he said I should contact the

Espoo police because I live in Espoo now. Leena said you used to work there. Who there can I trust?"

The first person who came to mind was Pekka Koivu. But instead of giving a name, I asked Jutta to give me more information. The threats had started when Jutta finally returned to work after her sick leave. She had just come back from an assignment covering the World Para Athletics Championships for STT, the Finnish News Agency, and was planning a series of articles about the rehabilitation of athletes after sports-related injuries that required surgery.

"There shouldn't be anything about that that's worth threatening me. I did think I might interview Toni Väärä too, but I'm not sure that would be ethical since we were in the accident together. I still need to talk to the editor who assigned the articles."

Leena rolled in, carrying a teapot. A tray holding a mug, two wine glasses, and a plate of hors d'oeuvres was attached to the armrest of her chair. Jutta poured the tea before continuing.

"It was a nightmare. I changed my phone number several times after Salo and Terävä were convicted, but somehow whoever's doing this always found it. I suspect one of my colleagues must be passing it on. After the accident, I did have a few months of peace. Maybe whoever ran us off the road thought he'd succeeded in intimidating me. That was what the messages before the accident always said: if I wanted to stay alive, I had to stop reporting on sports." Jutta took a sip of her tea and then looked me in the eye. "I know you've been a victim too, and that you were just doing your job, like I was. So I think you can understand where I'm coming from."

I nearly spat out my wine. This person knew what my attacker had done to me, just as he had wished—he'd wanted all of Finland to know how he'd humiliated me. Jutta looked at me quizzically, then took a mushroom hors d'oeuvre from the tray and asked Leena if it was gluten-free. With a napkin I wiped up the wine I'd spilled on the table.

"What were the death threats like?" I finally managed to ask.

"A couple of calls, a couple of letters. Just like before the accident, although now there have been much fewer of them. Last time the police caught a few cranks. Some of them were stupid enough to call from their own phones. Here are the letters, and the messages are saved on my phone." Jutta handed me two envelopes, which I did not take.

"How many people have touched them?"

"No one but me, I think. But how should I know?"

The fall was still warm enough that I didn't have gloves with me, so I went to the kitchen to get some rubber gloves. I might save the crime lab some bother if the letters ever ended up there. Both letters had been postmarked in downtown Helsinki, and the envelopes were the same, brown standard C5 size. The stamps bore a stylized Finnish flag and commemorated the centennial of the Olympic Committee. At first glance the letter paper seemed like normal printer paper you could buy by the ream. The font was Times New Roman, and the size looked like fourteen point.

I'd seen numerous death-threat letters during my police career. Some were genuinely scary, some formal, and some outright amusing. The first letter Jutta had received was mostly strange.

> *You lying whore leave Finnish Athletes in peace. You've caused enough trouble already. Now shut up or you won't get off so easy next time. I'll bury you.*

Of course, there was no signature. The second letter used even more direct language.

> *Didn't you understand my first letter? Leave Finnish Athletes alone or a big knife will stick you or your car will explode with you in it. We know what to do with people who foul the nest. If you get near Toni Väärä again, you gonna regret it. It be your fault he didn't go to the Olympics. Remember that, whore.*

"Apparently he doesn't know how to use spell-check. I thought they taught that in every beginning computer skills course," I said, mostly to myself. Some of the comments in the online message boards were written in the same bad Finnish, and you could never quite tell if it was intentional or not. I put the letters back in their envelopes and set them on the table, then took off the gloves. I didn't like the feel of the cold rubber. "Are the voice mail messages more of the same?"

"Listen for yourself." Jutta tapped at her smartphone. "I saved them in their own folder. Hopefully the fact that I moved them won't affect whether they can be traced, even though I'm sure the caller was using a prepaid phone."

"Did you answer them?"

"No. I never answer unknown numbers. If someone has important business, they'll leave a message. Here they are." Jutta handed me the phone. The voice that spoke into my ear a moment later was fuzzy, and the person had clearly tried to mask it. The first message said simply that Jutta was already a dead woman, and the second one threatened to rip her limb from limb if she didn't stop working as a reporter. I listened to the messages again, this time with the speaker on so Jutta and Leena could hear. It was a low mumble, and it was hard to tell whether a man or a woman was speaking. The tone was monotone and unaccented, the words betraying no specific dialect.

"Does the voice sound at all familiar?" I asked Jutta.

"No! It could be any crazy person. There are plenty of those. Nothing has changed. Those two discus throwers were slapped with a ban, but the federation is still full of the same old fogies. I'm not at all surprised what those boys did. It's no wonder that, when you've been working for something since grade school, you might get confused about the line between right and wrong, especially if someone comes along promising a shortcut to success. It's the same for the fans."

"I have such a hard time understanding why someone would make death threats over something as trivial as sports," Leena said with a sigh. "We don't need someone to put Finland on the map anymore. The world already knows we're here. We don't have to prove ourselves by running fast or throwing things farther than everyone else. Sports is just show business, plain and simple."

"Watch it. You're talking to a true believer!" Jutta said. "That was why I was so angry at those discus throwers, because they were ruining the thing I love!"

I let them argue, because I knew from experience that Leena would calm down once she'd said her piece, and Jutta Särkikoski seemed to be a good sparring partner. I considered the phone calls and the letters. The repeated nature of the threats and the fact that they were intended to infringe on a journalist's right to free speech made this a very serious matter. In Russia they killed political reporters who criticized the establishment, and elsewhere in the Nordic countries, bounties had been placed on the heads of journalists and comic artists who'd criticized Muslim extremists. So far Finland was satisfied to focus on sports reporters. But these threats still needed to be investigated, and that task would fall to my former colleagues. Of course, the police could try to trace the calls, but that probably wouldn't lead anywhere.

I had only a superficial relationship with my replacement as commander of the Espoo Police Violent Crime Unit, Anni Kuusimäki. According to Koivu, she was an OK boss. I'd have to tell Jutta to get in touch with him.

"Who's investigating the crash? The Raasepori police?" My question interrupted Jutta and Leena's debate.

"No, the Lohja police, since the accident happened just over the jurisdiction line. But they aren't the slightest bit interested in these death threats anymore. Their theory is that we were just hit by a drunk driver who didn't stop because he was afraid of the consequences. But there's a really weird connection I didn't see until a little while ago. The brother of the lead investigator in Lohja is married to Sami Terävä's sister. Shouldn't that mean he has to recuse himself?"

"Wait, whose sister?"

"Sami Terävä's, one of the discus throwers I exposed!" Jutta's eyes flashed as she described her conspiracy theory. She seemed passionate, not crazy. During my police career, I'd seen plenty of attempted cover-ups, and even though most of my colleagues handled their work irreproachably, there were always exceptions.

"That wouldn't create a true conflict of interest, because the relationship is distant and the cases are completely unrelated. Wasn't the investigation of the anabolic steroid smuggling handled by Vantaa and Nokia, the police departments where Salo and Terävä live?"

"Yes, but maybe the Lohja police swept my accident under the rug because of the lead investigator's conflict of interest!"

"When your accident happened, I was lying in the hospital myself and didn't have much to do but read magazines and watch TV," Leena said. "I'm not interested in sports, but I was interested in your accident because it had a lot in common with my own. And trust me, the media was screaming for the culprit's head on a platter, because the runner was hurt too. They really criticized the police."

"You can be sure it was high on the priority list of everyone involved. No cop likes an unsolved case. Do you think that Salo, Terävä, or someone close to them would be capable of orchestrating something like that?" I asked.

"I don't know them very well. I only interviewed Terävä once. Female sports reporters mostly get assigned to covering kids, women, and para athletes. The big boys are the men's territory." Jutta gave a crooked smile. "My impression of Terävä is that he isn't the sharpest knife in the drawer, and Eero Salo was probably the one who convinced him to start doping. Salo is all over the map. Back in the day he was always training, but now he mostly just practices tipping back pints, from what I hear. It wouldn't surprise me in the least if they were both in that van. Although . . . I only remember seeing one person."

"How would they have known you would be driving on that particular road at that particular time?"

"The federation would have known about the interview, and that I was going to bring Toni to the sponsor event. Maybe someone tipped off Salo and Terävä."

"But why take revenge on you when Toni Väärä was in the car?" Leena asked. I was starting to wonder whether she'd really asked me over to try to get Jutta to stop cooking up conspiracy theories. I took a careful sip of wine and a piece of the mushroom pastry. The sweet aroma of dusty waxcaps hit my nose when I took a bite. Leena couldn't go mushrooming, so her husband must have gathered them.

"There wouldn't be any sense to it, but on the other hand, that's exactly the kind of idiocy you could expect from Salo. Maybe it was mostly revenge with a little jealousy mixed in, since Toni was still competing, unlike him. Or maybe I'm on the wrong track, and the accident had nothing to do with me. Toni has always claimed he doesn't remember anything. But the first time we met in the hospital afterward, he asked me if I saw who the driver of the gray van was. He seemed to think it wasn't about me. Toni thought someone wanted to kill *him*."

3

The upshot of the evening was that Jutta promised to file a report about the death threats with the Espoo police, and I promised to give Koivu a heads-up. But if they weren't able to trace the phone calls or find finger-prints on the letters that matched someone in the police database, there was no hope of finding the perpetrator. Just as Jutta was preparing to leave, I asked her why she thought the death threats had started again.

"I thought Leena told you about the campaign. I'll be working with Toni again."

"What campaign?"

"The Adaptive Sports Association, the Mental Health Association, and the Athletics Federation's rehabilitation campaign. It's for people recovering from physical and mental injuries, specifically amateur athletes. They roped me into handling PR for it. I'm a freelancer, and after that doping scoop, it hasn't been easy to find work except with general-interest publications. I was a little surprised when Merja called—that's Merja Vainikainen, the current director of the Adaptive Sports Association. The campaign launch is next Tuesday, and it's sup-posed to run for a year. Toni Väärä is the mascot for the campaign, since he can attract media coverage. Leena, give Maria the brochures!"

"She can find all the information on the website," Leena said, but Jutta continued talking over her.

"The principle is that exercise helps both people with temporary injuries and illness and those who are permanently disabled. I'm working on a series of articles about professional athletes, which is loosely related, because the magazine that commissioned it is a sponsor of the campaign." Suddenly Jutta smiled broadly. "I love sports and exercise, and I intend to keep being active even if I never get rid of these crutches. That's why I hate doping. To me it's like the Nazis' human experimentation. After the war, East Germany continued the tradition by conducting clinical trials commissioned by Western pharmaceutical companies, and it just so happened that most of the guinea pigs at BALCO in the US were black athletes. That is, before they got caught a few years ago, in 2003."

"Here comes the sermon again," Leena said and sighed, but not meanly, and Jutta's smile spread to her eyes.

"They can't take my beliefs from me, no matter how much they threaten me. You're right, Maria, of course I have to contact the police. I'm not going to let these people frighten me."

"What are your security arrangements at home?"

"High-security locks and a burglar alarm. I live in Kauklahti, in the model development they put up for the 2006 housing fair last year, and there are security cameras, but unfortunately none of them point at my parking spot. I've asked the management to remedy the situation. I always have pepper spray with me. So yes, I'm looking out for myself. Thanks for taking the time to give me some guidance tonight. I really appreciate it." Jutta stood up and offered me her hand, then she hugged Leena. I didn't quite understand what had caused the change in her mood.

After Jutta left, I stayed for another glass of wine. Leena was trying her best to adapt to her wheelchair. After the initial shock, her attitude toward her mobility limitations had been emphatically courageous, so I was actually relieved when she started cursing about not being able to go mushrooming herself.

"Jouko tries, but he can't tell a chanterelle from a yellow birch leaf. And everyone says this year's mushrooming has been amazing."

"I thought I'd go check some of my mother-in-law's usual spots in Inkoo on Sunday. If I get a lot, I'll bring you some."

"Thanks. I'm green with envy, though. But it's nice you seem content with your life now. How are things going with Antti?"

"Better than ever. Things have just sort of fallen into place."

After the taxi dropped me off at home, I stood for a moment gazing at the stars, which were faint against the glow of the streetlight. I wished I could turn it off to make them brighter. Once inside, Venjamin greeted me with a testy meow, but Antti told me the cat had already had his dinner and was just trying to trick me into giving him more. I tossed him a few treats, and he played paw hockey with them on the living room floor before eating. When I sat down with Antti on the couch, Venjamin curled up at my feet.

Late the following Tuesday afternoon, I was in a client meeting when my phone, which was on silent, began flashing on my desk. I didn't recognize the number. By the time the meeting ended, I had received eight calls, six from an unknown number and two from Leena's cell phone. Just as I was dialing Leena back, the phone rang again. It was the same unknown number.

"Hi, it's Jutta. Särkikoski." Her voice was mixed with sobs. "Those threats . . . they weren't a joke. Pentti is probably already dead, though the sandwich was meant for me . . . What do I do now?"

I looked out the window onto the square, where it was raining so hard the clock tower of the railway station was barely visible. Jutta continued crying into the phone, but I could also hear someone talking to her. The voice was a man's.

"Where are you?"

"At home. Miikka brought me here."

"What on earth happened?"

"We had that campaign launch today in Tapiola at the Waterfall Building, in the MobAbility offices. They're one of our sponsors. Some media people were there, and everything went really well. Afterward, most of us organizers stayed to toast our success. MobAbility is a small company, so the Adaptive Sports secretary came along, and she organized the catering. I have celiac, and there was a little to-do because the secretary forgot to buy gluten-free bread. Merja made a huge deal about it. So the secretary went to get some rolls. I didn't have time to eat when she got back, though, because a reporter had called me to ask whether the images on our website were in the public domain. Just as I finished answering, Pentti collapsed. Merja shouted that he was having a heart attack and started CPR, but it didn't . . . Pentti lost consciousness before the ambulance arrived, and he was convulsing and vomiting so Merja couldn't even try rescue breaths."

"Did the police come?"

"No . . . Everyone thought it was a heart attack. According to Merja, Pentti'd had heart trouble before. Merja went in the ambulance, and Tapani Ristiluoma asked us all to leave. Miikka drove me home. He told me that Pentti ate one of the gluten-free rolls that was meant for me. It was no heart attack; it was attempted murder! Merja's phone goes straight to voice mail, and Jorvi Hospital won't even confirm that Pentti is there because I'm not family."

"Jutta, try to calm down. Do you have someone who can be there with you?"

"Miikka is still here. And Leena promised to come if she could get an accessible taxi."

Cramps and vomiting sounded more like symptoms of a poisoning than a heart attack, but I didn't want to jump to any conclusions. If the doctors discovered that this man named Pentti had been poisoned, they would alert the police immediately.

"Who is this Pentti person anyway?"

"Pentti Vainikainen. He's head of social affairs for the Finnish Athletics Federation and the husband of Merja, my boss at the Adaptive Sports Association."

In the background, I heard the muffled male voice again. I told Jutta I had to hang up. Work was calling, and I would get back to her. This was none of my business, I told myself. I couldn't do anything for her at the moment anyway.

I still had one client meeting that day, an old acquaintance from years ago. Anja Jokinen's husband had beaten her with increasing ferocity until the family's adult son ended the violence with a frying pan. Kalle spent time in prison for killing his father, and during that time his little brother, Heikki, followed in their father's footsteps. When Heikki was found dead in a snowbank, Kalle was the prime suspect, since he'd just been released from prison, but he was found innocent and eventually Heikki's death was declared an accident.

Nowadays Anja was a happy grandmother of two. She ran a support group for people who had been abused by their children, and she wanted to be included in my study. When I investigated Heikki Jokinen's death, I'd still been a wreck for a number of reasons, among them my colleague Pertti Ström's suicide and my own marital crisis, and I still wasn't sure whether the conclusion of the case had been entirely correct. But when Anja showed me pictures of Kalle's children, Mielikki and Onni, I agreed with her that the story of the remaining members of the Jokinen family had ended happily.

I didn't have time to call Leena until after Anja's interview, and she was still waiting in frustration for a taxi. Getting accessible taxis was a crapshoot, and even if the dispatcher agreed to make the order, the vehicle was usually late. I suggested a normal taxi van, because her husband was in a meeting, and I couldn't drive her either, since it was my turn to take Taneli to his off-ice training session.

"Maybe I'll invite Jutta here," Leena finally said. "Thanks for the mushrooms, by the way. They made a good soup."

Over the weekend I'd been in seventh heaven in the forest in Inkoo. The forest was overflowing with woolly milk caps and red-hot milk caps. Funnel chanterelles grew in mats, terra-cotta hedgehogs and the forest lambs practically jumped into my bucket, and I even picked some orange birch boletes. I'd brought Leena all the dusty black caps and some of the porcinis. Antti was our family's dedicated mushroomer, but his enthusiasm had rubbed off on me. His mom had scampered through the forest with us too, finally finding a trove of chanterelles. I'd felt pure joy at being alive and energized by the thrill of the hunt, rushing from boulder to boulder, looking for more plunder. In a way I almost started to understand what hunters liked about hunting. Of course, you didn't have to stalk mushrooms or kill them. They just appeared again every fall if there was enough moisture. Finally, we'd ended up on a cliff eating our lunch and gazing at the sea. Taneli had learned to recognize chanterelles and was exceedingly proud of himself, but Iida spent more time texting her friends than admiring the bounty of the forest. That had amused me, and my mother-in-law seemed to feel the same way. We'd exchanged looks of deep understanding.

I was supposed to be thinking about mushrooms, not suspicious deaths. I ran for the bus and, once onboard, tried to concentrate on my book, but my thoughts kept returning to Pentti Vainikainen. I had a vague memory of him—he'd been interviewed on *Sports Update*. At home I grabbed a banana and then rushed with Taneli through the rain to catch the next bus. He told me about his crafting class where he'd learned to do a chain stitch, and how he intended to crochet a phone case for his dad. I thought Antti would like that. Taneli chattered the whole short bus ride, making me forget everything else for the moment.

After he skittered off to the locker room at the gym, I went outside under the awning and called Koivu. Water was coming down in torrents, but the autumn air was still so warm that I had to unbutton my leather jacket. Koivu answered after the second ring, which was enough to tell me that he wasn't in the middle of anything important. Jutta

Särkikoski had contacted him the previous afternoon, and they had a meeting scheduled in a couple of days.

"That may be a colorful meeting," I said and then told Koivu what little I knew about the day's events at the Waterfall Building.

"So what you're telling me is you want to be a cop again."

"You wish! I'm just interested in all the commotion around Jutta Särkikoski."

"Puupponen suggested that this Vainikainen guy overdosed on Viagra. Just think: Puupponen is the same age as me, but his jokes just keep getting worse. Is that grounds for requesting a transfer?"

"Ask your boss."

"If only I could find her. She always disappears after our meetings. She's a fine boss, but she's gone a lot."

"Try Jyrki, then."

"Taskinen?" Koivu laughed. The head of the Criminal Division, Jyrki Taskinen, was still my good friend, but there had always been too many steps in the hierarchy between him and Koivu. Koivu was indebted to Taskinen since Taskinen had arranged for Koivu's wife, Anu Wang-Koivu, to move from Violent Crime to the Juvenile Unit, which kept eight-to-four hours, so things would be easier on their three kids. Koivu wouldn't have been caught dead admitting he wanted his wife and the mother of his children in the safest job possible, but that was clearly part of it as well.

"At least come over to watch the next qualifying match for the national team," Koivu suggested. "During the last game, my neighbor Mehdi screamed louder against Poland than I did, so it looks like he's starting to settle in to life in Finland. That would have been something for Ström to see. Just think how time flies. It'll be ten years soon."

I knew that he was referring to Ström's suicide. I'd told Koivu that I still had dreams about that, then said good-bye and hung up.

After his practice, Taneli and I ran together to the bus stop through the endless rain, which managed to seep into my rubber boots and through my Gore-Tex coat. Taneli had yet to complain about taking the bus to practice instead of the car. Iida, on the other hand, regularly took her father to task on the subject, and sometimes I had to excuse myself to go to the bathroom to laugh, since watching the two of them duke it out was just too funny. When it came to stubbornness, the apple didn't fall far from the tree.

We didn't notice the strange car in the driveway until we were rushing to the door. The storm lantern Antti had lit guttered on the porch. It was a silver Renault, but I couldn't tell the model in the dark. When I opened the front door, I heard a familiar voice: Leena was holding forth on some topic. The lovely scent of green tea found my nose, and Antti must have warmed up some of the chanterelle pie we'd made. While Iida told her godmother and Jutta Särkikoski stories about school, I changed into something comfortable and took my wet clothes to the laundry room. Then I went into the living room, where the women were laughing politely at Iida's imitation of her teacher.

"Hi, Maria! I'm sorry we showed up unannounced, but Jutta wanted to chat with you," Leena blurted out before I'd even managed to lean down to hug her. Jutta sat on the couch, petting Venjamin, who was curled up in her lap. Antti brought me a cup of tea and asked Iida if she would help him do some ironing. He closed the living room door behind them.

"Is there any new information about Pentti Vainikainen's condition?"

"No! Merja isn't answering her cell phone or Pentti's," Jutta said. "But if it was poisoning, as it appears, that poison was delivered to the wrong address. I have celiac, and everyone knows I eat gluten-free. Pentti took one of my sandwiches by accident."

"What was in the sandwiches?"

"I don't know! I never got a chance to taste them . . . Thank God. What kind of poison could act that fast?"

I thought for a moment. "Cyanide . . . A mushroom-based poison like gyromitrin would take effect more slowly, but ibotenic acid or muscarine can take effect in twenty minutes. I guess nicotine would be fast acting too."

"Our office secretary is incompetent enough to have used dried false morels that hadn't been boiled or some other poisonous mushroom."

"There's no point speculating since we still don't know anything yet. Maybe Vainikainen really did have a heart attack. That can be accompanied by nausea."

Jutta stared at the chanterelle pie, looking like she might never eat mushrooms again, although she was probably just examining the crust and wondering about its gluten content. Without her saying anything I returned to the kitchen and grabbed some rice cakes and cream cheese. What I really wanted was some peace and quiet. I was tired. Back in the living room, Jutta asked whether I could call the Espoo police to see if they knew something about the incident. I said I'd already spoken with Koivu.

"If Pentti survives, will they bother to investigate?"

"Of course, if they suspect poisoning. Try to calm down, Jutta. What you witnessed was horrible, but even if it turns out to be a case of poisoning, those sandwiches aren't necessarily to blame."

Jutta pursed her lips. Other than the one time I'd seen her smile on Friday, she seemed to always be in a constant state of tension. I remembered how my colleague Palo had reacted when a convict who'd threatened us escaped from prison. He'd literally been afraid of every little rustling, but even his hypervigilance hadn't saved his life.

Jutta's smartphone sat on the table, and she tapped at it for a moment. "There isn't anything new online," she said. "But I'll call Miikka. He might know something." Holding Venjamin under the front legs, she carefully shifted him onto the couch. Offended, he meowed and jumped to the floor to stretch. Jutta stood up, grabbing her crutches, and then hurried into the kitchen to make the call. Her movement was quick and jerky.

"What the hell is going on here?" I whispered to Leena. "Do you know anything about this Pentti Vainikainen? I only know his name."

"Of course I do, being a true sports authority," Leena said sarcastically. "I know the long-distance runner Lasse Virén, and that some guy named Räikkönen drives a car. All I have patience for is figure skating." Leena wasn't about to give up her sports-hater image, and she'd never admit to watching hockey on TV. It was funny that she'd become friends with sports fanatic Jutta, but the relationship made sense given their common experience.

"So you weren't invited to the campaign launch event?" I asked Leena.

"I was, but I didn't want to go because I was afraid I'd end up in the press photos. I'm not interested in pretending to be braver than I am or pretending that I'm OK with the possibility that I might never walk again. But the purpose of campaigns like this is to get people excited. Of course, I reviewed all of the campaign contracts, even though some of them were written up before my time. Toni Väärä still doesn't have a manager, so the Athletics Federation is handling his affairs." Leena cut herself a piece of the mushroom pie before continuing. "I haven't met Pentti Vainikainen, but his wife, Merja Vainikainen, is my boss. She's about my age, and about as grouchy as the two of us combined. But I get along with her just fine as long as I do my job. One day I overheard her laying into our temp, Miikka, and he's a grown man. All I could think was: so much for the myth of female leaders being easygoing and empathetic."

Jutta returned to the room. "Miikka hasn't heard anything either. He's planning on going to the office tomorrow. He says he's seen convulsions like that before and that it isn't necessarily anything serious." Jutta sighed, looking like a tightly strung bowstring that had been momentarily released. "Maybe it had nothing to do with me. Maybe I'm just self-centered and paranoid. Now where did that cat go?"

Before the visitors could leave, Taneli came in and insisted on showing them how he could do a turn and a half in the air, the equivalent of a single axel on the ice. Jutta scored some points by saying that a few years ago she'd interviewed his and Iida's top skating idol, Stéphane Lambiel, when he was just starting to make his breakthrough and had barely placed in the Finlandia Trophy.

I couldn't help but wonder what kind of person Jutta really was. She didn't seem like someone to get worked up over nothing. She'd flatly refused to reveal who had leaked the information about Salo and Terävä's doping, and when I'd gone looking for articles about the accident, I found that Jutta hadn't been the one to claim that someone had intended to kill her specifically. That was some other reporter's theory.

"Let me know when you hear something," I said as Antti and I helped Leena into Jutta's car. Once Taneli fell asleep and Iida went to bed to read, I turned on our home computer and googled Pentti Vainikainen. The search turned up a long list of results, including people with the same name who weren't the head of social affairs for the Finnish Athletics Federation. From the picture on the organization's website, it was easy to believe that the forty-eight-year-old Vainikainen still ran a marathon in under three and a half hours.

Vainikainen had degrees in business administration and exercise science, and his hobbies, besides marathon running, included floor hockey and fishing. His greatest sporting achievement was getting third place in the 10,000 meter at the Finnish nationals in 1983. That had landed him a spot in the Finland-Sweden Athletics International, which had been his last competition.

Vainikainen's first wife was Eva Fagerström, and they hadn't had any children. They'd been married from 1985 to 1998. His second wife, since 2003, was Merja, born in 1962. I didn't find mention of children from that marriage either. The name Eva Fagerström triggered vague memories, so I googled it. During my time at the police academy, I'd worked security at one of the Finland-Sweden Athletics Internationals and admired the final sprint of the Swede who won the women's 10K, although of course I should have been paying attention to the crowd. That Swede was Eva Fagerström. She'd represented Sweden in the 5K and 10K at the Los Angeles Olympics in 1984 but hadn't made it into the final round of either event.

My uncle Pena had bought a color television in 1976, just before the Montreal Olympics. During the summers I spent on his farm, we'd watched the Olympics with my father and Pena's cat. For Pena, a Finland-Sweden matchup was a great battle akin to the Winter War, but this time against our western neighbor instead of the Soviet Union. To him anyone who beat Sweden at anything was a great hero.

As a child I'd never thought to wonder about Pena's hatred of Sweden. Even though my uncle was generally tolerant, for him anything connected to Sweden was like a matador's cape to a bull. My mother teased her brother-in-law by sending him a postcard of the Swedish king whenever she found one, and later I adopted the same tradition.

Now the Finland-Sweden Internationals seemed like a silly relic of the time before the EU. The Swedish teams were full of second-generation immigrants, and sponsors' logos were larger than national flags. Switching nationalities in order to compete wasn't unheard of. I didn't have an opinion about these new developments, but there were many who did. Koivu and Ström had gotten into a big argument during a 1997 national hockey tournament about whether it was appropriate to use the charismatic General Ehrnrooth to pump up the home team. Koivu had talked about his grandfather and three great-uncles who'd died in the Continuation War, insisting that comparing hockey to war was an insult to the veterans and those who had fallen. That had shut up even Pertti Ström. Sometimes I wondered about the use of military terminology, like "destroy" and "enemies," in sports. Although I was also inclined to support Antti's half-joking notion that wars should be settled on the soccer field, because it was the world's most popular team sport and was as beloved in Muslim countries as in the Western superpowers.

I clicked back to Pentti Vainikainen. The pages that interested me most were the Athletics Federation press releases concerning campaigns or sponsorship deals with athletes. One page revealed that Merja Vainikainen, of the Adaptive Sports Association, who at the time used her second husband's name, Salminen, had started working as the youth-fitness project manager for the Athletics Federation in 2002. Wedding bells had rung a year later.

"What are you looking for?" Antti had come up behind me in the office, where we kept my bass guitar and Antti's piano. The kids were only allowed on the computer when neither of us was playing.

"Just information about Jutta." I opened a news site, which didn't mention that Pentti Vainikainen had fallen ill. I turned off the computer and followed Antti into the bedroom, where we engaged in my favorite relaxation technique. Right after, I fell fast asleep.

I'd left my phone on, and a message woke me up around six. It was from Koivu. *You asked about this Vainikainen guy. We just got word that he passed away at Jorvi Hospital. It looks like poisoning. This is going to be a mess.*

4

Soon after receiving the text from Koivu, my phone blew up with messages from Leena and Jutta. On the bus I replied to both of them. There would be a police investigation into Vainikainen's death. Even if poisoning was confirmed as cause of death, it could still be deemed accidental or at least noncriminal.

Behind me a group of kids were liberally using the f-word, and I closed my eyes and tried to ignore them. For a bit I kept a tally to pass the time, but when the number reached one hundred before the Lauttasaari Bridge into Helsinki, I started to get annoyed. Even though I cursed like a sailor when mad, I didn't approve of ten-year-olds swearing as punctuation. Iida would get an earful if she ever started talking that way.

At the office, I read my work e-mail and found that my first meeting of the day had been canceled. It was the third time Jarmo Paukkunen had failed to keep an appointment. He was a single parent with two children, and this time the excuse was that one of them had come down with a cold. Following the divorce, the court had granted him custody. Paukkunen had been referred to me by District Attorney Katri Reponen, who had brought charges against Paukkunen's wife based on a report of abuse from Child Protective Services.

With a sigh, I dived into some statistical work I'd been putting off, since placing numbers in columns and rows wasn't my favorite activity.

I heard the muffled sound of voices coming from Outi's office, then an ambulance siren as it sped along Vilho Street and over the tram tracks past the Ateneum Art Museum. My fingers fumbled some numbers, and I came up with 156 percent of male children as having been victims of domestic violence.

I couldn't count how many times people had asked whether I'd taken into account the risk of Taneli getting bullied at school because of his figure-skating hobby. As if bullying was a fact of life and anything that deviated from the norm, and therefore might attract it, should be avoided. Even though it had been ages since I believed we could have a world without violence, I still didn't want to give up. And these obnoxious spreadsheets were part of that effort.

My phone rang, and the screen identified the caller as Koivu. I answered, happy to put off statistics for a minute or two.

"Hi, Maria, how's it going?"

"Fine. Things are pretty quiet."

"Well, they aren't quiet around here. The death of this Vainikainen guy is turning into a circus. We suspect the poison was intended for that reporter lady."

"I know. I talked about it yesterday with Jutta. But that's none of my concern now, is it?"

"Don't gloat. Puupponen and I just had our first coffee in six hours, and time to piss is a rare treat. Anu already said I could go ahead and sleep here, and she'll ask her mom to help with the kids."

Koivu's account simultaneously amused and annoyed me. He was one of my best friends, so of course he could vent about his work troubles to me. And anyway I was the one who had asked him to do something about the threats against Jutta Särkikoski.

"Have you heard who made the poisoned sandwich?" Koivu continued. "It was Hillevi."

"Hillevi? Wait a second . . . You mean Hillevi Litmanen?"

"None other. She's the secretary at the Adaptive Sports Association. She was the one who ran over to the Stockmann in Tapiola to buy gluten-free bread. And apparently now she's going completely off her rocker."

"So it couldn't have been an accident?"

"I don't think so, and neither does Anni. By the way, I'm worried about Anni. She's pale, and she always seems upset. And she keeps disappearing. If I didn't know how ambitious and hard-working she is, I'd think she had the same problem as our old friend Pertti Ström. Booze, I mean. But I guess Anni is probably just nervous, since this is such a high-profile case. Half the planet is breathing down her neck."

"Poor Anni," I said sincerely. "Tell her she can call me if she needs advice. I know how reporters can be." I regretted those words the instant they left my mouth. Vainikainen's death had nothing to do with me, and I had no business trespassing on my successor's territory.

"Guess what just occurred to me?" Koivu said, almost talking over me. "Hillevi's ex-husband isn't out on furlough, is he? Maybe Jouni Litmanen thought she was buying those bread rolls for herself."

"Doesn't that seem a bit far-fetched? I think you've been spending too much time with Puupponen. But yeah, you should check. Have you identified the poison?"

"No, but the samples are being rushed through at the lab. Oops, Anni's calling . . . Gotta go. Good to at least hear from her, even if sightings are rare."

On my way to work I'd been distracted, so I hadn't noticed the newspaper headlines. Now I went online. Only one of the tabloids had managed to file a story so far, with the subdued headline "Sports Boss Dies at Campaign Launch." The story mentioned a health emergency. That would be updated as soon as someone provided more information. Much more column space was devoted to coverage of a bomb disposal team made up of Finnish peacekeepers who had been stranded in the mountains of Afghanistan for two days. Although even that was minor news compared to the latest twists and turns of reality TV: someone had punched someone else on *Big Brother*, and now everyone was wondering if assault charges would be filed. I didn't understand what the fuss was about.

I looked up Hillevi Litmanen. She'd never mentioned where she worked, just that she was a secretary. I could just barely imagine Hillevi poisoning her abusive husband, Jouni, but it was ludicrous to think that she would knock off anyone else. Though she did seem like someone who could make serious blunders when nervous.

An incoming e-mail alert interrupted these musings. The sender line said "The Snork Maiden."

> I haven't been going to school, and I don't know if I'll ever go back. The world is a black hole, but at least the Groke is gone at the moment. I don't know when she's returning, or if she's ever coming back. Maybe I'll be locked up in this house for the rest of my life. At least there's food and water. No one but the Groke can get in without breaking a window or calling the police. If only someone would. I'd tell them that even though I made some of the scars myself, some of them are from the Groke. I wish I could stick a knife in her throat and see if her blood is the same color as mine. Or is it black like orc blood? How can I prove that the Groke made these marks? No one would believe me.
>
> The Groke and Hemulen went off somewhere again and left me here. Maybe they're hoping I'll die, since the phone doesn't even work.
>
> Wait, someone's coming. Help! I'm

The e-mail broke off alarmingly. Maybe I finally needed to ask for permission to trace the address. It was strange that the school nurse or someone hadn't noticed the marks the Snork Maiden had mentioned.

At noon I went out for lunch with Jarkko and Outi. Passing a newsstand, I saw that the headlines were singing a different tune from the ones in the morning. "Sports Boss Dies Under Suspicious Circumstances. Poisoning Suspected," said a tabloid. "Wrong Person Murdered?" said another, the word "murdered" filling half of the front page.

Over lunch we compared the results of our statistical analyses and discussed how to craft the progress report we needed to deliver before Christmas. Outi suggested that we come up with a sensational title about violent women like "Mommy, Don't Hit the Baby."

"I can guarantee you there are people in Parliament who will be happy to give us more funding if we can prove that women are just as violent as men," she said in defense of her suggestion.

"Yeah, but show me one objective study," Jarkko said. I realized that if I wanted to use this material for my licentiate dissertation, I'd need to find out what law schools were currently interested in and what methods were in fashion. When I was doing my master's thesis, Finland had been in a deep recession, and that had impacted students' research projects. Now the old guard from the 1960s was retiring from academia, and you didn't have to be a fortune-teller to see that a new era was dawning in the legal establishment too. Liberalism was flourishing in the economy, but in jurisprudence we seemed to be swinging toward harshness, and one politician had even dared suggest the possibility of reinstating the death penalty.

Next on my schedule was an interview with someone for whom this would be the last session. Hinni had lived with her abusive boyfriend for a couple of years, and their final fight had ended with Hinni stabbing him, an injury that ultimately put him in a wheelchair. She was now on parole and trying to stay off drugs. I remembered one of my colleagues claiming that 90 percent of violent crimes in Finland wouldn't happen if not for drugs. Hinni and her boyfriend had been fighting over the last can of beer, but they'd also been popping sedatives, which in this case hadn't had the desired effect.

I was just putting the finishing touches on my report about Hinni's visit when a knock came at the door. I didn't have another appointment on my schedule, so I was a little surprised. There was a strict policy about who was allowed past the door downstairs; maybe it was just Outi or Jarkko.

"Come in!" I yelled, standing up just in case I'd have to face an irate ex or inebriated client. "Door's open."

Instead of danger, in walked two people I liked very much: my current superior, Senior Inspector Mikko Rajakoski from the Ministry of the Interior, and my former boss, Jyrki Taskinen, head of the Espoo Police Criminal Division.

"Hi! What are you two doing here?" I was going to hug Taskinen, but then I stopped in my tracks. Had something happened to Iida or Taneli? Or Antti? Taskinen's expression told me I wasn't going to like what he had to say. Anxiety replaced my initial shock.

Taskinen walked over to the window. "Nice view," he said. "It's too bad you're going to have to give it up."

"What do you mean?" I looked from one man to the other. A tram clattered by on the street below, and a car honked its horn. The four o'clock rush, eternal and immutable, worse and worse every year.

"Your assignment is changing, effective tomorrow," Rajakoski finally said. I stared at him in confusion. The project was supposed to continue through the end of the next year. Had Parliament suddenly canceled the funding? Taskinen evaded my gaze as Rajakoski continued.

"You're temporarily returning to the Espoo police. Just until this Pentti Vainikainen case has been solved. You'll take over the investigation. You can have whatever personnel and equipment you need."

I still didn't comprehend what Rajakoski was trying to tell me. Go back to the Espoo police? What the hell?

"What do you mean? Anni is there. You can't seriously want me coming in and walking all over her? And I'm not under the police administration anymore!"

"You are now," Taskinen said gruffly. "Maria, we don't have any choice because—" He cut himself off.

Rajakoski and Taskinen exchanged a glance, then Rajakoski nodded and Taskinen cleared his throat. "This requires revealing some personal information, but Anni is going on partial sick leave. After many years, her fertility treatments finally worked. She's expecting triplets in February. I'm sure you understand the risks, Maria." Taskinen spoke in a serious, warm tone, the purpose of which seemed to be to express that he was a good boss who understood his subordinates. But I wasn't falling for his nice-guy act.

"I have a contract for this project! You can't just drag me back into police work without my consent!"

"Did you read the small print in your employment contract?" I could have sworn Mikko Rajakoski was enjoying this a little bit. "Right at the end it says that if the organization that commissioned the project needs you for other duties, you can be reassigned as long as the contract remains in force."

"But that was about possibly expanding the project from domestic violence to workplace violence, if we got more resources. I signed a contract to be a researcher, not a cop!" I felt like slamming my fist on the table, but that would have looked ridiculous. Rage pounded in my chest and then moved to my head, and I could feel a rushing sensation in my ears. Was this what people meant by "a spike in blood pressure"?

"Yes, you signed an employment contract with the Interior Ministry Police Division. Today I spoke with the minister and the chief director of the police force. Here's your transfer order." Mikko took an envelope out of his breast pocket and handed it to me. I felt like ripping it up, but instead I opened it. The paper inside said plainly that Maria Kristiina Kallio, LLM, would be transferred effective the following day to a special assignment with the Espoo Police Violent Crime Unit, to investigate the death of Pentti Kalervo Vainikainen. The assignment would continue until the pretrial investigation was complete, and I would be given the right to form an investigative team of my choosing from the unit's permanent staff.

"We're focusing more resources on this than we usually would in a criminal investigation. Just think, Maria, you can have Koivu and Puupponen on your team. And what about Ursula Honkanen? She just came back from profiler training at the Police University College. Won't that be helpful?" Taskinen continued, still smiling warmly. "We can't get you a uniform right away, though this will mostly be a plainclothes gig anyway. Your phone, e-mail account, and business cards have already been ordered. This investigation will be an independent project separate from everything else the VCU is doing. Anni will retain control of the other cases. Come to the station at nine tomorrow, and we'll go through everything we know so far with Anni and Koivu. Which isn't much."

"Jesus Christ, you can't be serious! Isn't there someone else you could pull in? There are cops in this country who are fucking unemployed, and more are graduating all the time!"

"All junior officers, Maria." Rajakoski's voice was sharp. "The minister of the interior isn't the only cabinet member who's already been in contact with the police administration. Sports are important to a lot of people in high places, and you must understand that a homicide investigation is going to trump a domestic violence project. The crimes you're studying have already been solved."

"Not all of them!" I exclaimed, remembering the Snork Maiden. "We have anonymous subjects that need to be identified."

"Outi and Jarkko can handle that for now. You don't have a choice, Maria. And besides, you already have the background on this case, because you know both Jutta Särkikoski and Hillevi Litmanen, who most likely served the poisoned sandwich to Vainikainen. No, Maria," Rajakoski continued quickly when I tried to interrupt his torrent of words. "Not the kind of background that would create a conflict of interest. Don't even try it."

"What if I break my leg? Or my neck?"

Rajakoski laughed, but Taskinen remained serious. "Don't you understand, Maria, that you're going to concentrate on this one crime, and you'll have access to all available resources? If you want a car, we'll get you a car. This is a much bigger case than anything you've done before. Bigger even than the Petri Ilveskivi murder. See you tomorrow at the department, nine a.m."

"Are you going to tell Antti about this?"

"I can call if that's necessary. Is his phone number the same?" Taskinen pulled out his cell.

"Oh, give it a rest! And get out of here before the Helsinki police get a call that someone's throwing computers and binders around." Keeping my voice under control required considerable effort. I felt like screaming and shouting, and Taskinen and Rajakoski seemed to sense that now was a good time to leave. They skulked out like rabbits being eyed by an angry hunting dog.

After they left, I sat back down in my chair. I hit the desk once, but all that did was make my wrist hurt. Violence wasn't the answer. I listened as Rajakoski first talked to Jarkko and then Outi, the latter of whom gave an indignant yell. I felt like asking Outi out for a beer, but that wouldn't change anything. All I could do was head to the grocery store and then home as normal, tell my family the bad news, and then let my mother-in-law know that we were probably going to need her again. Antti might be able to do some of his research from our home office . . .

When I realized how quickly I was falling into line and reorganizing my family's life, I became even more irritated. Before going home, I traded a few words with Jarkko and Outi. Jarkko was confused and angry, and Outi was as furious as a cat with its head caught in a pickle jar.

"You're an expert, though. You'll solve the case and be back here in a couple of weeks," Jarkko said, trying to sound reassuring. I appreciated the effort.

On the bus I read through my transfer order but didn't find any loopholes. My employment contract didn't offer any either. According to the eighth article of the Police Act, the Ministry of the Interior can grant police powers to anyone it so chooses. According to the forty-first article, any official has to render assistance to the police, and according to the forty-fifth, even a civilian has a duty to assist in criminal cases. That was the legal web they'd used to catch me.

My heart had started to pound, and my breathing had sped up, so I closed my eyes and tried to take deep, calming breaths. This was a completely different case from the last one. No one was going to attack me, and I wasn't going to take any unnecessary risks ever again . . . My lawyer skills must have been really rusty for this application of my contract not to have occurred to me. When I got off the bus, I continued the deep breathing until my pulse returned to normal. As I trudged into the grocery store, I thought about the only good part of my temporary change of employment: now I could walk or bike to work. At the store, I bought Antti's favorite rye bread and ice cream for the kids.

At home I made pasta carbonara, which didn't require much culinary expertise. I poured Antti and me glasses of wine too. Fortunately, the children had a lot to report on, and I listened to their stories about school in silence. Once they'd disappeared to their rooms, I remained sitting at the table.

"So, Antti . . . I have something to tell you. Something you're not going to like."

Antti flinched, and the expression on his narrow face tightened.

"What? Do you have a new man or something? When do you fit him in?"

54

I laughed, although I didn't really feel all that amused. Antti stared at me with a confused look on his face.

"Well, no," I said after a moment. "It has to do with work. I'm transferring to Espoo."

"Why? Isn't your office downtown good enough? Or does the ministry no longer have money to cover the rent?"

"It isn't that. I'm starting another project. But it's only a project, just this one case. For the Espoo police. I'm leading the investigation into Pentti Vainikainen's poisoning," I blurted out.

Antti was quiet. Silence surrounded us like a fog, condensing into a cool wall between us.

I poured more wine into my glass. There were still fifteen hours until nine a.m.

"I don't get it," Antti finally said. Then comprehension dawned on him. "Oh, that! I saw the tabloids. There was a homicide in Espoo, and you volunteered to solve it since you already know about the death threats Jutta Särkikoski is getting. Is that it?"

"Not at all! Taskinen and Rajakoski just showed up at my office today and . . ." I tripped over my words as I explained the visit to Antti. His expression gradually changed, and I could tell that his anger was no longer directed at me.

"Can they really do that?" he finally asked, refilling his glass. "Something like that can happen at the university, since the administration considers us livestock, the only purpose of which is to pump out publications, but . . . since when did the police turn into the army?"

Bon Jovi started playing on my phone. That was Koivu's work phone ringtone. I picked up.

"Maria. I mean, boss. What the fuck!" Koivu said.

"Don't swear. I've already filled the quota for both of us today."

"But . . . so you're starting tomorrow?"

"Nine o'clock on the dot. What's the situation there?"

"I'm headed home to get some sleep. Things are frozen until you get here. We haven't had time to do much more than basic background. It looks like a poisoning, but of course, we still don't have the labs. Our assumption at this point is that the poison was in the bread. So far we've interviewed the wife, Merja Vainikainen, and the CEO of MobAbility, Tapani Ristiluoma. Hillevi Litmanen is still a zombie, so we can't get anything out of her. She's been taking a lot of sedatives."

Antti glanced at me, irritated. Our conversation had been interrupted, and now I was diving into a criminal investigation that he under no circumstances wanted me getting involved in. I watched as he emptied his glass. Antti usually didn't drink too much, especially not in the middle of the week and when the children could see. This seemed to be some kind of juvenile protest against me.

"According to the widow, Pentti Vainikainen didn't have any enemies. She knew about the death threats Särkikoski has been getting and said that Hillevi Litmanen is inept enough that she easily could have mixed drain cleaner with the sandwich filling. The gluten-free sandwiches had either garlic mayonnaise or parsley butter, both made by Litmanen. Wait . . . that moron just forgot to signal, and I almost rear-ended him!"

Iida walked out of her room to show us her math test. She'd inherited her math skills from her father. I told Koivu about his goddaughter's excellent grade, and he asked to speak to her. Antti continued staring at me as he started in on his third glass of red wine. Then he stood up and went to play the piano, taking his glass with him. The angry perfect fourths and fifths that began to thunder from the other room must have been a Bartok composition.

After a thorough reporting of her synchronized-skating practice, Iida gave the phone back to me. Koivu had made it home, and he asked me to hold on so that he could take his phone out of its car mount. I heard the car door slam, then Koivu greeting a neighbor, then the sound of a soccer ball bouncing on asphalt.

"This whole thing stinks, and I'd definitely start with the assumption that the poison wasn't meant for Vainikainen. Oh yeah, and the wife said he'd been complaining of chest pains recently, but she hadn't been able to get him to go to the doctor even by threatening to cut off sex. She must have been pretty upset to tell me something like that. And now I'm exhausted. I'll see you in the morning." Koivu's shoes banged on the stairs, and the sound of a door opening echoed in my ears as he hung up.

I cleared the dinner table, and Venjamin came to head-butt my shins. I tossed him a couple of pieces of bacon that had stuck to the bottom of the pot. The cat didn't know what profession I practiced to get his daily food, but he knew how to protest if I was away from home too much. Once the cat had eaten, I picked him up before going to see whether Taneli needed a reminder to do his homework. Then the phone rang again, and the cat leaped out of my arms. It was Jutta, so I answered.

"I'm sorry for bothering you so late. He called me again . . . the same voice. He said that unfortunately Pentti Vainikainen had been too greedy but that he'd make sure there were no mistakes next time. Then it would be my turn to die."

5

As was often the case, I woke up five minutes before my alarm went off. At first, I didn't remember what had happened the previous day and cheerfully scratched Venjamin, who'd started head-butting me when he noticed I was awake. Then reality hit me like two million volts of electricity. I'd been ordered to investigate a homicide that apparently had claimed the wrong victim. And the perpetrator was still threatening his intended victim, Jutta Särkikoski.

I felt like curling up at the foot of the bed between Venjamin and Antti. I tested my forehead, but unfortunately I didn't have a fever. Just to be sure, I checked Antti's body temperature too, but it was the same as mine. Yawning, Antti got up to make the coffee and oatmeal, while I went to wake up the children. They were healthy too, and Taneli was downright boisterous. Iida, on the other hand, was practicing her best teenage morning sulk. Antti and I only talked when we had to.

As I rode my bike the half mile to the police station, one military march after another played in my head, even though I wasn't on my way to war. Still, the fatherland was calling. *All rest, all peace, away! Begone!* went the "March of the Pori Regiment." Men didn't have to serve in the army anymore to get into the police academy. In theory, guys who opted for civil service instead were allowed in, along with the women. My dead colleague Pertti Ström was probably rolling over in his grave, and I knew plenty of other old cops who had choked on their coffee when they heard about the new law.

I was at the station at fifteen minutes to nine. The parking lot was overflowing, so I had to weave my way through the cars. A light rain was coming down, and my hair was damp and curly, so I put it up in a ponytail before I went through the all-too-familiar door.

Taskinen's office was located on the top floor. Because I didn't have a security card yet, I had to wait for him to fetch me. The duty officer was new, a young African Finnish woman who had a lot of jangly bracelets. The passport desk was busy, and I waved to a couple of familiar officers whose attention I managed to catch through the mass of people.

Taskinen wore the same suit as the day before. I had on a uniform-like dark-gray pantsuit, because I didn't know what the day would bring. Both of us were dressed more formally than we had been in the past.

"Morning, Maria. Here's your pass. Kuusimäki and Koivu are waiting in my office." Taskinen's speech seemed stilted, and I didn't try to put on a show of friendliness either. In a departure from his previous habit, Taskinen used the elevator, as if taking the stairs would have been inappropriate for the situation.

Koivu was eating a sandwich, and Anni Kuusimäki had a cup of herbal tea in front of her. She looked pale, and reflexively I glanced at her tummy. Under her loose jacket she wasn't showing yet. I settled for nodding to Koivu, since shaking hands would have seemed fake, and I didn't feel like hugging.

"So the purpose of this meeting is to provide you with information about the poisoning of Pentti Vainikainen two days ago," Taskinen said. "Unfortunately, the police were not called to the scene immediately, and the cleaner had already been through before officers arrived. But Anni can probably tell you more about the case."

I'd only met Anni Kuusimäki a few times. She'd attended the police academy five years after me even though she was only two years younger. She was tall and broad shouldered, and her dark hair was cut in a pageboy, which emphasized the pallor of her face. The situation must have been hard for her, having the Vainikainen case turned over to me without being given an explanation. Perhaps she felt like her superiors didn't trust her to lead the investigation. I understood that she didn't want to broadcast her pregnancy because it was still tenuous. I remembered how my own body had been like public property during my pregnancies, with everyone seeming to feel they had the right to pat my belly. Anni had been undergoing fertility treatments for years, and maybe she saw this as her last chance to have children. Likely she feared losing the triplets. Still, the decision about the partial sick leave had been hers.

"The victim was Pentti Vainikainen," Anni said and then repeated the same personal information I'd read online Tuesday night.

"According to his wife, he doesn't have any enemies. The possibility that the poison was meant for Vainikainen has been one of two lines of investigation. The other is that the poison was put in the sandwich for Jutta Särkikoski, the journalist. Maria, I understand you're already up to speed with this line?"

I told my colleagues about Jutta's call the previous night. Koivu stopped eating his sandwich. "That's weird," he muttered, his mouth full of white bread and ham. "Wouldn't it make more sense for the perp to keep quiet to avoid attracting attention? Did Särkikoski recognize the voice?"

"No, though she thinks the same person has called before. My first job is to get her phone records. Have we already requested the case files for Särkikoski and Väärä's car accident from the Lohja office?"

"They're e-mailing it this morning. Our interviews haven't gotten very far yet, and we haven't found enough evidence to confiscate anyone's passport. We should probably discuss how to divide our resources between this and our other open cases," Anni said.

"Yes, let's turn to that. As I've already told you, it's been decided that the Vainikainen case is our top priority and that we should use all necessary resources to solve it. You don't have any other violent-crime cases without obvious suspects, right?" Taskinen asked Anni.

"No, but there's no way to know what the future will bring. The Soukka neighborhood is still pretty restless, and we're working with the community police to prevent any more gang fights."

"Maria and her team can have two rooms on the second floor. You can use the conference room as a case room and shared office, and Maria, you'll have the separate office, where you can also conduct interviews."

"Is there a coffee machine in that conference room?" Koivu asked, clearly to lighten the mood. No one laughed.

"Requisition what you need. There's already a line item in the department's supplementary budget, 71-B. A phone and computer are waiting in your office, Maria, and your car should be in the garage by noon. Contact me if you have any questions. I have another meeting to get to." Taskinen stood up and left quickly, as if he expected us to throw sandwiches at him. Anni poured herself more tea, and I opened a bottle of mineral water. Koivu glanced back and forth between us like a boxing referee.

"So your case gets priority over everything else," Anni said. I nodded, trying to convey that I didn't want this, but I don't think I succeeded. "At the moment there are seven officers in the department besides me: Koivu, Puupponen, Puustjärvi, Honkanen, Karttunen, Lehtovuori, and Autio," she continued. "You know everyone but Karttunen, right?"

I nodded. It had started pouring outside, and pine needles flew against the windows with the water. A red umbrella escaped from its owner and tumbled across the parking lot. The umbrella rose six feet in the air before tumbling down again, and Officer Akkila, who was rushing toward the door, barely managed to dodge it. A cutup like Puupponen would have made a production of apprehending the killer travel accessory, but Akkila didn't have much sense of humor and didn't even attempt to grab it.

"You can have three officers, and a fourth part-time. I'd prefer not to give up Petri or Lehtovuori, since they're in the middle of a gang fight case. You'll be doing me a favor if you take Hon—or, no, never mind."

"Do you have an issue with Ursula?" I said before I had time to consider whether asking such a question was unwise. Anni glanced at Koivu as if to say that she'd like to talk about it later in private. I redirected the conversation to the matter at hand. "Since Koivu and Puupponen are already involved in the case, I'll take them. Pekka, I'll call your wife, because I have a feeling we're going to be working some long hours. What about this Karttunen? Does he have a family?"

"Yes," Anni and Koivu said in unison.

Anni continued, "A girlfriend and a one-year-old daughter."

"OK. So Honkanen can be our third, and Autio will be the alternate, since his kids are already teenagers." I thought about my own children, whom I would see shamefully little in the near future, and decided right then that this case was going to get solved with unprecedented efficiency. Then I could get back to my real life.

"So it's agreed." Anni eased to her feet. Even though her pregnancy wasn't showing yet, she moved as slowly as a woman in her ninth month. Suddenly I felt a wave of compassion for her. *Let Anni's pregnancy go well,* I prayed to what people surer in their faith called God.

"Anni, wait. You know I didn't ask to be on this case," I rushed to say before she could leave.

"I know." Anni held the door open for me, and I walked out, then waited for her. She closed the door behind us on a dumbfounded Koivu. "I also know Taskinen told you why I can't lead this investigation. I completely accept the situation—I was the one who decided not to tell everyone about my condition. I've been hoping for one baby for the last ten years, and now I'm expecting three. The most important murder investigation of the year can't be led by a person who might end up on bed rest at any moment."

We exchanged a gaze full of mutual understanding, and then Anni left. I already felt better, and even more so when Koivu came out and finally gave me one of his big bear hugs. He'd managed to develop a proper belly now. His fortieth birthday loomed on the horizon.

"You're furious, right?" he said when he let go of me.

"Yes. I never could have imagined walking into a trap like this."

"Well, I think Taskinen has been missing you since he got back from Canada. Puupponen and I have a conspiracy theory: Taskinen and Rajakoski intentionally engineered your research project contract so they could use it to drag you back here. And a couple of times I've heard Taskinen say you guys moved so close to the police station because you couldn't stand being away from us. Should we head down to our new HQ? Ville is probably already decorating."

I followed Koivu three flights down. On the second floor we turned away from the Violent Crime Unit. Our rooms were located right inside the glass doors, on the left side of the hall. Puupponen was in the conference room, hanging crime scene photos on the wall, and when he saw me, he started singing an off-key Schubert's "Ave Maria."

"Cut it out!" Koivu bellowed.

"But it fits the situation perfectly! Hail Maria, full of grace, the Lord is with thee!" Puupponen jumped down from the stool and gave me a combination hug and slap on the back.

"At what point did you turn into a Latinist?" I asked as I inspected the room's furnishings. It was as big as our break room in the Violent Crime Unit, but the furniture was newer.

"Last summer I dated a chick who was Catholic. I even went to mass a couple of times. But nothing came of it—the religious schism was too great." Puupponen gave a deep sigh like the male lead in a soap opera. I couldn't help but laugh. Outi and Jarkko were great colleagues, but apparently I'd missed Puupponen's dumb jokes.

Just then the door to the conference room swung open. Ursula Honkanen walked in, looking as impeccable as always. Her hair was in a stylish asymmetrical cut, and black lace pantyhose emphasized her long, beautiful legs, which ended in five-inch pumps. Her black dress looked as though it was sewn right onto her. I hadn't seen her in a while, and for a moment I couldn't help but stare. Puupponen and Koivu seemed to be immune to their colleague's charms, however.

"I was ordered to come over here," Ursula announced and then sat in the nearest chair. "Look, it's Maria. Did you decide that we couldn't get along without you?"

I didn't answer. Before I resigned, we'd managed to create a friendly rapport, but Ursula seemed to have forgotten that. I asked Koivu to tell me exactly where they were in the investigation.

"As you know, the doctor at Jorvi Hospital notified us about his suspicions of poisoning the night before last. Ville and I got straight to work. First, we interviewed the wife, Merja Vainikainen."

"In the middle of the night?"

"At six in the morning. That was when she called us back. She was pretty messed up. Then we visited the scene of the crime, but it had already been cleaned up. Hillevi Litmanen, who we also tried to interview, told us she'd thrown the sandwiches away. Of course, being the conscientious person that she is, she put them in the compost, which was emptied the following morning. Anni hasn't ordered a search of the composting facility. What do you think?"

Taskinen had promised me all possible resources. *Should I request a platoon of soldiers to search for a few gluten-free sandwiches in an ocean of compost?*

"Here are signed interview records for Litmanen, Vainikainen, and Tapani Ristiluoma," Koivu said, placing them on the table. "I put them together last night. Read them for yourself."

"Thanks. Ville, in the meantime, will you call the composting facility and find out how accurately they can identify the location of a specific load of garbage? If they know where we should look for those sandwiches, tell them not to dump anything more in that area."

"Got it, boss! Can we use this as an excuse to get them to shut the place down entirely? That dump is already overflowing, and you can smell the stink for kilometers around."

"Sure, give it a try. Ursula, will you see if the autopsy report for Pentti Vainikainen is ready? They already opened him up, right? Which one of you was there? And what about Forensics?"

"The body is in the queue, and we don't even have the drug panels back yet," Puupponen said.

"Well, Ursula, if you'll find out when the autopsy will be . . . Koivu, you start putting together a schedule of interviews. We need to get Jutta Särkikoski in here ASAP, or we can go to her home. I also want to visit the MobAbility office and Pentti Vainikainen's work and home. We'll continue with the lines of investigation Anni laid out, which means we're staying open to the idea that the poison was meant for Vainikainen even though it looks like it was intended for Jutta Särkikoski."

"What about the other possibilities?" Ursula asked. "Number three: the poison was meant for someone else entirely; and four: the whole thing was an accident."

"As in, Hillevi Litmanen intended to add some Tabasco to the mayonnaise but grabbed a bottle of drain cleaner by accident?" Koivu asked pointedly. Ursula still didn't seem to be one of his favorite people. Quite soon after her arrival in the department, Ursula had falsely accused Koivu of sexual harassment, and I had been forced to operate according to protocol and transfer Koivu to other duties until the harassment investigation was complete.

"We'll investigate every possibility," I said with a sigh and picked up the stack of interview records. "We'll split up into pairs as necessary to do the interviews. Pekka will come with me, and Ursula will go with Ville. Let's get going."

With that I went to look at my so-called private office. It was a tiny box, like most of the offices in the building. The desk was by the window, which provided a view of the parking lot and the nearby apartments to the north of the building. At least it was a change from my old view of the Turku Highway. A narrow couch with room for two just fit between the desk and one straight-backed armchair against the wall. The computer's wires hung unplugged. Ursula would be able to connect them more quickly than I would. On the desk waited a cell phone, which I picked up and turned on. Someone had left a note with the phone number and current PIN next to it. The model was new to me, and learning how to use it would take up valuable time. Maybe Iida could teach me its secrets. It was depressing to admit I was technologically behind my eleven-year-old daughter.

I sat down behind the desk and took out the interview with Merja Vainikainen. She had been completely out of her mind. According to her, her husband had occasionally complained of chest pain, but the doctor's examination hadn't found any indication of heart trouble. She had known about the threats against Jutta Särkikoski and considered it possible that the poison had reached the wrong person. When asked about the perpetrator, she responded that she didn't have a clue. Anni and Koivu had let the grieving widow off easy, so I would have to be tougher when I spoke with her. According to Tapani Ristiluoma, the three members of the staff of MobAbility, meaning himself, his secretary, and the bookkeeper, had participated in the campaign launch, but the other two had left the premises at the same time as the press. They'd been served coffee, tea, and cookies, while the sandwiches were reserved for the small group of invited guests, which had included Vainikainen, Ristiluoma, Jutta Särkikoski, Toni Väärä, and Ilpo Koskelo, and Hillevi Litmanen and Miikka Harju from the Adaptive Sports Association. Hillevi had handled the food. According to the crime scene pictures on the wall in the conference room, the kitchen at MobAbility was a typical small office kitchenette. Koivu had also included a floor plan of the office in his notes. There was only one door into the kitchen.

According to Hillevi Litmanen, she'd brought some of the serving dishes from home, and some were from the Adaptive Sports office.

Theoretically, anyone could have entered the kitchen, but Ristiluoma had claimed that he would have noticed if anyone from the media had gone in there. But Hillevi hadn't gone to get the gluten-free bread until after the media left. And she had made the sandwiches herself.

In her interview, Litmanen had obviously been confused. She'd responded to almost every question by saying that she didn't remember. We'd have to talk to her again as soon as possible. Had the Adaptive Sports staff all been coming to work as normal? We'd find out once Koivu contacted everyone.

What if Leena had been present for the campaign launch? Then could I have recused myself because a suspect was one of my best friends? For a moment I got lost in the fantasy, but then I realized how pointless it was to spend time on what-ifs.

At this point the only evidence I had of the most recent death threats was Jutta Särkikoski's word. I needed to trace last night's call to her phone. Then we could compare that to the other death-threat calls from before the accident. Receiving permission from the district court should be routine, given the possibility that someone had tried to kill Jutta. I didn't believe that the phone records would actually help, since the call likely came from a burner cell, but we had to try everything. And if we did find calls from a prepaid phone, that would at least prove that someone was trying to hide their identity.

I'd left the office door open, so Ursula walked in without knocking.

"They're performing the autopsy on Vainikainen today at three, and we'll have the report tomorrow morning. Do we need to go for it?"

"No need unless you really want to, since it's probably poisoning." I motioned to the computer. "This is a job for IT, but who knows when they'll come. Could you help with all these cords?"

Ursula laughed. "So you're trying to put us in our place from the get-go, is that it?"

"It'll just mean less swearing if you do it. I promise to watch and learn. Could you also handle the machine in the conference room?"

"Fine." Ursula sat down at the desk and started inserting cords into the computer and the electrical outlet under the window. Then she booted up the machine, checked the software, and made sure the firewall was up to date and that the connections to the intranet and Internet worked. Then she told me to create a password.

"I think this should be a shared computer, since you might need it too. I'll just protect my own files as needed."

"Whatever you want," Ursula said, sounding somewhat pacified. Maybe it had to do with the thought of getting on her boss's computer. "You don't know how to use Dragnet, do you?"

"What?"

"The new internal police messaging system. We started using it in October 2006. Come here, I'll show you." Ursula nearly purred with satisfaction as she introduced me to the new intranet application. I knew she would be even more pleased if I turned out to be completely hopeless with it, but I didn't feel like pretending to be an idiot. And besides, Dragnet was relatively user-friendly, so Ursula was free to get back to arranging the autopsy ten minutes later.

I opened the main folder for the Vainikainen case and divided it into subfolders. These were the routines that always kicked off an investigation. Forensics had visited the MobAbility office the day before, and I was waiting for a report to appear on my computer at any moment. Anni hadn't sealed off the office, so the employees had been able to get back to work once Forensics left. I called Tapani Ristiluoma and announced that we'd be coming by that afternoon.

He sounded extremely irritated. A crime scene attracted more than police. He thought the whole incident was insane, and he didn't like that their fitness campaign had been overshadowed. I understood his concerns. He was an entrepreneur, after all.

"Did you already know Pentti Vainikainen or Jutta Särkikoski?" I asked.

"I've been working with Jutta throughout the campaign, and I'd heard of her from the news. Pentti and I played a few rounds of golf together, but I wouldn't say I knew him. Hey, I have a client meeting soon with a rehabilitation facility in Russia. Can we talk this afternoon?" Ristiluoma said.

Puupponen had appeared at the door during our phone call. He was still as wiry as he'd been the first time I met him. Back then a mutual distaste for Pertti Ström had united us; having a common enemy created a strong bond. But it was hard to get to know the real Puupponen, because he concealed his feelings under a layer of buffoonery. Now was no different.

"The compost heap sends its regards! I could almost smell the place through the phone. We can look for the two leftover gluten-free sandwiches if we want to. They won't have decomposed completely yet, and there's only a meter of other compost and desiccant over it. We would probably have to take Hillevi Litmanen with us to identify the sandwiches, though if she's in the same shape as she was yesterday, she won't even remember if it was white or dark bread."

"Is there such a thing as dark gluten-free bread?" I asked as Koivu came into the room.

"Särkikoski is on her way here," he said. "Mrs. Vainikainen is ready to receive us at our convenience. Ilpo Koskelo and Toni Väärä are in Turku, and Hillevi Litmanen is on sick leave at home. She's still incoherent from the sedatives. She was just saying that this is a plot by her ex-husband to get her in prison with him so he can start beating her again."

"That's imaginative. OK. Pekka, first let's talk to Särkikoski, then head to the MobAbility offices at the Waterfall Building, then to Vainikainen's house," I said, then shooed the men into the conference room to join Ursula so all three of them could hear my instructions at the same time.

"Ville, find out who from the media was at the launch event. You may be able to get a list from Adaptive Sports. Miikka Harju would be the person to contact. Tell him we'll be expecting him here tomorrow at nine a.m. Also get the guys from Turku in here tomorrow. Don't let them give you any guff about interrupting their training schedule. Call every single person who was at the launch and get their impressions of the event. Ursula, search for any and all media material related to the launch. Wasn't there a TV camera there? Hopefully they haven't deleted the tape."

Ursula made notes, and then she lifted her head and gave me a pointed look. "Is it wise to talk to the media so soon? You've always been careful about preventing our cases from leaking," she said. "We haven't even held a press conference about this one yet."

"No, we haven't. I'll arrange that with the department press officer next. Thanks for reminding me. Anyway, I think those reporters will fall all over themselves to be the hero who comes up with the detail that helps solve the case. And I wouldn't be here if the big boys and girls didn't think this was going to turn into a media shitstorm anyway. Just keep your heads cool."

I returned to my office to call the press officer about holding a briefing late that evening. Maybe I'd be able to get home in time to read Taneli a bedtime story and chat with Iida. These days she only let me read to her in exceptional circumstances.

Deciding whether to search the dump could wait until the autopsy report came in. I didn't want to start an expensive operation that would attract public scrutiny without a good reason. If it looked likely that the poison came from the sandwiches, we would definitely have to go looking for the remaining ones, and fast. A search that big would have to wait until the morning, right when the sun rose at around seven. Hopefully Hillevi Litmanen would be of some help.

My phone rang. It was the receptionist from downstairs, calling to announce that Jutta Särkikoski had arrived. I stopped by the conference room to ask Koivu to escort her up. Ursula and Puupponen were speaking heatedly into their phones. I grabbed some water and an orange soda from the machine in the hall, then returned to my office.

"Maria! What are you doing here?" Jutta exclaimed when she arrived at the door. She looked as if she hadn't slept since Midsummer. I felt guilty because I'd entertained the idea that she'd lied about the death threats to get attention. Of course, I knew I couldn't completely write her off as a suspect for Pentti Vainikainen's murder. Perhaps she believed that he had something to do with her car accident.

"I've been ordered to take over this investigation."

"You? That can't be . . ." For a moment I thought she was going to cry. "How . . ."

"It's a long story. Anyway, have a seat on the sofa and let's get started. Who knew you have celiac disease? I mean, out of the people at the campaign launch?"

"Everyone at the ASA . . . so Merja, Hillevi, and Miikka. But probably everyone knew after Merja made such a big deal about Hillevi forgetting to buy gluten-free bread. Hillevi left for the delicatessen under Stockmann downtown, while some of the media people were still around. Oh, and Ilpo Koskelo and Toni might have known, since we ate together when I interviewed them before the accident. Do you think the poison was meant for me?"

"We haven't ruled it out. Do you have information that someone might want to keep quiet?"

A fire kindled in Jutta's eyes, and she leaned over the desk from the sofa and took me by the hand. "This isn't about that, Maria. This is about revenge. Just before I left to come here, I learned that Tapani Ristiluoma is Sami Terävä's cousin. That's right, the discus thrower I exposed. Apparently they're really close. Isn't it obvious? We were in Ristiluoma's office. What better place to get rid of me?"

6

It took a while before Jutta calmed down. She even looked askance at the water glass I set in front of her.

"I only found out about their connection by chance when I was chatting with a colleague. She was commenting on the campaign launch and said it was nice that there wasn't a grudge between me and Ristiluoma. When I asked why there should be, she said that Ristiluoma is Sami Terävä's cousin. How could I have known that?"

"How has Ristiluoma treated you?"

"Professionally, but of course he would do that if he intended to hurt me! Why would he attract suspicion?"

"Who suggested that the launch should be held at MobAbility instead of at Adaptive Sports?"

"Ristiluoma! They have a lot of their mobility aids on display there, and he thought it was a good idea to show that to the press. Free advertising. And I thought that was fine. Merja and I went to visit their office before we agreed. It seemed like it would work since we didn't expect a huge crowd at the launch anyway. About fifteen journalists attended, in addition to a sports news camera team."

"Were any of them your enemies?"

Jutta grimaced. "No. The ones who think I'm a traitor rarely write about disabled athletes, so they'd have no reason to be there. But how can I know who's a friend and who's an enemy anymore? I barely dare to eat anything that I haven't made myself from scratch. If someone really wants to kill me, what can I do? I can't spend the rest of my life cowering at home."

"Of course not." I thought again about the resources Taskinen had promised. Would that cover a police guard detail for Jutta too? For that I'd have to prove that the poison was intended for her. At the very least, she should have a friend stay with her for a few nights.

I drank from my own water glass as if to show Jutta that it was safe.

"I thought the whole to-do about the gluten-free rolls was completely blown out of proportion, but it was Merja's way of exercising power over Hillevi. Merja is used to things being handled quickly, and Hillevi is . . . well, slow. Hillevi came from the store just before the event started and hid in the kitchen making the sandwiches. The regular sandwiches, with the regular bread."

I didn't reveal to Jutta that I was previously acquainted with Hillevi, because that would be a breach of confidentiality. Jutta related what we already knew from Merja Vainikainen's and Tapani Ristiluoma's accounts: at the beginning of the press event, Ristiluoma had given a brief welcome speech, then Merja Vainikainen introduced the exercise campaign for the Adaptive Sports Association, and Toni Väärä talked about the importance of MobAbility products in his recovery. Jutta served as master of ceremonies. According to Jutta's recollection, no one besides Hillevi had gone in the kitchen during the event.

"At what point did the food service start? Did Hillevi or someone else distribute it? Was it person to person, or was it just set on a buffet table?"

Jutta thought for a while. Apparently the food hadn't interested her.

"The sandwiches weren't served to anyone specifically. They just appeared on a table before we started the toasts. And that was when Merja noticed that the gluten-free sandwiches were missing. The whole party was nearly derailed by it."

"Did Pentti Vainikainen have celiac?" I wanted to hear Jutta's answer, even though Merja Vainikainen had already stated in her preliminary interview that her husband didn't have any food allergies.

"Not that I know of, but I'd only met him once or twice, and we didn't talk about anything like that."

When I asked Jutta again whom she thought the poisoned sandwiches were meant for, she said it was obvious that she was the target. And that somehow Hillevi Litmanen had thrown a wrench into the murderer's plan.

"I'll have to call Merja. I assume she isn't at work. I wonder if anyone but Miikka is in the office," Jutta said.

"How well do you know Miikka Harju?" I asked. Harju had been the one who took her home after Pentti Vainikainen went to the hospital.

"Not very well. He's a former firefighter who had to leave his job because of back trouble. He seems trustworthy, and his own experience helps him empathize with people with disabilities. Wait. Does he have connections to . . . ?" Jutta was starting to sound more paranoid than an American conspiracy theory show. "I already have a burglar alarm, but do I need to start checking my car every time I go out too? Or would it be safer to take taxis?"

I didn't have any guidance for Jutta. Instead I told her that I was filing for a warrant to access her phone records, and that I would get back to her when I heard back. Finally, I asked whether she had gone in the kitchen at any point that day.

"What do you mean? Like, I tried to poison myself—or someone else?"

I scoffed mentally when I realized that Jutta's paranoia was rubbing off on me. I recognized it from years past: during the initial stages of a criminal investigation, when everyone was a stranger and the chain of events unclear, I wouldn't know who to trust. A couple of times I'd allowed my emotions to influence an investigation. I wasn't going to do that again.

Jutta described the death threats again, and now she seemed sure that the caller was Tapani Ristiluoma. I asked her not to answer any calls from numbers she didn't recognize. Of course, the best thing would be if the perpetrator were careless enough to leave a voice mail again. I needed to get that warrant for her phone records pronto.

After Jutta left, Puupponen came in to give me an interim report on his conversations with the media attendees. One reporter from a local paper in Southern Ostrobothnia had said flat out that he wasn't the slightest bit interested in the disability sports campaign and that he had only come to see what shape Toni Väärä was in. According to another reporter, Jutta Särkikoski had seemed extremely tense throughout the press event. The TV crew had promised to send over their tape by the afternoon, and Ursula said she would review it. I decided to take Koivu to see the scene of the crime, the MobAbility office in the Waterfall Building.

As promised, a car was waiting for me in the garage. The police department's car policy had changed since I'd left. Now the police didn't own any unmarked cars; they just rented them as necessary. A black Renault Scenic awaited us, and Koivu had to fight with the key for a while before figuring out how it worked. He also managed to kill the engine at the first stoplight.

"Thank God this isn't a cop car. That would be mortifying," Koivu said, finally getting the car started again on the third try as the Audi riding his bumper started honking. "Let's give him a ticket," Koivu said. "Isn't failing to maintain a proper distance a traffic violation?"

"Just drive," I said. Suddenly I missed the department's old fleet of 1990s Russian Ladas, which lacked elegance and required real strength to shift.

"I've been through the possible poisons and also got a preliminary guess from the forensic pathologist. So far Vainikainen's symptoms are consistent with nicotine poisoning. They present quickly. Could Vainikainen have received the poison before the event?" Koivu asked.

"What doesn't add up is the fact that nicotine tastes really, really bad. Vainikainen doesn't smoke, so he would have tasted it. Särkikoski doesn't smoke either. Do you remember how much nicotine it takes to kill?" I asked Koivu.

"Sixty milligrams will take out an adult, and twenty or so is enough for a kid. This one time, right after Juuso learned to walk, he stuck a cigarette butt in his mouth, but he spat it out because it tasted so bad. We called poison control, and Anu got the lethal dosage information from them. But nicotine is just a guess. We'll have to wait for the autopsy and drug panels."

I opened my laptop and looked up the forensic pictures from the MobAbility office, which I'd downloaded. Koivu managed to kill the car again in the middle of the ramp into the parking garage. I wondered whether I should offer to drive when we headed for the Vainikainen residence.

A flock of geese had gathered on the lawn in front of the Waterfall Building. A couple of ducks stood with them, looking like they were trying to blend in. In the lobby, two people stopped us, one of whom had a camera. I recognized the one without a camera as a crime reporter. Apparently one of the tabloids was staking out the lobby.

"Look, it's Lieutenant Kallio. Back at Espoo police, I see."

"Temporarily." I tried to pass him, but he was persistent.

"Why did you return to the police? Is this some sort of special case? Anything new you can tell us? Is it true that Pentti Vainikainen was killed accidentally?"

"We don't know yet. We'll see you at seven o'clock at the press conference at the Espoo police station. I'll give you an update on the investigation then," I replied, sidestepping the cameraman, who was trying to get a shot of me and Koivu together.

"Could the case have some connection to Pentti Vainikainen advocating for increased funding for star professional athletes at the expense of amateur programs? His opinion was that the only way to develop star athletes was to support star athletes, and the 'everyone plays' agenda is detrimental. You can find his latest statements on our website."

"We're investigating all avenues. Thanks for the tip. If you could allow us to continue our work now, we can move this case forward." I practically pushed the cameraman out of my way and stepped into the elevator with Koivu in tow. The MobAbility offices were on the second-highest floor. I rang the doorbell, and a large man of about forty with a beard answered the door. He wore a dark suit as if he was going to a funeral. I introduced us.

"Yes, come in. I'm Tapani Ristiluoma. I understand that you're trying to solve this case, but this is taking up an awful lot of our work time, and it doesn't help the situation that your forensic team took some of our sample devices. The papers are claiming that Pentti was poisoned. Is that true?"

I didn't answer and instead looked around. On the far side of the reception area were four doors. Three had nameplates: "Ristiluoma," "Häkkinen," and "Vainio," and the fourth was the restroom.

"May I?" I asked. Ristiluoma nodded, and Koivu and I started our tour of the office. A hall led to a glassed-in conference room, where there was a table that would seat six, two couches, and a few glass display cases, some of which were empty. Some contained elbow supports, water therapy belts, and various balls, which apparently were intended for arm and finger muscle therapy. The kitchen was located at the back of the conference room. The windows had a marvelous view across the sea toward Helsinki. The flock of geese was just taking off from the grass. The first birds rose to the south as others followed, and within seconds the grass was empty. Slowly the flock disappeared into the horizon. Antti and I had a habit of waving to migrating birds, and the children had adopted the tradition. I raised my hand but then quickly dropped it when I noticed Ristiluoma watching me. I didn't bother explaining. He could go ahead and think that waving at windows was normal police procedure.

The kitchen was a typical office kitchen with space for a small table. There were three chairs. The refrigerator, stove, and cupboards were the same as in my family's previous apartment, which we'd dubbed the "White Cube." Because Forensics had already visited, I didn't need to put on gloves. I opened the refrigerator. There was nothing but an unopened carton of yogurt and two apples, apparently someone's lunch.

"They took everything from the coffee machine to the sugar bowl," Ristiluoma said accusingly.

"You'll get it all back once they've taken samples. What do you usually store in this kitchen?"

"Mostly coffee and pastries. We usually go out to lunch, since there are a lot of restaurants near here." Ristiluoma pointed out the window at the center of Tapiola. His dark suit looked a little tight on him, and he stopped his arm motion halfway.

"I truly don't understand how someone could have poisoned Pentti in front of all of us. Are you sure he didn't ingest the poison somewhere else? I don't think anyone went in the kitchen except the woman who was handling the food."

"Not even when she was gone?"

"I don't know! Merja organized that part, and I didn't interfere."

"Who cleans your office? What time does the cleaner come?"

Ristiluoma smiled faintly. "I don't actually know. The property management company arranges the cleaning. Maybe my colleagues know. Just a moment." Ristiluoma left the room, and I heard him knock on a door.

I continued my inspection of the kitchen, opening all the drawers, the first of which turned out to be a cutting board. I told Koivu to pretend to be cutting bread and went into the conference room. The kitchen door opened in, and even at halfway open there would be no view of the cutting board.

Ristiluoma came back. "Satu remembered. Here's the name of the company. The cleaner comes at night, sometime around eight thirty or nine. I'm sure you can easily find out who cleaned on Tuesday night and where they took the trash. We haven't been in this office long, just since last spring, and our office secretary, Satu Häkkinen, handles these sorts of practical matters."

"Was hosting the campaign launch here your idea?"

"Both Merja Vainikainen and I came up with that. Merja is a great woman. She really wants to improve disability fitness services, not just competition sports. We offer mobility devices for anyone who needs them. Our factory is in Toijala, south of Tampere, and most of our employees are there, but we have to run our marketing operation here in the capital area. And business in Russia is really—"

I interrupted Ristiluoma's spiel and asked him about his version of events. Koivu taped our conversation. Ristiluoma's account didn't differ from Jutta Särkikoski's, other than he thought the media had been extremely interested in the campaign. Toni Väärä had shown how a custom-made hip belt had helped him keep his lumbar spine properly oriented so it didn't take too much stress when he ran.

"I have pictures. Look!" Ristiluoma took out his phone. On the screen, a shirtless Toni Väärä showed off the belt system, looking a little self-conscious. His upper body was muscular, since his race, the 800 meter, required power. At that point everyone's attention would have been on Väärä, and someone would have had no trouble slipping into the kitchen.

"Do you smoke?" Koivu asked Ristiluoma. "Do any of your coworkers?"

"No. Nicotine and sports don't mix. Satu quit a couple of years ago, and I don't think Anneli has ever smoked. Why?"

"What are your sports, in addition to golf?" I asked.

"When I was younger, I threw javelin, until I blew out my shoulder. Now it's mostly just golf and cross-country skiing."

"What about discus throwing?" Koivu said. "Your family seems to have a talent for that."

For a moment Ristiluoma appeared confused, but then the lights went on. "Oh, you mean my cousin Sami, Sami Terävä. Yes, he was a gifted discus thrower, but not gifted enough. And definitely not smart enough. Can you imagine throwing away a whole career over that doping nonsense!"

"You don't approve of doping?" I asked, giving Ristiluoma my best interrogator look. His face flushed a little, but that wasn't necessarily a sign of lying or even a rise in blood pressure.

"Of course not! Sami tried to convince me that everyone does it, but I didn't buy it."

"So you didn't have any trouble working with the journalist who exposed your cousin?" Koivu's voice was soft, practically gentle. Usually he brought out his sympathetic side with young people and women, and I wondered why he was trying it out on Ristiluoma. Ristiluoma stood up and nearly knocked Koivu's little voice recorder off the table.

"You can't seriously think that I . . . For a little shit like Sami? Hell no!" His guffaw surprised us both. Ristiluoma sat back down at the table. "C'mon. I wouldn't be stupid enough to try to poison Jutta Särkikoski in my own office. Or let some other innocent person accidentally eat the poison! Is that your theory? Excuse my laughing, but that's ridiculous! I can't tell you how angry I am at Sami for his doping shenanigans. There's more than fifteen years between us, and I tried to take him under my wing, but the kid is just a few bricks shy of a load, if you know what I mean. No, I think Jutta Särkikoski did Finnish sports a favor, and I tip my hat to her."

After we wrapped things up with Ristiluoma, we had a brief word with his accountant and secretary. Both were shocked by the incident. As Koivu drove toward the Vainikainens' home in an old neighborhood on the east side of Helsinki, I called the property management company to find out who from the cleaning company handled the MobAbility office.

"Waterfall Building . . . MobAbility . . . Hold on. Yes, our cleaner there is named Przemyslaw Siudek," an energetic-sounding woman said.

"What?"

"Przemyslaw Siudek. First name: P-R-Z-E-M-Y-S-L-A-W, last name: S-I-U-D-E-K. He's Polish."

"Could I have his cell phone number?"

"He doesn't have one. He doesn't even have a landline. But he's dependable, and we've never had a single complaint about his work. He starts at the Waterfall Building at eight thirty. I can give you his home address, if you'd like."

"No need, thanks." I said, knowing that we'd find him at work. I hung up, then I called Puupponen and asked him to hunt down Siudek in the evening. I didn't dare guess the nickname Puupponen would come up for a Pole named Przemyslaw.

Street signs flashed past as we neared the Vainikainen home. Most of the names were familiar to me, since during our house hunt Antti and I had looked at a house on Lynx Road. It had a wonderfully large lot, but the kids didn't want to move that far from their friends and the ice rink they were used to, and anyway the price of the home was more than we could afford. The trees in the neighborhood were taller than the apartment buildings, and the sounds of traffic on the East Highway were muffled.

The Vainikainens' house was the same subdued 1950s style of most of the housing stock in the area. The aspen in the yard already had some yellow leaves up high, and a few had fallen on the Volkswagen parked in front of the garage door.

"Is Mrs. Vainikainen our prime suspect at this point?" Koivu asked. He succeeded in stopping the car without it bucking too much.

"If the poison was meant for her husband, then yes. Mrs. Vainikainen hired Jutta Särkikoski to head up the campaign, so she must have known about Jutta's past. And you'd suppose she would also know who her husband's enemies were, if he had any. But let's treat her like a grieving widow rather than a prime suspect. According to you, she was all over the place when you last spoke."

"Yes. That's why I don't like this case. Too many hysterical women."

"Well, at least you have me." I patted Koivu on the shoulder. "Go have a look at Pentti Vainikainen's personal effects while I try to form a sisterly bond with the wife."

"OK, boss." Now Koivu patted me on the head. I elbowed him in the ribs and then rang the doorbell.

The woman who answered the door didn't seem at all hysterical. Her medium-length blond hair was styled in a fluffy helmet, and there was no sign of mascara running. She was wearing a black pantsuit and a white blouse, a work outfit clearly repurposed for mourning. I looked her in the eyes to see if her pupils betrayed the use of sedatives, but they revealed nothing. Her handshake was that of a person who was used to meeting visitors and giving an impression of dependability.

"Hello, I'm Detective Lieutenant Maria Kallio. I've taken over the investigation into the death of Pentti Vainikainen."

Merja Vainikainen said hello and motioned for us to enter. The entryway was narrow, and Koivu created a traffic jam as he paused to take off his coat. I looked at the patent leather men's shoes shining on the shoe rack. Pentti Vainikainen wouldn't need those anymore.

"I heard that leadership of the investigation had changed. Was there some particular reason?"

"Just prioritization. This case has been moved ahead of our other cases. Sergeant Koivu would like to inspect your husband's personal effects. Where are they, Mrs. Vainikainen?"

"In the bedroom and . . . Do you really have to rummage through everything?" Now there was a slight note of hysteria in Merja Vainikainen's voice.

"Did your husband have a home computer?"

"We share one. It's in the office, here on the main level."

"Was it just the two of you living here?"

"I have a daughter from my first marriage. She's at her piano lesson. Mona and Pentti didn't interact much, and obviously Mona doesn't have anything to do with this. She didn't know anything about Pentti that would be worth telling you." Merja Vainikainen seemed to want to protect her daughter, which was understandable. The population registry had said that Mona Linnakangas was sixteen years old, so she wasn't exactly a child anymore.

I was in no rush to interview her. Koivu went off to look for the office, and Vainikainen and I went into the living room. The furniture was a lime green that glowed strangely in the waning September light. Wavy patterns were painted on the walls, suggesting the sea at night in June when it never gets completely dark.

"You've been married for four years?"

Merja Vainikainen sighed. "That sounds like such a short time. We met at the Finnish Athletics Federation while I was working there as the youth-fitness project manager. We fell in love. We were both unattached, but we still tried to keep our relationship secret as long as possible. Of course, it came out eventually, and after that we got married quite quickly. I probably would have been able to get a permanent training manager position at the federation, but I didn't apply because I didn't want anyone thinking I was sleeping my way to the top. Perhaps you know what that's like, as a professional woman." Merja Vainikainen looked at me as if expecting an answer. I nodded; I remembered how Pertti Ström had accused me of getting a promotion by sleeping with Taskinen.

"That's why I moved to Adaptive Sports, even though I took a small cut in my salary. But Pentti's job was his dream. The government is appropriating funding for sports, and Pentti wanted to have an influence on that. It's so wrong that this had to happen right now when . . ." Merja Vainikainen stopped and took a deep breath.

"When what?" I asked, but Vainikainen shook her head. I let her calm down before continuing. "Did your husband have enemies, Mrs. Vainikainen?" I heard Koivu drop something and swear quietly, but Merja Vainikainen didn't seem to register the noise.

"Enemies . . . that's quite a strong word. I can't imagine anyone would have wanted to kill Pentti. He wasn't always the easiest person to be around, but he treated people fairly. Pentti was especially liked by the athletes, and he always looked out for his own. He wanted us to send the most complete teams possible to all the big competitions. Pentti may have had some run-ins with the press, because he didn't have much patience for criticism of our athletes. He always reminded people that Finland is a small country." Merja Vainikainen gave a brave smile. "Maybe this is typical defensiveness for a grieving wife, but I do think the poison was meant for someone else. I practically had to force Hillevi to buy those gluten-free rolls! Maybe if she hadn't . . ." Vainikainen's words trailed off, and I let her dry her eyes before I continued.

"Do you have an idea about whom the poison might have been meant for?"

"Well, Jutta. Särkikoski. She's been getting threats again, but I'm sure you know that. Or maybe Hillevi just got mixed up and put uncooked false morels in the sandwiches or something like that. I should have handled the food myself! I've tried to be understanding, and I know how hard Hillevi's life has been, but she is such a burden on our organization. I'm not sure if she's at all well."

"False morels? Were those in the sandwiches?"

"No! That was just an example. We had parsley butter and garlic mayonnaise, and I don't know which Hillevi used on the gluten-free sandwiches. Maybe the mayonnaise. Pentti loves . . . loved garlic. There was also smoked salmon, prosciutto, or chèvre, which were on the other sandwiches too. The one I ate, which was on normal bread, had parsley butter and prosciutto."

Those flavor combinations didn't seem strong enough to cover the bitter taste of nicotine, and Hillevi would have smelled it too. I glanced at my watch: ten minutes to two. We still had time before the autopsy would even start.

"Mrs. Vainikainen, I'm sorry for bringing this up, but I read that Pentti divorced his first wife. Do you know why? Did they keep in contact after the split?"

"Not really. Eva moved back to Sweden. All he told me was that their flame had died, and Eva never really got used to life in Finland. They'd also lived in Latvia, when Pentti coached long-distance runners there in the early nineties. Another reason could have been that they couldn't have children. For us that possibility had passed. And please, call me Merja. Being called Mrs. Vainikainen feels cold, like I'm being accused of something."

"OK. What brought you and Pentti together?"

"Whatever brings anyone together . . . Things just fell into place. And there's our love of sports."

"Are you a former competitive athlete as well?"

"Oh, yes. When I was younger, I was pretty good in the 100 meter and the long jump, but my best sport was speed skiing. Too bad it wasn't an Olympic event. Still, I have a silver and a bronze medal from the world championships. Maybe you remember? My maiden name was Ikonen. Merja Ikonen."

The name didn't ring a bell, but I nodded politely. Merja didn't seem to notice.

"I also tried ski jumping, but in the 1980s, they didn't want girls, and no one would coach me, even though I jumped farther than most of the boys. Sometimes on the hill they would announce that no women were allowed, and this one time, someone broke my skis when my dad forgot to put them in the car. But I landed more than forty meters on a thirty-meter hill . . ." Merja Vainikainen's expression was wistful. "Sometimes I watch the ski jumpers at the hill here and wonder if I would still dare. Maybe now . . . I don't have anything left to lose."

There was the sound of a door opening upstairs, and I saw Merja Vainikainen stiffen. "Oh my God, who's up there? Isn't the other detective in Pentti's office? Who could that be? You don't think . . ."

I acted on instinct. I didn't have a sidearm, but I grabbed a heavy candlestick off a table and rushed up the stairs, ready for almost anything. Fortunately, Koivu was in the house too. But upstairs there was no lurking murderer, just a young, scared-looking, obese girl. When she saw me with the candlestick, she howled like a cat with its tail caught in a door and rushed into the nearest room.

7

"Mona! What on earth are you doing here? You were supposed to be . . ." Merja Vainikainen had followed me up the stairs, and now she jerked open the door the girl had slipped behind. It looked like a bathroom. I turned away. As I walked back downstairs, I berated myself for my overreaction. I heard Merja Vainikainen speaking quietly, but I couldn't make out the girl's voice. Were there two ways to get upstairs, or had Mona been skulking inside this whole time, when she was supposed to be at piano practice?

I peeked in the office, where Koivu was flipping through binders.

"I haven't found anything interesting yet," he said. He seemed bored. "Not even any porn. And Vainikainen's finances seem to be in order. I went over his bank statements."

I thanked my lucky stars that Merja Vainikainen hadn't thought to ask us for a search warrant, since we didn't have one. We would need to get one for the Athletics Federation office.

The home office seemed to also serve as a spare guest bedroom, with a dark-blue pullout sofa against one wall. Vainikainen's workstation was orderly, with a bulky old desktop computer and a multifunction printer. On a separate writing desk there were a few pens and a picture of Merja Vainikainen smiling broadly in a bikini. It wouldn't have looked out of place on the cover of a fitness magazine.

I heard Merja Vainikainen's heels clicking on the stairs. She entered the office, an expression of irritation on her face, but her anger was not directed at Koivu's opening of drawers. "She canceled her piano lesson without telling me," Vainikainen said. "She hasn't been able to practice with what's going on. Mona . . . well, you saw her."

"Only a glimpse."

"She's sick, but what can we do? She has to go to school, but as soon as no one is watching, she goes and buys junk food."

"Does she suffer from bulimia?"

"If only she threw up! No, I don't mean that. I'm just so tired of all of this, and now Pentti is dead. That certainly won't help Mona's condition."

"Does she go to therapy?"

"We can't get public assistance, since she isn't in immediate danger. You should see the queue to get into the eating disorder clinic! I'm considering private therapy, if it gets any worse. I don't expect to get any support from her deadbeat father. He couldn't care less about her."

"Who is Mona's father?"

"Jari Linnakangas. He lives in a commune somewhere in Lapland and practices free love with his harem. I imagine they think they're artists, although mostly they're just welfare bums. Jari has two years of alimony judgements against him, but what are they supposed to garnish when he doesn't have any income and all his property belongs to those women? That man was the biggest mistake of my life—it's true what they say about love being blind. After him, I married his exact opposite, a career army officer, thinking he would be a stable father for Mona. Unfortunately, Olli believed he should be able to issue orders at home the same way he did at the barracks. The third time was the charm, but I guess that didn't last long either."

Even though Merja Vainikainen spoke calmly, she gave the impression of being on the verge of breaking down. Maybe she was one of those people who thought it impolite to show feelings to strangers.

I asked her to tell me about her deceased husband's friends, and she recited a list of names that were familiar not only from the sports section but also the financial and political pages of the newspaper. I was beginning to understand why the higher-ups at the Espoo Police Department had decided that his killing took precedence over all the other violent-crime investigations. Then I remembered the tabloid reporter's comment about Pentti Vainikainen's attitude toward support for fitness sports.

"I've heard that Pentti was a strong proponent of directing more funds toward competitive athletes. So why was your husband at the launch for the MobAbility and Adaptive Sports campaign?" I asked.

"The federation was one of the funding organizations. Why wouldn't Pentti have been there? Toni Väärä is an excellent example of how an injured elite athlete can use mobility devices designed for the disabled."

"Did he protest when you hired Jutta Särkikoski to handle public relations for your campaign?"

"How is that related? Of course Pentti was furious when he had to explain the nonsense with Salo and Terävä to the federation's sponsors, but that was part of his job. If Jutta hadn't exposed them, someone else would have, or they would have gotten caught eventually. The end result would have been the same no matter what. But yes, Pentti defended competitive sports. He is the social affairs director of an organization that supports competitive sports, after all. What else should he have done? Pentti was also at the campaign launch as my husband, but now I wish he would have stayed home . . . I'm going to blame myself for the rest of my life if it turns out Pentti is dead because I hired Jutta."

"Did your husband have celiac? Did he smoke?"

"Neither. I have no idea why he ate that gluten-free sandwich. Maybe he was curious about how it would taste. Pentti was always trying new things. That's why I liked him. He had a good head on his shoulders too, unlike Mona's dad. Pentti had a wide circle of friends, because he was interested in all kinds of people. He didn't have any prejudices. He didn't even condemn those discus throwers. He just said that actions have consequences."

Koivu came out of the kitchen with a cell phone and a fat brown wallet.

"This phone is locked. Do you know your husband's PIN code?"

"I'm sorry, no . . ."

My own phone started ringing. It was Ursula.

"I watched the tape of the launch event," she said.

"And?"

"The runner, Toni Väärä, goes into the kitchen after he gives his speech. There's also a man with dark hair who looks kind of shabby. He goes in the kitchen once too. I can't tell if he's a reporter or a representative from one of the organizations. He has a camera around his neck, so maybe he's a photographer."

"Find out who he is. Anything else?"

"I'm at the pathologist's lab now. Based on initial findings, the tissue damage makes it look like there was nicotine in Vainikainen's system, but that's just a guess, and there's no information yet about the amount."

I swallowed to stop myself from saying the word "nicotine" out loud. At least now we had an idea of what poison was used. "Pekka and I will be back at the station in a little while, if we don't get stuck in traffic. See you soon."

A clatter came from upstairs again, and Merja Vainikainen cast an irritated glance in that direction. Even though I'd only caught a glimpse of Mona, I suspected that Merja was ashamed of her daughter. The teen was the opposite of her elite athlete mother. I decided to have a little chat with Mona while Koivu questioned Merja. He'd just asked about Pentti Vainikainen's personal wealth and financial situation, and Merja was focused on answering and so didn't stop me from leaving the office and going upstairs.

I remembered which door Mona had come out of and knocked on it. Not a peep came from inside. I pressed down on the lever and opened the door. The room was nearly dark: the blinds were down, and the walls were painted black. The only light came from a reading lamp above the bed. The girl lay on top of her covers and didn't even turn her head. She had long, thick, slightly curly auburn hair. She was wearing loose sweat pants and a hoodie, both also black. "Hi, Mona. I'm Detective Kallio from the Espoo Police Department, and I'm investigating Pentti Vainikainen's death. I'd like to express my condolences. Would you mind speaking with me for a moment?"

Mona didn't look at me, but she did answer, in a voice so quiet I could barely hear.

"I don't know anything."

"What kind of man was your stepfather?"

I couldn't hear her muttered reply, so I stepped closer. Then she flinched and curled up in a loose fetal position, her round stomach and bulky limbs in the way so that she couldn't curl up tight.

"Mona, I didn't hear what you said. What kind of man was your stepfather?"

"Gone," she said.

"What do you mean?"

"Pentti was always gone," she repeated, pausing between each word as if speaking was an enormous effort. Then Merja Vainikainen was in the room.

"My daughter is a minor, and the police can't question her without me present! Will you please leave her in peace? This could set off another attack . . . She'll start eating potato flour straight from the bag."

"Mona, do you have anything you'd like to tell the police?" I asked anyway, but she didn't answer. The darkness of the room seemed to absorb all sound. The bedspread and curtains were black, and the wood floor was also painted black, with no rug. On the desk was a computer, and there were a few books and CDs on the shelf, but there were no pictures or posters, no photographs or decorations of any kind. There were also no stuffed animals or any of the other knickknacks teenage girls usually had. It was like a bare cave or a cell, whose owner was a prisoner within herself. I felt sorry for both mother and daughter.

"Get up, girl! You can't spend the rest of your life lying there!" Merja Vainikainen's voice had become shrill, and she half dragged Mona into a sitting position. Mona avoided my gaze, staring at the floor.

"No one keeps track of kids' school attendance anymore now that they all go to different classes every hour, and because Pentti wasn't Mona's father, she can't jump the line for therapy even though he just died. Mona and Pentti had a good relationship, didn't you, Mona?"

At first Mona didn't answer, but when Merja repeated the question, she nodded. Maybe that was all we were going to get out of her. Before her accident, Leena's son had responded to almost every question with "meh." So maybe it was just the usual teenage reticence. I left them to it; we could come back if needed.

As we drove toward the police station, Koivu related what he'd learned.

"Vainikainen's finances were in order, and no wonder. They had to be careful. The loan on the house is more than two hundred thousand euros. The Vainikainens bought it a little before they got married, and it's in both of their names. They have thirty thousand in debt on their cars, and those are also jointly owned. Vainikainen's salary was surprisingly small, just a little over three thousand a month. The wife barely makes two thousand."

"Sports associations run on government grants, so they aren't big moneymakers. It's a calling, almost like our job. Was there anything suspicious in the account statements? Repeating unexplained transfers? Anything that might indicate a mistress?"

"Everything was just as boring as my own accounts. And Merja Vainikainen didn't have anything to inherit from her husband but debt, unless there's some property he kept off the books. Who was hiding upstairs? An undocumented Polish maid?"

"Merja's daughter, Mona." I told Koivu about the girl, and he shook his head. If we had to interview Mona again, I'd put Koivu on the case. He knew how to make women of any age trust him.

Koivu's driving went better this time, but he couldn't do anything about the traffic on the Ring 1 beltway. He looked for some appropriate music on the radio and came up with Rammstein's "Mutter." He turned it up so loud that the bass thumping must have been audible in the car next to us, whose driver glanced at us in irritation. It was almost five o'clock by the time we reached the police station. I had exactly two hours to script my press conference. Koivu ordered takeout for our meeting, and only Ursula declined sharing the family-size tuna pizza, muttering something about dinner plans.

I watched the tape of the event while I ate. The disheveled, dark-haired man Ursula had mentioned went into the kitchen, and he also showed up in many of the shots with the Adaptive Sports group, so I assumed he was Miikka Harju, the office temp. When I visited the Adaptive Sports website, my guess proved correct. Puupponen had an appointment scheduled with him for first thing in the morning.

"The attendees from Turku are being more difficult," he said. "Koskelo is demanding that we go to them. That would take a whole day, four hours just traveling, so I said no dice. They're coming on the nine a.m. train, which will be at the Espoo station at about 10:45. Will we be done with Harju by then?"

"If not, we can interview them in shifts. Did you learn anything interesting this afternoon?"

"Some of the reporters expressed regret about not being on the scene when Vainikainen died. That would have been the scoop of the century. But I guess issues related to people with disabilities rarely interest the scandalmongers unless the story involves sex." Puupponen shook his head, and then a few minutes later, he and Koivu took off to question a couple of Pentti Vainikainen's coworkers, who had promised to keep the federation office open. That left me and Ursula alone. Finally, I had a chance to call Antti.

"Hi, it's me. I'll be home around eight. Is everything alright?"

"Yeah, we're fine," he said, sounding resigned. "Iida got a nine out of ten on an English test and is all bent out of shape about it. Taneli is out in the yard with the neighbor boys."

"Tell them I'll be home to read them their bedtime stories."

"Yeah, yeah."

"Antti, I didn't choose this! I'm working long hours so I can get this solved and be done with it. We still have a press conference tonight—" But Antti had already hung up.

Ursula had heard the call. She seemed restive and clicked the tabletop with her long fingernails.

"I've done everything I can. May I leave now?"

"Do you have a date?"

She glared at me. "My private life is none of your business! But yes, I have a date. A free dinner. On this salary, that's always welcome."

"See you back here at eight tomorrow for our morning meeting," I said. I would welcome some time to myself before the briefing. Once Ursula was gone, I put my feet up on the conference room table and closed my eyes. If only I at least had some salmiakki to give me a jump start, but in all the rush that morning, I hadn't thought to buy any.

Facing the press made me anxious. Too many of the reporters knew what had been done to me a few years before, and they might dredge that back up if they didn't have anything more interesting to report on. What if Iida's or Taneli's friends' parents read about the incident in the tabloids? I desperately wanted to deflect attention from myself and the fact that I'd returned to the police department to investigate this one case, but so far, I didn't have anything earth-shattering to share about the investigation.

I turned on the computer and looked up the article the reporter had tipped me off about. Pentti Vainikainen had been quite the orator. In the strongest terms he condemned the continued dependence of sports grants on lottery proceeds.

> Our runners put Finland on the map soon after independence, but things have changed now that we're in the new millennium. The stakes are much higher, and the impact is more far-reaching than in the days of Paavo Nurmi or even Lasse Virén. In order for us to defend the reputation and tradition of Finnish sports, we have to invest in our top athletes and stop begging for handouts. Our young people need star athletes as role models to inspire them to get away from their computer screens. In the past few years, there has been entirely too much focus on fitness programs. Nordic walkers don't need their own special paths, but track-and-field athletes do need indoor facilities here and proper training camps in warmer climates. Political decision makers are always ready for a photo op with a medalist, but few of them understand the day-to-day life of an elite athlete. The fight for medals can only be won through smart investments. We lost Vyborg in the Continuation War because our army ran out of bullets. Let's not let that happen in this struggle. Sponsors are important for our federation, but we can't build success solely on private money.

Through my kids' figure-skating hobby, I'd seen how strapped for resources most of the sports clubs were. Coaching was practically a volunteer activity, and parents also devoted enormous amounts of time to keep the whole thing going. To tell the truth, I was relieved when

Iida didn't turn out to have the kind of talent that could have made her a star. She was content to have fun. We didn't know yet about Taneli, though.

I tried to reach Liisa Rasilainen from Patrol Division to ask her to join me for coffee. Liisa was the most senior female officer in the Espoo Police Department, and even at nearly sixty she'd been a member of our soccer club. I hadn't seen her in far too long. Unfortunately, her voice mail greeting said she was at the EGPN conference in Amsterdam. The acronym stood for the European Gay Police Network, which Liisa was trying to expand into Finland. I left a message for her to say hello to a Swedish colleague I was sure would be there.

Pentti Vainikainen's preliminary autopsy report landed in my e-mail inbox at 6:15 p.m., earlier than I'd expected. Vainikainen had been in good shape. There were no signs in his lungs of smoking, and the rest of his internal organs were of normal size and weight. The apparent cause of death was poisoning, and the likely agent was nicotine. It had badly corroded the mucous membranes of his mouth. He'd recently had new dental veneers installed. Under his right collarbone was a bite mark a few days old, and there were external injuries present on his body sustained before death, probably related to the fall caused by his convulsions and subsequent attempts at CPR. That much I could share at the press conference, but because the role of nicotine was still uncon-firmed, I decided to mention poisoning without getting too specific. At fifteen minutes to seven, I freshened up my makeup and redid my hair. A clean blouse would have done me good, so I set myself a reminder on my phone to bring some extra clothes in the morning along with the salmiakki. Finally, the press officer and I went over the script for the briefing, and then it was time to face the lions again.

On the table were six microphones set up alongside the department one. A television crew was also present. When I revealed that this was likely a case of poisoning, many of the reporters immediately jumped to the conclusion that the poison hadn't been meant for Pentti Vainikainen and asked directly about Jutta Särkikoski. Apparently, Jutta had refused to answer her colleagues' questions, which was wise from a journalistic standpoint and good for our investigation.

When the press conference was finished, there were damp spots under the arms of my blouse and jacket. I spent a moment sitting in my office gathering my strength before heading home. I felt like I'd stepped into a nightmare. I didn't want this. Researching violence was one thing, hunting its perpetrators was something else entirely. Even though I could focus on only this case, to me that made the investigation feel all the more fraught. Before, at least I'd been able to rest my brain and nerves occasionally on more simple cases when a homicide investigation stalled. Why hadn't I told Taskinen and Rajakoski to go take a flying leap? I could go on sick leave. I could get a doctor to certify that homicide investigations were too psychologically difficult for me.

That possibility was comforting, even though I knew that withdrawing from the case would definitely make the media dredge up the events of three years ago. In short, all of my options were bad options. Angry at the world, I pedaled home furiously, dodging the birch leaves that had already dried from the morning's showers and now flew at my face.

At home it was the usual weeknight chaos. Taneli had spread his Legos across the living room floor, and Iida sprawled on the sofa, reading with Venjamin at her feet. I put the tea kettle on to boil and enlisted Taneli to clean up. Antti went out for a walk. Soon it was time for bedtime stories, and Iida came to listen to Pippi Longstocking too. We were reading the second book in the series, *Pippi Goes on Board.*

Puupponen called at eight thirty as Taneli was brushing his teeth.

"Hi, it's Ville. I found the office cleaner Siudek. I'm talking to him soon. We're going to have some language trouble, but I'll do my best with English."

"If he knows something important, let's get an interpreter. We have an unlimited budget, after all."

"In that case, let's go to the Savoy for lunch tomorrow," Puupponen said. "Although with me and Koivu, it would be tossing pearls before swine. Ursula's probably there right at this very moment . . . Have you heard who she's dating?"

"No. I expect she's moved up to government ministers by now."

"I'm sure she'll tell you soon. Our Ursula is never one for keeping quiet. Pr . . . przem . . . the cleaner is on his way. I'll have to ask him how to pronounce his name. Bye!"

I drank my tea and ironed clothes while I chatted with Iida about her day, then talked to my sister Eeva on the phone. I hadn't bothered to tell my wider family about my sudden change of jobs, mostly because I knew my mom would worry. She'd had to take sleeping pills for months after I was assaulted. Before, whenever I'd been involved in a violent incident, I'd been able to gloss over it because we didn't release all the details to the media for investigative reasons. Now I had to tell my parents and sisters what was going on before they read about it in the paper, so, being the coward that I was, I chose Eeva as my messenger.

Puupponen called again at nine thirty, even though I hadn't asked him for a report. Iida had just gone to sleep, and Antti, whose hair was still wet from the shower, gave me a glare that let me know it was his turn for some attention.

Przemyslaw Siudek had gone to MobAbility at around eight thirty as usual the night of the event and was surprised to find that everything had been rearranged. The conference room tables were pushed against the walls, as were the chairs, and one of the tables was still full of dirty plates and coffee cups. Siudek had put them in the dishwasher and thrown out the milk souring in the pitcher, along with a thermos of room-temperature tea. He had returned the tea bags to the kitchen cupboard. According to our other interviews, Hillevi Litmanen had taken home her own dishes and the leftover sandwich makings. Apparently, she'd washed the dishes immediately, believing that Pentti Vainikainen had suffered a heart attack, rather than being poisoned. However, for some reason Hillevi had left out all the picked-over food in the conference room, and Ristiluoma hadn't cleaned up either, since that was a job for someone else, in this case Siudek. Hillevi had thought the food belonged to the ones who paid for it, meaning MobAbility.

"But the most important thing is that Siudek took the leftover sandwiches and cookies home," Puupponen said.

"Including the gluten-free rolls? Did he try them?"

"No! He ate some of the rye sandwiches, but the gluten-free ones are still at his house. He lives in Leppävaara with eight other Poles."

"Holy hell! Has anyone warned them?"

"We're still trying. There isn't a phone in the apartment, and Siudek only had one roommate's work number. Contacting him took forever. Apparently another one of Siudek's roommates took one of the sandwiches for his lunch. Some of these guys are cleaners, and a couple deliver newspapers. Siudek was worried we were going to charge him with stealing, so at first, he didn't want to give us any names. He was protecting his fellow Poles, sticking to the old Lech Wałęsa Solidarity tradition."

I laughed, and Venjamin, who was crawling into my lap, made a quick about-face.

"I left a message for the landlord of their rental apartment, but there isn't a superintendent on site. I sent a patrol car over. Six-two was close. That's Akkila's car. I'm sure he'll enjoy raiding some foreign workers' refrigerator. I'm driving to Leppävaara now to check on the situation."

"Well done! Now check to make sure there aren't any Poles in the hospital for poisoning. That's all we need right now."

I hung up and tried in vain to catch Venjamin on the floor. Part of me wanted to rush to Leppävaara, but there wasn't any sense in that. Tomorrow would be long enough, and I needed rest. I took a shower, and when I came back into the living room, I heard my own voice on TV. Antti was watching the news.

"It's like you never left," he said dryly.

"Well, it doesn't feel that way to me."

"Are you sure you can handle this? Remember how long your recovery took?"

"If I can't handle it, I'll go on sick leave," I replied, not mentioning the fact that I'd been having the same thoughts. Instead I just said I was going to bed and turned my phone to silent. Antti didn't join me until later, and sometime around three Venjamin jumped into bed and started purring between us, which I noticed because I was sleeping so fitfully. I checked my phone every half hour to see whether Puupponen or one of the others had texted me. I didn't fall completely asleep until almost four.

In my dream, Iida and Taneli happily ate white death-cap mushrooms, and I tried in vain to force them to vomit by shoving my finger down their throats. The Iida in the dream bit me, and I woke up to find Venjamin with his claws sunk into my hand because I'd been waving it around, and he thought I was playing. It was six o'clock, and Antti was also awake.

"So is this how it's going to be again?" he asked and rolled toward me, taking my face in his hands. "If you're going to be up all night every night, I'll go sleep in the guest room. How can I function without sleep?"

I didn't have the energy to answer, so I just dragged myself into the kitchen to make coffee. Outside it was raining heavily, else I would have gone for a run. As I grabbed the newspaper from the mailbox, Venjamin came to the door but decided to stay inside. Antti had fallen asleep again, and I woke him up at seven thirty because I had to leave. I managed to spend ten minutes with the kids and make sure that Taneli put on his rain clothes. After outfitting myself with an umbrella, raincoat, and rubber boots, I set off tramping toward the Espoo police station. Part of the route was under construction, and cars splashed water on me, but the rain was warm, and the air smelled of the falling leaves.

I planned the day's schedule: first the morning meeting, then Miikka Harju's interview. I assumed that Puupponen's Operation Sandwich had gone off swimmingly, because I hadn't heard anything from him.

As I began to cross the final intersection before the police station, I was nearly run down by a large black SUV turning left. I jumped out of the way just in the nick of time, and when the SUV driver braked, I barely restrained myself from kicking the bumper. Instead I memorized the license plate number, thinking that the driver would receive either a phone call or an e-mail from me later in the day.

But I ended up not having to track the license to discover the identity of the SUV's owner. The vehicle pulled up to the police station, and Ursula Honkanen got out of the passenger side, her five-inch heels treacherous in the rain. The man driving the car gave me an arrogant wave. I realized it was Kristian Ljungberg, my law school boyfriend and currently an extremely successful criminal attorney. Even though twenty years had passed since our breakup, I still didn't want to see him. Kristian was just behaving true to form, and I knew that few people would dare chastise him for idling his car in a no-parking zone. But I wasn't afraid of him.

"Hi, Kristian. So nice to see you. I'll be sure to send you the dry-cleaning bill. I'll get the address from Officer Honkanen," I sang out sweetly through the open passenger door, and seeing his irritated look lifted my own mood.

8

The sandwich farce had indeed ended happily. One of Siudek's roommates had taken a bite of one of the gluten-free rolls, but he'd spat it
out immediately because the filling tasted so bitter. He'd thrown both
the sandwiches in the trash, from which we retrieved them and sent
them to the crime lab. The results would take two weeks, even though
the case was a top priority.

"Siudek's roommate, Jurkiewicz, already thought Finnish food was
strange. He told me that in the spring they'd bought some leftover
mämmi, because it went on sale after Lent. But apparently Poles like
their desserts sweet, and our beloved gloop left them with some serious
prejudices," Puupponen said. "But Polish foreign workers don't have
the same kind of pull as Silvio Berlusconi. If they complain about the
food, let them go home."

"Mämmi is terrible," Koivu said. "But because it's healthy, it's sure
to be the next trend. Mark my words. They're already making pasta out
of it." Then he contentedly bit into his donut.

"It was quite a place. A run-down, thirty-five-square-meter one-
bedroom apartment with a dozen men crammed into it. Good thing I
went over, because they were as frightened as rabbits facing a pack of
wolves. They kept repeating that their work permits were in order and
that they're EU citizens. Akkila's partner was only a trainee from the
academy, so he could bully the Poles as much as he wanted. How did

that old commie song go about carrying your bedroll to the barracks or something? It came to mind when I saw that dump. Although I guess no one's breaking the law by living that way."

"Aren't you the hero! You know, you don't have to suck up to the boss," Ursula said angrily. "What do you want me to do today?"

I decided not to comment on Ursula's romance with Kristian, since it was none of my business. The last time I'd heard, he had still been married to a woman named Mikaela, but that had been a couple of years ago. And the fact that a man was taken had never bothered Ursula before.

"I just got the warrants from the district court, so, Ursula, you can analyze Pentti Vainikainen's and Jutta Särkikoski's phone records. Compare the latter to the death threats she received before the accident. Then we'll see about how to approach questioning the Turku contingent. Pekka, you'll come with me to interview Miikka Harju. Ville, you write up a summary of everything we've found out so far, including the forensic findings. Then contact the Athletics Federation office. Even though we've already been there, we should go again. Vainikainen's coworkers were still in shock when they were interviewed. You and Ursula handle that once we're done with the guys from Turku. That's it for now. If you need me, I'll be in my office."

Because I didn't have overlapping cases to worry about, I decided to focus on interviews. The normal hierarchy didn't apply to this investigation. Koivu checked Miikka Harju's personal information and found one drunk-driving conviction from a couple of years back. He'd been stopped at a routine checkpoint and registered 0.07 on the breathalyzer at seven in the morning. He got off with a fine.

Harju was on time, and Koivu had him standing at the door to my new office at exactly nine o'clock. He was a little over thirty, and his dark hair extended nearly to his shoulders. It looked cleaner than in the pictures taken at the campaign launch, and he'd shaved. He was a tall man, about six foot six, and weighed north of two hundred pounds. He seemed remarkably nervous.

Koivu took a seat on the chair next to the wall, and Harju sat on the couch and tried to fit his long legs between it and my desk. The ornamental buckles of his black boots glittered, and his legs nearly reached my own. He watched me set up the recording device for the interview with interest.

"How long have you been working at the Adaptive Sports Association?" I asked. I was surprised by the torrent of words that followed.

"Since the beginning of July. I'm on a six-month unemployment relief contract. I'm trained as a firefighter, but about three years ago my back went out, and I had to change jobs. I ended up drinking too much, and my girlfriend left me, and then I drank even more," Harju said with a grimace. "I hit rock bottom and realized I had to either slit my wrists or give up the bottle. I chose the latter. I slip sometimes, but this job keeps me on the straight and narrow. I just don't know what will happen when—"

I interrupted. "How well did you know Pentti Vainikainen?"

"I didn't really know him. We met a few times in the office when he came to pick up Merja. But I don't have any idea who would've wanted to kill him."

"We're not asking you that. What was Pentti like during those meetings?"

"We didn't talk enough for me to say. But he seemed to really be in love with Merja. He would come in to say hi in the middle of the day, even if they didn't have time to go to lunch together, and once, I think he brought her flowers for the name day for her middle name. But don't ask me what that name was. I don't remember things like that."

"What kind of a workplace is Adaptive Sports?"

Miikka Harju grimaced again. "Well, it is a little tiring . . . But maybe that's just because I'm the only man there. Luckily there are other guys around the Sports Building, so I can get away from all the nattering every once in a while." Miikka glanced at me. "I don't mean any offense. Women are just so different. All my previous coworkers were men. Hillevi Litmanen is sweet, but she's like the Energizer Bunny. She just won't calm down. And then there's Merja, who has a real short fuse. That combination doesn't work well."

I asked Miikka to tell me about the campaign launch. His job had been to start the PowerPoint presentation and to take pictures.

"The event went really well. We didn't think anyone would show up. Disability issues aren't very sexy. Toni Väärä was a good crowd puller, though."

"Whose idea was it to hire him?"

"Merja's, and I guess she arranged it through Pentti. Väärä visited the office a few times to get the rundown. Nice guy. Of course, there was a little tension since he was injured riding with Jutta . . . Although the accident wasn't Jutta's fault, if what the newspapers said is true." Miikka Harju shifted in his seat and inadvertently kicked the desk, sending it banging painfully into my knee. I barely stifled a curse.

"Did you participate in the food preparation?"

"No, I only helped moved the tables and chairs around with Ristiluoma. The work was divided up the old-fashioned way. Which was fine with me."

"Did you go into the kitchen at any point during the event?" Koivu asked. Harju, who had directed his last sentence at me, turned toward my partner.

"No. But . . . I went to the bathroom once."

I woke up my computer and searched for the video I'd received from the TV crew. Harju turned back around and looked at me curiously. "Watch this," I said when I found the right file. I turned the computer display toward him and went behind him to watch. At the twenty-three-second mark, Harju walked through the kitchen door.

"This picture contradicts what you just said. Why is that?" I came around to face Harju and leaned back against my desk, and still his face was only a little below my own. A faint stench of sweat rose off him.

"Well, I guess I did go in there. How am I supposed to remember everything? I went to wash my hands. They were a little dirty. I was only there for five seconds. And why is the kitchen so important?"

"Do you smoke?" I asked.

"Not anymore. I gave it up when I stopped drinking. I figured if I was cleaning myself up, I should go all the way. Why? I don't have the faintest idea what you're getting at. I don't know anything about anything, and Hillevi certainly didn't do anything, even if Merja blames her for Pentti's death. It must have just been some sort of crazy accident."

"Why do you think Merja Vainikainen blames Hillevi?"

"Because that's what Hillevi told me! She didn't come to work again yesterday, and I gave her a buzz to ask about a couple of things. She said that Merja had called her on Wednesday and interrogated her about what she put in Vainikainen's coffee. And now Hillevi is scared to death you'll believe Merja."

Merja Vainikainen hadn't told me anything about this phone call. Most likely she had overreacted and later regretted it, and maybe she also understood the seriousness of the charge. But why did she think that the poison was in the coffee rather than the sandwiches?

I asked Harju to tell his own version of the events surrounding Pentti Vainikainen's death. His story didn't differ from Merja Vainikainen's, Jutta's, or Ristiluoma's narratives, besides his having helped Hillevi pack up the dishes she'd brought and throw away the extra spread for the sandwiches, among other things. Harju remembered that it was the garlic mayonnaise, since the parsley butter had run out earlier. He flushed the mayonnaise down the toilet. Harju and Jutta had then taken Hillevi home in Jutta's Renault, after which Harju drove Jutta's car to her house.

"They were both out of their minds. Luckily, from my old job I'm used to dealing with distraught people. Hillevi was afraid she'd done something wrong, and Jutta thought the gluten-free sandwiches must have contained poison meant for her. And I guess she was right. She asked me to stay with her for a little while, at least until she could call someone . . . Hey, wait, you're the one she called!" Harju said, finally making the connection. "She said something about a Maria. But I didn't realize you were a cop then."

I didn't bother explaining, since it wasn't any of Miikka Harju's business. And he didn't wait for me to reply anyway.

"I stayed while Jutta checked to make sure no one was in the apartment. She said she'd been getting death threats again, like before her accident. I felt sorry for her. She still doesn't know if she'll ever walk without crutches."

"When you went in the kitchen to wash your hands, what did you see? Had the gluten-free sandwiches already been made?" I sensed that Harju was trying to convince me what an empathetic guy he was, not the type who could poison anyone.

"I don't remember. Like I said, I was only in there for a minute. The kitchen was closer than the bathroom, and I didn't want to have to go through the crowd. I came out right away to take pictures of Toni Väärä's presentation. That was what the reporters were most interested in."

The television recording showed Toni Väärä talking about his lumbar spine support belt and the utility of the other products MobAbility provided during his recovery. None of the journalists had said that Väärä or his trainer, Ilpo Koskelo, had gone in the kitchen. Merja Vainikainen's mention of coffee bothered me, but maybe Pentti had eaten first and then taken a sip of coffee. We'd have to ask her. Harju testified that no one else had any trouble from the coffee. So maybe I wouldn't pay too much attention to the whole coffee angle.

"Couldn't it have been an accident?" Harju asked again. "There are so many solvents in kitchens these days, and wasn't there goat cheese in some of the sandwiches? That can be dangerous if unpasteurized.

Once, one of my old coworkers got listeria from cheese he brought from France."

"We'll look into that. Did you know anyone at the campaign launch from before you came to work at Adaptive Sports?"

"No," Harju said quickly. Then he began to backpedal. "Well, of course I knew who Toni Väärä was, and Ilpo Koskelo. I went to that Finland-Sweden meet with my buddies. It was a pretty boozy trip, but we were in the stands to cheer for Väärä's win. And I guess I knew about Jutta too. I followed that doping story back when I was unemployed and had time to hang out online and watch TV. In a way it was comforting to know I wasn't the only person who had screwed up his life."

I asked again about visiting the kitchen and received the same answer. Harju was facing unemployment, and I didn't entirely swallow his story about his back going out being the reason why he left his original job. I thought it was more likely that he'd gotten canned for drinking. Out of everyone at the campaign launch who might have been hired to poison either Pentti Vainikainen or Jutta Särkikoski, I'd put my money on Harju. I said as much to Koivu once we'd let Harju go.

"I had the same thought," Koivu replied and rubbed his temples. "I need to get stronger glasses. I can't see a thing, and my head always hurts. But who would have bribed Harju to poison Vainikainen? The wife?"

"That'd be my guess. Maybe we should look into what kind of company Harju keeps. I'll tell Puupponen."

Puupponen was sitting in the conference room, and there was no sign of Ursula. I headed for the ladies' room, and as I walked into the hallway, I nearly ran into Taskinen.

"Good morning, Maria! How are you getting along?" Taskinen tried his best to look encouraging. My own face reflexively contracted into a scowl.

"No breakthrough yet. The cause of death isn't certain, but we still suspect nicotine poisoning. We're trying to interview all the key witnesses today."

"Do you have time for lunch?"

"Not by a mile. I have more interviews," I said, glad for the excuse. I was angry more at myself than Taskinen. I just should have said no and held to it. I pushed past him and walked to the bathroom, since he wouldn't dare follow me there.

Inside I found Ursula. She was touching up her already devastatingly glossy red lips, looking satisfied.

"I never would have thought we'd end up as pogo sisters," she said, giving a crooked smile. "Kristian sure is great. I like a man with balls, if you know what I mean. I'd thought I would find real men at the police academy, but nowadays the recruits are mostly a bunch of pansies. But Kristian has some kick to him."

"Well, then he's learned a lot since the late eighties," I replied and immediately regretted it. Ursula cackled.

"Do you want to hear what he says about you? Or . . . maybe I shouldn't. I don't want to be accused of sexually harassing my boss or something." She snapped the cap on her lipstick and walked out. The clicking of her heels echoed far down the hall.

Kristian had left me, partially, because he couldn't stand that I scored better on tests than he did. I hadn't been too upset about it. We were so different, and Kristian had expected more traditionally feminine behavior than I was capable of. We were just kids then, and I was infatuated with Kristian's exoticism. You didn't run into Swedish-speaking Finns in my hometown. Now it just amused me that Kristian had apparently felt the need to belittle me. I'd heard that he'd spent the past few years working for the EU's criminal division as a consulting official, and I imagined that he was stationed in Brussels. Ursula would be sure to bring me up to speed with his current activities, whether I wanted her to or not.

The coffee maker was percolating in the conference room by the time I returned. Ilpo Koskelo and Toni Väärä had arrived at the Espoo station, and Puupponen had directed them to take a taxi here. I ordered Puupponen and Ursula to question Koskelo first, while Koivu and I took Väärä.

"You two be the bad cops, and then Koivu and I can be the good cops," I suggested. "Koskelo has been coaching part-time for decades, so he's been in contact with Pentti Vainikainen longer than anyone else, even Merja Vainikainen. Try to dig into that. Possible enemies, scandals, or other dirt. I'd also like to hear about how Merja and Pentti Vainikainen's romance started. If it caused any bad blood, et cetera."

"You don't have to hold our hands! We've been doing just fine here without your micromanaging," Ursula snapped again. For some reason I found her outburst funny—I did my best not to smile.

I returned to my office and called Merja Vainikainen. She answered on the third ring. Her voice was tentative, maybe expecting it to be someone from the media.

"You accused Hillevi Litmanen of putting poison in your husband's coffee. What made you suspect that?"

Merja was silent for a long time. "I don't remember anything like that . . . When did I say that?"

"Wednesday. The day after Pentti died."

Merja was silent again, and then she sighed. "I may have said that. I don't remember. I didn't sleep at all Tuesday night, and I must have been confused. I didn't really mean it. I was just trying to figure out what Hillevi put in the coffee and the sandwiches. She's such a scatterbrain. I wouldn't be surprised if this were an accident and she caused it. I don't believe she would intentionally kill someone. What I'd like to know is why didn't the police notify me about the poison? Why did I have to read that it was nicotine in the newspaper?"

"For the time being, that's unsubstantiated," I said, then immediately realized my mistake. The next of kin weren't supposed to learn these sorts of details, however unsubstantiated, from the media; she should have heard it directly from me. My investigation skills were rusty, that much was clear. Merja Vainikainen accepted my awkward apology with grace.

A moment after I hung up, the duty officer announced that Väärä and Koskelo were downstairs, and I sent Koivu to fetch them. I'd make a show of my authority by waiting for Toni Väärä in my office. If the two men had something to hide, they would have had plenty of time to get their story straight even before the train ride. I heard them approach, and then Koivu knocked on my door.

"Lieutenant, may we come in?"

"Enter!"

Koivu nearly shoved the shy-looking young man into the office. I'd seen Toni Väärä run on TV, and his shy smile in press pictures. In the real world, he seemed fragile and younger than his twenty-one years. He was the kind of man you could pick out as a Finn in any airport in the world. The skin of his bony face was pallid, and all that was left of his summer tan was a slight browning on his high cheekbones and the end of his narrow nose. His hair was blond, thin, and stiff, and stuck up all over his head. The blue of his eyes was pale. He'd obviously bought his jeans and hoodie from the nearest department store, but his shoes were from his sponsor. Toni Väärä looked like a young man who didn't want to attract attention.

I asked whether Väärä wanted coffee, but he had his own sports drink with him. He poured some in a glass and politely offered us some as well. Koivu took a cupful, then moved to the chair by the wall. Väärä sat down on the sofa. I tried to look at him as sternly as a principal questioning the only witness of a bathroom hazing incident. According to Jutta, Toni thought that the purpose of the accident was to hurt him, not Jutta. But I didn't start with that. Instead I asked Väärä's impressions of the MobAbility campaign launch, just to get the ball rolling.

"I was so nervous about my own presentation that I couldn't pay much attention to anything else until it was over. I've never liked being in front of cameras. Jutta talked for a while and then Tapani Ristiluoma. The mood got better once the reporters left. There were toasts, and then we ate, and then suddenly Pentti started moaning and having a fit. It was horrible. It reminded me of the time one of my little sisters tried a red poisonous mushroom . . . Mom shoved her fingers down her throat and made her throw up."

"Do you have many siblings?"

"There are twelve of us. I'm the third oldest and the oldest boy."

"That's a pretty big family." I remembered that Väärä was from somewhere in Ostrobothnia, the Wild West of Finland, known for its knife fighters, religious fervor, and high proportion of Swedish speakers. "Did you know everyone who stayed after the reporters left?"

"I did, more or less, although I've never talked to Hillevi Litmanen. She's so shy." For some reason Väärä blushed. "And then there was that tall guy, Miikka. He talks a lot, and he's sort of . . . curious. He kept asking the whole time about my recovery as if it was the most important thing in the world."

"Isn't it?" Koivu asked, but I didn't let Väärä answer.

"According to Jutta Särkikoski, you suspected that the accident was an attack on you. What made you think that?"

Väärä looked miserable and didn't answer. He just squeezed his sports-drink bottle as if it was some sort of talisman. I asked the question again. The answer came out of Väärä's mouth very slowly.

"Maybe I exaggerated a bit . . . It was such an awful thing . . . the accident. Just after I set my record and everything. Although maybe there was something good about it too, since I got some time to myself. Setting that record caused so much excitement, and it wasn't all fun."

"Why not? You were a hero."

Väärä's wandering gaze met mine for a moment, and I saw a flash of anger. "The newspapers hounded me constantly! 'Oh, you're religious?

What church do you belong to? Do you have a girlfriend? What, no? Aren't you allowed to date? So sports is your life?' Garbage like that. And then Pentti . . ." Now the young man blushed even redder. "You shouldn't speak ill of the dead, I know that, but Pentti . . . well, we had a fight, and I think he was the one who sent that van after us. It was a good plan, since he could take revenge on me and Jutta at the same time, even though she'd done the right thing."

Väärä stopped abruptly and took a swig from his bottle. I tried to make sense of his download. Koivu managed to fashion a question first.

"Why did you suspect that Pentti Vainikainen wanted to hurt you?"

Väärä wrung his hands and then asked, "Do I have to answer?"

"You're being interviewed as a witness to a homicide. Lying would be a crime," I said, taking back control of the interview.

"So you don't suspect me of poisoning Pentti . . . or was it meant for Jutta?"

"Should we suspect you?"

"No! I didn't do anything."

I let Väärä pause and indicated to Koivu with a glance that he should do the same. Väärä clearly wasn't the kind of athlete who could come straight from a race and give a detailed statement about his own and his competitor's tactics.

"I just thought that Pentti didn't want me to talk about . . . the offer. I guess he was afraid I'd talk to Jutta about it, and she'd put two and two together. Pentti came to my hotel room after the Sweden meet. My roommate was somewhere celebrating, but I don't drink alcohol, and I'm not interested in parties anyway. Pentti said that Ilpo is a perfectly good coach, but that his last real accomplishments were in the eighties. In the 2000s you need new methods to succeed. And that would put me on the highway to heaven. Sponsors, professional coaching, a nice car, women . . ." Toni Väärä laughed and then fell silent.

I remembered what Jutta had said about the discus throwers she nailed for doping. *"You might get confused about the line between right and wrong, especially if someone comes along promising a shortcut to success."* Toni leaned back in his chair and stretched his arms, his slender wrists poking out of the sleeves of his hoodie.

"Pentti asked if I could keep a secret, then told me that the federation was founding a new, modern biomedical training project for promising distance runners. They already had sponsors behind it, big companies. Help was coming from Norway, from the same guys who took Vebjørn Rodal and Geir Moen to the top in the nineties."

I laughed before I could stop myself. I thought Moen had been an extremely attractive athlete, but I surely wasn't the only one who had wondered how his incredible improvements had been possible.

"I asked whether we could try this biomedical thing with Ilpo. Pentti said no, that it required special training that someone Ilpo's age wouldn't have time to learn. But I couldn't tell Ilpo that. Of course, I could think about it—I didn't have to decide right then. But wouldn't it be amazing to stand on the top podium and listen to the national anthem?" Toni grimaced. "I didn't even have the sense to ask what 'biomedical training' really meant, and it never even crossed my mind that the federation would suggest doing anything illegal."

I didn't respond, giving him time to think. Väärä took a sip from his bottle. He obviously wasn't the kind of person to rush. He was only fast on the track.

"The day before Jutta was scheduled to interview me, Pentti called and warned me against saying anything about our conversation. He said she would take everything out of context. The best thing would be to cancel the interview. I could claim I had the flu."

"How did Vainikainen know that Jutta Särkikoski was coming to interview you?"

"He heard about the sponsor event and that I was going to be getting a ride in her car. That van started following us pretty soon after we dropped off the photographer in Kisko, when Jutta and me were alone. It was like someone didn't want us talking . . ."

"Before the accident, did you have a chance to tell Ilpo Koskelo that you were considering changing coaches?"

"No! And now I wish I had. All you have now is my word, since Pentti is dead. But so many things were going on, and I was pretty messed up after the accident, and I didn't know how fast I would recover . . . or if I'd recover at all. And Vainikainen never brought it up again. I only saw him a couple of times before the event on Tuesday. Ilpo handled things with the federation."

"How much do you remember about the crash?"

"Not much. The roads were terrible, and I didn't really trust Jutta's driving. Not because she's a woman, but because I'd never driven with her before, and I'd heard that there were lots of moose on that road. It was like I sensed the trip was going to end badly. Probably it had something to do with Pentti's warning. But the strangest thing was that Ilpo didn't want me driving with Jutta under any circumstances. He told me to take the train to Helsinki. As if he knew something. I've thought and thought what that could be, and sometimes I feel like I'm going crazy. But I don't understand, and I don't remember. If only I'd seen who was driving the van, and maybe I did. But now all I see is blackness and—" Suddenly Väärä stopped talking, on the verge of tears. Koivu looked at me in confusion.

"I don't even know if I want to recover and start the climb back to the top. Not if it's going to be like this. I now understand what he meant by biomedical training, even if I didn't at the time. What do I know? Maybe Ilpo was part of it too. What if now they're feeding me something that I don't even know is banned? But what choice do I have? If I don't succeed, I lose my sponsors. If I do succeed, I don't get to have my own life. It's like I'm public property. Everyone expects me to win, and if I fail, they'll laugh at me." Väärä took a deep breath and looked me in the eye. "I don't know what happened at MobAbility, but I think something evil was present. Something I don't want to be a part of. Ever."

9

"So, evil, huh?" Koivu said once the door had closed after Toni Väärä, and Ursula and Puupponen had joined us.

"What church does Väärä belong to, the Laestadians?" Puupponen said, taking a seat on the sofa. Ursula joined him. "Twelve kids in the family, coming from Ostrobothnia . . ."

"Yes, maybe so. But few Finnish athletes are openly religious, except at the end of their careers when they find religion and decide to confess their sins, like doping."

"Don't forget Matti Nykänen. He doesn't regret anything, not the drinking, not the bar brawls, not the restraining orders," Puupponen said. "That's my kind of athlete—follows the road he chose to the bitter end."

Koivu laughed, and Ursula looked bored. I steered the conversation back to Väärä and Koskelo, who were both waiting in the conference room. When I'd asked Väärä what he thought they might be feeding him without his knowledge, he said he just meant that you could never trust anyone completely, not even doctors. So far Ursula and Puupponen had mostly asked Koskelo about Pentti Vainikainen. Now sixty-three, Koskelo had started his coaching career around the time Vainikainen was retiring from running and moving over to the administrative side of sports. According to Koskelo, Vainikainen hadn't been a prodigy and had earned his success through hard work. He was also well-liked and a good networker. A talent for making friends with important politicians and sports figures hadn't hurt his career prospects in the industry.

"Last year Vainikainen attended one of the government's National Defense Courses. That has to say something about his social standing," Ursula said. "He and Koskelo weren't close friends by any means, but they respected each other."

"Toni Väärä paints a different picture," I said. "Specifically, about what Vainikainen thought of Koskelo."

"Väärä hinted that Vainikainen encouraged athletes to dope," Koivu said. "Wouldn't that be reason enough for some people to want to get rid of him? What if he was endangering the reputation of Finnish sports?"

"Then all they had to do was fire him. That's how they 'cleaned up' the Ski Association," Puupponen said, stretching his arms over his head. Ursula glowered at him as if he'd done something obscene. "Remember Kyrö and Petäjä? They got the boot, but all the other old white guys in charge must have known what was going on long before the Lahti scandal broke. Just like how the Athletics Federation bigwigs pretended to be in the dark about what Salo and Terävä were up to. That's reality, Pekka! Everyone uses. Some of them just have access to drugs that don't show up in the tests."

Ursula seemed contemplative. She rolled a pen between her lips in a way that was downright pornographic. I saw Puupponen look at her, and then his mouth twitch.

"OK . . . so we're back to Salo and Terävä," Ursula said. "They swore they got their growth hormones from Estonia, without the blessing of the federation or their coaches. The public had to believe them because there was no evidence otherwise, and Jutta Särkikoski refused to reveal her sources. And then we come to the fact that Tapani Ristiluoma is Sami Terävä's cousin. Shouldn't we question Terävä too?"

"Yes. But first you and Puupponen take a turn chatting with Toni Väärä while Pekka and I take care of Koskelo. Väärä seems like a pretty inexperienced kid. It's time for you to turn on the charm," I told Ursula.

"So I'm supposed to whore it up to get information?" she replied coldly. "If you want that, then you'll have to leave me alone with him. Or should I take him to the lounge?"

I sighed. There was no point trying to rein Ursula in. As long as she did her job well, I would have to endure her. I was the one who chose her for this team, after all. And I hadn't responded to Taskinen's invitation to lunch any more warmly than she was responding to me now.

"Just do what you can do under Ville's watchful eye. Send Koskelo in here on your way."

I was cold because the cuffs of my pants still hadn't dried properly, but at least I had extra shoes with me. Ilpo Koskelo padded into my office in rubber boots; it must have been raining in Turku too. His beard and mustache were almost entirely gray, and he sat carefully, as if his back hurt. According to his personal information, Koskelo lived in Rusko, about ten miles north of Turku. He'd worked as a physical education teacher before he retired. Koskelo had been married to his wife, Sinikka, for forty-one years, and, in addition to their three daughters, they had three grandchildren.

"Such an honor to be able to speak with so many detectives," Koskelo said. He had a southwestern accent, which sounded funny to my eastern Finnish ear. "I already told those other ones everything I knew about Pentti Vainikainen. Do I have to repeat everything again?" Koivu adjusted the video camera lower than it had been with Väärä, since Koskelo was quite short.

"We're going to talk about some other things. Why didn't you want Toni Väärä to ride with Jutta Särkikoski on the twenty-sixth of last September?"

The question surprised him.

"What does that have to do with Pentti Vainikainen's death?"

"I'm asking you. What were you afraid Toni would tell Jutta during their drive? Or had you been warned ahead of time that her car would be involved in an accident?"

Koskelo tugged at his beard, seeming confused. "I don't understand what you're asking. Of course I didn't know they would be in an accident. It was a terrible shock. The boy had just run the best race of his life, and then he had to start over from zero. I felt so guilty when I heard. It was like I'd sensed something would happen, though I don't believe in things like that."

"Did you know that after the Swedish meet, Pentti Vainikainen offered Toni a chance to switch trainers and take advantage of some experimental biomedical training techniques?"

Koskelo's astonishment seemed to deepen.

"Who said that?"

"We have our sources."

"Was it Jutta? Well, even if Pentti made that offer, the boy must have said no! He's been working with me like always. And Pentti never hinted to me that he'd talked with the boy. He and I designed the next season's training plan together, which the federation approved. We had long camps planned and everything. He wouldn't go behind my back like that . . . Is this crazy story from Jutta?"

"Do you think Jutta Särkikoski is a liar?"

"I didn't say that!"

Koskelo's indignation seemed genuine. Had he known about the attempt to lure his protégé into using shady training practices, he would have had good reason to hold a grudge against Pentti Vainikainen. But Toni Väärä had refused to join up, so there was no fight between the two men, as far as I knew. Although we only had Väärä's word for that.

"When was Toni Väärä's last drug test?" Koivu asked, once again baffling Ilpo Koskelo.

"Not since that international meet more than a year ago. That was the last time he competed. He isn't even licensed for this season! During his recovery he's had to take medication that's on the banned substances list. You have no idea how tough he's been fighting the pain. It shows true Finnish grit." Suddenly Koskelo wiped his eyes and glared at us, as if expecting us to dare claim otherwise.

"How did Toni Väärä get you to coach him? Or did you find him?"

Koskelo was more than happy to speak on this subject. Five years previously, Koskelo had been watching the junior track-and-field competitions and noticed a thin slip of a boy running with spikes that looked too big for him, against boys who were larger and a year older than him.

"He's from Nurmo, which is baseball country, and their sports club had some serious wrestlers back in the day. But the boy wanted to run. He says in running you get to compete mostly against yourself, and he doesn't have to be dependent on other people's training schedules. He also didn't have time or money for the more expensive sports, since he had to help out at home. I hear his mom is eating for two again, even though she's forty-six, but for them children are a blessing from God."

"Is the family Laestadian?" I asked.

"No, Smith's Friends. It's another one of those sects, but I'm no expert on the distinction. I'm just a weddings-and-funerals Christian. Although I did get down on my knees to pray for Toni right after the accident." Koskelo sighed. "The Vääräs are a good family, but they don't have much, living on his dad's wages as a welder. I don't charge Toni my regular coaching fee; I make up for it with my other students. And soon I'll start getting my pension. I already told those other detectives that I've known Pentti Vainikainen for thirty years, and I have no idea who would have wanted to hurt him. Are you sure it wasn't just food poisoning? The spread in those sandwiches was strange. I've always told the boy, and everyone I train, to watch what they put in their mouths. When we go abroad for camps and meets, we always take our own food."

As with the others, I asked Koskelo to recount the events of the campaign launch. He'd come to Espoo with Toni Väärä, because "the boy," as he called him, had been nervous about the public appearance and wanted his coach there for moral support. At the event, Koskelo had stayed in the background, although a few reporters had asked him about Väärä's recovery and prospects for the next season. He told them that Väärä was shooting for a spot on the Olympic team.

"I felt a little sorry for the woman taking care of the food. She was so upset when they realized she forgot the special bread. I said I could help her, since I wasn't doing anything, but she wouldn't hear of it because I was a guest. Vainikainen's wife told me to mind my own business. I'm surprised there's speculation that it might be a heart attack. I've seen enough of those to know right off that it wasn't that, but heart attack is an easy explanation for a healthy person suddenly keeling over. After that, the boy and me left to drive home, because there was nothing we could do for Pentti anyway."

"Did you know everyone who stayed for the after-party?" Koivu asked. I noticed that the audio recorder wasn't working. I picked up the device and pressed record, but the cassette was full. I turned it over. It would be stupid if we had to question Koskelo again because of a technical error. Fortunately, Koskelo's words would be caught on the videotape.

"I only knew the boy and Pentti and, of course, Pentti's new wife, since she used to work at the federation. I guess that's where they met. I already told the other detectives: even though I'm a track-and-field guy, I remember when Merja Ikonen was skiing like a bat out of hell and when she tried jumping too. Matti Pulli and all the other coaches couldn't wrap their head around a girl who was more promising than most of the boys her age. But she wouldn't have become a jumper anyway. Merja has a woman's body. Too much air resistance." Koskelo glanced at Koivu.

In interviews I'd encountered dozens if not hundreds of times this same "only a man will understand this joke" look. I was immune to it. Even though Merja Vainikainen had told me only a little about her sports background, I could well imagine the sexism a girl who wanted to be a ski jumper would have encountered in the early 1980s. In my teenage years, I'd played soccer on a boys' team and bass in a punk band as the only woman. The music world had made more strides toward equality than the sports world. In pairs figure skating, men and women competed together, but the gender roles were still rigid. Still, that was one of the few sports in which female athletes were admired as much as the male ones, and both sexes received similar prize money.

"Did Toni share with you his suspicions about the car accident being intentional?"

"Jutta started talking about that in the hospital. I didn't take her seriously. But I guess it's possible, especially if it turns out that Pentti took poison meant for Jutta. I don't know what to believe . . ."

Koskelo stroked his beard again, which seemed to be a habit. I tried to remember of whom the gesture reminded me, and my uncle Pena came to mind. He had done exactly the same thing. Koskelo's gray pullover jacket had a little dandruff on the shoulder, and a few white hairs stuck out from his ears. According to Pentti Vainikainen's logic, Koskelo was a relic from another era, a man incapable of coaching Finland's next great runner.

"I meant to ask whether Toni told you that he suspected *he* was the target of the accident, not Jutta Särkikoski," I said to clarify, and received another baffled stare.

"No! How would he have gotten something like that into his head? Everyone was happy about Toni's win. Even his dad said that if God blessed him with fast legs, then he had to use them to show his thanks. And we haven't had anyone running Olympic-level times in the 800 meter since the days of Ari Suhonen. Who would wish evil on someone like that? The boy has his own demons, and he's a pessimist sometimes, so maybe that's why he thought that. But he hasn't said anything like that to me, and if he did, I'd tell him to shut his trap!"

That was all we could get out of Koskelo. Koivu and I took him and Väärä to the train station on our way to Hillevi Litmanen's apartment. In the car, Koivu tried to strike up a conversation about the upcoming ice hockey season, but the track-and-field men had nothing to add other than that TPS, the Turku team, were sure to play better this year than last. Thankfully Puupponen wasn't around to plug KalPa, the Kuopio team.

After we dropped them off, Koivu demanded that we get something to eat before going to see Litmanen, so we turned toward the Big Apple Mall. Espoo was often criticized for lacking a proper single city center. But instead of having an outdoor square, Espoo had large shopping centers like the Big Apple and Cello. Why develop artificial outdoor spaces when climate change was going to stretch November across a third of the year? Their heated concourses were perfect for hanging out on a cold winter day, and restaurants offered a range of food and drink. The sound of traffic didn't disturb conversation, and the music and advertisements coming from the shops created an urban, hectic feel that some people liked. And at the Big Apple, there were places you could go for free, like the library and the chapel. This was city life for the new millennium.

We ended up at Chico's, because Koivu was an avowed aficionado of spicy Mexican food. "What do you think about Koskelo and Väärä?" I asked as we gorged on fajitas as if we hadn't seen food in weeks. This was another familiar phenomenon: during a really intense investigation, I was constantly on overdrive and rarely remembered to eat until my blood sugar dropped dangerously low.

"I was just thinking that Koskelo doesn't have a son. All his grandchildren are girls too."

"And?" I asked with intentional impatience in my voice, because I knew where Koivu was headed.

"Maybe Koskelo thinks of Väärä as some sort of foster son, always calling him 'the boy' like that. And Väärä would have had a hard time getting attention in his own family, what with eleven siblings and number twelve on the way."

"What you're wondering is: Would Koskelo kill to protect his foster son?" I licked some guacamole off my lip, and Koivu took another bite of tortilla and meat. I felt pleased in a way, now that, after the slow start, we had at least two people with a possible motive for killing Pentti Vainikainen: Toni Väärä and Ilpo Koskelo.

"How are we supposed to answer that? What does it take to put poison in a sandwich? It's too bad the television crew was only there at the beginning of the event. Let's see what Hillevi can tell us. This is probably going to be brutal. Let's take some napkins along in case she's out of tissues," Koivu said.

After divorcing her husband, Jouni, Hillevi Litmanen had moved from their two-bedroom apartment in Lippajärvi to a studio in Matinkylä. In the divorce settlement, Jouni had received more than half of their assets, because his abuse hadn't figured into the division. And, he pointed out, he had paid the mortgage, and as an electronics technician, he earned three times as much as Hillevi did pushing paper. I'd never visited Hillevi's home, but she'd told me about her apartment and the things she'd filled it with. She was planning to adopt her grandmother's maiden name, Sydänmaanlakka, once she was finally done with Jouni Litmanen.

Hillevi's apartment was in a high-rise a couple of blocks away from the Big Apple, so we left the car in the mall garage and walked. Being outside, if only for a few minutes, was pleasant despite the drizzle and the wind that blew raindrops in our faces. It was bracing. Koivu wanted to take the elevator to the second floor, because his stomach was so full, but as his boss, I ordered him to climb the stairs. Hillevi's apartment door had a peephole, and I heard her approach and then fumble with the security locks before opening.

Koivu had told me what kind of shape Hillevi had been in during the domestic violence investigation. Even so, I was shocked at
the appearance of the woman who stood before me. In our meetings, Hillevi had always been almost compulsively well-dressed and
groomed. Now she was wearing grubby pajamas, and her short dark
hair was plastered to her head. She didn't have her glasses, and without
them she appeared half blind. The apartment smelled the same as train
smoking cars used to. Full ashtrays were scattered around, and the bed
in the alcove was unmade. My first thought was to open the door to the
balcony and the kitchen window to get a little airflow. Then I realized
that my comfort was not the most important thing here.

"Hello, Hillevi. How are you?"

"Fine, I guess."

"How long do you have off work?"

"I'll be back on Monday. The person who died wasn't my family
member, so . . ." Hillevi lit a cigarette and sat on her bed. Koivu collapsed on the couch, and I took the armchair. Koivu had brought the
tape recorder and set it up on the coffee table. This time he made sure
he had a new cassette. We'd left the video camera at the station.

In theory it was an attractive apartment. The decor was white and
blue in a vaguely French farmhouse style, and Hillevi had many knickknacks and a few still life paintings of flowers. On the bookshelf there
were more videos and DVDs than books. Jouni had broken Hillevi's
stereo, so she'd bought a new one as soon as she received the damages
the court awarded her. I could see Jari Sillanpää's latest album sitting
on top of the unit. Hillevi had told me that Sillanpää's music kept her
alive during the worst times, but of course Jouni had mocked her idol.
I wondered whether it would put Hillevi in a better mood if we played
some music. But she began speaking before I could put it on.

"I didn't do anything. You believe me, don't you? I made the
sandwiches exactly how Merja told me to. Didn't I already tell you

everything?" These last words were directed at Koivu. Then Hillevi turned to me.

"And you look familiar . . . But I can't find my glasses. You are . . . Who are you? Are you one of Jouni's girlfriends?"

"I'm Maria, from the domestic violence research project. But right now I'm a police detective," I responded reassuringly. Koivu stood up and started rearranging pillows and lifting stacks of magazines. He must have been looking for Hillevi's glasses. He went into the kitchen, and I heard him opening cupboards. Then the tap turned on, there was a rustling of paper towels, and Koivu returned with the glasses.

"I rinsed them off because you accidentally left them in the freezer. Here." Koivu's voice was kind. Hearing him, Hillevi made a sound like a cat whose tail had been stepped on but then extended her hand and accepted the glasses. She put them on her nose and looked at me in surprise.

"It is you . . . But why?"

I explained briefly, although Hillevi didn't seem to fully understand. Her first interview after Pentti Vainikainen's death had been muddled and fragmented, and the transcript was nearly impossible to make sense of. Officer Autio had handled it, and in my experience, he did significantly better with hard-boiled repeat offenders than he did with hysterical women. "Should I make you some coffee or tea?" Koivu asked, in the same voice I'd heard him using to talk to his children when they were sick. "Or would you like some food? When did you last eat?"

"I'm not hungry," Hillevi replied. "I just end up thinking about Pentti . . . throwing up. And Merja said I put something in the sandwiches! I didn't do anything. Believe me!"

"We do believe you. We just want to know how you ended up being the one handling the food at the launch event." I smiled at Hillevi, even though I was having trouble breathing due to the smoke. Hillevi lit another cigarette immediately after stubbing out the first.

"I know how to make beautiful sandwiches. I always have. Before, I always organized all our food, before Jouni . . . Before my sick leave that is. Jouni tried to say I didn't know how to do anything, but I don't have to worry about Jouni anymore, right, Maria?"

"Right. You can forget Jouni."

"Neither of the MobAbility women were cooks, so Merja said we would have to use a catering service, but that would be expensive. So I said I could handle it. I enjoy being in the kitchen. Merja was pleased with me for once. We planned the menu together. It was very simple. We would buy ready-made cookies and make the sandwiches ourselves. Everything was going well, but then I forgot the gluten-free rolls . . ."

"What was the filling for the sandwiches? Who bought it and who prepared it?" Koivu asked quickly before Hillevi had time to start sniveling. I started to cough, and Koivu stood up and walked to the balcony door. He opened it. Outside, the drizzle had become full-fledged rain, and the fresh air, scented with fallen leaves, penetrated the cigarette smoke. I took a breath.

"I made the sandwiches. Miikka commented on how nice they looked. They had ham, goat cheese, smoked salmon, parsley butter, and garlic mayonnaise. I set the garlic ones separately from the others in case someone was allergic. Jouni hates garlic. He never eats it. When I was making the mayonnaise, I thought 'Ha, Jouni, hopefully all the food in jail has lots of garlic.'" Hillevi gave a little giggle. "The parsley butter I made at home and chilled, but I made the mayonnaise at the office. I brought my immersion blender from home."

Koivu had sat back down, and now I walked to the balcony door. The view was the yard of the neighboring building. The sound of traffic was much louder now that the door was open. For a minute I watched the people driving to the Big Apple for their Friday shopping. Only a week earlier, I'd met Jutta Särkikoski for the first time, and I hadn't had a clue where meeting her would take me. It was almost like Jutta was responsible for reordering my entire life. An idea popped into my head but flew away when Koivu continued.

"Were the extra spreads and meat and such still in the kitchen when you went to buy the gluten-free rolls?"

"Well, of course I put them in the refrigerator so they wouldn't spoil! It isn't far from the Waterfall Building to Stockmann, and because I was only buying a few rolls, I could use the express checkout. Still some of the reporters arrived before I got back, and Merja was terribly angry. I went into the kitchen to make the sandwiches and didn't dare come back out until the official part of the event was over."

"So you were alone in the kitchen the whole time you were filling the gluten-free sandwiches? What did you put in them?"

"I put garlic mayonnaise in two of them and parsley butter in one. The butter had goat cheese with it and the mayonnaise had ham. I was alone, except Miikka came in at one point and asked if he could help or maybe take the sandwiches out to the table, but he didn't touch anything."

"Tell me the recipes for the mayonnaise and the parsley butter," I said, and Hillevi did. They were the same recipes everyone had in their cookbooks, without any mysterious ingredients. The parsley butter had been at Hillevi's home, and then in the common refrigerator at the Sports Building, and then the refrigerator at MobAbility. I asked Hillevi if there was anything else in the kitchen, and she didn't remember anything out of the ordinary. No eyedroppers in the refrigerator, no drain cleaner on the counter. But lots of people had eaten sandwiches with both fillings, including Merja Vainikainen, Miikka Harju, and Ilpo Koskelo, along with the media representatives, and suffered no side effects.

Koivu and I made Hillevi repeat her account several more times, but no inconsistencies cropped up. The others had told the same story. Hillevi remembered meeting Pentti Vainikainen only once, when he came to bring Merja flowers. As we interviewed Hillevi, we gradually tidied up: we emptied ashtrays, loaded used coffee mugs into the dishwasher, and stacked old magazines. Maybe a few of our words were beyond the recorder microphone's reach, but that didn't matter much.

"Have you spoken with Merja Vainikainen since Tuesday?" Koivu asked as he poured detergent into the dishwasher dispenser. Hillevi instantly grew agitated again.

"Merja? She called. I don't remember what day it was. She was angry and said something about the coffee. That Pentti's stomach couldn't handle it and that was why he died . . . But I don't really remember. What day could that have been?"

"What exactly did Merja Vainikainen say?" Koivu started the dishwasher and wetted a dishrag, which he then used to wipe down the sink.

"I don't remember! Are you blaming me too?"

We struggled to calm Hillevi down. I gently suggested that a shower might do her good.

"Are you sure Jouni is still in prison? Have you checked recently?" Hillevi asked once we'd shut off the recorder and were preparing to leave. Hillevi had moved to the balcony, and at that moment she didn't have a cigarette. Even though the apartment was only on the second floor, the drop from the balcony would be about twenty feet. For some reason the thought of Hillevi alone on the balcony terrified me.

"No one has escaped from any prison in Finland for ages, and Jouni doesn't have the right to furloughs at this point. Why do you ask?" Koivu inquired.

"Could it have been one of Jouni's friends, then? Maybe someone saw me buying the rolls and thought they were for me. I wouldn't have noticed anything since I was in such a hurry. And then I had to pee so bad, which is always what happens when I'm nervous. Jouni made fun of me for that too." Hillevi sniffed. She'd told me previously that sometimes she lost control of her bladder when she was frightened. "I didn't want to go to the bathroom at MobAbility because there's only one and everyone can see it and the men use it too, so I used the bathroom downstairs in the lobby. I was so rushed that I left the rolls on the edge of the sink. What if someone went in there and put poison in them! How do I know Jouni didn't tell his friends to kill to me? He swore he wasn't going to let me get rid of him so easily . . ."

"I can't imagine anything like that happening. Hillevi, you shouldn't be alone right now. Who could you ask to come be with you? Could you go stay with your parents?" I asked. Her friends had gradually fallen out of her life because Jouni never let her go anywhere alone, and for the final months before the stabbing, they had only socialized with Jouni's acquaintances.

"I don't know . . . Everyone has read the newspapers and probably blames me."

In addition to her parents, Hillevi had a brother who lived in Lohja. I looked up his number and asked Hillevi to call. I said that I could tell him I was the detective in charge of the Pentti Vainikainen murder investigation and that Hillevi wasn't being accused of anything.

I couldn't swear that Hillevi wasn't a suspect, because that would have been a lie. She smoked so much that her sense of taste must be damaged, and maybe she wouldn't have smelled the nicotine if there had been a small amount of it in one of the spreads. Hillevi's brother promised to come pick her up for the weekend, so Koivu and I left the apartment. We'd be wearing its stench for the rest of the day.

I wanted to get home as soon as possible to change my clothes and wash my hair. Koivu made it out of the Big Apple parking garage with only one clutch failure. Just as we merged onto Ring 1, my phone rang. Puupponen had news.

"Hi, it's Ville . . . The shit just hit the fan. I'm here with Ursula in Pasila, at the Sports Building. There's been an explosion. Not in the building but in the parking lot. A car, and there was a person inside it. There's no way they survived the blast. Maria, it was Jutta Särkikoski's car."

10

Installing the emergency light on top of the moving car wasn't easy, but somehow I managed it. With sirens blaring we sped toward the Sports Building. Ring 1 and the Turku Highway had the usual Friday traffic, but we still made reasonably quick progress. The surface streets closer to Helsinki were a different matter, though. Some cars pulled over onto the sidewalk, but a few drivers didn't seem to notice the flashing light and wailing siren. Fortunately, no one's life was in our hands. It was already too late—I'd failed to catch whoever tried to murder Jutta. He had gotten a second chance, and she had gone up in flames with her car. Jutta had told the police about a possible bombing; one of the death threats had mentioned it. I'd failed her. Should I ask to be relieved of duty?

Koivu finally managed to get back on a thoroughfare, and I put out an APB to pick up Salo and Terävä. Steroids increase aggressiveness, and there was no knowing what else the pair had taken. They had every reason to hate Jutta. Now I regretted wasting so much time on Pentti Vainikainen. This wasn't about him. The poor man had just happened to eat the wrong sandwich.

We came upon some construction, and Koivu swerved dangerously between the concrete barricades, banging the passenger-side mirror hard enough to bend it. I opened the window and straightened it. We weren't actually in a hurry. There was nothing we could do, at least not for Jutta. And although Ursula and Puupponen happened to be at the building when the crime occurred, investigating the explosion would fall to the Helsinki police unless I could convince my colleagues there that the explosion was linked to my case. Still, we would need all the help we could get tracking down and interviewing eyewitnesses. Dozens of sports associations had their offices in the Sports Building, along with some other companies, so there would be hundreds of people on the scene.

The road was blocked at the MTV3 building, but we got through after showing our badges. A television camera was hunting for shots, and the cameraman began filming me, apparently recognizing me from the previous day's news conference. Damn it. The reporters didn't have access to the scene of the explosion yet, but it wouldn't be long before they were grilling me again. Even the dimmest reporter would realize that, for those who wanted to silence Jutta, the second time had been the charm.

The central Helsinki police station was only a couple of blocks from the Sports Building, so the place was crawling with cops. The gate that led to the Finnish Broadcasting Company campus was closed, and the next intersection was blocked by police tape. That didn't stop the FBC's crew from trying to capture what they could. I managed to catch a glimpse of an ambulance speeding south with its lights and sirens on. Maybe Jutta hadn't died. Or maybe someone else was injured. We'd know soon enough.

Koivu parked in front of the Sports Building. Police in tactical jumpsuits were everywhere, and a hearse was pulling out of the court-yard. So there was Jutta. I bowed my head. What else could I do? The smell of the explosion still hung in the air, and I could see several dam-aged cars in the courtyard and several lower-level windows that had been blown in. The bomb squad was already checking the other cars for explosive devices. In the middle of the chaos were the remains of a silver Renault. Around it were spatters of blood. I saw Puupponen and a couple of plainclothes cops I knew from Helsinki conferring near the door to the building. I didn't even bother saying hello. I wanted to know the truth as soon as possible.

"Was anyone else hurt?" I asked Puupponen, the words nearly catching in my throat.

"Jutta Särkikoski caught some shrapnel in her face and torso, but her injuries aren't life threatening. She was conscious when we put her in the ambulance."

"Särkikoski? Jutta Särkikoski? She's alive?"

"Yes," Puupponen replied. Relief washed over me like a warm shower after a long day of skiing, but then I realized there was no reason to be relieved.

"But what about the hearse? Who was in that?"

"According to Särkikoski, a man named Tapani Ristiluoma was in the car at the time of the explosion. There isn't much left of him for his family to bury," Detective Perävaara from Helsinki said. "Do you suspect this is connected to the poisoning case you're investigating in Espoo?"

"It is the same target," I said, feeling helpless. "What was Ristiluoma doing in Jutta's car?"

"We don't know yet," Puupponen replied. "According to the receptionist, they were holding a meeting at Adaptive Sports about extending their campaign. Miikka Harju was with them. The receptionist also remembers Ristiluoma, because he had to sign him in." Had Jutta offered Tapani Ristiluoma a ride?

"Pekka, order twenty-four-hour security for Jutta Särkikoski. Are you in charge of this investigation?" I asked Detective Perävaara, who confirmed that he was the senior detective on call. I suggested we meet to coordinate our efforts. He and I had always worked well together, since neither of us had any grandiose professional ambitions, and Perävaara's team included a couple of pleasant female colleagues with whom I went out for drinks occasionally. I didn't expect Perävaara to make this a power struggle, but there was no telling what our bosses might do.

While Perävaara was talking to the leader of the bomb squad, I retreated a bit to call Antti.

"I don't know when I'll be home. Things just got complicated." Antti wasn't one of those people who always kept the radio on or spent his days surfing online, so he probably hadn't heard about the bomb yet. I gave him the short version of what had happened, and he didn't bother commenting. He was going to be a single parent until this case was solved. For a moment I missed my children so badly that I felt like I'd been the one to take a shard of metal to the chest. I hung up the phone and put it in my pocket, and I noticed my hands were shaking. Jutta had been given another chance. My job was to stop the person who was trying to kill her before they got lucky.

Ursula walked out of the building looking tense, and a tall man in a police jumpsuit tried in vain to stop her. When Ursula noticed me, she walked over.

"Kallio, what the hell is going on?" she asked as if I'd been the one who'd rigged Jutta's car. "We're here interviewing Pentti Vainikainen's coworkers, and everybody thinks he's the most decent guy in the world. A bona fide saint, if not the second coming of Jesus Christ. Then the parking lot explodes, and surprise surprise, one of our persons of interest is lying in her own blood outside. We don't even know whether she's the intended victim or the prime suspect! I think I set a new Finnish record for the 400 meter running down the stairs. Ville called it in while I was responding."

"Did you see the explosion?"

"Not the explosion itself. I didn't happen to be looking out the window since I was talking to the chairman of the Athletics Federation. Strange guy. He stared at me the whole time like he'd never seen a woman before. Or not so much me as my tits."

"Were you the first one in the courtyard after the explosion?"

"There were a couple of other people too: one woman screaming her head off and some old man who'd called the police. Maybe they heard the bang at the Pasila Station, since there were sirens going by the time I got to Särkikoski. At first, I thought she was dead too, since she was just lying on the ground motionless. But she was just in shock. I'd left my coat upstairs, so I made the old guy with the phone give me his. He was none too happy about that, but I can be very convincing when I need to be. I used it to warm up Särkikoski before the ambulance got here."

"The alarm came in at 15:43," Perävaara said. "The first patrol car arrived within two minutes of the alert, but the ambulance took nearly fifteen minutes."

Now it was 4:15. Perävaara had already organized all the officers on scene to interview the employees in the building. We went into the lobby, which was buzzing with people. No one would be allowed to leave until their contact information was recorded, and anyway the cars in the parking lot were still being searched in case there was another bomb. Everyone would have to get permission before they could go.

The guest parking cost one euro per hour. According to Perävaara, there was no video surveillance of the lot. The bomber had taken the risk of being seen, but enough people visited the building for it to be easy to get lost in the crowd. Now only one name was on my mind, the name of the person who had been at this building today and at MobAbility on Tuesday. I asked Puupponen to figure out whether Miikka Harju was still inside. I wanted to have a word with Perävaara alone, so the receptionist let us into a conference room.

"The owner of the exploded car has been receiving death threats, and we're in the middle of investigating. I propose we work together: Helsinki investigates the explosion itself, and my group investigates the Jutta Särkikoski angle."

"So we do all the dirty work and when the case is over Espoo gets all the glory?" Perävaara grinned.

"Trust me. You can have all the glory if you figure out who set that bomb in Jutta Särkikoski's car. Do you have any idea about the type of explosive yet?"

"We'll send the car to the lab as soon as rush hour is over and the flatbed can get here. I've mobilized all of our terrorism and explosives resources, and I assume we can borrow more from you if we need to, right?"

I nodded, although I didn't know who worked in the ad-hoc Espoo police terrorism and explosives group nowadays. That work was sporadic, so the experts tended to have other assignments as well.

"Who was the dead guy?"

I told Perävaara what I knew about Tapani Ristiluoma, then called the hospital. Jutta Särkikoski was still being stitched up. She'd lost some blood and was in mild shock, but according to the doctor, we could visit her as soon as she was out of the procedure room. A guard was already in place. I ended the call since another was coming in from Puupponen. He was in the lobby with Miikka Harju. I went out to find Harju white as a ghost, his hands trembling so much that he could barely shake my hand. He immediately shoved them back in his jeans pockets. How much would a former firefighter know about explosives? Harju confirmed the receptionist's account of why Ristiluoma and Särkikoski had been at the Sports Building.

"Tapani called pretty soon after I got to work from our interview at the police station. No one else was in the office. I don't know who has official sick leave and who doesn't. Ristiluoma demanded to know how we intended to continue the campaign, and of course I said I didn't have a clue, that he'd have to ask Merja. I didn't dare disturb her, since she's in mourning, for God's sake, but Ristiluoma said he would contact her himself. I didn't know what to do, so I just tidied up, and every once in a while, someone from elsewhere in the building would come in with some excuse for stopping by, although they probably just wanted to see a glimpse of the scene of the drama. I wondered if I should start charging admission!" Harju laughed nervously.

"Then Merja came in. She was on her way to the Athletics Federation to get Pentti's things. She returned after not too long, and she was irritated. They wouldn't give his effects to her, saying that the police were coming later that day to look through everything . . ." Harju stopped talking and turned his face away when a television cameraman peeked through the door. It looked like Perävaara had allowed the media in. We hadn't arranged anything about public relations yet, but apparently Perävaara thought that fell within his jurisdiction. For the time being, that was fine with me.

"Did Merja Vainikainen arrange the meeting with Tapani Ristiluoma?" I asked Harju.

"I don't know who arranged it! Jutta came to the office sometime around two. Merja was just sitting at her desk, doing nothing. It was horrible to see, since she's usually so full of energy. She's the kind of woman you would think could handle anything. I'd imagined that she was as cold as steel, but apparently I was wrong. I asked her if it wouldn't be better for her to go home and told her that Jutta and I could handle talking with Ristiluoma, though Jutta wasn't in any better shape. It seemed like the women didn't dare look at each other for fear that if they did some facade would crumble. And it did finally crumble when the lady with the dark hair poked her head through the door. I don't know which organization she was from. I don't know all these women. She brought flowers. Merja started bawling and left, saying she wasn't ready to be there. As she went she said something to Jutta about calling the executive committee together next week. And she said to apologize to Ristiluoma for not being there when he came. I heard her burst into tears again when she got into the hall. I wondered if she'd be safe behind the wheel, but I didn't offer to help. Is Merja alright?"

That wasn't my first concern, but one of my subordinates would need to contact her.

"This explosion has something to do with Jutta, doesn't it? At least Jutta has the same kind of car as the one that exploded. I drove her home in it a couple of times."

I didn't respond, because the people around seemed to be listening to our conversation. The first cars were pulling out of the courtyard. They must have been cleared. The bomb squad was still moving from car to car in their blast suits, but they didn't have the extreme caution in their movements as they had a few moments ago. But everything had to be inspected, even though it was unlikely they'd find another bomb.

I guided Miikka Harju to the conference room, and Puupponen followed. Harju sat without being asked, his hands still in his pockets and a couple of beads of sweat running down his nose. He answered my next question only after a long delay.

"Oh, when did Ristiluoma come? I guess sometime around two. I was in the meeting, although I wasn't much use to anyone. Ristiluoma thought that the show must go on, and he seemed to believe that Vainikainen's death was a strange accident, not an intentional act. He and Jutta left together, and I stayed to arrange the papers."

"What exactly do you mean by 'arrange the papers'?"

Harju blushed, his color going from pale to brick red.

Puupponen sat down next to him, and compared to Harju's red face, Puupponen's looked nearly green even under all his freckles. Puupponen had seen the remains of Ristiluoma's body, and that wasn't a sight you soon forgot, even if you were an experienced police officer.

"I stayed behind and played solitaire on the computer. Nothing ever happens in that office without Merja's instructions. It's better to do nothing than to do things wrong, but when you've got a time card, it isn't like you can leave early. I guess I should have been arranging the winter athletes' competition licenses. People with no feet skiing, blind people skating, deaf people dancing . . ." Harju giggled, but then he suddenly shouted, "A fucking hearse came! Tell me who died already! Jutta, probably, since you keep asking about her. Tell me, God damn it!" He'd taken his hands out of his pockets, and they were clenched in fists. He stood, staring in turn at me and Puupponen.

"Why do you think it's Jutta Särkikoski who died in the explosion?" I asked.

"Because I saw her fucking car out the window! Jutta's car! I already said I recognized it. I took her home in it after Pentti died. I don't have my own car, not on this pay. Jutta was as frightened as a rabbit caught in a trap. I felt like staying to keep her safe, but she didn't trust anyone, not even me, and why would she? Why the hell didn't the police do anything? Jutta should have been taken somewhere safe. Why did you let them kill her?"

"Them who?" I tried to catch Harju's gaze, but his brown eyes avoided mine. The phone rang again. It was Koivu calling from outside to confirm what we already knew: the car was definitely Jutta Särkikoski's. I asked him to get ready to go with me to the emergency room at Töölö Hospital. Harju had slumped back down in his chair, and he was crying. Puupponen looked at him and rolled his eyes. Harju had put on quite a show, and his hysteria nearly outdid even Hillevi's. But where Hillevi's terror had felt genuine, there was something carefully calculated about Harju's act, or at least that's how I felt.

"Jutta Särkikoski was only injured in the explosion," I announced, because I wanted to see Harju's reaction. He shot to his feet again, and instantly his head hovered sixteen inches over my own.

"What the hell? Then, who died?"

"Tapani Ristiluoma. We don't know yet why he was in Särkikoski's car." I tried to assess Harju's expression. At least he wasn't crying anymore. He just stared in bewilderment at an old picture of the ski jumper Jari Puikkonen hanging on the conference room wall as we left the room.

Once we were out of Harju's earshot, I asked Puupponen to find out from the employment office how he had ended up working at the Adaptive Sports office. Had he been assigned there, or had he chosen the job himself? Puupponen was already working on finding out more about Harju, but so far he'd only had time to question a couple of neighbors over the phone, all of whom thought Harju was a respectable fellow now that he'd stopped drinking. According to the neighbor he shared a wall with, goings-on in Harju's apartment before he sobered up about a year earlier had been rowdy. Of course, an alcoholic fired for drinking on the taxpayer's dime would have been a perfect bribery target for someone who wanted to get rid of Jutta Särkikoski.

Koivu was waiting in the courtyard while the bomb squad finished up its work. "They picked up Salo near his home in Siuro. He was sitting in his usual bar. According to the local police, he practically lives there. They asked if they should keep him locked up until he dries out. He blew a 0.25."

"Was Salo in that bar all day today?"

"Probably. And yesterday. And all last week. The Nokia cops said they chatted up the bartender and some of the regulars. They said Salo has been a wreck since he got nailed. Terävä hasn't shown up at his apartment in Tikkurila or at his job at the Tikkurila Sports Park. He got to keep his cushy job despite the bust, but today no one has seen him, and he hasn't called in. Are we heading to the hospital now? Juuso sent a text message. Look." Koivu tapped at his phone and then turned the display to me.

When are you coming home dad. We can play table hockey again. Juuso.

"Have I told you what a good table hockey player he is for a boy his age?"

I snorted. I was feeling guilty too, but that wasn't going to change anything. I told Perävaara where we were going, and we agreed to keep in touch. He would retain responsibility for public relations. But as soon as the media realized whose car had exploded, I would have to get in front of the cameras too.

I decided to take the wheel for a change, even though readjusting the steering wheel, seat, and mirrors took time. Traffic to the south was at a complete standstill because of the police roadblocks, but I didn't bother turning on the siren. Sitting in traffic would give Koivu and me time to chew things over. I told him about Miikka Harju's behavior. Koivu also wondered if Harju might be bluffing.

"Does he go to AA? Not many people can get sober without it. They're bound to keep everything they say confidential, but do you think Ursula might be able to bribe his sponsor or something? They admit all their evil deeds there, right?"

"Koivu, come off it. AA meetings aren't Catholic confession or something to joke about. And maybe I'm getting too stuck on Harju since we have so little else to go on. If only someone saw whoever messed with Jutta's car, or maybe, say, Sami Terävä in the Sports Building just before the explosion. But I doubt we're going to be that lucky. What about what Hillevi said about the bread rolls being poisoned while she was in the bathroom? It sounds far-fetched, but there was a small window of time when they were unguarded."

"So . . . you're suggesting Terävä followed Hillevi and knew that the gluten-free rolls were purchased specifically for Jutta Särkikoski? Come on, Maria. That's ridiculous!"

"If I was going to kill someone, I would definitely find out about all their movements and habits beforehand." I stopped at a crosswalk for an old man with a walker who had been waiting at the median. "Come on already, grandpa!" I said more to myself than anyone else. Someone honked behind us, and Koivu shook his head, opened the car window, and thrust his right hand out. We were in the left lane, and the person driving in the right lane had to brake hard when they noticed the old man appearing from in front of our car.

"Last week I was talking to one of the women in Traffic Division. She said that it isn't actually a good idea to stop at a crosswalk on a four-lane road. If I wouldn't have waved my arm at that car coming on the right, they would have hit that guy. And don't start preaching to me about traffic laws. The only law now is might is right."

I watched the old man, who struggled to turn his walker onto the sidewalk. The walker had a basket, which had a cloth bag with rye bread and a bag of flour poking out. I recognized the generic packaging from the Salvation Army bread line.

"Might is right, huh? OK, turn on the siren and let's scare some poor elderly people," I said to Koivu as I took off, engine revving hard. Koivu did as ordered, and I felt like Moses parting the Red Sea. When we reached Mannerheim Street, I turned off the siren, since I didn't want to gridlock all of downtown Helsinki. Antti would have detested my behavior, and I wasn't particularly proud of it either.

A police emblem did allow us to leave the car in an otherwise illegal spot. The Töölö Hospital emergency room was in its normal state of chaos. This was where all the most serious and urgent cases were treated, and the junkies and confused elderly that shuffled the halls of other metro hospitals were conspicuous in their absence. After announcing ourselves at the reception desk, we were told that Jutta Särkikoski was out of the procedure room and had been taken to a carefully guarded private suite. I set off following the lines on the floor leading toward the correct ward. Apparently, the entire staff had been put on alert, because when we reached the ward, the duty nurse stopped us immediately. She carefully inspected our police identification before informing us of Jutta's condition.

"Ms. Särkikoski has lacerations on her face and upper torso, but thankfully she didn't lose too much blood. She's received a heavy dose of pain medication and sedatives. Does she know you?"

When I replied in the affirmative, the nurse agreed to allow us into Jutta's room but ordered us to be quick. At the door waited a guard who made Koivu look slender. We had to show him our badges too. I suggested to Koivu that he stay outside and have a conversation with the guard about ensuring Jutta's safety. The fewer the people coming and going, the easier it would be for Jutta to talk. This was just a preliminary interview, not an official interrogation.

Jutta's room was dimly lit, the blinds down and only a small bedside lamp switched on. Jutta lay on a pile of pillows with her eyes closed, but at the sound of me entering, her eyes snapped open. A bandage covered her left cheek, but apparently her vision was unharmed.

"Maria!" Her voice was barely above a whisper, but there was no doubt of her terror. "Maria, they tried again! They tried and failed. How . . . was Tapani still in the car?"

Rather than answering, I grabbed the chair by the window and moved it next to Jutta's bed. I took her by the right hand, noted the bandage around the wrist, and asked what happened in the parking lot. Jutta hesitated, not wanting to remember. I let her think in peace. Next to the bed was a cup with a sip top, which Jutta motioned toward. I handed it to her. She drank carefully, then handed it back. As I was setting the cup back on the table, Jutta began to talk.

"I tried to start my car, but it just sort of jammed, and I couldn't get the steering wheel to turn. Like it was locked. Ristiluoma was there, on the way to his own car, and I asked him to help. Sometimes the steering wheel in that car would stick, and getting it unstuck took some strength."

"So you drove your car from home to the meeting?" I asked, interrupting.

Jutta nodded.

"Did it work normally then, without any trouble starting it?"

"Yes, it was fine. I thought I would take the bus this morning or maybe a taxi, but since it was raining, it was easier to drive my own car. If only I'd left it home. I got out of the car and Ristiluoma took my seat. And then it just exploded! What . . . what happened to Tapani?"

"I'm sorry, Jutta. He died."

Jutta began to cry. I held her hand, and I felt like crying along with her, but that wouldn't have helped anyone. Blubbering wouldn't bring back the dead. I told Jutta that we had arranged for a guard to be with her around the clock until we discovered who was trying to kill her. There was every reason to believe the perpetrator wouldn't hesitate to try a third time. In the hospital, Jutta would be safe, but we would have to think about what would happen once she was released. Police had their ways of protecting people. It was expensive, but I remembered the unlimited budget Taskinen had promised. This was so different from what I was used to. Usually we counted all costs carefully and only ordered expensive lab work if it was absolutely necessary. What had caused this sudden change in spending culture? Was it this case, or that Taskinen wanted to lure me specifically to investigate it? But why?

I urged Jutta to remember anything strange that had happened during the day, but she was sleepy and couldn't focus. I felt bad leaving her alone to think about Ristiluoma's death. She hadn't caused it, and neither had I, but we were both wallowing in guilt. When I stepped out into the corridor, I realized that I had no clue what to do next, whom to interview, or what questions to ask. I wanted out of this situation, so I could enjoy a normal Friday where the biggest question would be what to fix my family for dinner over the weekend. Whoever killed Pentti Vainikainen and Tapani Ristiluoma had stolen the weekend from dozens of people. Merja Vainikainen's life would never be the same, and neither would Jutta Särkikoski's. If I wanted my life back, I had to endure this trial by fire. I had to find a solution. And we absolutely could not allow for any more victims.

"I'm hitting the restroom. Then we can go," I said to Koivu in the hospital lobby, because I didn't want even him, one of my best friends, to see how lost I was. I rinsed my face with cold water. The makeup I'd thrown on that morning was long gone, and only waterproof mascara came off in little smears on my hands when I rubbed my eyes. And then my damn phone rang again. I recognized the ring tone. I didn't have the energy to talk to Taskinen. It would have been easy to blame him for this, to say that it was his fault Tapani Ristiluoma had died, because he'd assigned the wrong person to this investigation. I let the phone ring, and finally it pinged with a message notification. Before I went back out, I pinched the skin around my eyes. Giving the car keys to Koivu, I told him to drive me wherever he thought best. So he turned us toward Espoo and our home base.

11

I couldn't get rid of Taskinen that easily. He was waiting in our conference room when I walked in. Taskinen's expression was agitated, and he grabbed my arm when I tried to walk past him.

"Hi, Maria. Is your phone not working? You didn't return my call. I need to know about the explosion in Pasila."

"Why did you need to hear it from me? You could see the report on the Dragnet." I looked Taskinen in the eye. He was significantly taller than me, and he had bags under his eyes and wrinkles deepening around them.

"Isn't the explosion connected to your case?"

"It is one of our lines of investigation. I've already arranged cooperation with Lieutenant Perävaara in Helsinki, so no need to worry. As I recall, I wasn't ordered to file regular reports with anyone. Let me know if that's changed since I last heard." I tried to push past him, but Taskinen grabbed me again, this time by the shoulder. My subordinates watched the situation unfold. Ursula's face bore a crooked, amused smile, and Puupponen looked resigned. Koivu was pouring himself some coffee and had his back to us. Taskinen tried to avoid my gaze, so I pushed in even closer. I could smell his aftershave.

"I just thought I'd ask if you need any additional resources," he finally said gently and dropped his hand from my shoulder. As he did so, his hand brushed against my hair. I was sure Ursula noticed it. "In theory I'll be home all weekend, but you can contact me anytime. If your phone is working." Taskinen tried to give a conspiratorial grin, but the attempt was clumsy. And then to top it all off, my phone started ringing. There was no reason not to answer.

"Hi, it's Liisa Rasilainen. So you snuck back into the department, did you? Do you have time to catch up over coffee?"

"Hi! You're back from your conference! Sorry, but it doesn't look good for coffee. It's nice to hear your voice, though," I replied, and meant it. Liisa had always been one of my favorite colleagues.

"I also called to let you know you have a package from Vantaa. It answers to the name of Sami Terävä. They caught him at the Tikkurila train station. He's waiting in a holding cell. And he wants to know why he's been brought to Espoo."

"Thanks for the heads-up! Terävä can wait for a while. If you have enough guards, take him downstairs to one of the interrogation rooms to wait. If not, keep him in a cell. See you soon!" I hung up and turned to look at my team, then announced that it was time for a summary. Ursula and Puupponen had just returned from Pasila too.

"The initial analysis suggests a bomb with a combination of a timer and a contact detonator. So it was set to go off after a certain time at the first touch," Ursula said. "That means this wasn't a complete amateur job."

"What was the explosive?"

"Don't know yet, but probably not your basic dynamite. They're doing a full search of the area, and supposedly this will get priority over everything else. Plenty of people wouldn't mind an explosion at the Parliament building, but the Sports Building is a holy shrine. That's where they hatch the plans for winning gold medals, even though you don't see an athlete like Tero Pitkämäki walk through the doors every day. He's too well-behaved for my taste, even though his body is fine," Ursula said. She seemed remarkably calm, given that she'd nearly been the first on the scene of the explosion and had had to provide first aid to Jutta Särkikoski. I hadn't even thought to praise her for how well she'd handled that.

"The Helsinki boys stayed behind to interview everyone with a window facing the inner courtyard, but they aren't going to have any luck. Mark my words. My guess is the bomb was placed in Särkikoski's car last night. Wasn't the meeting at the Sports Building arranged just this morning?"

"Tapani Ristiluoma called it." I walked across the room to switch on the electric kettle. Even a bag of Lipton tea would be better than nothing at this point. Ursula continued her report. Apparently, she'd also gotten along very well with Detective Perävaara. I told the team about my conversation with Jutta and the other things I'd found out during the day, like Hillevi's theory about how the poison ended up in the bread rolls. That made Ursula roll her eyes.

Puupponen had contacted the fire station where Miikka Harju had worked before his supposed back trouble began. He'd arranged meetings that evening with a few of Harju's former coworkers, on the condition that they weren't out on a call. Puupponen had learned that Harju was from Parikkala near the Russian border and had attended the Emergency Services College in Kuopio before getting a job in Hyvinkää and then Espoo, apparently following the girlfriend who eventually left him.

"Ristiluoma didn't have a family of his own. Ursula, will you look into his extended family and any new girlfriends when you have time? But first come with me to interview Sami Terävä after this meeting is over."

"What about me?" Koivu asked, seemingly surprised. He'd probably assumed he'd be the one to go with me.

"You're going home to count your children," I replied. Koivu looked even more surprised, and Ursula cried out.

"I'd forgotten that you always favor those with families! Recharging is just as important for the rest of us. Is Anni going to turn out like this after she has her kid too?"

"How do you know about Anni's pregnancy?" I replied angrily before I realized that I'd just let confidential information slip. Ursula smiled triumphantly.

"I was right. It doesn't take a genius. First there were the appointment reminders on her desk for the fertility clinic, then her crying fits, and now the puking in the women's restroom. It's been like working with an alcoholic. What the hell kind of drive to reproduce controls you two? Taskinen should have given this case to me to lead, then we wouldn't have to schedule the investigation around nap time!" Ursula crossed her arms and stared defiantly at Koivu.

"No one is forcing you to have children," Koivu said. "And I can stay at work."

"No, you go home and see Juuso," I said sternly. "If you die tomorrow, you won't regret not being chosen as police officer of the year or never visiting New York City. You'll regret that you didn't play table hockey with your son. Get going! We'll meet tomorrow at nine unless you hear different from me. And Ville can head off to play cards with the firefighters. Or . . ." For a moment I considered the possible dynamics of the situation, but Puupponen had already made the appointment, so I couldn't replace him with Ursula. "And keep your traps shut about Anni's pregnancy. The department gossipmongers already have enough to talk about."

"Does she have more than one baby on the way?" Ursula asked, but Puupponen told her to give it a rest, and to my surprise she did. The men then beat a hasty retreat.

"Let's go deal with Terävä. You can take the lead," I said to Ursula. "I'm just going to drink this tea first. Although I guess I can have it on the way," I said and poured hot water in a cup and threw the tea bag in. I took a sip. The flavor experience was just as terrible as I'd imagined.

You would have thought that during a century of tsarist rule, the Finns could have learned the art of tea making.

Terävä was still in cell number six because there weren't enough personnel to guard him in an interrogation room, the guard on duty explained to us. He left for a minute, then returned with a man who, at first glance, looked far too short and narrow-shouldered to be a discus thrower. In her heels, Ursula had a couple of inches on him.

Sami Terävä had brown hair that reached his shoulders, along with a carefully shaped mustache and pointed beard. His rings would have made a nice collection for a table at a flea market, and he had enough necklaces and piercings that it must take him several minutes to prepare to go through an airport metal detector. The guard hadn't found it necessary to take his jewelry, maybe thinking Terävä couldn't have hurt himself much with it anyway.

We sat Terävä down in Interrogation Room 1, and Ursula recorded his personal information on the tape. Sami Kalevi Terävä was born on May 2, 1984, in Vantaa. He worked as a sports-field maintenance technician and lived in Tikkurila in a Vantaa city rental apartment. Terävä had less than a year remaining on his competition ban, and by his own account was in constant training.

"Why did you drag me down here? I don't have anything to do with spiking those sandwiches."

"When did you last have contact with Jutta Särkikoski?" Ursula asked and leaned over the table toward Terävä. I moved my own chair farther back into the shadows so Terävä couldn't see my face well, only Ursula's.

"I haven't been in contact with her at all! Why would I?"

"Do you have a prepaid SIM card for your cell phone?"

"No! I don't have anything to hide from anyone. Eero Salo and me got fines for possession and sale of anabolic steroids and a two-year ban on competition for using performance-enhancing substances. Is that really enough to make me murder someone?" Terävä looked around in agitation. According to Jutta, Terävä was the less intelligent half of the pair, but it was likely neither of them was the brains of the doping operation. Someone else had orchestrated it. Still, Terävä had coped better during his competition ban than his supposedly more intelligent companion.

"Why were you allowed to keep your job after your conviction?" The clicking of Ursula's nails on the table was familiar and irritating, and for a moment it felt as if three years had been erased from my life, and I would never be able to extricate myself from the Espoo police.

"What does my work have to do with doping? I have a job with the City of Vantaa, and I've always done it well! I guess the federation probably spoke in my favor. Pentti Vainikainen might have called the sports-program manager at the city and asked them to give me a second chance. Everybody makes mistakes. Pentti was a good man, and I never would have done anything to hurt him. You're crazy if you think I did. Can I please have something to drink? I haven't eaten or drunk anything since breakfast."

"You just said you handled your job well," Ursula said, completely ignoring Terävä's request. "But today you didn't show up to work. Why is that?"

"I was at the doctor. I think I tore my left trap, so I went to get some anti-inflammatories. I have to be careful about what I take if I want to be able to compete. Can I have some water? The pain meds make my mouth dry. I'm supposed to take them three times a day. I can do that in jail, can't I?"

"What doctor did you visit? And why were you at the Tikkurila train station instead of on your way back to the sports park?"

"It was the company doctor! I got sick leave. All the prescriptions and receipts are in my bag—the other cops took it when they brought me in here. At least tell me why I'm here!"

Ursula didn't answer him, instead slowly turning her chair toward me. "What do you think, Lieutenant, shall we give this turd some water? Otherwise he might take us to the European Court of Human Rights."

"Coke good for you, Terävä?" Those were the first words I'd said since introducing myself. Terävä nodded, and Ursula left the room after marking the time of the pause in the interrogation on the tape. Once the door closed behind her, Terävä turned to me.

"Are you that one's boss? Tell her I was at work at the field all last Tuesday. Lots of people can back me up, like half the elementary school students and teachers in Vantaa. They were having a track meet, and I was superbusy all day. I was moving equipment around, and I even had to tape one little boy's sprained ankle. I never could have gone down to Espoo."

"Repeat that for Sergeant Honkanen and the tape," I managed to say before Ursula returned with a bottle of cola and a pitcher of water. Terävä opened the drink and chugged greedily. His thirst wasn't an act. Then he repeated his statement for the tape, but Ursula didn't react in any way. Terävä's alibi would be easy to check, since he was well-known at the Tikkurila sports park.

"Did you threaten Jutta Särkikoski after she exposed you? Did you send her letters?"

"No!"

"Postcards?"

"Not that either."

"E-mails or text messages?"

"I didn't send her a fucking thing!"

"Did you call her?" Ursula continued her bombardment. Terävä shook his head at this last suggestion. It was as if the soda affected him like water would a wilted flower: he now seemed more confident and aggressive than thirsty.

"I haven't had anything to do with that bitch! What would I gain by it? Somebody tipped her off, and we got caught. I should have known it

151

would happen. Everyone uses; the Russians and the Americans and the others just have better drugs. We just need to invest in better technology and hope we can finally clean up the sport."

"Well, aren't we righteous now? Druggies like you are treated far too leniently in Finland. In Italy doping gets you sent to prison. You said Särkikoski got a tip. From whom?"

Terävä drank more of his Coke, and Ursula asked her question again.

"Ask Särkikoski how much she paid for her information, and to who." Terävä looked Ursula up and down as if to evaluate how far she would let him push it. Ursula immediately responded.

"You're just trying to change the subject. You don't know who talked to Särkikoski. Otherwise you would have told in your interrogation." She glared at Terävä as if he were a rat she'd found in her pantry. Terävä looked away, then directed his next words to me.

"I didn't threaten anyone. Believe me! Of course I was pissed that someone I trusted blabbed to Särkikoski, and yes, we know who burned us. But what good would it have done to name names when we were still claiming that we were innocent?"

"Which was idiotic, since the evidence from your samples was so clear." Ursula smiled sardonically. "Anyway, why not out the person who exposed you to Särkikoski? Are you planning to take revenge later, when everyone's forgotten about the scandal?"

Terävä stared at Ursula in shock. "I'm not going to take revenge on anyone. He was just shooting his mouth off. He didn't realize Särkikoski was a reporter. At least that's what he said."

"Did it cross your mind that a newspaper might pay good money to know who ratted you out?"

"But they wouldn't pay! There wasn't enough evidence, and he claimed Särkikoski already knew. The newspaper people just laughed at me." Terävä appeared genuinely offended.

"Whoever turned you in did the right thing anyway. What about your partner in crime, Salo? Maybe he was sending your mutual friend Jutta Särkikoski little notes or calling her at night."

Seeing his opportunity, Terävä responded bitterly.

"I'm not sure about Eero. Throwing was all he ever had in his life. Maybe he did make some calls to Särkikoski from the last pay phone in Nokia—even he wouldn't be so stupid as to use his own phone. If he even has a phone anymore. He probably pawned it to buy more beer at the pub. He has friends there who think he's a good guy despite the drug bust. We haven't been in touch much lately."

"That Coke really seems to have loosened your tongue. Are you saying that Eero Salo threatened Jutta Särkikoski?"

"No."

"So this is just your courageous attempt to shift the blame to your friend." Ursula tsked. "So manly of you. What did you think about your cousin working with Jutta Särkikoski?"

"What do you mean? Why would I think anything?"

"Isn't thinking one of your strong suits? If not, what is? Explosives?"

The consternation on Sami Terävä's face seemed genuine, and I started to get the feeling that interrogating him was a waste of time. Salo's and Terävä's alibis at the time of Jutta and Toni's car accident had been checked, and there'd been abundant evidence that they had been far away from that particular road.

"How close is your relationship to your cousin Tapani Ristiluoma?" Ursula intentionally avoided using the past tense.

"Tapani? We're eighteen years apart. His mom is my mom's oldest sister. She never really cared much about her relatives. The Ristiluomas were higher class than the rest of us, according to my other aunt. I saw Tapani sometimes at sports events, but we don't have much in common. If you're asking whether I ever dropped by his office to say hi, the answer is no. His mom died about a year ago, but none of us cousins were invited to the funeral. I think maybe my mom went. After I got busted, Tapani didn't exactly advertise that we were related. He joked that we barely even had the same blood flowing through our veins, since I'd diluted mine with so many other things." Terävä drained his soda and crushed the can between his hands. "But I wasn't using EPO, just steroids, and they grow your muscles, not your blood-oxygen uptake."

"Were you ever offered an opportunity to participate in a new bio-medical training research project?"

I'd been expecting this question from Ursula. When Terävä asked what that even meant, I guessed that he hadn't been promising enough for anyone to invest in expensive doping technology for him. Eero Salo had been the more successful of the two. As I remembered, Terävä's greatest accomplishment had been fourth place in a Finnish junior nationals meet. In the adult men's division, he'd placed fifth in the last Kalevala Games, while Salo had taken the bronze medal, although there had been a ten-meter difference between the number-one and number-two performances.

"What research project?" Terävä asked again, but Ursula didn't respond. In court, Salo and Terävä had sworn up and down that no one knew about their doping. They'd had different trainers. They'd only become friends because they'd been in the army sports league at the same time.

Exhaustion had begun to creep over me. Ursula finally began to press Terävä about his exact movements during the day. He said that he'd woken up at around six with significant pain in his shoulder and had taken the last over-the-counter pain medication he could find in his medicine cabinet. Since the occupational health clinic opened at eight, he called and set an appointment for nine. It didn't occur to him to notify his workplace because there wasn't much going on at the field in the morning besides physical education classes from the local schools. After visiting the doctor, Terävä went to Helsinki and "just hung around." According to the receipt, he picked up his prescription at the pharmacy on Three Smiths Square at 12:37.

"The police tried to call you, but you didn't respond to their messages. Why?"

"My battery was almost dead. I was saving it for really important calls." Terävä grinned.

"So you were in Helsinki. Did you stop in Pasila, perhaps at the Sports Building, to say hi to old friends?"

"No! I jumped on the 5:21 train to Tampere. Yes, I know city passes aren't good on those trains, but no one ever checks tickets before Tikkurila. There's your crime. I confess. Can I go now?"

"When did you last see your cousin Tapani Ristiluoma?" Ursula asked.

"I don't remember! Not since the beginning of my suspension, at least." Terävä stood up, but Ursula's voice stopped him midmovement.

"You're not going anywhere. We're going to test you again." Ursula should have asked me first about taking samples from Sami Terävä to test for explosives residues, but his account of his day was undeniably vague, so there was good reason for heightened scrutiny. And we did have Taskinen's miracle budget, so the cost was no issue.

"What the hell do you mean?" Terävä sat back down, then turned to me. "OK, sure, maybe you're going to find more painkillers than I was prescribed, but who cares? I didn't drive a lawn mower, let alone a car today. I don't have anything to do with that poisoning. Two hundred people can testify that I was in Tikkurila—I wasn't anywhere near Espoo!"

At this point I thought it only fair to tell Terävä why he'd been detained. "Your cousin Tapani Ristiluoma was blown to bits in the parking lot of the Sports Building while trying to start Jutta Särkikoski's car."

I'd rarely seen anyone go so white. It was as if even the color of Terävä's eyes dimmed, and all his self-confidence instantly disappeared.

"Tapani . . . What? He's dead?"

"My condolences."

"He was killed instantly," Ursula said. Terävä looked back and forth between the two of us.

"We're going to test your clothing for explosives residues," I said. "If the tests come back clean, you will be free to go. You're going to have to stay here overnight."

"But . . . I didn't . . . I didn't have any reason . . ." he sputtered and then began to shake his head. Ursula had the sense to keep quiet while Terävä arranged his thoughts. "So my cousin and Pentti Vainikainen are both dead," he finally said, as if to himself. "And the police think that I had something to do with it. Now I've heard fucking everything! Are you ladies crazy? I'm just trying to live my life. I'm planning to compete again once my suspension is over! Why would I make everything even worse?" Terävä stood again and started for the door, but Ursula stuck out her long leg. He stumbled, and I grabbed his wrist and wrenched it behind his back. I hadn't grappled with anyone in years, and if Terävä had really tried to get away, I would have been no match for him, but Ursula was there to help. And Terävä wouldn't have made it far anyway, because the next door was locked, and the guard would have been waiting for him even if he did manage to slip out of the interrogation room.

"Should we cuff him?" Ursula asked and, to my surprise, pulled a pair of handcuffs out of her breast pocket. My investigation kit was upstairs in my office, but apparently Ursula was always prepared to make an arrest.

"Are you going to behave yourself?" I asked, and Terävä nodded. I released my hold, and Ursula followed my lead. Terävä shook himself like a dog after swimming.

"Seriously . . . I've got really bad claustrophobia. The guys always laugh at me because I never take the elevator. I'd run up the stairs at the Olympic Tower if I had to. Please. I'll go nuts if I have to be in a cell overnight."

"Do you have an official diagnosis?" Ursula asked coldly. When Terävä said no, I considered our options. Terävä did have motive to kill Jutta Särkikoski, so I wanted him screened for explosives, and that couldn't happen until tomorrow morning. And we couldn't let him go before the samples were taken. When Terävä realized we wouldn't relent, he began to struggle again, and Ursula's handcuffs became necessary after all. I asked the guard to give Terävä a sleeping pill if he wanted it. I then gave instructions to release Terävä as soon as the samples were taken, and to let him know that I was issuing a temporary travel ban.

"Let's check his cell phone and those prescriptions too," Ursula suggested as we were about to head back upstairs.

I asked the guard for Terävä's belongings, and we pulled on exam gloves. The painkiller prescription was in his wallet, along with a bank card, an athletic club membership card, a bus pass, twenty euros, and a few coins. Apparently Terävä didn't carry any keepsakes around. He hadn't worn a watch. In addition to the wallet and phone, Terävä's shoes and jacket would also be tested. Ursula looked at Terävä's cell phone with interest. I reminded her that we didn't have a warrant to inspect his call records yet.

"That is such a stupid law. It only makes our job more difficult. Shouldn't the police be able to automatically check everyone's phones, contact lists, calls, messages, and stuff like that when investigating a crime? Plenty of us do it anyway—we don't have time to deal with the pointless bureaucracy. And then there's all the prepaid burner phones, which we can't do anything about."

I didn't bother answering. When Ursula had joined our unit five years before, I'd chalked up her excesses at least partially to inexperience, but she didn't seem to have mellowed, despite her years of service.

We left Terävä's belongings in Holding and headed back upstairs to our floor. As we were leaving, Ursula's phone rang, the ringtone a familiar male voice:

"It's Kristian, baby. Answer the phone."

Glancing at me, Ursula lifted the phone to her ear. I didn't hear Kristian's replies, but I could infer plenty from Ursula's half of the conversation.

"Hi, honey. No, I'm still at work. Yes. Longer and more complicated. I don't know what the boss is going to want me to do next. But I'll come when I can. I have a key. Mmm . . . kisses!"

I knew Ursula meant for this cooing to annoy me, but I found the entire situation immensely amusing. No way Kristian would have been so brazen as to give Ursula a key to the home he and his wife shared. Apparently the Ljungbergs were at least separated. I didn't bother to ask Ursula for the gossip.

On the stairs, I bumped into my old friend Katri Reponen, the prosecutor, whom I hadn't had time to inform about my change of employment. Katri worked in the same building, in the Espoo District Court, and in previous years we'd often handled the same cases. She was currently specializing in family law, so our collaboration had continued during my research project. A lot of lawyers considered family law a fluff specialty, and the group who handled those cases only included one man—who had been forced into the position so the grumbling about men always getting steamrolled during divorce proceedings didn't grow even louder.

"Hi! I was just looking for you! Why didn't you tell me you were back? I had to read about it in the paper," Katri said. I was surprised at her outfit, a violet sweat suit and gym shoes, but I didn't say anything. Usually Katri was more the two-piece suit type, at least on trial days.

"I didn't have time. I've been swamped. Do you want to get some tea?"

"I wish I could, but yoga is about to start. Have you heard our department started a yoga club? We just got a new chief judge, who thinks the whole thing is nonsense. We're waiting for him to disband the group. Come try it out. You look like you could use some stretching and calm breathing."

I admitted that was true, but I didn't have time, and my mind was in overdrive. There was no way I'd be able to relax.

Back at my office computer, I found three e-mails from Perävaara. The first was a public relations plan. We would hold a joint press conference the next morning at ten o'clock at the Helsinki police station, as long as that fit with my schedule. Could I be there half an hour early? I quickly scanned through the other messages, which mostly reiterated that, so far, they hadn't identified the explosive or pinpointed its location in the car. The third e-mail was a summary written up by one of Perävaara's subordinates about the eyewitness testimony they'd collected, which basically said that in the Sports Building it had been business as usual, and no one had seen anyone crawling around under any of the cars in the parking lot or anything else out of place. Behind the parking lot was a forest with a walking path, and someone could have come from that direction too, but the area around the building itself was so open that going unnoticed would have been nearly impossible.

I replied to Perävaara about the press conference and let him know about Terävä's detainment and that we would be testing him for explosives residues. I received a quick, happy reply.

> Good. At least we have one arrest to tell the media about. See you tomorrow.

I heard Ursula talking on the phone in the other room, still dealing with arrangements for Ristiluoma's remains. The digital news had reported the explosion and said that all train traffic toward Turku was delayed due to technical difficulties.

That reminded me of our Turku suspects. I'd completely forgotten about Ilpo Koskelo and Toni Väärä. They'd been in the metro area today too. I wasn't certain whether they took the first train back to Turku after their interviews or not. Maybe one of them paid a little visit to the Sports Building. Or maybe both of them.

12

―――――――◆―――――――

When I finally got home, Taneli was already asleep. Iida was still up reading, so I sat next to her on her bed for twenty minutes. She wanted to know why my work situation had changed so suddenly, and since she was eleven, I could almost tell her the uncensored truth. And besides, she'd already seen the headlines and the tabloids.

"Do you like investigating murders?" Iida asked. Deciding how to answer wasn't easy.

"I wouldn't say I like it, but it's necessary. We can't let killers run free."

"Does it scare you?" The gaze of her brown eyes was intense. Iida had inherited them from her father. Slowly I stroked her hair, which had become greasier when she began puberty.

"Not exactly. I know my job has risks, and I've been in danger a few times." I hadn't told Iida about the time I'd been pregnant with her and had to flee a murderer armed with an ice skate across the rink where she now trained. "We're all trying to solve this set of crimes as quickly as possible, and then I'll be home more. Dad will take you guys to practice tomorrow."

"Will you even be here for dinner?"

I didn't dare promise anything, so I just wished her a good night.

Antti sat in the living room with a book and a glass of wine. Venjamin had climbed into his lap. I went and poured myself a glass too, and then we talked through practicalities. He was still a little aloof, which wasn't at all surprising. My sister-in-law and my mother had called—they both stubbornly continued calling our landline—and asked what on earth I was up to. My personal cell had been on silent all day, so they couldn't have reached me that way anyway.

"I have to be up before seven tomorrow. If you want to sleep longer, you'll need to go to the guest room. Or I will," I suggested once I'd drained my glass. I'd begun to feel sleepy.

"No, we're going to sleep together. Otherwise I won't see you at all," Antti replied.

I sent my mother a text message telling her not to worry. In bed, I tried to focus on my book, but it was no use, and I turned the lights off as soon as Antti joined me.

"How are you doing?" he asked and wrapped his arms around me. I pressed my face against his shoulder and smelled his familiar, slightly salty scent.

"I'm fine. I'm staying unattached," I said, knowing as I did that I was lying to both Antti and myself. I knew that I'd been ordered to be a cop, so I needed to think like a cop, and now I had to sleep so I'd be able to deal with whatever came my way tomorrow. The Maria who lay in Antti's arms did not belong to the police station, but the woman who went there tomorrow must be fully committed to the role of homicide detective.

"Do you have a gun?" Antti whispered.

"No. We're handling it so that I won't need it. Let's sleep now."

Antti kissed my cheek. It was good to fall asleep in his embrace. In the night, I woke up to Taneli padding into our room. Nowadays that was extremely rare, but it felt good when he curled up between us. I could smell the shampoo in his hair. When Venjamin settled down at my feet, the bed was more than warm enough.

In the morning, I left the family to sleep and paid a visit to the Espoo station to leave instructions for my team and inform them that our morning meeting would be at eleven instead of nine due to the press conference. I considered leaving the car at the station and taking the train to the Helsinki suburb of Pasila, but the transit schedules didn't work out right. Thankfully it was Saturday morning, so there was plenty of parking at the Helsinki headquarters.

It felt like an eternity had passed since my stint in the Helsinki PD. That assignment had included my first lead on a homicide investigation. My boss at the time had been a hopeless drunk, and everyone had tried to cover for him. These days that wouldn't fly, since tolerance for drinking in the workplace had diminished considerably. As I understood it, Lieutenant Kinnunen had taken a disability pension about five years ago and then ended up in the ground soon after.

The police station in Pasila felt foreign. The building had been remodeled since I last visited, so I had to ask directions to reach the right room. Oddly enough, the building smelled differently than when I'd worked there. I'd always had a good memory for smells, and now the unfamiliar scent confused me. It was the same on the floor where the Violent Crime Unit was housed. The walls had been painted, and everything seemed strange. Eventually I found a door with a sign that said "Perävaara" and knocked on it.

Detective Perävaara looked like he hadn't slept since I'd last seen him. Compared to him, with his stubble, wrinkled shirt, and red eyes, I must have looked downright perky. But there was nothing lethargic about my colleague's brain function, and his team had managed to interview the majority of the people working at or visiting the Sports Building the day before. People were helpful, especially since the attack had been directed at someone who worked in the same building.

"Almost everyone in the building knew who Jutta Särkikoski is and that she is currently working there. Some of them even knew her car. The head of the Fencing Association, whose car was right next to Särkikoski's yesterday, said he'd known whose car it was when he parked. His vehicle was also totaled in the explosion. Maybe not everyone liked the fact that Särkikoski was working at Adaptive Sports. Apparently, there had been some grumbling about it in the weight-lifting wing. But only a few people knew Ristiluoma, mostly the Athletics Federation folks because he was Pentti Vainikainen's occasional golfing buddy." Perävaara yawned and scrolled down in his file. "I sent these interview documents to you, but I bet you didn't have time to read them this morning, right?"

"Right. I slept until a luxurious 6:45."

"You've picked up bad habits since leaving the police. I spent the night in the lounge down the hall. Anyway, a few people claimed they saw someone sneaking around Särkikoski's car, but we're still checking on that. A couple of our detectives are going through the tapes from the security cameras at the building entrances, but so far, they haven't found anything. The terrorism and explosives task force think we may be dealing with something as simple and accessible as TATP. Theoretically you can even make it at home, but it's pretty unpredictable stuff. A lot of terrorists use it, and professional criminals."

"Is it possible to use it to make a bomb that goes off when you start a car?"

"As I said, it's a pretty unpredictable substance, so offhand I'm thinking no. We're going to talk to a few folks who've messed around with it before, and we'll see if they can give us any insight. One of our detectives is also looking in the online message boards for any clues. How about at the press conference, I talk about the bomb, and you answer questions about the victim and the car, OK?"

"Great."

"Do you know much about where Särkikoski's car has been the past few days?"

"It's mostly been in the parking lot at her apartment building. No cameras there, unfortunately. She doesn't have a garage, just an engine heater plug spot. And anyone could have asked the Bureau of Motor Vehicles for her license plate number."

"You interview the neighbors, since Särkikoski lives in Espoo. Are you also considering the possibility that Ristiluoma really was the target? As I understand it, Särkikoski has cheated death twice now. Maybe she set the trap herself." Perävaara noticed my expression of disbelief and laughed. "Don't you suspect everyone and everything anymore? Paranoia is our number-one occupational hazard. Or did you recover from that during your leave of absence?" I didn't have time to correct his characterization of my departure from the police before he stood up. "I'm going to go clean myself up. My wife gets on my case if I look like a slob in press photos, not to mention my mother-in-law."

After he left, I thought about what he'd said. Was it possible that the car accident and the death threats had messed up Jutta to the point that she'd started taking out the people she thought were threatening her? Jutta seemed frightened but not insane, and she'd been injured in the blast too. What if this was a case of Munchausen syndrome? Maybe Jutta missed the attention she'd gotten during the doping case and after her accident, and now she was trying to recapture the spotlight by faking threats against herself? I shook my head—there had to be some limit to our paranoia.

About ten minutes later, I got a text from Koivu, letting me know that Terävä's tests had come back clean, so they'd let him go.

"Ready to face the lions?" Perävaara asked from the door. I looked up from my phone. A shave, a shower, and a clean shirt had worked miracles on him. He must have even put concealer on the bags under his eyes, because the skin there was a normal color again. The glasses he wore hid most of the redness in his eyes.

"Let's go. You can start." Perävaara took me by the arm but released me well before we stepped into the briefing room.

Naturally the room was crowded. Bombs didn't go off in Helsinki every day. I declined to name the hospital Jutta Särkikoski had been taken to for treatment, but I did say she was under constant guard. Hopefully the person I was looking for followed the media. Perävaara and I both appealed to the public for useful information. Puupponen would check the tips that came in and investigate any possible connections between Perävaara's list of known bomb makers and our suspects. Perävaara's presence next to me was reassuring, and he immediately shut down one of the crime reporters when he asked about the possibility of a serial killer. I remembered that Ursula had just finished profiler training. Those skills might be useful in this case after all.

As I drove back to Espoo, I felt satisfied that the collaboration between the Espoo force and the Helsinki force was going smoothly. Perävaara had the same troubles I did: he'd promised to take his kids to the face-off between the two rival Helsinki hockey teams, but the case had to come first.

On the way, I called Töölö Hospital. The nurse on duty told me that it had been peaceful overnight, and no one had tried to see Jutta Särkikoski. Her condition was good, given the circumstances, and I would be able to interview her later that afternoon.

As I exited the freeway, I looked wistfully at a jogger on the sidewalk. It looked like the day would be sunny for a change, and I longed for fresh air. The fall colors were at their best, the birch trees blazing yellow and the aronia bushes full of striking red leaves. With its white facade, the Espoo police station looked like an animal that had donned its winter coat too soon.

Inside, my team was already assembled in the conference room, Koivu with his customary cup of coffee and Ursula wearing an abnormally restrained pantsuit and only two-inch heels.

I conveyed Detective Perävaara's regards, and that he suspected the bomb was made by a professional. Puupponen whistled upon hearing that piece of information.

"Särkikoski must know something she doesn't know she knows! This can't just be about doping. What if her unnamed source is still dealing steroids, or maybe something stronger, and he's afraid that Särkikoski will eventually turn him in?"

"Yes, we have to get that name," Ursula said. I reminded her that Terävä claimed to know who exposed him and Salo. Ursula could question Terävä again even though we'd let him go after he was tested for explosives. If she talked to him long enough, he was likely to let the name slip. And maybe Eero Salo had sobered up enough for the Nokia police to grill him about what he was doing on the day of the crime. If they discovered anything significant, we could have Salo shipped to Espoo. Hopefully Jutta would finally reveal her source. My impression was that she didn't think her source was the one who'd been threatening her, but now we'd need to be the ones to decide if he was a suspect.

"OK, let's turn to Miikka Harju and Ristiluoma. Ursula, did you find anything about Ristiluoma that could lead you to believe the bomb was meant for him?"

"How could it have been meant for him? No one knew he would be in Särkikoski's car—except, of course, Särkikoski herself. Do you suspect her? She has always seemed a little strange to me."

I shared my Munchausen idea, but Puupponen and Koivu didn't warm to the theory, and Ursula thought it sounded pretty far-fetched too.

"Could you work up a criminal profile based on these two cases?" I asked her. "I understand you did some training in Tampere."

"Male, under thirty-five, lives alone, unemployed or in danger of unemployment, problems with mental health or drugs, no long-term female relationships. Probably short." Up until that last point, Ursula had us going. "Reads Woody Woodpecker comics and listens to Paula Koivuniemi, who serves as a mother figure." She burst out laughing. "It isn't that easy, but I'll think about it! Although male and living alone are probably good guesses."

After grinning at us long enough to make Koivu scowl, Ursula returned to the topic of Ristiluoma. She pulled up a photo of him on her computer and projected it onto a screen that she must have ordered from IT the day before. In the picture, Ristiluoma's bearded face smiled as if he didn't have a care in the world. Now all that was left of that face was a shattered skull and scraps of flesh.

"Hemmo Tapani Ristiluoma, who went by his middle name, Tapani. Originally from Kotka, now living here in Espoo, in North Tapiola to be precise. Has a master of business administration. Thirty-nine years old and unmarried, both parents deceased, father of lung cancer and mother of breast cancer, so he didn't do that well in the gene lottery. His one sister, two years younger, lives in Kerava. I spoke with her on the phone, although I don't know how reliable she was because she was so upset about her brother's death. Ristiluoma was never married, but he did have two long-term girlfriends. Ristiluoma's sister gave me the first one's contact information, but she didn't remember the second one's last name. She promised to let me know if it comes to her. The property management office was closed when I called yesterday, but I'll call back later—they should be able to give us the second girlfriend's contact information from the lease on the apartment she and Ristiluoma shared." Ursula paused and took a sip from her bottle of pear-flavored French mineral water. My phone rang, and I saw from the display that it was Leena, so I didn't answer. Somehow she'd gotten hold of my work cell number. Maybe the switchboard had given it to her.

"According to the sister, Ristiluoma was afraid of commitment, and that was why his girlfriends left him, because they wanted to get married and have children. Girlfriend number one, Eija Heikkinen, confirmed this. They started dating in their early twenties, when they were still in school, and Ristiluoma was throwing javelin. Then he got injured, which ended his athletic career. She said he'd been really upset about it, but he managed to turn his attention to his schooling, ultimately going for an MBA. That isn't the easiest switch for an active athlete, but Ristiluoma wasn't some dumb hick, even though he came from a small town. What is it, Ville?" Ursula asked as Puupponen waved his hand enthusiastically.

"Ristiluoma fits your profile. Male, lived alone."

"Good point. And I think you fit it too, don't you? Now let me finish. Because of his arm injury, Ristiluoma became interested in mobility assistance devices for athletes and founded MobAbility with an occupational therapist and a physical therapist. Five years ago, he bought them out, which turned out to be profitable for him. I spoke with his former partners. One used the proceeds of the sale to start a physical therapy practice on the Costa del Sol and had nothing bad to say about Ristiluoma. The occupational therapist is an academic now. He mostly writes textbooks, but he also designs devices for MobAbility as a subcontractor. He was a little bitter about not receiving an invitation to the launch party, because the lumbar spine belt Toni Väärä showed off was one he designed. So everyone but Toni Väärä thought Pentti Vainikainen was a perfect angel, and now we have another guy who everyone thought was just swell too, except maybe his exes. But his not wanting a wife or kids isn't a crime. I'm meeting with the MobAbility office staff today if you don't have anything more important for me to do. The secretary, Satu Häkkinen, has been with MobAbility since the beginning and probably knew her boss better than anyone."

"How long had Ristiluoma been without a steady girlfriend?" Koivu asked.

"About two years, as far as I can tell. Are you wondering where he was getting sex during that time? Trust me, Koivu, there are nonmarital options. You can always pay for it or get it for free if you aren't too picky. According to ex-girlfriend number one, Ristiluoma was very active in that department, at least when he was younger."

"Should we check Ristiluoma's bank account to see if there's anything that points to his using prostitutes? Like regular deposits to strange accounts or unexpectedly large cash withdrawals," Puupponen said, trying to redeem himself.

"I still think Ristiluoma's death was an accident," I said. "And that for our main line of investigation, we should assume that the bomb was meant for Jutta."

"So I don't get to try the Casanova angle . . ." Puupponen said, trying to be funny again. The rest of us just stared at him. That fall, there had been public discussion about the sexual harassment female police officers encounter in the line of duty, because more than a fifth of us had been victims at some point, myself included. Someone who didn't know him well could easily take Puupponen's joking as harassment. But over the years I'd learned to accept Puupponen's corny jokes as simply part of his personality, or a way to cope with a job in which beauty was less frequently on display than misery.

The sound of Antti's ringtone startled me. My husband wasn't in the habit of calling me at work unless it was important. I went into my office to answer.

"Sorry for bothering you." Antti's voice was tense. "Your friend Leena has already called me three times demanding to know what hospital Jutta Särkikoski is in. She says you aren't answering her calls."

"You shouldn't answer them either" was the only guidance I could give him. "You can't officially know anything beyond what can be found in the newspaper. As a lawyer, Leena should understand that."

"But she's so damn persistent! She seems to feel involved in the case because she introduced you and Särkikoski."

"As I said, don't answer her calls. And if you go by the liquor store, buy a bottle of Laphroaig. I think I'm going to need a stiff drink once I get out of here. Give everyone a hug from me."

After Antti hung up, I sat at my desk and stared at my phone. I didn't have any obligation to keep Leena informed about the progress of the investigation, but I knew my friend well enough to guess how concerned she was. So I typed out a quick text message: *This case is intense, but Jutta is fine. I'm meeting with her later. Want me to tell her something? I'll let you know as soon as you can see her.* That would have to suffice.

I returned to the conference room, and Puupponen filled me in on the progress investigating Miikka Harju. Coincidentally, the fire and rescue crew Harju had worked with had been called out to the explosion in Pasila the previous day, and they had been very open to Puupponen's questions. Most of them had known Harju, and they didn't bother to hide their opinions of him. Harju's claims of back trouble had elicited hoots of laughter.

"Booze was Harju's problem," Puupponen said. "They asked him to turn in his resignation after he came in not quite sober and blew a 0.06 on the breathalyzer. That wasn't the first time he'd gotten in trouble—he'd already received a couple of reprimands. Still, according to his coworkers, when he wasn't intoxicated, he was a damn good firefighter and was always the first one into the flames. He seemed to enjoy taking risks, which is something of a prerequisite for both firefighters and cops. He hasn't kept in touch since he left the fire station. One of them tried to call him early on, but Harju hung up on him. They didn't even know he'd sobered up and was working at Adaptive Sports." Puupponen had also met Harju's former fiancée, whose name and cell number he'd gotten from Harju's old boss. She said she'd grown tired of Harju's drinking, although the relationship had been on the rocks for a while before he'd really started losing it.

"She said she fell in love with the uniform and the feeling of familiarity. Apparently, her dad and brothers were firefighters too. I guess I should go back to Patrol, since apparently uniforms really do bring luck with the ladies," Puupponen said with a laugh and then blushed. He had never been in the habit of talking about his private life, and sometimes I'd wondered how such a great guy managed to stay single. Ursula's wiles had had no effect on him when she tried to seduce him early on, so she must have come to the same conclusion that I had: either Puupponen was asexual or gay.

"This woman, her name is Teija Koskivuo. She's a pharmacist, and she actually tried to patch things up with Harju about six months ago, after she heard he was in recovery. But Harju said there was no going back. Apparently Harju's finances have always been a mess. He still owes money to some of his old coworkers at the fire station, and Koskivuo said she'd basically supported him. Occasionally he'd go gambling and hit a jackpot, but he always just blew it right away. When he lost his job, he also lost his credit, but he managed to keep his apartment because it's privately owned rather than by the city, and Harju always paid his rent even if he didn't keep up on his credit card bills. A guy who always has a hole in his pocket is awfully easy to bribe."

"You mean, like pay to commit a homicide? Are you suggesting that Harju went for the job at Adaptive Sports because he thought that would be the best way to get at Jutta Särkikoski?" Ursula asked.

"The employment office is closed on the weekend, so I won't be able to ask them until Monday. But maybe Merja Vainikainen would know, since she hired Harju. Maria, can we contact the grieving widow?"

"The grieving widow was at her office yesterday, and I imagine she wants this case solved quickly too. But who would have hired Harju to kill Jutta? Who did he used to drink with?"

"I got a few names, but they aren't interesting. A couple have drunk-driving convictions and speeding tickets, but they aren't exactly career criminals, and there's nothing about drugs. And nowadays Harju is on the straight and narrow and spends his evenings at AA. And as we've already said, getting information out of his pals there would be like questioning a Catholic priest. Although I guess we could try to bribe his sponsor with a bottle of the hard stuff."

"Ville, come on. That's over the line."

"Don't you remember that with Maria, you're only allowed to tell politically correct jokes?" Ursula said, and I found it necessary to count to ten in my head. I still blamed myself for not intervening more when Pertti Ström was drinking on the job, because he still might have been alive if someone had interrupted his downward spiral in time. But to Ursula, Ström was just a name, since he'd died before she'd entered the department, and all she knew about him were colorful stories. Even though we hadn't gotten along, these days I tended to remember Ström's rare bursts of humanity more than his rages. I also honored his memory whenever I happened to visit the urn cemetery at the old Espoo church, where there was a space reserved for remembering those buried elsewhere.

"Ville, you continue digging into Harju. Ursula, you work on your profile and bring Terävä back in," I managed to say before my phone rang again. I didn't recognize the number, but the voice I heard when I answered was familiar from many of the Women's Police Days I'd attended.

"Hi, it's Anne Kauppinen from the Nokia Police Department. Do you have a second? We just finished talking to a very hungover Eero Salo."

I put my phone on speaker so the others in the room could listen. "I'm here with my team. Go ahead."

"We sent him over to the health center to get treatment. Eero Salo hasn't left Siuro in the past month. In August he went to the theater festival in Tampere, although I get the impression that the only culture he imbibed was beer culture. His friends are all drunks, but the staff at the pub can vouch for him. He's been sitting there with a pint in front of him every day. There's always someone willing to treat the hometown boy who definitely would have won Olympic gold if that pesky suspension hadn't gotten in the way. Back in the day, Eero stole the county discus record from a guy in Tampere, and the folks in Siuro are still proud of it."

"Does Salo have any friends who might have wanted to take revenge on his behalf?"

"Well, those guys certainly know how to talk, but the cases you're investigating are more complex than Eero's crew would be capable of. The only one that could have built a bomb is named Rissanen, and he's already doing a three-year stint. He's about to be moved to the new prison in Turku. I doubt the views will be as nice as those at the old prison up on the hill. You know, I've known Eero for practically his whole life." Anne had been a police officer in Nokia for more than twenty years, since before Salo was born. "He was always up for some petty shoplifting or sneaking beer out into the woods. That is, if someone else suggested it. But he was never the instigator. Thankfully Harri Timonen started throwing shot put, and Eero got into sports too. At the time I thought that we weren't going to have to worry about him anymore. But I guess down at the pub they knew before the doping commission and the Athletics Federation that Eero was using something."

Before hanging up, Anne promised that she and her team would keep their ears open for rumors circulating in the area about Salo having a part in the homicides we were investigating. They had their local sources. Anne had always been good at finding informants, and she claimed that it was because she was a country girl. She'd actually come from the same village as Eero Salo. She seemed to have real pride about it—a few years before, at a Women's Police Day karaoke event, she'd sung Kari Peitsamo's "From Shanghai to Siuro." She'd brought the music herself because the song wasn't on any of the karaoke lists.

"So no immediate need to go to Nokia," I told my team. "What about Turku? Did Toni Väärä and Ilpo Koskelo go straight home after their interviews?"

"Koskelo did, but we haven't been able to get in touch with Väärä," Koivu said. "Koskelo took the train, and he said that Väärä had jumped on the 109 bus to go visit some friends. I must have left ten messages on his phone. Koskelo took the two o'clock from Espoo Central and was home in Rusko around four thirty. He met people he knew on the train, including the mayor of Rusko, coming home from a meeting. Should I check the alibi?"

"Not at the moment. Doesn't Väärä have training with Koskelo today?"

"He should, at three o'clock at the Kupittaa Sports Park. If he hasn't called me back by then, I'll get in touch with Koskelo." Koivu stretched, and when I asked him how the table hockey had gone, he reported with feigned dejection that Juuso had wiped the floor with him over three ten-minute periods, five to one.

"You let him win," Ursula scoffed.

"I did not! I just didn't wear my glasses, and without them I can barely tell where the puck is. And the kid really is fast. He takes after his mother that way. Speaking of which, Maria, Anu has tickets to the ballet for Tuesday. Can I have that night off?"

"Unless the sky falls on us," I said. "OK, let's get back to work. Koivu and I are going to Töölö Hospital. I'll call when we're free, and we can all go out to Kauklahti to figure out who's been skulking around Jutta Särkikoski's car lately."

On the way, Koivu and I stopped at an Indian fast food joint. As Koivu was maneuvering the car out of the ridiculously cramped parking garage, I received a call from the forensic lab.

"Hi, it's Pirre from the lab. We're still running drug panels, but I have one result for Pentti Vainikainen. It looks like it was nicotine poisoning. That is, we found nicotine in his stomach, but only about thirty grams. It seems like it was in the sandwich spread, probably the garlic butter. But let me emphasize: it was only thirty grams. That's not enough to kill a person."

13

I asked Koivu to pull over so I could get the autopsy report open on my laptop. The lab had started its analysis with the stomach, since we'd assumed Vainikainen ingested the nicotine with the sandwich. But could someone have injected him with something? The autopsy report listed in detail every mark they'd found on the body, but there was no mention of a needle site. They would have noticed that, and Ursula would have told me that already, since she attended the autopsy. The mucous membranes in Vainikainen's mouth were badly burned, but that was assumed to have been caused by the nicotine. According to the eyewitnesses, Vainikainen had downed the sandwich in two large bites.

"We still don't have the drug panels or the nicotine concentrations in his blood or internal organs. But maybe we're just dealing with a measurement error. These initial results aren't always very good," I said, trying to comfort myself.

"Yes, or maybe the killer thought a small dose of nicotine would do for Jutta Särkikoski, since she's so slight."

"But Jutta Särkikoski didn't eat the sandwich, and Pentti Vainikainen wasn't a small woman! Damn it to hell. And Vainikainen didn't even smoke, so that can't explain the nicotine either. And his wife didn't mention any sensitivity to nicotine."

"We just need to be patient and wait for the full results," Koivu said. "Ready to go? There's a bus coming, and the driver isn't going to be happy with us taking up the stop."

As we continued driving, I noticed boats still out in the bay enjoying the sunny, windy weather. We needed to get the family boat into dry dock for the winter, but Antti could probably handle that with his nephews. Right now, I should have been shivering in the ice arena watching Iida's practice. Although the thought of the cold ice rink wasn't the most appealing thing in the world. At least the car was warm.

Outside Töölö Hospital, I paused to breathe the autumn air for a moment, but Koivu marched right inside so that he could call Toni Väärä again without having to deal with the noise of the wind. Did the kid have a girlfriend in the Helsinki area that Koskelo didn't know about? There was hardly any information online about the Smith's Friends. There were only about three hundred members of the sect in Finland, mostly in Kirkkonummi and Inkoo. Smith's Friends were supposed to marry within the religion, and that meant few options. Many seemed to go looking for spouses in northern Norway, where there were more of their brothers and sisters. The Smith's Friends had no priests, and anyone could speak in their meetings, even the small children. That part at least sounded charming, since in that respect it promoted equality. But overall, their doctrine emphasized that men were in charge.

The duty nurse said that Jutta had called her parents in the morning. Was that alright? She didn't know whether Jutta had revealed her location to them. The guard at Jutta's door had changed, and the new one also carefully checked our badges before letting us in.

Jutta was propped up in a partial sitting position, and she already looked spryer than she had the previous evening. Koivu had brought a tape recorder, since this would be an official interview.

"How are you doing?" I asked as I sat down in the chair I'd pulled over to the bed while Koivu attached the cords and tested the minicassette. I understood that some of our colleagues were recording interviews directly onto the computer, but I hadn't learned that new system yet. Learning to use the Dragnet was already enough to keep me busy.

"Hi. Is there really a guard outside all the time?" Jutta asked in a scratchy voice and then sipped some water from her cup. She must not have spoken much today.

"Yes, and the police aren't telling anyone where you are. I didn't tell Leena, even though she's worried and keeps demanding to see you. You didn't tell your parents where you're being treated, did you? I heard you called them."

"I did . . . I really need to see them. Can't they come visit?"

The paranoid police officer in me thought that Jutta's parents could be followed, but I didn't share that thought. Even if someone did follow them, it wasn't that easy to barge into a hospital. Whether the reporters might be able to wheedle Jutta's location out of them was another matter. Jutta assured us she'd asked her parents not to tell.

"They aren't stupid. They understand the seriousness of the situation. This is the third time someone's tried to kill me. Maybe in this case the fourth time will be the charm." Jutta tried to sound jaunty, but there was fear in her eyes that she couldn't conceal.

"There won't be a fourth time. I'm sorry we didn't assign you a security detail after Pentti Vainikainen's death. We won't take any more risks. Would you be willing to let us apply for a wiretap warrant on your phone?"

"Absolutely! I'm never going to answer that number again. But can we even trust these nurses? People are always talking about how small their salaries are, and then there were those cases of nurses poisoning mentally handicapped people. A lot of the handicapped athletes that Adaptive Sports works with were really upset by those incidents. What if someone bribes one of my nurses? I'm afraid to even go to sleep."

"Testing, testing, one, two, three," Koivu said into the microphone and then listed the names and titles of everyone present, along with the date and time. We were interviewing Jutta as a witness, so I reminded her that she was bound by law to tell the truth.

"Why on earth would I lie? I want all of this to be over."

I didn't immediately press her for the name of the source that exposed Salo and Terävä. I'd work up to that.

"Did your car work as usual when you came to the Espoo police station on Thursday?"

Jutta said that nothing had been wrong with her car on Thursday. From the police station she'd driven home and left it in her assigned spot in the apartment complex parking lot. Later in the day she visited the corner store, but that was only a few hundred yards away, so she'd walked. She didn't start her car again until Friday. Jutta lived in a row house in a model housing development built during the recent 2006 housing fair. The streets were open and well trafficked, so she hadn't been afraid of someone attacking her out there in the middle of the day. The car had been in her parking space until she left to meet Tapani Ristiluoma at the Sports Building, at his invitation. Jutta had last filled up the gas tank on Tuesday before she drove to the fitness campaign launch.

"My car has—had—an alarm. I don't understand how someone could have tampered with it. It was really sensitive, and sometimes the neighbors complained that they didn't dare walk near it for fear of setting it off. They wondered why I was so worried about a regular car that was fully insured. But I wasn't so much concerned about the car itself as I was about those who might try to break in."

"I understand. And I also understand that now is the time for you to name your source. Salo and Terävä claim they know who ratted them out. Who was it?"

Jutta opened her mouth but then closed it again.

I repeated my question, and two large tears began running down her right cheek. Strangely she only cried with one eye. The other stayed dry.

"I promised. No, I swore with my hand on the Bible and on my honor as a journalist. You police officers have your own set of professional ethics, don't you? Why are you demanding that I betray mine?"

I stood up from my chair by the bed, and the movement made Jutta flinch. I walked to the window. The room had a view of the central courtyard. Maple leaves were blowing in the wind. One came loose from a branch and began to float higher and higher until an opposing current of air ended its flight. It slowly glided down toward the ground. I took a couple of deep breaths to keep myself from yelling, which wouldn't help in this situation. I turned back to Jutta and tried to keep my voice calm. Koivu still sat at the table, watching the tape recorder next to him, his expression inscrutable.

"We aren't talking about your professional ethics; we're talking about the fact that someone is trying to kill you. You may not see your source as a threat, but the situation may have changed. Your source is obviously someone with connections to drug dealers. If Salo and Terävä know who this person is, then we can be sure that the big players in the steroid racket know too. Are you sure you didn't accidentally step on some toes and make yourself part of something larger than you'd intended? Or are you still secretly working on a story that's so important you're willing to sacrifice your own life to publish it? No one asked Vainikainen or Ristiluoma whether they wanted to be martyrs for free speech. You have to answer me. Who are you protecting?"

Jutta continued crying quietly, and now tears ran freely from her left eye too. "You have to believe me! My source would never want to hurt me in a million years and isn't involved in the drug trade. The information was obtained by chance."

"You didn't just make the whole story up like some in the sports press claim, did you?"

"No! Do I have to listen to this? My head feels like it's going to explode. I think I have a migraine coming on . . ."

179

I didn't know whether Jutta was just acting, but I interrupted the interview momentarily so she could calm down. Koivu gestured to ask whether I wanted him to step out, but I shook my head. I wanted everything Jutta said to be in the official record. I did have ways of being persuasive, like threatening to arrest her for concealing information, but what good would that do? I had to go back to square one.

"Interview continuing at 1:36. Lieutenant Maria Kallio and Sergeant Pekka Koivu still present, interviewing Jutta Särkikoski, location Töölö Hospital. Ms. Särkikoski, did your source indicate that Pentti Vainikainen encourages athletes to dope? You might as well tell us—the dead can't sue you for slander."

"Pentti . . ." Jutta sounded contemplative. "I don't believe that Pentti would have directly encouraged anyone to dope. I guess he might have done it in a roundabout way. As far as I know, Pentti had nothing to do with what Salo and Terävä were up to, since they were barely good enough to qualify for domestic events, let alone international competitions. Pentti knew who to invest in. For example, Toni Väärä."

Väärä had claimed he didn't tell anyone about Vainikainen's offer, not even his trainer.

"Is that why you were interested in interviewing Väärä? Did you believe he was doping?"

"I wasn't the only person surprised by the sudden improvement in his results. And Väärä would have been a perfect guinea pig for the so-called biomedical training they've been marketing to the sponsors. Fancy code name for doping, eh?" Jutta's voice became brighter, and she visibly perked up as she began to talk about something less personally relevant. "The 800 meter is a demanding event. Steroids help with sprinting, and that's what the BALCO lab developed for the American runners and anyone else who could pay. But in the 800, extra muscle mass becomes a liability, and you need endurance in addition to speed. There also haven't been any international superstars in the 800 lately, unlike some in the shorter and longer distances, so it hasn't been nearly as lucrative. And there isn't as much money in the throwing sports as in running, but in throwing you can better use growth hormones to improve. In the 800, you'd benefit more from EPO. That's what our national ski team got caught using. So now they need new drugs that won't show up in the tests, but skiers are watched too closely to try it on them. One more bust, and competitive Nordic skiing will be done for in Finland, at least in the eyes of the public and the sponsors. So the doping labs need new guinea pigs. And who better than someone like Toni Väärä, someone who is clearly gifted and wants to improve but isn't yet the kind of superstar who would be constantly tested?"

"So . . ." I interrupted Jutta's monologue.

"So if I was a sports boss who wanted to test new drugs, I'd go look-ing for someone like him. And that's why my alarm bells went off when Pentti Vainikainen went to such great lengths to keep me from meeting Toni. His coach practically hung off the bumper of my car to stop Toni from riding with me to Helsinki. What did they have to hide?"

Jutta paused and took a sip from her cup. Koivu pulled a pack of gum out of his pocket and offered me a piece. I declined. Outside, the wind was blowing harder, and I heard a cry in the hallway, followed by quick footsteps. A little color had returned to the Jutta's cheeks, and after taking a third sip, she continued.

"The other people involved are still alive, so I can't mention their names, but I will tell you that Pentti Vainikainen was working with some of the sponsors to develop this new biomedical training thing. The sponsors are happy to contribute when it's pitched to them the right way. Having your logo on the jersey of an Olympic champion sure is great. And no one is going to question the victory as long as no one gets caught."

"Was Toni Väärä Olympic medalist material?" I asked, to buy time. Jutta didn't know that Väärä had told me more or less the same thing, and I didn't want to reveal that, at least not as long as she continued to conceal her source.

"Of course not, at least not without some serious chemical help! He might be up for a European championship, although the continent is getting so many runners with African heritage that whites with their slow genes are mostly out of luck."

A knock came at the door, and a nurse entered. "I know you have visitors, but it's time for your medication, and I need to change that bandage on your face. We want to leave as little work as possible for the plastic surgeon." The nurse's tone was firm, so I said we could wait in the corridor while she did her work. I'd decided to drag Jutta's source out of her even if I had to sit in her room until Sunday morning.

Koivu used the opportunity to go get us some coffee. The guard asked Koivu to get him one too and left me to watch the door while he used the restroom. I wondered if the job requirements for a security guard included a bladder that could go eight hours without being emptied. I was just sending Iida a text message asking how her skating practice had gone when Ursula's name began flashing on the phone display. I picked up.

"Hi, Ursula."

"All that time with Terävä yesterday was a waste," she said bitterly, cutting to the chase. "I didn't have to sweet-talk him much before he agreed to meet me at the coffee shop in the Tikkurila ice arena. I'm just coming from there. The name we were looking for is Petri 'Pete' Heiskanen. He's an old school friend of Jutta Särkikoski's. They were in the same class. Heiskanen has a suspended sentence for drug dealing, and he goes to the same gym as Terävä and Salo, the gym where they got their steroids. I got the impression from Terävä that he thought doping was somehow more honorable if you supplied your competition too. Because then everyone has the same chances of winning."

"So, Petri Heiskanen. Find out what you can about him. Koivu and I are taking a break at Töölö Hospital, but I'll drop that name to Särkikoski once we get back in with her. Good work, Ursula!"

"That guy would have told me anything. All I had to do was leave my bra at home. It never ceases to amaze me what worms men are."

"I think the worm is in their pants," I said, and Ursula laughed. Apparently if I wanted to build some kind of rapport, I had to meet her at her level.

Now the guard and Koivu were talking about what was happening in hockey. The guard said that he'd been a juniors player for the Blues, but he'd had to quit due to chronic groin injuries. I only half listened; I thought Jutta's wound cleaning was taking a long time. Ten minutes had passed. I poked my head through the door, and the nurse angrily shooed me away. When she finally allowed us back in, she said that the patient's blood pressure was alarmingly high, and that Jutta was complaining of a migraine. We wouldn't be able to stay long. Once the door shut, I got straight to the point.

"Pete Heiskanen. What does that name mean to you?"

Jutta looked me straight in the eye. "He's an old school friend. We lived in the same neighborhood. What does Pete have to do with this? I haven't seen him in years."

"He's been in trouble for selling drugs. Salo and Terävä got steroids from him."

I wasn't prepared for Jutta's reaction: she burst out laughing. The lines on the monitors measuring her vital signs began to fluctuate, and her bed shook. Gradually the laughter turned to a coughing fit, which made her eyes water.

"Did you call Salo and Terävä while you were in the hall? And they claimed Pete Heiskanen was my source, because of course I would protect Pete at all costs. I can understand those meatheads thinking that, but I thought detectives were smarter . . . seriously, Pete Heiskanen! If he ever tried building a simple nail bomb he'd end up with no fingers, and the poor thing would never get mixed up in intravenous drugs! He always fainted in school when it was time for shots. My God, Pete Heiskanen!"

So either Terävä only thought he knew Jutta's source or Jutta was such a good actor that I should suspect her of being mentally unstable, as Detective Perävaara had suggested. But gradually Jutta calmed down, and the lines on the monitors stopped jumping around. Soon she was speaking in a normal voice again.

"In theory Pete Heiskanen could have made threatening phone calls to me after Salo and Terävä were caught. The police told me that some calls came from a pay phone at the Nurmijärvi bus station, and Pete used to hang out in the bar there. I can see him thinking pranking me would be a good idea after a few beers. But Pete isn't my source."

The nurse had moved my chair back to the wall, so I sat on the edge of Jutta's bed, careful not to touch her body, which was covered in bruises. Jutta avoided my gaze and began staring out the window, even though the sky was empty.

"You're right. Police detectives do have professional ethics," I said. "But the reality is there have been three attempts on your life. How can we find the guilty party if you won't work with us? If you'd told me your source the first time we met, Pentti Vainikainen and Tapani Ristiluoma would still be alive. It's time for you to talk."

Jutta was silent for a long time. Finally, she spoke, almost in a whisper. "I'm protecting my source because they committed a crime by reading an e-mail intended for someone else. They were shocked by the contents and forwarded it to me. I checked the accuracy of the information with another source. Salo and Terävä were so clumsy that half the world knew their secret, probably even Pete Heiskanen. If I hadn't written about it, someone else would have eventually."

I took a moment to digest Jutta's words. "So you really had two sources: the one who sent you the e-mail intended for someone else, and the one who confirmed Salo and Terävä's doping."

"Yes."

"Who was the e-mail originally intended for?"

"That person never received it and to this day doesn't know that in their own way they were part of this chain of events. That's all I'm going to say. The person who forwarded the e-mail to me would never hurt me or anyone else. And the original sender of the e-mail probably didn't realize they set off this avalanche, or if they did, they were probably happy about it. They wanted Salo and Terävä to get caught." Jutta leaned back on her pillows and closed her eyes. Her face was gray like ice formed on a puddle, and there were beads of sweat on her forehead. The nurse returned, looked at her patient, and then turned an imperious gaze on us.

"She has to rest. It's time for you to leave."

We complied, because I guessed the only way to get the information I wanted was to have this same conversation over and over again. A street sweeping machine was running through the parking lot outside the hospital, so we had to wait a couple of minutes to leave, but I didn't bother turning on the lights or sirens.

"So our heroic journalist used some shady methods to get her information," Koivu said as I turned onto the street, "considering reading a message intended for someone else is a criminal violation of privacy."

"Yes, but we don't know whether Jutta realized the message wasn't meant for her. If the person who forwarded it added their own message, then she must have known. Call Ville and Ursula, and let's head to Kauklahti. It's Saturday, so we'll just have to hope that at least some of Jutta's neighbors are home. That's where I'd rather be too."

After a few blocks, I stopped at a red light. A family of beggars sat on the sidewalk, a mother and two children who looked too young for school. "We are hungry" read the cardboard sign leaning against a plastic box. The woman's age was difficult to determine. She was very thin, with a scarf covering her hair and felt shoes on her feet. The children were seriously underdressed—although the fall day was sunny, the wind was biting. I didn't have time to see if there was any money in the woman's cup before the light changed.

"Those children shouldn't be on the street, even if they don't need to be in school yet," Koivu said sternly. "I'm calling a patrol."

"What will that help? Begging isn't illegal per se. My guess is they're from Romania or Hungary, and there the police aren't always friendly. Calling social services would be better. Or . . . I don't know. Should we turn back and intervene somehow? That isn't a good spot anyway. Not enough people walk by there. Or has Helsinki been divided into begging turfs, and that corner belongs to that family?"

A few times I'd stopped to chat with the increasingly prevalent beggars in downtown Helsinki, although finding a common language was often difficult. Some of the Romanians spoke spotty Russian, and some knew a few words of German. Hardly any knew English. They rarely appreciated my inquiries. Occasionally I gave money out of pity, even though I knew that doing so propped up the begging system. I tried to forget the woman's anguished gaze and the children's frozen faces. Koivu called Puupponen to tell him we were headed to Kauklahti.

"Put together a flier with our contact information. If we can't track down everyone who lives there, we can at least post it on the bulletin boards," Koivu said into the phone, acting on his own initiative. Maybe simply placing a notice requesting the public's assistance in the local paper would be enough, but I wanted to see with my own eyes the parking spot Jutta used so I could picture how and where the bomb might have been placed.

I'd visited the Kauklahti Housing Fair area a couple of times out of curiosity, and I remembered the apartment building Jutta lived in. The parking lot was relatively open, visible from the road and the neighboring building. However, the windows of Jutta's apartment faced the other direction.

We started by interviewing the residents of Jutta's building and then moving on to the other buildings nearby. People were inquisitive, and we often had to give more answers than we received. When Ursula and Puupponen joined us, we began to cover more ground. It was Saturday afternoon, so many families were cooking, and some were working outside, although the tiny yards probably didn't require much upkeep. Jutta's immediate neighbors did their best to recall anyone strange they might have recently seen in the area, but when we finished our interviews, we weren't much wiser than when we started. One old man in the next stairwell over claimed he'd seen a man fiddling with the undercarriage of a car, but when I dug deeper, we established that the mysterious car mechanic had been at a single-family home on another street, one that the old man had walked along the morning before.

The housing area was large enough that the residents didn't all know each other, and the neighborhood often had visitors coming to gawk at the houses they'd seen in magazines and to tour the ones that hadn't sold yet. Jutta's building had a sparse, chic style, with commercial space on the first floor. She'd moved to Kauklahti immediately after the housing fair, a month before the car accident. The change of address had been a relief, because she'd still been receiving hate mail at her old apartment.

"Are there any security cameras around here?" Puupponen asked. We were sitting at a picnic table in the courtyard between the apartment buildings, going through the information we'd gleaned so far.

"Not in the parking lot, but there should be cameras that cover the entrances and the street, since now they automatically set those up in all new housing projects. Check with the building manager and then maybe ask Lehtovuori to go through the tape. At least that will tell us who was in the area before the bombing. My guess is that the bomb was placed at most one day before the explosion. Koivu and I didn't learn a damn thing. Did you have any better luck?"

Ursula shrugged. "I think these days you could sink a hatchet into someone's head without the neighbors intervening. No matter how close people say they are, tragedies always seem to be a surprise." We posted Puupponen's flier on a few bulletin boards and then left, all of us in low spirits. Because no more progress was going to be made that night, I thought I'd just drop by the station briefly and then head home.

Ursula must have turned on her sirens and sped back, because she and Puupponen were already sitting in the conference room when Koivu and I arrived. Puupponen was typing furiously at his computer.

"I have Särkikoski's phone records. Your number is listed," he said.

"What conclusions should I draw from that?"

"Don't even start with me." I marched into my office and closed the door. I would take a moment to collect myself and then call Merja Vainikainen and arrange a meeting. Then it would be time to go home and heat the sauna. I could come back to the station if the results of the forensic analysis demanded it.

Puupponen burst into my office before I could make the call. His face was flushed.

"Maria, I think we got a hit! I went through the death threats Särkikoski received right before Pentti Vainikainen's death. There are a couple of calls from burner phones, and we can't trace them because they aren't from numbers connected to any previous cases. Then there was one number I was able to trace. It belongs to a phone registered to an eight-year-old named Olivia Kämäräinen from a village named Vahto, north of Turku."

"Why would an eight-year-old threaten Jutta?"

"I doubt she did. But guess who her grandfather is? None other than Ilpo Koskelo, Toni Väärä's trainer. Should I have the Turku police pick him up?"

14

Puupponen had certainly found something interesting in Jutta's phone logs from the past week. The timing of the call from Olivia Kämäräinen's number matched with the timing of the threat Jutta had received. According to Jutta, that particular call hadn't been a direct threat to kill her, just a prediction that she might have another accident if she meddled with things that were none of her business. Jutta had noted that the caller seemed to be a man trying to alter his voice, and that there were sounds of traffic in the background.

I looked up Ilpo Koskelo's number and called him.

Koskelo answered immediately.

"Hello, this is Detective Lieutenant Maria Kallio. I'd like to talk to you—"

"I'm glad you called! I'm here outside the boy's apartment. He didn't come to the gym for circuit training today, and his parents don't know where he is. I don't think he's home either. At least, he won't come to the door. He isn't answering his phone, and I haven't heard a word from him since we split up outside the Espoo police station. I'm really worried. Should I ask the super to open his door?"

Ilpo Koskelo sounded as if he was on the verge of tears. It felt like an eternity since we'd sat face-to-face in this same room, but it was only yesterday. Puupponen had tried in vain to reach Väärä too, but we hadn't worried too much about the young man not returning our calls.

But according to Koskelo, missing practice was very out of character for Väärä.

"The boy's very diligent about training. He always shows up. Something must have happened."

"Then yes, it's a good idea to get in touch with the building superintendent. Call me back when you're in his apartment. I was thinking about coming for a visit anyway."

"To Turku? Today?"

"First let's see if we can track down Toni Väärä. Stay in touch."

When I hung up the phone, Puupponen stared at me, dumbfounded. The fervor in his face had dimmed.

"You didn't say anything to him!"

"Toni Väärä is missing. He didn't show up to practice. Koskelo was out of his mind with worry."

"But we only have his word that Väärä stayed in Helsinki and Koskelo went to Turku alone. Koskelo was seen on the train, but Väärä could have snuck off anywhere. What if they're working together, and Koskelo arranged for Väärä to leave the country? Didn't you and Koivu say that Koskelo would be willing to do anything for Väärä?"

"That is the impression we got. But why would Koskelo and Väärä team up to kill Jutta?" Different scenarios ran through my head, each more ridiculous than the last. Covering up Väärä's doping was the obvious motive, but he'd been hurt in the car accident too. Maybe when Jutta had gone to Turku to interview Toni Väärä, she'd seen or heard something with a significance greater than she realized. Were Väärä and Koskelo up to something we couldn't even imagine? Were they in a relationship? Koskelo was a married man, but that commitment had failed to stop plenty of people before. Admittedly, that idea seemed pretty far-fetched.

I went back to the conference room with a confused Puupponen in tow.

"You probably already heard Ville's discovery about the phone number. I called Koskelo—"

"Did he confess?" Ursula asked, interrupting.

"I didn't have a chance to ask about the death threat because he was too preoccupied. Toni Väärä is missing. Ursula, check with the airlines and ferries to see if Väärä left the country yesterday or today. Koivu, you call the hospitals, and Puupponen, you check the jails. Let's assume that Väärä is still in the Helsinki area. Koskelo is calling Väärä's building super to get into his apartment."

"Does this mean Väärä's our perp?" Koivu asked, sounding startled, but then he got to work on his phone. My heart beat faster than normal, and I expected my phone to ring any second with Koskelo's number on the display. What if Väärä blamed Jutta for his injury and wanted revenge? He claimed he didn't remember anything about the accident, but that could be a lie.

Ursula had headphones in, and Puupponen moved into my office to talk because he couldn't hear over Koivu's and Ursula's chatter. Should I have issued travel bans for Toni Väärä and the other suspects from the beginning? It'd be crazy to start an international manhunt for Väärä without solid evidence. And there was still the possibility that Ilpo Koskelo was lying. He'd managed to conceal at least one threatening phone call.

My colleagues' voices rolled over me in a steady stream in which it was impossible to make out individual words. I was tired, and I felt as if I'd received so much information in the past few days that my head was going to explode. Four days had passed since the poisoning, and the bomb had exploded at the Sports Building yesterday. I realized that I hadn't heard from Detective Perävaara since our press conference. They were probably pulling long days in Helsinki too.

"He isn't and hasn't been in police custody anywhere in Helsinki, Espoo, or Vantaa." Puupponen had finished his task first. "Should I put out an APB? Väärä is famous enough that a lot of sports-loving cops will recognize him without a picture."

"I don't think an arrest warrant is necessary yet, but spread the word that we want to know if anyone sees him. The fact that he's missing doesn't mean he's guilty of anything. And let's see what we find out about his apartment."

We could drive to Turku in two hours, and a train would take an hour and forty-five minutes. The thought of the steady, calming rhythm of a train was appealing. I could have more than three hours alone with my thoughts. But if I went today, I'd have to stay overnight in Turku. That would mean getting a hotel room. Since I had an unlimited budget, Taskinen wouldn't mind if I booked a suite at the Marina Palace. But what would I do there alone, without my kids? Should I send someone else to handle it? Ursula?

We didn't hear anything from Koskelo; it seemed to be taking forever for the building superintendent to arrive at Toni Väärä's apartment. While we waited, Koivu established that no one matching Väärä's description had been admitted to any of the hospitals in the metro area. Checking whether he'd left the country was more difficult, and Ursula cursed between each phone call. Koskelo finally called back after forty minutes.

"That took a while, and now I don't know whether to be relieved or more worried. There's no sign of the boy in his apartment. The morning paper and a stack of junk mail were on the floor under the mail slot, so he probably didn't return to Turku yesterday. Can't the police track a missing person using their cell phone? If you can, for God's sake, do it now."

There was pleading in Koskelo's voice, but all I could tell him was that the situation didn't warrant such dramatic action yet.

"The boy's parents promised to call me if he shows up there. I never should have let him stay in Helsinki alone. Who knows where he could be now. His parents said they'd ask their church members in the area, since he knows a lot of them from summer revivals. Maybe he ran into one of them. Kids like that can lose track of time—"

I interrupted Koskelo's agitated monologue. I said that I would take the morning train, which would leave Espoo at 9:21 and arrive in Turku at 11:00. Koskelo told me that he and Väärä were supposed to meet at the track in Kupittaa from ten to twelve. I said we would meet there, and Koskelo promised to wait for me even if Väärä didn't show up. I asked him to notify me immediately if he heard anything regarding his protégé.

After I hung up with Koskelo, Detective Perävaara finally called on his way home for a sauna. The bomb technicians had determined that the explosive had been placed under Jutta's car near the front, and the evidence still pointed to TATP.

According to the technicians, at least part of the explosive had gotten wet and failed to go off, so the bystanders had been lucky. More people could have been killed.

"Remember to get some sleep too, Kallio. I asked a patrol car to give me a ride home. I'm so tired I don't dare get behind the wheel. Until tomorrow!"

When I passed along the latest about the bomb, Ursula nearly exploded herself.

"That bitch is hiding something from us! She must have stepped on some big toes for anyone to go to so much effort to try to kill her. Is she working on a report about drugs or arms trafficking that she hasn't told us about? She's making fools of us. Just think what a great marketing stunt it would be. 'Two people died but I just kept courageously digging . . .' We need to search her apartment, impound her computer and all her disks and memory sticks. We could get a warrant by tomorrow, couldn't we?"

Ursula's fury only grew when I said that instead of searching Jutta's apartment, I was going to meet Koskelo in Turku the next day. Because everyone had their hands full, I would take Koskelo with me either to the local police station or bring him back here to Espoo if an official interview was necessary.

"That bastard threatened Särkikoski!" Puupponen was stunned. "You make me go through all those Goddamn phone numbers, and then suddenly none of it matters. Why, Maria?"

I didn't have the energy to explain. Of course the information Puupponen had found was valuable. And Ursula's insistence that we execute a search warrant on Jutta Särkikoski's apartment was reasonable. But I still had the feeling that this tangled web was even more complicated than we thought, and I couldn't quite shake the paranoid idea that Jutta was the killer, not the intended victim.

None of us left the police station feeling very triumphant. The evening sky was clear, and I walked home under a moon that was nearly full. It was the autumnal equinox, and the hours of darkness would only increase. Every year, that seemed to affect my mood more. The mild, mostly black winters of southern Finland were far from the frozen paradise of my youth in Arpikylä, with ski outings through glittering white fields and the blaring music at the skating rink, which called me alternately to play ice princess or throw on my dad's old hockey skates and join a game as if I was one of the boys. Even though Arpikylä had a couple more hours of darkness than Espoo, the winters in my memory were full of light reflected from snowbanks at every hour of the day. For Iida and Taneli it was a rare treat to skate on an outdoor rink like their mother did as a child. The artificial ice built in Arpikylä in the early eighties had seemed like a great miracle, but nowadays even there they had an indoor facility.

It smelled good at home. Antti was emptying the dishwasher. Taneli was building a skating monster out of Legos, and Iida was reading a collection of scary stories, wide-eyed on the couch in her room. Venjamin was curled up on her lap, and she had a half-eaten *pulla* roll next to her.

"We baked them with Dad," she said. "Taneli put raisins in his pulla, but I think they're nasty."

I sighed in satisfaction. "Pulla and sauna. My favorite." All that was left to complete the Saturday evenings of my youth was a bottle of Omenapore apple soda, which I'd loved as a ten-year-old. It had been almost the same color as Coca-Cola, which my progressive parents refused to buy for us. My younger sister Helena would always secretly buy it at the ice cream stand, which was her way of rebelling.

I helped Taneli with his building project, even though he was much handier, and then we went to get more wood for the sauna stove. A traditional wood sauna was our little luxury and a big reason why we'd bought the house. I felt slightly guilty that I'd be leaving again in the morning before anyone else was up, but for now I could enjoy the normalcy of home. Instead of bubbly apple soda, I shared a bottle of dry French cider with Antti, and after we'd had enough of the sauna, we all played cards and munched on more warm, cinnamon-scented pulla. For the moment, explosions and poisonings felt far away. After the children went to sleep, I lured Antti back into the sauna, and for half an hour, with skin on skin, I forgot everything that was happening outside.

In the morning I accidentally slept in. I thought I'd set my alarm to go off at 7:45, but when I woke up to Venjamin jumping on my stomach, it was already 8:30. I started some coffee and rushed to dress. As I sipped my coffee, I called a taxi, because Koivu had taken the department car and Antti needed our family car to take the children on a mushrooming expedition after their skating practice. Antti came to the door to say good-bye.

"There isn't anything dangerous in Turku, is there?" he asked. The taxi was waiting at the curb, so I pulled myself from Antti's embrace.

"No." It was hard to imagine Ilpo Koskelo trying to hurt me.

"I'd stopped being afraid every time you leave, afraid that that might have been the last time I'd see you," Antti said seriously.

"Well, don't start again. Everything is going to be fine, OK? I have to go, or I'll miss my train!" I stretched up to kiss Antti and hit the end of his nose. The taxi driver, who had clearly seen everything, made no comment on my acrobatics in the back seat as I did my makeup, even when he braked suddenly before the Espoo train station, to avoid a drunk who'd stumbled into the road, and I smeared mascara across my forehead. I didn't have time to buy a ticket, because the train was about to leave, so I ran to a car where I could pay a conductor onboard. I sat down in the first empty window seat I found and nibbled the pulla I'd grabbed on the way out the door. Based on the number of raisins, it had to be one of Taneli's. My phone hadn't buzzed all night, which didn't bode well for the fate of Toni Väärä. I called Puupponen. He hadn't heard anything about Väärä either.

As the train left Espoo behind, Koskelo's concerns began to worry me too. I tried to tamp it down by telling myself that Väärä had probably just found his first girlfriend and refused to leave her side. The great North Karelian thinker Seppo Räty had claimed that in addition to sports, a young man's mind only had room for either studying or dating—although Räty had stated the latter in somewhat different terms—and maybe now Väärä had temporarily forgotten about sports. But did his religion allow him to date outsiders? Maybe Väärä's family thought he was out sinning, because he hadn't been in contact with them either.

"Tickets, please. Anyone who boarded in Espoo." The conductor snapped me out of my reverie. I bought a ticket to Kupittaa and then turned back to the window to watch the yellow-and-green landscape speeding by, past the suburbs and into the forest. Just before the Siuntio station, I caught sight of an idyllic pink villa with a calico cat in the yard. In Inkoo I saw a line of horseback riders in single file. When my mother had visited Antti's parents' cabin in Inkoo, she'd demanded to be driven to see former president Koivisto's house, which was still a local attraction.

I thought of Antti's parting words. Things had been hard for him too after my assault, and it had taken months before I'd been able to have sex. It probably would have been easier for him to face danger himself than to fear for my safety, and that had nothing to do with gender. Antti wasn't worried about me because I was a woman but because I was his wife and the mother of his children. He knew full well that a detective was rarely in danger at work, but logic didn't always win out over emotion.

Had Ilpo Koskelo been able to sleep, as worried as he was? At least Jutta got to take sleeping pills at the hospital. And what about Merja Vainikainen . . . ? That was where I shut down this train of thought. My job wasn't to grieve for victims or their loved ones; it was to make sure the crime was solved as quickly as possible. Until then we would all live in limbo, and only by learning the truth could we move forward.

About halfway to Turku, I received a text from Ilpo Koskelo. *No sign of the boy at the track. I'm going to the restaurant at the soccer field for coffee. Call when you get here.* Ursula had determined that Väärä hadn't left the country by plane, by ship, or on the train to Russia, but no one monitored car traffic across the borders with Sweden or Norway. Of course, it was possible that Väärä's phone had been stolen, but then wouldn't he have borrowed a phone to call his family and Koskelo to let them know where he was?

I didn't know the city of Turku very well. The last time I'd visited was a couple of summers earlier when we'd toured the castle and the *Suomen Joutsen*, a three-masted square rigger on display in the harbor. The distance from Arpikylä to western Finland had always been bigger in my mind than on the map, and when I was studying at the police academy in Tampere, I'd adopted some of the locals' ridiculous prejudices against Turku, which had taken time to shake. Unfortunately, I probably wouldn't have time for lunch at any of the floating restaurants along the river or to stop by the art museum or the market square, which always seemed to be bustling. I understood that for a country boy like Toni Väärä, Turku was a big city where he could be free and anonymous.

I caught a taxi at the Kupittaa station. When I told the driver to take me to the sports park, he cast me a strange glance but didn't say anything. I could have walked, but the driver knew the exact door at which to drop me off. I called Koskelo, who said he was still in the restaurant at the soccer field, on the second floor of the building. I took the stairs to a large open lobby and then found my way to the restaurant, which was nearly empty. The only people there besides Koskelo were a middle-aged couple holding hands and looking blissful. Koskelo shook my hand, his fingers trembling slightly. I ordered a cheese sandwich, because one piece of pulla had been a light breakfast.

"I talked to the boy's mom, Liisa Väärä, again. She doesn't know where he could be, and she already called everyone they know in the capital, but no one has heard from him. They just said that they'd pray that nothing bad had happened to him. He couldn't have been in Pasila when that bomb went off, could he? What if he went to the Sports Building and somehow . . ." Koskelo covered his face.

"That isn't possible. Jutta Särkikoski was alone when she tried to start the car. Then, when she couldn't, she got out and asked Ristiluoma to try. There was no sign of a second body. And we've already checked the jails, the hospitals, and all the border crossings in southern Finland. Are you absolutely sure Toni doesn't have a girlfriend in Helsinki?"

If the girl wasn't a Smith's Friend, Väärä might want to conceal the relationship so that his parents wouldn't hear about it. And Koskelo was so attached to his athlete that I could imagine him being jealous of a possible love interest.

"Toni doesn't have a girlfriend," Koskelo replied, almost angrily. "He's putting sports before everything else right now. Only another athlete would understand him anyway. It was too bad he got in that accident last year and didn't make it to the national camps. A lot of romances start there, with all those kids training together. Another coffee, please," he said to the server, who'd arrived with my tea and sandwich. The first bite of the whole wheat bread tasted heavenly. I hadn't realized how hungry I was.

"Toni is a really great boy, and he's going to go far. Kids these days don't know how to work hard, and everything's about instant gratification. They'd rather get drunk and have sex in front of the whole country on reality TV than take the time to accomplish something. Toni's not like that. People like that get forgotten, but medals get remembered." Koskelo stopped and wiped his nose with a crumpled tissue. I handed him an extra napkin.

"Toni's been running seriously his whole life. There wasn't much else to do out there in the country, and I worried a little when he moved to the big city. But everything was fine, since he put running front and center. He did his school work, of course, but training was his top priority. The only thing I was concerned about was that he didn't really have any friends. He stopped going to church too, which was probably his way of rebelling against his parents. That's only natural, for a young person, and it usually passes in time."

The server brought another coffee, into which Koskelo dropped two sugar cubes. The sun peeked through the large windows, shining right into his eyes, and Koskelo moved his chair slightly to get out of the glare. "I said he could go out and have fun, but he wasn't interested. Once Toni came to practice really upset, and I couldn't figure out what was going on. He claimed it was nothing. We went through our normal routine, and then I asked if he wanted to go for a sauna. When he hesitated, I said it was coach's orders. While we were in there, he told me that his back had been bothering him, and he'd needed some extra massage. Our club has a regular sports masseuse, but she was out sick. So the boy decided to try a Thai massage place over by the train station. I guess it really shocked him, when he realized they offered more than the usual treatment. He was horribly embarrassed to tell me, and he never would have dreamed of talking about something like that at home. He doesn't even like it when the other guys tell dirty jokes, even though that's just how it goes in the locker room."

The female half of the middle-aged couple stood up and walked past us. Her face bore a wide smile, so euphoric that it was almost frightening. Had the man proposed, or had the woman just learned that she was pregnant at long last? Koskelo didn't pay any attention to her. But my next question made him spit his coffee out on the table.

"Why did you call Jutta Särkikoski on your granddaughter Olivia Kämäräinen's cell phone on Thursday the thirteenth of September?"

I'd clearly taken him by complete surprise. Face red, he coughed and coughed. For a moment, I was afraid he'd choke, and the server looked over at us with concern and then brought a glass of water. Once Koskelo was into his third minute of coughing, I realized he was playing for time.

"Särkikoski taped all of the calls," I lied. "And we checked her phone records. But you didn't think of that. Really, sending death threats from an eight-year-old's cell phone!"

"It wasn't a death threat!" Koskelo said, walking into a classic trap. He suddenly tugged at his beard as if to punish himself.

"Technically not, but it was still a threat. How many other calls did you make to Jutta Särkikoski from prepaid phones? Were you the one writing her letters? We'll need to go down to the police station to take your fingerprints and a DNA sample," I said, continuing to bluff.

"It wasn't anything like that! I swear that was the only time I called. The boy and me didn't have any idea that Jutta Särkikoski would be part of the MobAbility campaign. Seeing her wasn't good for the boy, and his recovery was going so well. It only reminded him of that terrible accident. It wasn't just his hip that broke in that crash. Part of his mind went too. No one wants to remember a thing like that." Koskelo's southwestern accent became more prominent as he became more heated.

"So you only called Jutta Särkikoski to scare her away from the campaign? Did you think one threatening call would do the trick, even though you didn't even say what it was about?"

"If I had, she could have guessed who was calling her! I'm not that stupid. And they never solved the car accident. How do I know she didn't intentionally sabotage the boy's career? Maybe she thought he was using banned substances and that if he ended up in the hospital they'd find it in his blood. But he wasn't using! When we were leaving the police station after our interviews, he said he never would have given in to Vainikainen, and he didn't want any coach but me. Everything was fine between us, and I can't stand the thought of that being the last time I see him!"

Now the tears in Ilpo Koskelo's eyes weren't from his coughing fit. Because his own napkins were wet from the coffee, he grabbed another one of mine and wiped his eyes. "I didn't tell you or the other detectives because it wouldn't have mattered. I didn't poison anyone or put a bomb in anyone's car. Why would I do something like that? You won't tell my daughter about the call, will you? My daughter and my son-in-law will never speak to me again if they knew I'd used my grandchild's phone for something like that. And I didn't know the call would affect Särkikoski so much. I promise I'll apologize to her. I won't go to jail for this, will I?"

"The maximum sentence for criminal intimidation is two years in prison," I replied. Koskelo could chew on that for a while. People thought threats were no big deal as long as words didn't turn into actions. He wiped his eyes again, apparently concerned for himself now. I considered whether I should tell him that in his case the court would probably apply a lesser punishment, and that he would get off with a fine if the prosecutor bothered pressing charges at all.

Down below, a women's soccer team was jogging out onto the grass to warm up. The coach was a man, as usual. Was I too traditional as a mother because I hadn't encouraged Iida to take up soccer or the shot put and instead put her in figure skating, traditionally a girl's sport? But that's what she'd wanted. It was probably discouraging for those on the medal-winning women's team to have to listen to the whole country talking about the men's national team just because they'd made it past the qualifying round at the European championships. Although I had to admit that I went to more men's games than women's games. So maybe I should just keep my mouth shut.

"Should we go?" Koskelo asked once he finished his coffee.

"Go where?"

"To the police station. To take those samples. They already took fingerprints in Espoo, 'to rule me out' was what that grouchy blond lady cop said."

"That will do for now. You said Toni Väärä damaged more than his body in the car accident. Was his mind damaged enough to make him want to take revenge on the driver?"

"The boy isn't like that! He thought he was a sinner, so he was to blame for the accident. He thought he was being punished for having too much pride about his win at the international competition, and because he was lusting after more gold and glory, getting above the station God had allotted him. They're good people, his parents, I mean, but some churchgoers have really strange ideas about sin and hell. When we started working together, Toni was sad I was going to hell because I don't believe like they do."

I thought of my friend Terhi, who was a priest, and how angry that idea would make her. She'd been told plenty of times she was going to hell because women aren't supposed to be in the clergy. Fanaticism could lead to delusions of persecution and grandeur no matter what the religious persuasion. Even though Koskelo claimed otherwise, it was possible that Toni Väärä had demonized Jutta and then decided to take God's judgement into his own hands. It was possible but seemed unlikely.

Koivu called and reported that a woman who lived in a building near Jutta Särkikoski's had contacted him. She hadn't been home the previous day but had seen our flier. According to the woman, on Thursday evening a man had been hanging around the yard and taking pictures of Särkikoski's building, especially the balcony. The man had seemed suspicious and likely foreign, and the woman had feared he was planning a robbery. From Koivu's tone, I took it that he considered this eyewitness to be unreliable, maybe even a little flaky, but he still intended to interview her and then spend a little more time canvassing the neighborhood.

"Ursula is still talking about that search warrant. What if I just took a little gander inside, if I can get the keys from the property manager? Maybe Särkikoski would like it if we brought her a book from home or something."

"Don't you dare!" I'd thought about an unofficial visit to Jutta's apartment myself, and I knew that Leena had keys. Maybe I'd give her a call on the train ride back to Espoo.

As I hung up the phone, I heard Koskelo's breath catch. He grabbed my arm with his left hand and pointed with his right at the parking lot in front of the soccer stadium. Jogging toward the practice track was a young, slender man. Toni Väärä.

Koskelo didn't hold back as he sprinted out of the restaurant and down the stairs. I left the server thirty euros, which hopefully would be enough since I had no idea what Koskelo had ordered while waiting for me. I followed behind, glad that I'd worn jeans and sneakers.

"Toni! Wait!" Koskelo shouted.

Väärä turned and started to run toward his coach. We reached Koskelo at the same time, but Väärä didn't seem to notice me.

"Ilpo," he said and was about to hug Koskelo, but then he drew back. "I couldn't stand it anymore . . . All the lying. I had to . . . Even though it's a sin straight from Satan. I couldn't face you yesterday, and I can't go home ever again. Ilpo, what have I done?"

203

15

I understood from Koskelo's expression that he hoped I would leave, but I had no intention of doing anything of the sort. Now I understood why he hadn't wanted Väärä talking to Jutta Särkikoski, and why Koskelo had been so uncomfortable when I asked him about Väärä's girlfriends. Toni was gay, and he'd wrongly thought that Koskelo hadn't known. Hiding in the closet seemed like wasted effort to me, but I had to admit I couldn't name a single openly gay professional Finnish athlete offhand, at least not a male one. And it was probably safe to assume that Väärä's church reserved sex for marriage between a man and a woman, which might explain Väärä's feelings of guilt and the demons Koskelo had mentioned.

"What have you done, Toni?" Koskelo asked gruffly. "You can tell me. You're like my own son. But you can also keep it to yourself." He glanced at me. "The most important thing is that you're OK."

"I'm not sure if I am. Maybe I've just been running from this my whole life . . . from my real self." Väärä brushed from his forehead a lock of hair displaced by the wind, and that was when he noticed me. He stiffened.

"What are the police doing here? They already interviewed us on Friday."

"Hello, Toni," I said and extended my hand, which Väärä took reluctantly. "Haven't you been following the news over the weekend?"

Väärä blushed deeply. "No, I haven't . . . what do you mean? Did something happen?"

Väärä wasn't sweating, and his breathing had leveled off quickly during the conversation. Maybe I could question him right now before he started to get too cold.

"A bomb went off in the parking lot of the Sports Building. It killed Tapani Ristiluoma."

The color disappeared from Väärä's cheeks. "Ristiluoma is dead? What's going on?"

"You tell me. You're going to have to cancel training today so that we can talk. Can we go to your apartment? Do you have a car, or should I call a taxi?" Väärä looked as if he wanted to run away. Koskelo offered to drive us to Väärä's apartment, which was near the main railway station. It was a studio apartment that belonged to Koskelo's aunt, who was spending the rest of her life in a nursing home.

"I had to hunt down the super last night," Koskelo said as he pulled out of the sports center parking lot. "It would have been a lot easier if I had a spare key."

"Why on earth did you go in my apartment?" Väärä asked angrily from the back seat. I could see his tense expression in the rearview mirror.

"To make sure nothing had happened to you! I was worried. You've never disappeared like that before! I didn't touch anything. I just wanted to make sure you weren't injured or something. Two men have already died, and I was afraid you might be next."

"Yeah, yeah," Väärä said, suddenly sounding like a bored teenager.

"Where were you?" Koskelo asked.

"I'm right here now."

We drove for a little while in silence. Koskelo clearly didn't want to talk in front of me, but I planned to talk to Väärä before his coach could coach him about what to say. He parked his car illegally in a small plaza in front of the building and followed us to the downstairs door.

"Come to the house for sauna tonight, and we'll think about how to rearrange the training schedule after this break," Koskelo said. "And answer my calls from now on!"

"My battery died, and the charger was in Turku," Väärä explained as he opened the door. Politely he let me in first and then turned back to his coach. "I can come over tonight if it's OK with Sinikka. I'll call you later."

"Sinikka always likes it when you visit," Koskelo said and then stood watching as Väärä and I started up the stairs to the second floor. Väärä had taped a "no soliciting" sign above the mail slot. Again, he let me through the door first. I stepped into the cramped entryway. There were two rows of shoes on a rack, mostly different running shoes and spikes. I took off my coat and hung it on a hook next to Väärä's track jackets and a dark Ulster wool coat.

"Come on in. I'm going to put on a fresh shirt," Väärä said and disappeared into the bathroom. I doubted he would try to make a run for it, and if I needed, I could have everything in his apartment tested for explosives residues.

Some of the furnishings must have been left by Koskelo's aunt. It was hard to imagine a young man buying himself a heavy, ornate period furniture set with matching dressers, armoires, dining table, and sofas. Even though the studio apartment was relatively big, the furniture took up so much space that it was difficult to avoid bumping into things. In the alcove was a single bed that didn't belong to the same set as the rest of the furniture. Above the head of the bed hung a simple metal cross, and at the foot was a poster of the runner Sebastian Coe. It seemed the great runner from the 1980s was Toni Väärä's idol. I heard water running in the bathroom, and over it came the sound of Väärä humming a song that seemed vaguely familiar.

There weren't many books in the room, and the TV and DVD player were on one of the small tables, which likely had been for flower arrangements at one time. I sat down in one of the two armchairs. This wasn't a reclining lounger; instead it forced you to sit up straight like you were visiting the pastor's wife for coffee. When I shifted my legs into a more comfortable position, I kicked a dumbbell under the chair. Luckily, I hadn't taken off my shoes as was customary in a Finnish home, so they cushioned the impact. Over the years I'd concluded that a police officer was more authoritative with shoes on than in her socks.

Väärä stepped out of the bathroom, wearing just a T-shirt and a towel around his waist, to grab a pair of jeans from a closet in the entryway. Out of consideration, I turned away. After another minute he came into the main space, now dressed but his hair still wet.

"Did you come to Turku just to look for me?" he asked as he went to the kitchen nook and opened the refrigerator. He pulled out a half liter of mineral water and took a drink straight from the bottle. "Can I offer you anything?"

"No and no. I came to see your coach, but since you're here now, you can tell me what you've been up to since you left the Espoo police station on Friday. Senior Officer Puupponen has been trying to reach you. It seems awfully convenient that your phone ran out of battery."

Väärä bustled in the kitchen, then brought a pitcher of juice and two glasses to the coffee table. "Currant juice my mom made. Please, help yourself. We don't let visitors go thirsty where I'm from, including police. And I didn't lie to you about my phone battery. I left the charger at home and . . . and where I spent the night there wasn't a charger that fit." Väärä sat on the couch, which, judging from his posture, was just as uncomfortable as the chair. I waited for him to continue, but he remained silent. His face looked young, somehow unformed, but in ten years he might be a good-looking man. A phone rang somewhere, and Väärä jumped off the couch and returned to the kitchen. On closer look, I could see a cell phone charging there.

"Hi, Dad. I'm at home. No, there's nothing to worry about. My battery was dead. I'm sorry, but I have a guest, a police officer. No, I didn't do anything! I'll call later. Blessings to you too, and to Mom and the kids." Väärä returned to the couch, carrying the phone, and then dropped it on the table and flopped down hard enough that the sofa springs complained.

"Why is everyone always calling me? Can't a grown man have two nights of peace? It's no one's business where and with who I spent the night! But I guess I have to tell you what I did, since . . . since Ristiluoma is dead, and you think I had something to do with it." Väärä gave me an angry stare as if I was denying his right to a private life. I forced a friendly smile onto my face, which seemed to encourage him.

"When I left the Espoo police station, I jumped on a bus to downtown Helsinki. I got off in Kamppi. I didn't have a clue what I was going to do, but I wanted . . . Ah!" Väärä pushed his wet hair back from his forehead with both hands and avoided looking at me as he continued.

"I wanted to see if I really belonged there . . . with them . . . I found a couple places online, but I was nervous. Do I really have to tell? I didn't go near the Sports Building, and I never saw Ristiluoma! When I got off the bus, I went for a salad and then bought new jeans and a shirt that I could wear to the club. I changed in the bathroom at the bus station and thought about booking a hotel room. The last train to Turku leaves at eleven, and I decided to take it, because . . ."

"Can anyone attest to your movements Friday? Do you still have the bus tickets or receipts from the stores?" It was possible that someone in one of the stores or restaurants had recognized Väärä, but finding out would take time and resources. We only needed to establish his whereabouts for a few hours, from the time he left the police station to the time of the explosion. If he had been at the Sports Building, someone would probably remember. I couldn't quite picture him poisoning someone or planting a bomb, although I knew that extreme feelings of guilt could drive a person to strange behavior. A lot of people thought Väärä had good reason to hold a grudge against Jutta Särkikoski—because of the accident, he'd missed an entire season, just as he'd been on the verge of an international breakthrough. And if he didn't remember the crash, it would be easy to blame Särkikoski.

Väärä took his wallet out of his pants pocket and rifled through it.

"Here's the bus ticket," he said and handed me a single-ride fare, which had been stamped on Friday at 1:25. I didn't bother reminding him that he just as easily could have used the same ticket to travel to Pasila, which was only one stop north of the central Helsinki railway station and the nearby Kamppi shopping district.

"And here's the receipt for the clothes. I paid for them with my credit card. So this proves I was in Kamppi," Väärä said triumphantly. The timestamp said 3:15. He searched for the last receipt, but then looked at it and snorted.

"I don't think my mineral water from Don't Tell Mama is going to help, since they didn't ring me up until 11:45. Obviously, I didn't make that last train." Väärä held the receipt in his hand as if it were a precious treasure and then pressed it flat before returning it to his wallet. "Do you think he really meant it?" he asked after a pause, staring at the tips of my shoes.

"Who meant what?"

"Ilpo, when he invited me to sauna today."

"Why wouldn't he have meant it?"

"Because I'm sure he can guess where I was! We only talked about it once, back before the accident. I told you that Pentti Vainikainen promised me anything I wanted if I joined his biomedical training program and dropped Ilpo as my coach. I wasn't interested in the women, but I thought that Vainikainen probably knew lots of people, so he might know men like me. I started toying with the idea that I could . . . that I wouldn't have to hide anymore. I was going to Helsinki for that sponsor event, and they'd promised to pay for a hotel room. I told Ilpo that maybe it was time for me to look for some companionship and be more open about who I am, and that I could do that in Helsinki. But Ilpo . . . he lost it and started yelling at me. He said that I couldn't say anything like that ever again and that I'd lose all my supporters if I didn't keep my mouth shut. He was probably right, but it still felt like the end of the world. We didn't talk any more about it—I considered maybe I should join up with Vainikainen, since those people have seen more of the world and think differently. Then someone from our club came in, and then Särkikoski showed up. Ilpo was probably afraid I'd tell her."

Jutta had thought Koskelo was trying to hide Väärä's doping by preventing the interview. But in reality, Koskelo was worried Väärä would tell Jutta he was gay. And apparently Vainikainen had been afraid that Väärä would tell Jutta about the offer he'd made. Quite a merry-go-round.

"Did Koskelo change his mind after the accident?"

"How should I know? We never talked about it! In the beginning, I really didn't remember much about the days before the accident, and later, when I started to remember, it seemed best to claim I didn't since Ilpo was acting like nothing had happened anyway. And he has his reasons. Ilpo's son-in-law's company has the same kind of van as the one that tried to run us off the road. What if Ilpo tried to come after us . . ."

"Which of Ilpo's daughters are we talking about?"

"Minna. Her husband's name is Mikko Matilainen. He gives me rides sometimes. I can't afford to get my own car."

"So you really didn't see who was driving the van?"

"No. It was rainy and dark, and I was sitting in the passenger seat." Väärä took a sip of his juice and grimaced slightly because it was so sour. "I'm actually relieved that Ilpo hasn't brought it up. I mean, about who might have forced Jutta off the road. Not the other thing. I haven't talked about the other thing except with some people online, and they don't know who I really am. When I was a kid, I didn't know there were others like me, and then I heard at church that those kind of people are monsters. But now that I know what it's like to be with a man, I don't think I can pretend anymore!"

Väärä looked at me, a challenge in his eyes. I'd heard confessions like this before. People thought police took the same kind of vow of confidentiality as a priest or a therapist. Väärä barely knew me, and it was probable we'd never meet again. And clearly he needed someone to talk to. If he'd had his first real sexual experience this weekend, it was no wonder he felt his world had been turned upside down.

"When my dad was the same age I am now, he was already a husband and father. A couple of years ago, our family started looking for a suitable wife for me from the Smith's Friends. Luckily, I've been able to put them off because of sports. I don't have the money to support a family on random stipends and sponsorships. I can barely pay Ilpo. I only pay the maintenance fees for this apartment, and another person wouldn't fit in here anyway . . ." There was panic in Väärä's voice.

"I can tell you for certain that Ilpo Koskelo was truly worried about you. Worried the way you worry about someone you really care about, about someone you love. Are you sure your family would reject you if they knew you were gay?"

The word startled Toni. He was so used to using euphemisms, even in his own mind. That seemed to trigger him, and he started talking again about all the things his religion considered sins. It was like he was giving himself a spiritual scourging, because sexual sins were the very worst and were sure to open the gates of hell.

"It's the same in sports. When I was younger, I played club baseball and wrestled, but I couldn't stand the other kids. The constant homo jokes were too much. It's no different now. 'Go run for Sweden, faggot' is what they'll say if I tell, and they won't let me in the locker room, let alone the sauna."

"The whole world doesn't think that way. You must have found that out this weekend. You had fun, didn't you?"

I'd already missed one train, but I didn't want to leave Toni Väärä yet, as worked up as he was.

"Fun? Is that what you call something that's wrong and sinful but also completely right and natural? I did have fun, at least after I met Janne. At first I didn't give him my real name . . ." Toni's voice had the semihysteria of someone who hadn't gotten much sleep lately. "If we had the same laws today as we did forty years ago, you'd have to arrest me for indecent behavior!"

"Good thing we're living in the twenty-first century. All kinds of people work at the police station, and I know a family made up of a male couple, a female couple, and their four shared children. They all live in the same house. You can do what you want, and you have no obligation to tell anyone about your personal life. It isn't like I go around advertising that I'm hetero." I nearly added that one of my colleagues, meaning Ursula, did put that front and center, but that was beside the point. "If I were you, I'd go over to Koskelo's house for that sauna. He wouldn't invite you unless he wanted to. I'll tell Detective Puupponen that I met with you. The next time, answer your phone when the police call. We spent six man-hours just trying to figure out if you were in jail, the hospital, the morgue, or out of the country. We have much more important things to do." I considered whether I should ask Väärä for the phone number of this Janne person he'd mentioned, but that didn't have anything to do with his alibi for the time of the explosion.

I drank the rest of my juice and stood up. Väärä's apartment was a few hundred yards from the train station, and I'd have just enough time to grab a bite before the next train. I gave Väärä my card and told him to call me if anything new occurred to him. I hoped he understood that I was referring to the car accident and murders, not that I was available as a personal confidant.

Next to the park across the street from the train station was a quiet Chinese restaurant, where a couple of families were having Sunday dinner. Decorations from the previous Christmas still hung from the ceiling, or they'd been put up three months early this year. In the corner was a children's play area, inside of which a toddler had nodded off. His parents were in no hurry as they ate their deep-fried bananas. I ordered jumbo shrimp in chili sauce and managed to eat nearly all of it before I had to rush out. It wasn't until the train was pulling away from the station that I noticed the Thai massage parlor next to the restaurant. Was that where Väärä had been surprised by the add-on services?

During the ride, I called my team to ask them to meet me at the police station. Koivu had already made it home, but Ursula and Puupponen were still out working. I told Ursula to look at the original accident report to see whether a van registered to Mikko Matilainen had been checked. After a moment's thought I said that the vehicle might also be under the name Minna Matilainen or Minna Koskelo, although the name Koskelo probably would have attracted the investigators' attention. Maybe Ilpo Koskelo made a habit of borrowing his relatives' property when he was up to no good.

Töölö Hospital reported that Jutta's condition was stable, and her recovery was off to a good start. Her parents had just left. I had the nurse transfer me, then asked Jutta whether she needed anything from home. I told her that I could drop by with Leena, since she knew where everything was. Jutta mentioned a few books, clean underwear, and some cosmetics, and gave me permission to reveal her location to Leena, who had a spare key because she was the only person Jutta trusted. Lucky for me.

I changed to a local train in Espoo and quickly realized, given the stench, that someone had just vomited in the car. The car didn't offer ticket sales, so the conductor wouldn't be doing a walk-through. I went off to find someone to report it to. Even in the other car I could smell the reek of vomit clinging to me. That reminded me of Hillevi Litmanen and her constant smoking. How had she managed over the weekend? I couldn't picture her in Pasila rigging a bomb under Jutta Särkikoski's car.

Because my route from the train station to the police station passed my house, I stopped at home to grab my bike from the yard. Our car wasn't in the driveway, so apparently the family had gone on the outing they'd planned. Only Venjamin stood guard on the windowsill. I inhaled the scent of apples, and someone was baking a mushroom quiche somewhere. The crisp air rinsed me clean of all the nasty smells of the day.

Koivu's report was brief. He'd talked to the man the neighbor had spotted, the one who'd been taking pictures of Särkikoski's apartment. He turned out to be a magazine photographer who later realized that publishing a photo of the apartment of a person who'd escaped death three times wasn't necessarily a good idea.

Puupponen hadn't made any new breakthroughs with the phone records. Mikko Matilainen's van hadn't been inspected after the accident, since there had been no reason to suspect it was the cause of the crash. Ursula could call the family and ask where the van had been on the night in question. Koskelo's daughter would probably remember the night when her father's protégé was injured. The rest of the information I'd gathered in Turku mostly aroused amusement.

"There's typical Finnish male communication for you! One thinks one thing and the other thinks something else, and they never clear up the misunderstanding because they refuse to call a spade a spade," Ursula said in exasperation. "When are these hicks going to come out of the woods and catch up with the rest of us? For God's sake, turn on the TV and you'll see three gay people an hour. But of course religious people like them don't have TVs."

"Sure they do," Puupponen said. "A family of Smith's Friends used to live next door to me, until they moved to Siuntio to get a big house for cheap. At that point they already had six kids, with number seven on the way."

"Uh huh," Ursula said, shuddering. "Did Koskelo really think Särkikoski could get Väärä to tell her something that he'd never told anyone else before, that all that was needed was a two-hour car ride? Especially since her feminine wiles weren't going to work on him . . ."

"Not everyone uses your methods," Koivu snapped. "Anu's brothers and their families are coming over for dinner soon. We arranged it a couple of weeks ago. Is this going to take much longer?"

I went through the rest of our business as quickly as possible and then dismissed the team. Then I forwarded my most innocuous work e-mails to my personal address, so I could read them after the kids were asleep and I'd returned from Jutta's apartment. As I biked home, I called Leena, who had just finished a half-hour phone call with Jutta. She could go with me to Kauklahti any time that night, since she didn't have any meetings the next morning. She'd need to go in to the Adaptive Sports office at some point, because they had to figure out how to keep the MobAbility campaign going now that Ristiluoma was dead. Apparently Merja Vainikainen did the same thing as me, avoiding her troubles by overworking and demanding the same of everyone else. Leena had spoken with Hillevi Litmanen, who would also be going to the office in the morning.

I rode home quickly, my thigh muscles complaining on the uphill. Our kitchen smelled of fried chanterelles, and Antti was threading mushrooms on a string to hang them to dry in the sauna. The children had seen three deer in the woods.

"And then there was this really neat dog. His name was Haiku," Taneli recalled excitedly. "I threw a stick for him, and he fetched it every time. Mom, Dad already said no, but . . ." What followed were the same pleas we heard every three weeks or so, and which Antti always countered with an appeal to his nonexistent dander allergy. A dog was all that was needed to make our three-ring circus complete.

Five days had passed since Pentti Vainikainen's death, four since my appointment as lead investigator, and three since my return to the department. It felt as if an enormous clock was ticking somewhere nearby and I was Captain Hook, always listening for danger. I knew that I wouldn't be able to relax until I solved this case. My mind and body screamed for rest, but after Iida turned off her light, I took our family car to pick up Leena, since I'd left the official car in the department garage. The moon was almost full, illuminating everything, even the blind spots where the streetlights didn't reach, painting the leaves on the ground a deep yellow, and burnishing the apples waiting to be picked in the trees. A brown hare stood guard in Leena's front yard, glaring at me before bounding off to the left of the house.

Leena opened the door almost immediately after I knocked. I pushed her wheelchair down the ramp built over the front stairs and across the yard, part of which had been paved to make it easier for her to get around.

"I don't believe for a second that we're stopping by Jutta's apartment just to be nice. This isn't only about collecting the mail and watering the plants," Leena said as I backed out of her driveway. "You don't have probable cause for a search warrant, so you need an excuse to snoop around. In which case, you should have taken one of your colleagues instead of me. I'll know the instant you overstep your bounds."

Actually, I'd brought Leena with me as a sort of shield, and I'd had no doubt she would notice. Most of all I hoped I would find some indication of Jutta's source at her apartment. No major clues had shown up in her phone records, even though Puupponen had contacted each number.

"Jutta's apartment has a burglar alarm," Leena said as we pulled into Kauklahti. "What will you give me if I tell you the code?"

"You know I'm trying to solve a double homicide, right?"

"Using traditional Maria Kallio–style law-bending. Fine. The code is seven-one-seven-one. Is that simple enough to remember?"

Not many people were out and about in the model neighborhood anymore, so I was able to park across from Jutta's building. A couple of teenage boys were skateboarding, the sound of their boards echoing off the walls. A pair of dog walkers were so deep in conversation that they didn't noticed that their pets' leashes were wrapping together until one of the dogs was so tightly wound that it began howling pitifully. The light of the moon shining between the buildings formed a path to the courtyard, which I pushed Leena's chair along. The main door to the building opened with one of the two keys Leena handed me, which were connected by a blue-and-white sleeve bearing the logo of the state lottery, presumably swag distributed to sports journalists. The wheelchair fit in the elevator, and we proceeded to the second floor. I was just about to open Jutta's door when everything inside me started to scream danger. The sensation of a ticking time bomb disappeared, replaced by the feeling of a steam engine about to boil over.

"Maybe this isn't a very good idea after all," I whispered to Leena, since I didn't know what the soundproofing was like in the landing. "Jutta's apartment has been empty for two days. Whoever failed at MobAbility, and then with Jutta's car, is sure to try her home next. There may be explosives inside. Wait here!"

Leena stayed on the landing outside the elevator, and I ran down and across the street to my car. In the glove box I found a flashlight and the small binoculars Antti used for incidental birdwatching. Pointing the flashlight beam at the balcony I assumed to be Jutta's, I brought the binoculars to my eyes. I had to refocus them twice before the image was sharp enough. On the balcony was a small, round rattan table and a chair of the same material, along with a folded lounge chair and a few potted plants. The balcony was about fifteen feet up, so accessing it would require a ladder. There would be a high probability of being seen, but an intruder could try to pass for a window washer or something. *Too far-fetched,* I thought, but then again someone had managed to set a bomb underneath Jutta's car. The balcony door appeared to be shut.

Walking around the building, I tried to determine which windows belonged to Jutta's apartment. The opposite side of the building had no balconies, and I saw no telltale signs of forced entry on Jutta's windows.

Just then someone opened a third-floor window. All I could make out was a man's silhouette.

"What the hell are you doing with those binoculars, bitch?"

"I'm from the police."

"So they all say. You're a reporter, right? This place has been crawling with you people. Give it a rest and let us sleep!"

I turned off the flashlight and returned to the stairwell. If the Cerberus I'd just met was any indication of the kind of people who lived in Jutta's building, no way a bomb maker would have been able to get into her apartment or onto her balcony.

I didn't want to call in the bomb squad unnecessarily, and I certainly didn't want to end up a laughingstock if they failed to find anything. Still I ordered Leena to stay in the hallway while I opened the three deadbolts and stepped into Jutta's entryway, which was illuminated by a narrow shaft of moonlight. The steam engine in my chest continued to boil, and even though my eyes were wide open, all I could see was red. The burglar alarm flashed on the wall, so I entered the passcode. Nothing happened other than that the light stopped flashing. Where was the light switch . . . there. Did I dare? Sweat broke out on my forehead as I pressed the switch.

The light felt blinding, but only silence followed it. I stalked from room to room, wary as a cat who knows she's crossed into another feline's territory and is ready for a fight. There were no signs of any break-in. For safety's sake I even turned on the coffee maker, the microwave, and the TV before helping Leena over the low threshold. Now the search could begin.

16

If Toni Väärä's studio was full to overflowing with furniture, Jutta Särkikoski's one-bedroom apartment was the opposite. Furniture and other objects were kept to a bare minimum, and everything was modern and economical. In the bedroom was a narrow bed and an exercise bike, and one corner in the living room was devoted to a computer and printer. The kitchen fixtures were stainless steel, so I felt as if I'd entered a laboratory, but the stench wafting from the compost bin shattered the impression of sterility. I glanced in the refrigerator for spoiled food that needed to be thrown out. A half-empty milk carton had passed its expiration date the previous day, so I poured the contents down the drain and placed the carton in the recycling. A head of lettuce was a little wilted but wouldn't start crawling on its own for a few more days. Jutta didn't seem to be much for home cooking, based on how bare her cupboards were. She must have lived on packaged soups, dried fruit, and green tea, plus the berries and espresso I found in the freezer.

The doctor hadn't wanted to predict when Jutta would be released from the hospital, and I didn't feel any need to rush her. Guarding her was simpler in an institutional setting than at home.

Leena collected everything Jutta had asked for in a plastic bag while I watered the plants, except the cacti and ficus, which I left alone. Jutta's computer seemed to call to me, but I knew that anything interesting would probably require a password. On the desk, shelves held binders full of her archived stories. I opened the first one. Jutta had started writing articles in 1992, when she had been seventeen years old. She'd landed a summer job at the local paper in her county and been assigned to cover local news and interviews as well as sports. Jutta had studied journalism at the University of Tampere, graduating in 1999. During college, she'd written for *Aamulehti* and the *Valkeakoski Times*, where she gradually came to specialize in sports reporting. Her writing was fluid and nimble, and she often wrote about coaching methodologies and, very critically, of abuses of power in the sporting world.

A familiar face in the picture that accompanied one story happened to catch my eye, and the caption confirmed my initial impression. The photo was of Mona Linnakangas, whom Jutta had interviewed for an article named "Physical Education in Schools: Worthless or the Best Thing Ever?" Jutta's point was that many children and teenagers didn't exercise at all on their own time, so getting them active while in school was important. Five years had passed since that article, and Mona had been eleven at the time. In the photograph, she looked unsmilingly into the camera, a little embarrassed. The heading for her section was "Competition is Stupid." None of the other interviewees had been nearly as critical as Mona.

> The boring thing about PE is that we always have to compete, and all the results are measured. PE would be a lot more fun if we could just skate or dance without all the pressure. I don't like team sports, because I'm bad at them, and no one wants me on their team. My mom says that competition is a part of sports, but schools should teach exercise, not sports. Those are two different things.

I wondered whether Jutta had known who Mona's mother was when she interviewed the girl. I couldn't imagine Merja Vainikainen being pleased about her daughter stating opinions like that in public. On the other hand, it took a pretty smart eleven-year-old to recognize the difference she'd identified. Maybe she'd heard conversations about sports and exercise at home, or maybe Jutta had gussied up Mona's statements.

Jutta had often written about women's, children's, and handicapped sports and exercise. She wasn't an expert in motorsports or soccer. In addition to track and field, sometimes she reported about skiing and women's ice hockey and ringette. Jutta had written a series of articles about javelin thrower Aki Parviainen's preparations for the 2001 IAAF World Championships, concluding with Parviainen's winning a silver medal and returning as a conquering hero. Even there, she had managed to insinuate her doubt that a second-place finish for a woman would have been celebrated quite as widely as Parviainen's accomplishment. In a different article, she offered a perspective on sports celebrity and the place of female athletes in the media. She mentioned a few athletes who received more public attention for their appearances than for the strength of their performances. Public interest could be guaranteed if the loveliness of the competitor matched the violence of the sport.

One of the few articles Jutta had written for a women's magazine covered track-and-field athletes' winter training camps in the south. She'd cited the sports managers' and the coaches' names, but kept the female athletes anonymous, because "women's issues aren't something we talk about." Of course, the camps' main purpose was intensive training for the competition season, but sometimes hard work demanded hard play, and in such an isolated environment, hormones often run wild.

> National team competitor "Maija," age 22, not long ago considered leaving her January training camp in South Africa. "I don't need to listen to filthy stories and comments about my ass while I'm training. This is my job. Some of the male athletes are outright chauvinists, but the worst thing is that the managers don't do anything about it. They just laugh or sometimes even join in. They

consider peeping in the shower and throwing condoms onto my balcony to be harmless practical jokes. Do other people have to put up with that at work?"

I remembered reading the tabloid headlines the article spawned, and the online forums had been full of discussion of who this brave "Maija" could be. When a B-level 100-meter hurdler failed to qualify for the European Athletics Championships, even though others with the same results found spots on the team, I suspected that she was the straight-talker Jutta had quoted.

Doping and attitudes toward it were among the subjects Jutta had written about the most. She'd even written a full-page article about Pertti Hemánus's book *Doping: The Good Enemy.* I skimmed the article, since I'd read the book soon after it appeared.

Jutta's printer was also a copy machine. I turned the power on, startling Leena.

"What are you doing?"

"I'm copying one of Jutta's articles. Just because I'm interested. Do you know if Jutta keeps a diary or a blog?"

"There's definitely no blog. And she probably would have asked us to bring her diary to the hospital if she kept one, unless she had it with her at the time of the explosion."

I looked around for a diary, but all I found were some old calendars from the last few years. I picked up the previous year's calendar and flipped through the entries Jutta had made. The 2006 calendar was A5 size, with plenty of space for notes but no address book. Maybe that was with this year's calendar. I put the calendars in my bag, even though I knew it was against protocol. I hadn't filed for a search warrant, and any evidence I collected illegally wouldn't hold up in court. And I was mixing Leena up in my law breaking.

Next to the computer was a small metal box. I opened it and found it full of memory sticks. Some were labeled, some weren't. I also took this box. Ursula and Puupponen could go through the files, if they could get past the passwords. Now I might also be causing trouble for my subordinates.

On the shelf above were a couple of photo albums, which depicted the life of a typical Finnish woman: baptism, Jutta riding a tricycle, her first-grade portrait with eight more following it, then confirmation and graduation. Jutta didn't smile in the pictures, instead simply looking directly into the camera. There were a few sports photographs mixed in, with Jutta sometimes standing on the top of the podium and sometimes on the lower steps. In one snapshot, Jutta posed with Aki Parviainen. That seemed strange, because as I'd understood it, Jutta generally tried to keep a professional distance from the athletes she wrote about. In the newer pictures there were dates automatically superimposed by the camera, ending in 2003. Apparently after that Jutta had moved to a digital camera. I didn't find any printed versions of later pictures.

"Maria, come help!" Leena yelled from the bathroom. "I can't reach Jutta's face creams. This is so frustrating!" She backed her wheelchair out of the bathroom. "The night cream and the eye cream, please."

Jutta favored domestic cosmetics, and the firm that made them was also a sponsor of the Finnish women's ski team and, if I remembered correctly, the figure skaters. In addition to the creams, there was also cleansing milk and toner, and an electric toothbrush and toothpaste. I glanced in the mirror cabinet, where I found hair care products and medicine. Beyond the usual over-the-counter medications, Jutta still had some strong prescriptions left over from after the accident, including sedatives and sleeping pills. That last package was almost empty. At the back of the cabinet I also found a pack of condoms. Jutta hadn't said anything about her love life, and she hadn't mentioned any exes who might be threatening her.

"Jutta still won't tell us who her source was for the Salo and Terävä doping story. She thinks it's impossible the source has anything to do with these crimes. You know her better than I do. Who would she go this far to protect?" I couldn't tell Leena that Jutta's source had obtained the doping information illegally.

Leena pondered my question for a long time. "Someone defenseless," she finally said. "An older person or a child. Maybe an elderly person who happened to go to Salo and Terävä's gym and happened to see them doing a drug deal."

It couldn't be that simple, could it? Jutta's calendars were heavy in my bag. I wanted to look through them, but that would have to wait. Instead I went into Jutta's bedroom. On the nightstand were a couple of translated paperbacks and a clock radio. In addition to the bed, there was an armchair and a rattan dress form torso with dozens of press-credential lanyards from various competitions hanging around the neck. The large window faced the parking lot, and I realized that during my Peeping Tom routine, I'd been off by one window. But there was nothing around the window or on the sill that indicated explosives. Another wall was full of clothes cabinets. The bed was against the third wall, and the wall next to the door was decorated by framed sports photos of Finnish track-and-field athletes. It seemed as if the same photographer had taken them all, because they all had a slightly unusual perspective, and the feeling of motion was so strong that I almost expected Tommi Evilä to finish crashing into the sand or Markus Pöyhönen to break the tape in the 100-meter sprint and run right out of the picture. They weren't just press photos, they were works of art.

There was plenty of space in the cabinets, since Jutta obviously didn't collect anything unnecessary. The bedding was ironed and folded, and in one of the cabinets I found a small clothes wringer. Jutta's clothing was sporty and practical, tending toward the inconspicuous. She clearly didn't want her appearance to call attention to her gender.

The apartment was clean and thoughtfully decorated but gave an impression of . . . something I couldn't place. Then I realized what it was: loneliness. Not just because Jutta lived alone. It was more that there were no signs of her having anyone else. No drawings from godchildren.

No pictures of parents. No funny postcards from friends on vacation. Everything focused on work, on sports. The apartment wasn't a place where people stayed late or came over for a drink. When I asked Leena how often she had visited Jutta here, she replied that she'd only come over once before. Usually they met in the city.

Jutta was an only child, and her parents cared for her to the point of fussing, in Jutta's opinion, Leena said. "They're relatively old. Her dad turns seventy-five next year, and Jutta tries not to worry them with her own problems. Apparently, her mother's greatest fear after the car accident was that Jutta might not be able to have children. She can," Leena continued when she saw my expression.

"Is she seeing anyone?"

"I don't actually know. She hasn't mentioned anyone. And I didn't ask, because Jutta tends to go into lockdown if you ask her anything too directly." Leena rolled over to the balcony door and requested that I water the arborvitae outside. It was hard for her to get through the door with her wheelchair.

After I did, I looked in the kitchen cabinets and cleaning closet again, but I didn't find anything interesting. Leena had started to yawn, and my own bed was calling to me too. We took the trash with us, set the alarm, and outside the door I carefully turned each of Jutta's locks. The building was quiet, and I banged the elevator door needlessly. Espoo was the second-largest city in Finland, but it already felt sleepy despite it being not quite midnight. Urban life was far removed from the neighborhoods of Espoo, although there were a couple of restaurants still open in the city center.

I'd lived in Espoo for the past twelve years and watched it become increasingly urbanized. Five distinct districts had gradually grown together, forming a band of dense rows of single-family homes and new high-rise apartment buildings bordering the train tracks. The metro extension would bring even more intensive land use, and the building of a tunnel over the beginning of the Ring 1 beltway, with new structures on top of it, would mean expansion in the Tapiola area. The city planners had to find solutions to the lack of housing and commercial space, because Finland was a free country and companies could transfer their operations wherever they wanted, which almost always meant south. And we'd all need to use public transit more. If I intended to stay in Espoo, at some point I'd have to stop mooning over the fields of Hentta or any other undeveloped oases. I couldn't have both city life and wandering through untouched forests with the moose.

I dropped off Leena at her house. She'd agreed to take Jutta the books and cosmetics in the morning. As I backed out of her driveway, my eyelids began to droop. I turned on the radio, and after some scanning, finally found a decent station. Hector was singing about lost children, and I joined in to stay awake. My next rehearsal with the Flatfeet was scheduled for Wednesday, but I was probably going to miss it. The rest of the band would understand. I'd been so busy I hadn't even dropped in to say hello to our guitarist, Söderholm, who worked in the Espoo Police Department as a ballistics expert. So far, I hadn't needed his help with this case.

I made it home in one piece. For a moment I stood in our front yard in the light of the moon. Our house looked safe in its normalcy, one modern Espoo single-family home among tens of thousands. I thought about all the people who didn't have the patience for routine, who thought it was boring and meaningless. It wasn't until a car accident or a violent death disrupted normalcy that it rose to its true value. I was willing to bet Merja Vainikainen would have preferred to be a nobody living with her husband rather than the grieving widow of a famous sports figure known by the whole country. Tomorrow I'd go to Adaptive Sports, and hopefully I could kill several birds with one stone at the Sports Building. Merja would be at work despite it all.

My eyes started drooping again, and a cold wind whipped my hair against my cheeks. I went inside and managed to sneak under the covers without waking anyone except Venjamin, who soon settled down and purred me to sleep.

In the morning I dragged myself up at 6:30, because no matter how tired you are, the body needs exercise. I jogged around the neighborhood, organizing my thoughts as I went. In the exhaustion of the previous night, I'd completely forgotten Jutta's calendars, and my first job after the morning meeting would be to study them.

The run woke up my brain better than another hour of sleep would have. The others were having breakfast when I returned. I gave the morning paper a glance. Everything they reported about my case was true. Also, the missing peacekeepers in the mountains of Afghanistan had been found, cold but alive. A drunk had run down a cow in Heinävesi.

Iida was worried about an English language vocabulary test. She had a tendency toward the dramatic, and I anticipated her full-fledged adolescence with horror. Antti promised to practice with her while he took them to school. I hopped in the car and drove the few minutes to the station, since we might need an extra car during the day. In the garage I ran into Anni, who looked exhausted.

"How's the investigation going?" she asked politely in the elevator. I didn't have the nerve to leave and take the stairs, which Anni's doctors must have encouraged her to avoid.

"I guess it's moving along, but you know how it is. Do you have a lot of cases on ice right now because so many of your detectives are working with me? Things must have piled up over the weekend."

"Actually, it's been pretty quiet. Summer vacations are done, and the Christmas party season hasn't started yet. There are always plenty of house calls and bar fights, of course. Since the staff doesn't monitor the sidewalks and alleys outside their bars, and after a few drinks people like to start arguments, which sometimes escalate. I'm not really sure about the new smoking law's impact at this point."

The elevator stopped, and I opened the door for Anni. Then, out of nowhere, she asked me if I would fill in for her when she went on maternity leave. In other words, she wanted me to take my old job back.

She'd probably end up taking the longer parental leave too, since triplets would be a handful. I hated to disappoint her, so I said the thought had never crossed my mind.

"But I'll think it over," I added. That was as much lying as I could manage. Hopefully Anni wouldn't share her bright idea with Taskinen.

Ursula was already in the conference room, sitting with her back to the door and speaking on the phone so heatedly that I felt sorry for whoever was on the other end of the line.

"Why didn't you inspect it? You morons, why didn't you crosscheck all the cars? Because it belonged to one of the victim's coach's son-in-law. Do I have to spell it out for you? The coach's son-in-law. It's no wonder you never catch anyone! If you'd bothered to actually do your jobs, two people would still be alive. No, there's no point doing it now. Matilainen or his father-in-law has had plenty of time to repair any damages. Thank you ever so much!"

After she hung up, Ursula turned her belligerent gaze on me.

"Rough morning?" I asked, aware that the question would probably only add to Ursula's irritation.

"Minna Matilainen, maiden name Koskelo, returned my call. Surprise, surprise, she didn't remember if her dad borrowed their van on the night of Väärä and Särkikoski's accident. And there's no way to find out, thanks to those nitwits in Lohja. Did Särkikoski say something about the lead investigator having a conflict of interest? There might be something to that, since they handled the case so incompetently."

"So it was the cops in Lohja that got under your skin?" I asked, trying to commiserate. I never could tell when Ursula might be feeling friendly.

"Not just them, men in general!" Ursula put her feet up on the table and put a pen in her mouth. Her attempt to look tough didn't quite work.

"Is it Kristian? Did he not tell you the whole truth about the status of his divorce?" I remembered all too well his tendency to paint himself in the most advantageous light.

"No, Kristian's divorce has been final since May. But guess what he had the nerve to suggest to me yesterday? It's insane, because he already has three kids with his ex-wife. Now he wants to breed with me too."

I would have expected to see triumph in Ursula's expression, but instead she only looked mad and sort of disappointed.

"Isn't it pretty common for people in love to want to have children together?" I asked.

"Who said anything about love? He wants to tie me down and then leave me in five years for someone younger and more fertile!"

"You certainly have a sunny outlook on men," I said. Just then Puupponen walked in. Ursula didn't notice.

"What reason is there to think otherwise?" she asked. Puupponen snuck up behind her and covered her eyes. She screamed. Koivu arrived just in time to witness Ursula trying to stab Puupponen in the face and groin with a pen. Fortunately, Puupponen had the sense to let her go before suffering bodily harm.

"I can't listen to insults to my sex without retaliating," he said in his defense. "And besides, I had to test these new shoes. Look! I ordered them all the way from the Unites States—supposedly they have special soles that make your footsteps perfectly silent. They cost five hundred dollars, but I think they're worth it."

To my surprise, Puupponen's buffoonery seemed to put Ursula in a better mood. I used the opportunity to take the box of memory sticks out of my bag and put it on the table. "Here's a new job for you. They're Jutta Särkikoski's."

Ursula glanced at the USB drives and nodded. There wasn't much to go over, so we quickly disbanded to start on our tasks. Leena had told me that the meeting at the MobAbility office would be held at eleven, so I would try to be at the Sports Building a little before noon to catch them as they finished.

I withdrew to my office to go through my e-mails. The bomb investigation had progressed: The explosive had almost certainly been TATP—acetone peroxide—which was commonly used by terrorists but had only been seen occasionally in Finland. The risks associated with it were well-known, but some terrorists were prepared to risk their own lives, not to mention the lives of bystanders. The whole incident seemed increasingly bizarre: Why would an international terrorist group be hunting Jutta?

I'd received the official report saying that no explosives residues had been found on Sami Terävä's body or clothing. There was no new information from Pentti Vainikainen's autopsy. Ristiluoma's would be the following day. The law required that the autopsy be performed, though not much was left of the body. There was no rush, because the cause of death was already known.

Perävaara called and we discussed public relations strategy, ultimately deciding not to publicize the nature of the explosive at this point. We needed to buy some time. While I was still on the phone, a knock came at the door. "Come in," I said, expecting a member of my team. Instead Taskinen stood on the threshold.

"Hi, Maria," he said once I'd wrapped up my conversation with Detective Perävaara. "How are things progressing?"

"As I understand it, I'm still not obligated to report to anyone, or have the orders changed?"

Taskinen walked in and closed the door. I turned my chair toward him but didn't stand to shake his hand. Suddenly I felt like I understood Ursula.

"Are you still sulking?" Taskinen sat down in the armchair. He'd been the one to encourage me to look for a position outside the Espoo Police Department, and we'd always gotten along well, despite tensions over the years. At times our working relationship had lapsed into friendship, but neither of us had ever been ready for more than that. Now I couldn't comprehend how I'd almost become infatuated with Taskinen, though I still liked him, despite this unpleasant assignment.

"I'm just doing the job I've been ordered to do. That was Detective Perävaara on the phone. They've identified the explosive. So we're moving along. I'm about to head to the Sports Building."

"Good. I was just talking to Anni and—"

"Me too," I said, cutting him off. "I've thought about it, and the answer is no. Shouldn't you be asking around to see who might want to go for commander training? I think Ursula Honkanen is just about ready to move up to lieutenant."

"Can you really imagine Honkanen leading your old unit?"

"Yes. It would probably bring them all together in a whole new way."

Taskinen burst out laughing, and I joined in, not because I thought what I'd said was all that funny, but simply because I wanted to laugh with him. Then I told him honestly how far we'd made it in the investigation. Naturally he was angry that I'd taken the calendars and memory sticks from Jutta's apartment. I said I'd return them before Jutta got out of the hospital.

"You needed her permission. Hopefully the wrong person doesn't hear about this. I've heard rumors that there's a pretty big internal affairs investigation going on in the Helsinki Narcotics Division about breaches of protocol like this. I don't want that happening here."

"I understand the importance of the rule of law, but no one can fire me, since I don't work here anyway," I said sarcastically. "Listen to me, Jyrki. I'm sure the identity of Särkikoski's source is going to be key to the investigation. It has to be significant, or Särkikoski wouldn't be so tight-lipped."

"I guess you know what you're doing," Taskinen said with a sigh. "Tomorrow it will be a week since Vainikainen's poisoning. The Interior Ministry called again this morning. The Council of State is watching this case closely, since it's the perfect test for the new supplementary police appropriations law. I'm not quite sure whether you should succeed or fail in order to get them to loosen the purse strings."

"I imagine the prime minister is happy to have the media savaging someone else for a change. Could there be something political in this, what with the explosive possibly pointing to terrorists?"

Taskinen's face twitched, but before he could say anything a knock came at the door. This time it was Ursula, who glanced curiously at Taskinen. He stood quickly, said good-bye, and left.

"I hadn't noticed how Jyrki has aged. How many grandchildren does he have now?"

"Two. What's up?"

"I went through those memory sticks. There were nine of them. Three are completely locked down, and four had no passwords at all. On the other two, I can see the files, but they all have individual passwords. So I just looked through them superficially. Nothing about the file names stand out. I suggest we take the ones with the most security to our experts right away."

"We can't take them to IT because they were obtained illegally. You can ask IT how to crack the passwords, can't you? Use those feminine wiles we keep talking about!" I hoped that the sisterly comradery I'd felt between us earlier was still in effect, but Ursula sneered.

"You're so out of the loop. The department's new head of information technology is a chick. She's under thirty, she has a doctorate and three kids, and she's the former aikido world champion. Apparently, they're paying her twice the last guy's salary because she's so valuable to White Collar Crime. But I can go beg. White Collar always takes priority these days, so don't hold your breath."

When I told Ursula what Taskinen had said about the Council of State's interest in the Vainikainen and Ristiluoma murders, her expression brightened. Once she left, I finally had the chance to look through Jutta Särkikoski's calendars. I started with the oldest one to get a general idea of how she took notes. After working through the first two, I was sure that Jutta recorded both her work and personal meetings in the same calendar. There were significantly more of the former than the latter, which were usually walks or movie nights with girlfriends. I wrote down names as they appeared. Maybe Jutta had confided in someone about her source.

The first reference to the doping story was from January of the previous year, when Jutta wrote *Call P. Heiskanen* in her calendar. The number that followed had been erased and rewritten, so she must have started out with the wrong number. Then there were several days of normal entries, including the names of some athletes I recognized, with addresses sometimes written next to the appointments. Jutta had also visited Toni Väärä during that period. Here and there I saw an entry that read simply *M*, once with *Forum Mall 4:30* and once with *Free Record Shop Forum 6 p.m.* They didn't seem like dates with a boyfriend. Within her circle of friends, I knew of a couple of names that started with *M*, for example two other journalists, Milla Kettunen and Ulla Martikainen, whom she also called "Marsu."

On the day of the car accident, she'd entered *Pick up Hande 1:30 at Karjalohja Neste Station*, then *Väärä 3:00 Kupittaa Sports Park*. After that, several weeks of calendar entries were blacked out, as if Jutta hadn't wanted the reminder of the work she'd missed.

I'd collected a long list of names, addresses, and phone numbers, but I wasn't any closer to figuring out who Jutta's source was. I peeked into the conference room, where Puupponen was just finishing a call.

"Great, thanks. Same to you!" He hung up with a flourish and gave Ursula a wink as she looked up from her computer screen, apparently still delving into the secrets of the USB drives.

"I just talked to the employment specialist Miikka Harju worked with. She remembered Harju, because he'd been such an active, positive job seeker. According to her, Harju found the listing for the Adaptive Sports job on his own. He insisted on applying for it."

17

Since I was already planning to visit Adaptive Sports, I could leave grilling Miikka Harju until then. I returned to my office, because my brain seemed to work better when I was alone. I wondered whether the *M* in Jutta's schedule could mean Miikka. Working as a firefighter required physical strength, and maybe Miikka had been getting supplements from the same people as Salo and Terävä. Perhaps his finances had been a mess after losing his job, and so he betrayed them for money. But why would Jutta protect Miikka Harju?

At Adaptive Sports, I would see Leena, Merja Vainikainen, Miikka Harju, and Hillevi, whose sick leave had ended. The two remaining MobAbility employees were also supposed to be there. What would happen to the company now that the primary owner was dead? Ristiluoma didn't have children, so his parents would probably inherit his assets.

I read Pentti Vainikainen's autopsy report again. The mucous membranes of his mouth had been badly corroded, but the small amount of nicotine in his stomach didn't match up with the severity of those injuries. Would the medical examiner be able to explain that? I tried to reach her, but she was on vacation. Of course. I left a message.

My phone rang as soon as I hung up. It was a TV crime reporter who had played a key role in helping me solve a previous case. I couldn't deviate from the information-sharing policy Detective Perävaara and I had agreed on, but I told the reporter as much as I dared. I owed him.

Public relations was usually a tightrope walk, and I always did my best to ensure that a victim's family got information from the police first, not the media. When the next of kin were suspects, the situation could get dicey. The worst-case scenario was when the media revealed information too early and labeled an innocent person as guilty.

I began to browse the news online. The newspapers put forth that Jutta Särkikoski was the intended target of the killings. A reporter from one of the tabloid websites had interviewed Sami Terävä and Eero Salo. In the accompanying photo, Salo's face was puffy, and he looked ten years older than he really was. He leaned on a lamppost, apparently in need of the support.

> Since the doping scandal, Eero Salo has learned who his real friends are. At his local pub, we found a group of loyalists who are quick to point out how many Olympic medals have been earned using banned substances. Among his own, Eero Salo isn't a villain, he's just a regular guy. No one at Salo's table believes the revenge theory, and the attempts on reporter Jutta Särkikoski's life, which have resulted in two other homicides, are considered just as shocking as anywhere else. "This is Finland. We don't want any of that American nonsense," says a man who introduces himself as Stode.

I continued to search, reading everything I could find about the case. Sometimes reporters' speculation could be useful. Vainikainen's connections to the high and mighty, and his famous golf partners, were mentioned repeatedly. That made me wonder again if Pentti Vainikainen might have somehow managed to kill himself out of carelessness. Could he have given something to Hillevi and ordered her to put it in the sandwiches and just not realized that it ended up in the gluten-free ones that he ate? What if Vainikainen had known all about the doping? I couldn't entirely trust anything Hillevi told me, because she'd been forced to lie to her ex-husband to protect herself, and maybe she'd gotten used to it.

Once I'd exhausted the online news, I went to see if Ursula had extracted anything from Jutta's files. In the conference room, Ursula's fingers were flying across the keyboard. The printer hummed, apparently spitting out everything she found the slightest bit interesting.

"Don't get your hopes up yet. There were a couple of good pictures in this story about athletes as sex objects. It included men too. They're pretty yummy, but Särkikoski didn't take the pictures. Then there's a story about all the foundations that support athletes. Some of them seem to have an awful lot of money to throw around. State grants are carefully regulated and have strict criteria, because they come from the Ministry of Education budget. But the Finnish Field Sports Fund, for example, has a board made up entirely of people in sports. She's certainly written a lot. Särkikoski, I mean."

"A freelancer has to work hard. Did IT give you any advice for cracking those passwords?"

"It depends how smart Särkikoski was about protecting her files. There's one drive here that she obviously copied her e-mails onto. The security is pretty light, so I can read the senders, the recipients, and the subject lines."

"We have to treat e-mails like letters. Check the senders and subjects anyway, even though we're breaking the law."

Ursula smiled. "Look at you! What happened to all the chickenshit nitpicking? I was sure you were going to order me to hand over the drive. Are you finally realizing that we can't follow every last letter of the law when the people we're up against don't give a rat's ass about any of them? Anni just looks the other way. Seems like you have to do that to survive as a mother too. Is your daughter checking out boys yet?"

I stayed to gab with Ursula for a moment, taking advantage of the chance to build rapport. Though I did steer the conversation away from

Iida. Puupponen kept talking on the phone, and Koivu wasn't around. Ursula said he'd gone to the cafeteria. "He heard the siren call of the meat pie. Or maybe it was his wife."

I hadn't seen Anu Wang-Koivu in ages, so I went downstairs to the canteen too. She and Koivu were hiding behind a fake fern. Anu didn't look particularly glad to see me, so apparently I'd interrupted a serious family meeting. Pekka, on the other hand, seemed overjoyed at my arrival. He jumped up holding his half-eaten meat pie wrapped in greasy paper and asked if we were leaving for Adaptive Sports. I told him to finish his food and went to get myself a sandwich.

I knew a lot of the people in the cafeteria. Among them were many young police officers who looked fresh from the academy. To my surprise I saw Visa Pihko, who had worked in our unit ten years earlier but had left for law school and now served the fatherland as a member of the fraud team at the Helsinki Police Department. Pihko was an ambitious guy, and he'd be perfect as temporary VCU commander for the Espoo police, if he was interested in getting back into violent crime. I was already walking over to him when I realized that the search for Anni Kuusimäki's substitute was not my problem. But Pihko noticed me and closed the distance.

"Hi, Kallio! I hear you've returned to the scene of the crime?" Pihko gave me a friendly handshake; we didn't know each other quite well enough for a hug.

"Only temporarily. What brings you to Espoo?"

"A meeting with your White Collar Division. We've had a long-running money laundering investigation that's about to come to a head. There's a salon here in Espoo that's part of it. They're known for their low prices, but the receipts tell a different story. Fifty euros for a men's haircut, that sort of thing. We know the money is coming from prostitution. Luckily it isn't my job to prove that part of it or to track down the johns."

That reminded me of Ursula's suspicion that Ristiluoma had been paying for sex. What did it matter if he had?

After lunch, Koivu and I walked down to my car. We mulled the thought over, then tried to imagine motives for Vainikainen's and Ristiluoma's slayings. It was possible that the sandwich was meant for someone other than Jutta, but the bomb must have been for her—unless Jutta had wanted to get rid of Ristiluoma.

We kept talking as we drove to Pasila. "I've met victims of domestic violence who will lie to protect the person who beat them," Koivu said with a sigh, "but never the target of two murder attempts who still won't talk. Which means I don't get to go home to see my kids. Speaking of, are you going to fill in for Anni while she's out on maternity leave?"

"No," I said firmly. Koivu sighed and opened his mouth but closed it again immediately. Traffic was a mess again. At one point no one would let in a little green Nissan trying to merge from the right, until Koivu acted magnanimously. The driver was an old man with silver hair, who drove so slowly that someone started to honk behind us.

The Sports Building parking lot still had signs of the explosion. There was plenty of space to park.

"Could the explosion be a coincidence? What if someone had wanted to protest something at the Sports Building and just chose a car at random to blow up?" I said to Koivu as we walked toward the main entrance.

"It could have been an eco-terrorist protesting cars in general. Why don't you mention that theory to your husband?"

"Yeah . . . maybe not."

Security at the Sports Building had been heightened, with a uniformed guard in the lobby and another watching the parking lot with binoculars. Our identities were carefully checked before we were allowed to pass. Because I hadn't caught whoever was after Jutta following Vainikainen's death, the hundreds of people who worked in this building now had to live in fear.

The Adaptive Sports Association was located on the fourth floor, at the end of the north hallway. On the inner doors I saw familiar names: Harju, Vainikainen, Litmanen. I knocked on the final door, guessing the meeting would be in there. When no one answered, I opened it.

Inside a girl dressed in black sat at a table reading. When she saw me, she jumped up and closed her book. She bowed her head, her hair hanging down over her eyes and concealing her expression.

"Mona? What are you doing here?"

Now she looked up at me in fright. She didn't seem to recognize me.

"I'm Detective Lieutenant Maria Kallio, from the Espoo Police Department. I'm investigating your stepdad's death. We met at your house, in your room. I'm here to see your mother. Do you know if she and the others are in the conference room?"

The girl continued to stare at me as if I were a ghost or an alien.

"Who did you say you were?" she asked. I repeated my name and rank, and Mona repeated after me. Then she sort of woke up and informed me calmly that her mother and the rest of the staff were in the conference room down the hall.

"What are you reading?" I asked, trying to connect with her. She blushed but showed me the cover of the paperback. *The Coarse Salt of Andalusia*. I knew the book, which was a cookbook-memoir. What might Merja Vainikainen think of her daughter's taste in books?

"Why aren't you in school?" I asked.

"Doctor's appointment," Mona replied quietly. "After Mom's meeting. Mom always comes with me to the doctor . . . to make sure they don't take me away."

From what Merja Vainikainen had told me, I'd thought that she would have liked her daughter to be admitted for eating disorder treatment, but our visit to their house had been so chaotic, and Merja had been so addled, that maybe I'd heard wrong, or she'd misspoken.

"Oh," I said. "Well, enjoy your book."

Koivu and I set off to find the conference room. It didn't take long—we could hear Leena's agitated voice through the door. "According to the contracts, the campaign can go on!" she was saying. "It will take time for Ristiluoma's estate to be settled, and the fate of MobAbility to be decided. I can speak with the remaining board members. We have to keep operating, even though two of them are dead. Merja, why weren't we informed that your husband, Pentti, was on the board of MobAbility?"

I hadn't known that Pentti Vainikainen was a member of the board of MobAbility either. That seemed potentially problematic, given their sponsorship activities, although that wouldn't necessarily mean that he or his wife would receive any direct financial benefit. And anyway, he didn't own any MobAbility stock. Maybe that was why not even the crime reporters at the tabloids had noted it.

"It didn't matter from a practical perspective—" Merja Vainikainen replied. I knocked on the door and opened it. Merja stopped midsentence as all five heads in the room turned toward me. In addition to her and Leena, there sat a haggard-looking Hillevi Litmanen, Miikka Harju, and a tall, sturdy woman in her sixties, whom I'd caught a glimpse of during my visit to the MobAbility offices. Merja looked annoyed.

"Detective Kallio. Hello. As you can see, we're in the middle of our meeting. Hopefully your business can wait." She turned back to Leena and continued. "Of course the campaign will go forward as planned. You contact the remaining members of the board, and I'll speak with Toni Väärä. Kai Toijala's factory can produce the devices at the usual pace, since it's the foreman, not the CEO, who's in charge of that."

Apparently Merja Vainikainen was still in the denial stage of grief, trying to live life as though nothing was wrong. She was just as well-groomed as ever. The only sign of distress was the darker shadows around her eyes.

"When will Satu return from sick leave? Did she tell you, Anneli?" Merja asked the other MobAbility employee. She looked at Merja in surprise.

"I already told you, the doctor gave her until the end of next week! I visited her yesterday because she needed company. The poor girl was so attached to Tapani."

"Well, it isn't like she was married to him!" Merja said curtly. Hillevi trembled at the sharp tone.

"No, but maybe she wanted to be." The woman named Anneli leaned back in her chair and looked at me. "So you're from the police. I met other police officers the last time they came to our office. At that time I didn't think it mattered, but I guess I should tell you that poor Satu was infatuated with Tapani. That's why she's so broken up. She must have thought something was going to happen between the two of them. At least she hoped it would, ever since he left his ex."

"And she wasn't exactly subtle about it," Merja Vainikainen said with a snort. "That's probably why Satu didn't like Jutta much. I sensed some coldness between the two of them." Vainikainen didn't address her words to anyone in particular. Koivu and I exchanged a glance. Ursula and Puupponen had interviewed Satu Häkkinen and Anneli Vainio after Pentti Vainikainen's poisoning, but with meager results.

"Of course, I don't believe Satu could have hurt anyone," Anneli Vainio continued. She seemed to enjoy having our undivided attention. "But when you work with someone for a few years, you get to know them pretty well, and Satu tends to confide in me, because she's younger. She fantasizes about having a family and children. She's getting to that age."

"Let's take it one thing at a time," I said. "Once you've finished your meeting, I'd like to speak with each of you individually. Perhaps starting with you," I looked at Anneli. I didn't intend to question Leena, but the others didn't need to know that. "For how long do you have this conference room reserved?"

"For the rest of the day," Hillevi replied quietly.

The conference room could have been located in any office building. The furnishings were as bland as those at the Espoo police station, and the photocopier was exactly the same model as ours. The only thing that gave the room some personality was the couple of basketball posters on the wall.

"I think we've handled everything," Merja Vainikainen said. "My daughter has a doctor's appointment in an hour and fifteen minutes, so if you need to speak with me, could we do it first?" This question, which was addressed to me, sounded more like a command.

"Certainly, as long as Mrs. Vainio has time to wait." I was guessing at Anneli Vainio's marital status from the rings she wore. There were three of them on her left ring finger, two narrow gold bands and a flashy diamond ring, presumably an anniversary present.

"Where would I need to be? And of course I'd like to help the police. Poor Tapani. He was only trying to help, and look where it got him . . ."

With Koivu's help, I shooed everyone but Merja Vainikainen out of the conference room. Then he set up the computer and tape recorder. Merja remained sitting at the head of the table, and we sat to either side. First, I asked if she had any idea why someone would want both her husband and Tapani Ristiluoma dead.

"I haven't thought of anything earth-shattering," Merja Vainikainen replied. "It just seems so unfair that two people have lost their lives because of Jutta Särkikoski. I feel indirectly responsible, since I'm the one who hired her. I was only thinking about how her name would attract attention, just like Toni Väärä's. I wanted publicity for our cause, but not publicity like this."

Vainikainen shook her head, but her hair helmet didn't stir. Her hairspray must have been really strong.

"Have you discovered anything new? I can't bear to read the news about Pentti's death. In line at the grocery store I turn my head away so I don't have to see him smiling on the front pages. Before, I never paid attention to those gruesome headlines. Nothing like that could ever happen to anyone I knew. Now I'm living the news." Vainikainen's voice trembled, making her seem more . . . human. I told her what the autopsy had revealed, but I didn't mention the small amount of the nicotine in his stomach. Technically, Merja was still a suspect.

"Our main line of investigation assumes that Jutta Särkikoski was the intended victim, but we're also looking into other possibilities." Just then I remembered that I'd applied for a warrant with the district court to open Pentti Vainikainen's phone records. I'd probably received it this morning, but Ristiluoma's death had distracted me.

"How is Jutta doing? I assume you're protecting her from any more attacks. I was surprised that she came to the meeting on Friday, but she's made of tougher stuff than other people, like that sniveling Hillevi." I confirmed that Jutta was safe. A quick smile flitted across Merja Vainikainen's carefully made-up face. I felt like telling her that losing control wouldn't be the end of the world. It would be perfectly natural for someone whose husband had been murdered and whose child obviously suffered from a mental illness.

The rest of the interview was like trying to squeeze blood from a stone. One thing Vainikainen did admit was that Ristiluoma had seemed to be interested in Jutta. Jutta hadn't mentioned anything about that. Had she intentionally concealed it, or had she not noticed his interest? Frustrated infatuation could be a motive for violence. Even though I'd only met Ristiluoma once, he didn't seem to me like a person who might accidentally poison someone or blow himself to kingdom come over unrequited love.

"What kind of explosive killed Tapani?" Merja Vainikainen preferred to be the one asking questions. "I mean, was it the sort of thing anyone could whip up with instructions from the Internet? Haven't there been cases like that? I've heard of kids doing that, kids like Mona . . ." Vainikainen's voice cracked. "I haven't been sleeping, and

Mona's condition is getting worse every day. Yesterday she made cakes out of rye flower and water and ate them raw. Then she passed out like an alcoholic. You don't think that she could have had something to do with these crimes, do you?" It hadn't occurred to me that Merja Vainikainen might suspect her own daughter.

"Did she have a reason to hate your husband or Jutta?" I remembered the article about physical education in schools. Maybe kids had bullied Mona after its publication. Might she blame Jutta for her recent troubles? Merja Vainikainen pulled a white handkerchief out of her pocket. It looked to be freshly ironed. She wiped her eyes, though I couldn't see tears in them. Her makeup remained perfectly intact.

"Not really. I know my daughter! Pentti and Mona had a decent relationship, and she barely knew Jutta. But of course I keep thinking over and over about how all of this could have happened. At one point I imagined that Mona gave Pentti poisoned chocolate or something like that . . . I know, it's silly. But her condition has gotten worse, ever since she spent two weeks with her father before school started. Who knows what happened between them."

"Do you suspect sexual abuse?"

Vainikainen's eyebrows rose in surprise, and she tried to force a smile, but all she managed was an uneasy grimace.

"Not as such. I don't think Linnakangas would touch her. But Mona might have seen her father having orgies with girls almost her own age. I'm sure that gives a wonderful impression of male sexuality. That reminds me—I need to take her to the doctor now. Maybe I'll finally be able to convince him that Mona needs to be admitted to a hospital!" Merja Vainikainen stood up and left without saying good-bye.

"Let's hope so," I called after her. Koivu verified that the recorder had been working and labeled the tape containing Vainikainen's interview.

"Who next? Vainio?" he asked.

"Let's wait a minute." A strange idea had popped into my head, and I was trying to find the words to express it. I stood up and walked to one of the two windows, which faced the courtyard. To the north I saw the MTV3 and Channel 4 buildings. The Sports Building was in the center of the media district and close to the Helsinki police station. Exploding Jutta's car had been a daring, public crime, a veritable feat of cold-bloodedness.

"Listen, Koivu. What if we have two perps? Perp number one kills someone during the campaign at the Waterfall Building in Espoo, though whether the intended victim was Jutta or Vainikainen, or maybe even Toni Väärä, is still unknown. Then perp number two sees an opportunity and blows up Jutta's car, believing that we'll assume the crimes are connected and so overlook him, because he doesn't have a motive for the first crime."

Koivu sighed. "So does that make one of the perps Satu Häkkinen since, according to Anneli Vainio, she was jealous of Jutta? Let's pump Vainio for information about that. Should I get her?"

"Go ahead, and tell Harju that he'll be next. Then we can use the thumbscrews on him."

Right away, Anneli Vainio gave the impression that she didn't completely comprehend that her boss was dead. She still talked about Ristiluoma in the present tense.

"I wondered why Satu declined to stay and organize the food for the campaign launch, since she usually does anything to please Tapani. I helped set up but couldn't stay at the event, because every Tuesday I watch my granddaughter while her parents are at their ballroom dance class. Satu just snorted and said that if Jutta Särkikoski was organizing the event, then she could organize the food too. So we both left before people started to arrive."

"Was Hillevi Litmanen already working in the kitchen at that point?"

Vainio frowned and put on a pensive look. "I didn't know who was working in the kitchen. I only caught a glimpse. I didn't realize it was her until you asked. She's amazingly skittish. She practically hugs the walls. Although that's no wonder after what's been going on. Anyone would be scared. I spent the whole weekend trying to figure out a way to retire immediately. I'm already sixty, but I need to hang on for a few more years. I'm just not excited about getting a new boss, and I have no interest in staying at MobAbility after all of this. But an old lady like me isn't going to find work anywhere else. I've done OK in this small firm, since we control when and how often we update our computer systems. I thought I'd be able to survive until retirement on last year's new system, but now I'm not so sure . . ."

Crow's feet surrounded Anneli Vainio's eyes, and her lower lip had begun to narrow. Even so, she looked much younger than my grandmother had at sixty. Would Iida's generation be allowed to age at all, or in fifty years would wrinkles be considered so uncouth that getting a face lift would be like a civic duty?

Vainio frowned again and fingered her rings nervously.

"Forget what I said about Satu! Delete it from your tape! She's a good girl. There's no way she had anything to do with these incidents. At most I could imagine her slipping laxatives into Särkikoski's coffee. And Satu could never build a bomb. She's just a regular small-town girl, and her mom works at the MobAbility factory."

Vainio stood up, straightened her black-and-gray woolen jacket, and from her inside pocket took out a grave candle of the kind that would burn for three days. Then she took me by the hand and led me to the window.

"That's where Tapani died, right? Where the asphalt is cracked? Where the police tape is?"

"Yes."

"There isn't anything down there to remind us of him. I'm going to go light this candle. I asked the building manager if he would put the flag at half mast, but he said not until the day of the funeral. Is there anything left of him to bury?" Anneli Vainio started to cry, and after a moment I let her go.

Koivu fiddled with the tapes again while I stayed at the window. After a minute, Vainio appeared in the parking lot, raised the police tape enough to slip under it, and lit the candle with a cigarette lighter. When she crouched to set the candle on the asphalt, the guard rushed out. I didn't hear the exchange that followed, but in the end the guard allowed the candle to remain where it was. After he left, Vainio bowed her head and crossed her arms. Even though the Monday afternoon hadn't begun to darken yet, the lone candle in the sea of cars looked as bright as a fallen star. Passersby stopped to stare, and few moments later someone brought another candle from inside. Soon a third person came to take pictures of them.

"Maria!" Koivu's voice snapped me back to reality. "I'll go get Harju now, but first I'm going to go on a treasure hunt. I'll be back in a minute."

I kept looking out the window at the parking lot. A young woman placed a vase of African violets next to the candles. The guard returned to the parking lot, speaking into his cell phone and looking agitated. I wondered whether he was taking orders from his security company or Detective Perävaara.

Koivu returned with Miikka Harju, both men carrying cups of coffee. The smell nauseated me. Was I coming down with something? As Koivu sipped his mug, I opened the recorder, inserted a new tape, and then rattled off the usual formalities of time, location, and participants. I'd thought I was done with that forever.

Harju had taken a seat at the end of the table by the window, so we were side by side. I remembered how upset he'd been on Friday after the explosion, but now he seemed calm, if overly alert, like a hunting dog expecting the command to set off after prey.

I asked a couple of warm-up questions and then got to the point.

"How did you end up in your position at the Adaptive Sports Association? Did the employment office randomly assign you the job, or did you ask for it?"

Harju sipped his coffee, and the sight of oiliness on the surface brought back the nausea. From the street side of the building came the wail of a siren, which made us all jump. The sound gradually receded.

"I don't remember anymore. I think I got to pick the job myself. They gave me a list . . . A job is a job. I guess I thought that working with disabled people would be useful."

Harju wore all black: a sports coat, T-shirt, and jeans over the tops of his boots. There was a silver ring in his left ear, which I didn't remember from the previous interview. When Harju lowered his coffee to the table, I saw that his hand was shaking.

"The agent you worked with at the employment office remembers it differently. According to her, you specifically requested work at Adaptive Sports. You practically begged. Why?"

Harju's right wrist was on the table, so close to me that I could see his rapid pulse. A polygraph machine would be redlining right now.

"Well maybe I did! What does it matter?" he suddenly bellowed so loudly that Koivu knocked over his coffee. Fortunately, only a splash of liquid was left, which formed a coin-size puddle on the tabletop. Harju looked at it, embarrassed, and then threw his own almost-empty cup into the trash can. Then he stared at me intently.

"The papers say you believe that the person who's recently tried to murder Jutta is the same one who ran her and Toni Väärä off the road last fall. Is that true?"

I knew how to stare too, a look my husband called my angry cat face. I turned this on Harju, trying to make my expression as intense as possible.

"That's one possibility, but only one."

"Then you're on the wrong track!"

"What do you mean?"

248

"You think that the purpose of the car accident was to kill Jutta Särkikoski, right?"

"Yes, that's our assumption. Doesn't everything that's happened recently suggest that someone wants to get rid of her?" I continued to stare at Harju, and he didn't turn away from my gaze. Out of the corner of my eye I could see a vein throbbing in his forehead. His heart rate must have been twice its normal speed.

"I don't have a clue about what's happening now, but the car accident last year was just that: an accident. I should have confessed earlier. I was the one who ran them off the road."

18

Koivu's jaw had dropped, and his eyes widened behind his glasses. Maybe I didn't look quite as astonished, since I'd suspected all along that Miikka had some connection to Jutta's accident.

"Did someone order you to run Jutta's car off the road?" I asked.

"No! Weren't you listening? It was an accident. If you can really call it an accident, since I was drunk as a skunk. I was coming back from my friend's cabin. We'd been drinking since the previous night, and I was supposed to stay for another night, but then there was some sort of disagreement, and we'd thrown back a lot at that point, and then he started talking about knives, and I thought it was best to leave quickly. At the time it seemed more logical to stay off the freeway and drive through Inkoo. I didn't remember that the 51 has traffic cameras. I was in a big hurry to get home because I still had a half bottle of vodka and some beer there. Normal alcoholic thinking."

Harju finally dropped his eyes. His fingers tapped the table, and his breathing was rapid. The wind had picked up outside, rattling the windowpanes. Harju took another deep breath, and I wondered whether he was hyperventilating. There should be a paper bag in my investigation kit. After a minute, he continued.

"I was going over a hundred easy and wasn't paying much attention. And I probably would have blown close to 0.2. Hard to say. I'd already almost hit someone out jogging, and the rain was really coming down.

I had maybe a millimeter of tread left on my tires, and when I tried to pass that Renault . . ." Harju whimpered, then lifted his gaze and looked at me. "The van started slipping and sliding, and I couldn't get traction. I remember screaming—I was so afraid, I thought I would die. I hit the other car again, and that's when it went off the road. I kept going, and my bumper was rattling like a demon from the impact. I just kept driving. I was such a coward I didn't even stop to see what I'd done. What a fucking bastard I am!"

Koivu's phone rang. He dug it out of his pocket and then set it down after glancing at the display. Harju continued staring at me as if I was a judge about to hand down his punishment. I didn't say anything, not wanting to interrupt the flow of his story. The time for that would be later, once we'd established whether he was telling the truth.

"The next day I woke up in Kirkkonummi without any idea how I got there. I must have found some dive to drink in, and they gave me as much as they dared before I went and passed out in the back of the van. That's where I woke up, soaked in my own piss. I must have taken back roads the rest of the way because I was afraid of the cameras. What a fucking genius. And like I said, when I woke up, I didn't remember what had happened. I thought I was just imagining the accident, until I saw the state the bumper was in. That was when I got scared. Then the magazine headlines started screaming about a reporter and a star athlete's tragic injuries, and I knew I'd really stepped in it. I'd already lost my license once and . . . Well, you've seen my record. Prison wasn't an option. I'd been tossed out of the fire department, and my old lady had left me. I had to get my life back together."

"The van—what happened to it? As I understand it, the police contacted every body shop in southern Finland to ask about a dark-colored van."

"It wasn't in my name! It was my uncle's. He started going blind a couple of years ago, and they took away his license last year. I didn't have the money for a car since I spent it all on booze, but my uncle kept the van insured, and I brought him a few cases of beer, some potatoes, and a vat of pea soup every week. He lives out in the woods behind Siuntio, and he doesn't have any neighbors. By the time the cops came to check his van, my friend Sakke had already fixed the bumper. He's got a little shop of his own, and he kept the job off the books. And the cops didn't visit him anyway. They did stop by my uncle's place, and he swore the van hadn't left his yard the whole week of the accident. Who was going to argue with an old blind man? I guess the cops asked if someone might have borrowed it, but my uncle said they should go see if they could even get it started. I'd drained the battery and cut the fan belt after Sakke and me brought it back to Siuntio. Destroyed a perfectly good van. So that's what happened, and that's the kind of man I am." Harju looked away. His breathing had calmed, but I heard him swallowing.

"I haven't told anyone about this at AA, although I've come close. During my last relapse I almost confessed everything. Luckily no one died, or it would have been the end of a rope for me."

"Is that what made you get sober?"

"Try to get sober." Harju grimaced. "I'm still struggling. Seeing this job at an organization for disabled people was a twist of fate. There were so many stories in the newspaper about how this young kid, this Olympic hopeful, might never run in the white and blue again. I guess I was just being naïve, thinking maybe I could make amends some-how . . ." Harju laughed mirthlessly. "So what I'm saying is no one tried to kill Jutta or Toni Väärä. It was just a drunken idiot who happened to run his van into theirs."

"Where is your uncle's van now?"

"At a recycling factory somewhere. I took it to the scrap yard in the spring."

"Why are you telling us this now?"

"So you won't keep wasting your time on the wrong track! God!" Harju almost yelled. "I thought getting this off my chest would make things better, but you're acting like you don't believe me!"

Harju must have known full well that there was no way to verify his story, and any lawyer would tell him to at least deny drinking before he drove or, preferably, recant the whole confession. A few times I'd run into criminals who'd found religion and wanted to confess their past misdeeds in order to atone. But it wasn't as simple as they imagined or hoped it would be. In theory, driving under the influence and two counts of vehicular assault could result in jail time, but as a first-time offender, Harju wouldn't serve long. Two or three months would be no big deal, if someone was paying for him to take the fall. How much would Harju charge for his incarceration? Would twenty thousand euros have been enough? And who would have that kind of money? Pentti Vainikainen might have, but he was dead.

The investigation of the accident was still the responsibility of the Lohja Police Department, so Harju would have to repeat his story for them. His friends and his uncle could corroborate, but would Sakke, who'd helped him hide evidence by fixing the van, admit to anything? What about the friend at the cabin who'd scared Harju off with talk of knives?

Part of me wanted to believe Harju's story, though it didn't simplify my investigation or negate the fact that Jutta had received death threats both before and after the accident. It was an amazing coincidence that Harju had ended up working at Adaptive Sports, although of course a poor sports-promotion organization would be happy to accept assistance from the state employment office. And if Harju had reason to assume that he might be found out, it would be in his best interest to confess and try to maintain his image as a decent human being.

"The investigation of the accident isn't my responsibility," I told Harju. "I'll send copies of our interview report to the police in Lohja, and they'll contact you."

"Can I talk to Jutta before they do? And Toni too, of course. I have to apologize to them."

I wouldn't reveal Jutta's location to Harju, but he could do whatever he wanted in regards to Toni Väärä. Once more I asked how well Harju had known Pentti Vainikainen and received the same answer as before: he hadn't known him at the time of the accident, and he'd only seen Vainikainen around the office later on.

"You don't believe me, do you? I was trained to save lives, not take them. Just like you're trained to solve crimes, not commit them. I thought I was helping by telling you the truth about the accident."

Harju looked at each of us in exasperation, and Koivu gave him a crooked smile.

"Were you expecting a pat on the back?" he asked.

"No! But what happens now? Are you going to take me in, or do I turn myself in somewhere else?"

"Now you go back to work. The Lohja police will be in touch. Your crimes haven't passed the statute of limitations, and the maximum sentences for driving under the influence and vehicular assault are two years in prison. Those are the maximum sentences," I repeated when I saw Harju flinch. He must have known that his confession might lead to prison.

Harju remained seated, as if expecting the interrogation to continue. I asked him for contact information for his uncle, Sakke, and the owner of the cabin, even though that was really the Lohja police's job. We were slated to become the same large police district soon anyway—the Espoo police would be, that is, since none of that had anything to do with me, I reminded myself, startled that my mind had gone there. It was so easy to slip back into my old role. Sweat broke out on my forehead, and I felt nauseated again.

"Maria?" Koivu asked carefully, and I realized that both he and Harju were staring at me. I wiped my brow.

"What? Oh, you can go," I said to Harju, who stood up.

"Stay reachable!" Koivu added, though saying that didn't bear any force of law. It would be Lohja's job to file his travel ban.

"Will you ask Hillevi Litmanen to come in?" I called out to Harju as he opened the door. He stopped with his hand on the doorknob.

"You can't really suspect Hillevi! She wouldn't hurt a fly. Once when we were leaving the office, we found a seagull that had been hit at the bus stop. She couldn't even watch me put it out of its misery. And I don't think she's ready to be back at work either. She's afraid of Merja, and Merja takes every chance she gets to put Hillevi down. This isn't a nice place to work, and I'm glad I'll be leaving soon. Don't scare Hillevi any more than she already is!"

With that, Harju left. Koivu rolled his eyes.

"Quite the knight in shining armor. You think they're in cahoots?"

"Who?"

"Harju and Hillevi Litmanen. With someone paying them. As Harju said, Hillevi is easy to frighten. Her husband broke her. Are you alright? Your face is totally white."

"I'm fine," I replied and poured myself some water from the pitcher on the table. I felt the same way I had on the worst days of my pregnancies. But my IUD couldn't have failed a second time. That would be ridiculously bad luck. Koivu must have had the same thought.

"You aren't having a third, are you? Hi, Hillevi," he continued as Litmanen walked in. As usual, Hillevi stank of tobacco. It seemed she'd been outside having a smoke.

"Hi." Hillevi stood in the doorway. I asked her to sit.

"How was your weekend?" I said and refilled my glass, because the smell of cigarettes made a new wave of nausea churn in my gut.

"How do you think?" Hillevi's voice was as shrill as a frantic three-year-old's. "I heard about the explosion on the radio on Friday night and knew instantly that somehow it had something to do with me. You have to believe me. Jouni must have hired one of his prison friends to kill me, but first he wants to toy with me. I told you before: Jouni liked threatening even more than hitting. Now he's killing people around me, and maybe I'm next . . . Number three. I don't know who I can trust.

On the bus today, this bald, tattooed man sat next to me. It was horrible. I couldn't change seats because the bus was full, but I was afraid
the whole ride that he was going to stick me with a poison syringe
without anyone noticing. At least the guards keep me safe here, but
what about at home?"

Hillevi's fear was familiar, as were her darting eyes. I tried to calm
her down, but she seemed to trust Koivu more than me. She probably
still thought of me in my role as an Interior Ministry researcher with no
executive authority, whereas Koivu was a real police officer.

Once again, we reviewed the previous Tuesday's events—the making of the sandwiches and Hillevi's trip to the grocery store—but she
didn't remember anything new.

"Is Merja still blaming me for Pentti's death?" Hillevi's hands groped
in the pockets of her cardigan, and she took out a packet of nicotine
gum. "Merja keeps scolding me for smoking. She says it isn't appropriate for a person working for a sports organization. There are plenty of
other people in the building who smoke or use snuff, but in me it's this
huge flaw. I don't understand how that woman can be so mean. Even
her own child is afraid of her. She calls her daughter her ball and chain
and tells us how fat and stupid she is. I can't work here anymore! I'm
going to move somewhere in Lapland where Jouni will never find me.
I thought I might change my name to my grandmother's last name,
Sydänmaanlakka. Isn't that pretty? Jouni never remembers things like
that. He'd be lucky to remember his own mother's maiden name."

Koivu and I had been at Hillevi's apartment when the bomb
exploded at the Sports Building. Her state at the time made it seem
likely that she hadn't left home in days, and I couldn't believe she was
just pretending to be so helpless. I asked her about Ristiluoma, but
Hillevi didn't have much to say. He'd always been friendly to her.

We offered to take Hillevi home if she was free to leave work, but
she declined. She had to finish some calculations by the next day, and
she'd lost the whole previous week to the campaign launch and then sick

leave. I remembered what Miikka Harju had said about paper pushing. Maybe Merja Vainikainen wasn't very good at organizing their work.

After we wrapped up the interviews, we stopped by the Athletics Federation to look over Pentti Vainikainen's office, since Ursula and Puupponen's investigation there on Friday had been interrupted by the explosion.

Vainikainen's office still looked as if someone had been rummaging through it: binders were spread across the floor, and the top desk drawer was open. A framed, full-page picture of a smiling Merja Vainikainen had fallen on its back. It was strange the cleaner hadn't tidied up the room, or had he been unable to get into the building after the explosion? The secretary confirmed that the cleaner usually came at eight every weeknight.

"My office has been cleaned, and no one else has complained. But our cleaner is some . . . well, an immigrant, from one of those Arabic countries," the woman said coolly. "Maybe their kind don't like going in rooms that belonged to dead people."

I called Puupponen, who confirmed that they had left Vainikainen's office more or less in the state I described. So for some reason the cleaner hadn't worked on that room.

The binders contained business documents, including memos from sponsorship negotiations, notes from Athletics Federation board meetings, and archived e-mail correspondence. The spine of a green binder was labeled "Pictures," so I opened it.

Inside I found sports photographs, mostly of female athletes' scantily clad posteriors. Was this how Pentti Vainikainen relaxed during tough days at work? The athletes were mostly from track and field or tennis, but a few figure skaters were included. Jutta's article about the objectification of female athletes came to mind.

I didn't find anything more interesting in Vainikainen's binders, although I only flipped through them superficially. Koivu was on Vainikainen's computer, which was a sturdy, older desktop model.

"Can you believe the idiot used 'Merja' as his password?" He pulled a USB drive out of his investigation kit and started copying files. Apparently Vainikainen hadn't done much by way of extra security.

Because Koivu had his hands full, I went to do some informal interviews with the staff who were still in the office. The CEO of the Athletics Federation was on a business trip, and the head of coaching was off training coaches. Life goes on. The board had met in emergency session on Saturday to find a new director for social affairs.

"Pentti was a great colleague, and he knew how to do his job," the chief financial officer told me. "He was especially good at networking; he must have known at least half of Parliament, all the most important ministers, and everyone who makes decisions about the economy in Finland. The CEO of Nokia answered Pentti's calls himself. When Pentti died, at first I thought someone wanted to hurt the federation, but I guess it was just about that reporter. It's kind of ironic—Pentti loved attending events and meeting new people, and that was his downfall."

After I'd briefly checked in with everyone present, I returned to Vainikainen's office and sat down in the armchair next to the bookcase, while Koivu continued to slave away at the computer. I'd been forced into this investigation because Taskinen and company considered Vainikainen such an important figure that solving his murder took precedence over every other case. I'd initially assumed that Vainikainen wasn't the intended victim—I'd thought it was Jutta, and the car bombing had only confirmed my suspicions. But what if I was wrong? Could blowing up Jutta's car have been a diversion? Or was the target Ristiluoma after all? What connected these two men? Who would have wanted to kill them both?

I repeated my questions for Koivu as we drove back to Espoo. We all needed a break to clear our heads, so I drove him home, despite his objections. I also called Puupponen and ordered him to knock off. I couldn't reach Ursula, so I left her a message.

I drove myself to the station. It was already gloomy, but I didn't turn on the lights in my office, instead sitting in silence with my feet up on my desk and my hands linked behind my head. I tried to breathe slowly in and out, to get my thoughts flowing freely. I mulled over my conversation with Miikka Harju. It was possible that the poison and the bomb had been meant for Jutta, and the car accident had been a completely unrelated and random occurrence. But I couldn't dismiss the possibility that someone wanted to get rid of both Vainikainen and Jutta. What if Jutta had seen something important during Vainikainen's poisoning but didn't realize it, because she thought she was the intended victim?

My head started to hurt. I was fumbling for the bottle of painkillers in my bag when I heard the conference room door open and the click of high heels that could only mean Ursula. A man began speaking loudly as soon as the door closed behind them, and I immediately recognized the voice. It belonged to Kristian.

"Ursula, listen to me! You can't just leave me like this. Everything was going so well! Better than well! You're the woman I've been looking for my entire life. I want to marry you and have children with you. I make enough money so that you could quit the police, and if you want to do something else, I have connections. Just tell me what you want, and I'll get it for you!"

"Don't even bother, Kristian. We're through."

I'd thought I'd heard Ursula's voice at its coldest, but the rage she'd directed at me was nothing compared to the anger that radiated from those last two words. I heard her sit in her usual chair, followed by Kristian's footsteps, then a sound like a kiss and what could only be a slap.

"Don't touch me! Get out of here! Do you want me to call for help? I don't think that would look very good for you. A top lawyer attacking his ex-girlfriend at her workplace, which also happens to be the Espoo Police Department. Leave me alone. I gave you back your key. I can mail you the jewelry you bought me."

"Ursula." Now Kristian was pleading. "I don't understand what's gotten into you. We were so good together. Did Maria say something bad about me? Don't believe her. She's just bitter I dumped her all those years ago."

"This doesn't have anything to do with Maria. If you don't leave now, I'm going to start screaming. Or do I need to get the pepper spray? Leave!"

I heard steps again, and the door opening. Now Kristian's voice was also hard with anger.

"You'll change your mind. You'll be begging me to come back before you know it. Trust me. We'll just have to see what I say."

The door slammed after him. I waited a couple of minutes, but Ursula didn't leave. How long would I have to lurk as a prisoner in my own office? I didn't want Ursula to know that I'd heard their conversation.

Then I started hearing sounds from the conference room. Ursula blew her nose once and then again. Then she started to cry. I'd rarely heard such inconsolable weeping. It was like a small child being left at day care for the first time, absolutely sure that her parents weren't coming back. I never would have imagined that Ursula could cry that way, because she'd always given the impression that she could survive anything and didn't care about much of anything.

When the crying didn't subside after a full five minutes, I decided to go find out what was going on. I tried to stand up out of my chair as loudly as possible to give Ursula a chance to calm down or escape. I opened the door and stepped into the dark conference room, which was illuminated only by the streetlight outside. Ursula lay with her face buried in her hands on the table. When she heard the sound of the door, she lifted her face and groaned.

"Maria! Were you here the whole time?"

"I was. I'm sorry. I should have made myself known earlier. Can I help?"

I expected her to tell me to go to hell and mind my own business, but instead she burst into tears. Her handkerchief was soaked through, so I got her some napkins from near the coffee maker and looked in the refrigerator for the mineral water I'd brought with me in the morning. Crying makes you thirsty. I took the napkins and water to Ursula and carefully sat down next to her. I didn't dare touch her, afraid she'd lash out at me.

"Tell me that Kristian is a bastard. You have experience with him! Tell me it's good to be rid of him!" Ursula wailed.

"But you were the one who dumped him," I said in confusion.

"What else was I supposed to do when he wouldn't shut up about having kids? I thought he wouldn't want any more. He already has three from his last marriage. I guess he's too young for me. I'll have to stick to the sixty-year-olds. Like Assistant Chief Kaartamo or that vice president from Nokia." Ursula burst out in what was either laughing or crying—I couldn't tell.

"Are you absolutely sure you don't want children? Is that a red line for you?" I was still prepared to beat a hasty retreat if she lost her temper, and now Ursula did look at me. Her heavy makeup was smeared around her eyes.

"It isn't a choice I get to make! When I was seventeen, I had a tumor in my uterus. They had to do a hysterectomy, so there aren't ever going to be any children! Of course, you can't understand. You already have two beautiful brats. You can't imagine how much I envy you!"

At the risk of being shrugged off, I wrapped my arms around Ursula, because I couldn't find any words of comfort. Ursula's sorrow was catching, and my own eyes began to tear up. For a long time, we sat side by side in the darkness, listening to the hectic pulse of the police station slowing down. Cars pulled out of the parking lot, leaving only the bare-bones duty staff. Finally Ursula began to shift, and I let her go and stood up. Ursula uncapped the mineral water and greedily drank.

"You aren't going to tell anyone, are you?" she finally asked, her voice still lacking its familiar tone of defiance. "Especially not Kristian?"

"Of course not. But don't you think this might change his mind about having kids? Like you said, he already has three."

Ursula sighed and wiped her face on a clean paper napkin. "It doesn't matter. He's a great guy, but you heard how he wants to make me a housewife."

"Kristian ditched me when I started getting better test scores than him. Back then it stung a little, but now it only makes me laugh," I said. I felt like I was walking on thin ice, where any misstep could mean a sudden plunge into frigid water.

"He told me a different story. But to hell with him. He's gone! And besides, the only man I've ever really wanted since I've been in Espoo is Ville Puupponen!" Ursula burst out laughing. "Isn't that crazy? Ville's the only man in the whole department besides your Taskinen who's never drooled over me. Ville Puupponen!" It sounded like Ursula was slipping toward hysteria. Tomorrow she would regret her admissions, and I would have to pretend I'd never heard it.

"I've always liked Puupponen," I said lamely, wondering how I could wriggle out of this situation without Ursula feeling she'd lost face. Her cell phone started ringing, with Kristian's voice as the ringtone. Ursula declined the call and then began tapping through the menus, presumably throwing the ringtone into the digital garbage can.

"Did you learn anything new at Adaptive Sports?" Ursula asked once she'd finished. When I told her about Miikka Harju's confession, she whistled.

"Särkikoski seemed to think the whole world revolves around her!" The old Ursula was back. "But this means we're back at square one."

"Unfortunately. Koivu copied Vainikainen's computer files onto a USB drive. The machine itself is still in his office. We forgot to get a search warrant to go through it, but we can do that retroactively. Vainikainen didn't seem to be any cryptographic genius. His password was his wife's name. I thought I might take a look at his files before I go home."

I'd never been to the sauna with Ursula, or in any other setting where she might be without her mask of makeup. Now that mask was cracked, though her lips were still perfectly glossed. She gave a cautious smile.

"I can do it. I don't have anything else to do. You go home to your kids since you have them, you lucky bitch!"

"Are you sure you'll be OK?"

"I'd love to have something to distract me from my life right now," Ursula replied. "Get going already! What time is the meeting in the morning?"

"Nine. OK, I'm going. Thank you!" I grabbed my coat from my office, and when I returned to the conference room, Ursula was already immersed in the exploration of the memory sticks and only muttered a vague response to my good night.

As I walked home, I thought about what had just happened. The fact that I now understood Ursula better wasn't going to make our working relationship any easier. Her inability to have children didn't justify her periodic peevishness. And what had she said about Puupponen? I would have liked to gossip with Koivu, but unfortunately, I would have to keep my mouth shut.

At home dinner was still on the table, since Antti's sister had dropped in unexpectedly and thrown off the family's schedule. I enjoyed my husband's homemade macaroni casserole with saffron milk cap mushrooms while listening to Taneli's description of his art class, in which he'd traced the shapes of fallen leaves on paper and then colored the outlines in with hues not usually found in nature. Taneli was scandalized that someone named Sissi had only used green. "I had at least three colors on every leaf!" he told me.

We were all tired, so we went to bed early to read Pippi. The book was one from my childhood, and the covers had been taped multiple times and bore my sister Helena's attempts at coloring in the pictures. The result was a mess that Taneli found especially amusing. Iida stroked Venjamin, who was curled up on her stomach, and I could feel her warmth on my right side and Taneli's on my left. He leaned against me, breathing straight into my ear. This was pure joy. Fortunately, we weren't at the book's emotional final scene, which I wouldn't be able to read without crying—Iida and Taneli hated that. Instead, Pippi was shipwrecked and sending messages in bottles. I read Pippi's lines, familiar from my own childhood:

> *"Let's see," said Pippi, thinking hard.*
> *"Write: Save us before we perish! For two days we*
> *have pined away without snuff on this island."*
> *"Pippi, we can't—"*

"Mommy, what's snuff?" Taneli asked.

"It's gross stuff that's worse than cigarettes but doesn't stink. People put it in their mouths," Iida explained. "You've seen it at practice, when Julia's dad's upper lip looks all fat. That's because he uses it, even though it's illegal."

I realized that I hadn't asked if Pentti Vainikainen used snuff. I'd asked about smoking, but snuff hadn't even crossed my mind, even though Swedish *snus* and American snuff were common in the sports world. Was it possible that the excess nicotine dose had been from snuff or snus, in addition to the sandwich spread?

I had to force myself to keep reading. Once the children were asleep, I looked up the autopsy report on my computer. I'd skipped past the damage to Pentti Vainikainen's oral membranes, because I thought they were a result of the poisoning. Regular use of snus could cause the same kind of damage. Yellow teeth were another common side effect. Vainikainen had recently gotten dental veneers.

Snus tasted of nicotine, so maybe someone wouldn't immediately notice an extra dose. The poison in the sandwich had just been a ruse. The real target of the first homicide had been Pentti Vainikainen.

19

The next morning, I woke up before the rest of the family as usual. In the bright light of day, I wasn't as sure of my theory as I had been the night before. I turned on the coffee maker and then padded outside with Venjamin, me to get the paper, him to sniff the autumn air. He'd been so happy to leave our high-rise apartment for a place where he could come and go as he pleased. He ran off into the neighbor's yard, and I tried in vain to lure him back. The sun was shining for once, and my face looked tired in the entryway mirror.

I could hardly taste my breakfast and had to force myself to eat. As I was brushing my teeth, any contact of the brush with the roof of my mouth triggered my gag reflex.

On the walk to work I considered the possibility that extra nicotine had been slipped into Vainikainen's snus. It seemed possible to inject a snus pouch with a syringe. Thinking about this felt strange on such a beautiful fall morning, as the last wagtails chirped their good-byes, and a Jack Russell terrier pup chased leaves in its yard before trying to follow me to the police station. I told it to stay home, and unlike Venjamin, it obeyed me.

First thing at our morning meeting I told my team my nicotine theory. I'd been afraid of how Ursula would react to seeing me, but she acted as if our conversation the previous evening had never occurred.

"We should look at the pictures and videos from the campaign launch event again," she suggested. "Maybe one of them will show Vainikainen with snus in his lip. That won't prove anything, but it would confirm your suspicions."

Ursula fetched the binder with the pictures and handed it to Puupponen, who flipped through the pages as she set up the DVD player and turned on the TV. Pentti Vainikainen only showed up occasionally in the pictures, since he hadn't been the most important person at the event. We all examined the still shots, but none of us could spot a bump under his upper lip. Puupponen finally began inspecting them with a magnifying glass.

"You're a regular Sherlock Holmes," Ursula said, but she stopped laughing when Puupponen gasped. "Look at that!"

Vainikainen was only half an inch tall in the picture, but with the aid of the magnifying glass, we could make out a bulge in his cheek. "It could just be tongue in cheek," Puupponen said.

"You're killing today, Ville," Ursula said dryly. "Why don't we ask his wife or coworkers?"

According to the autopsy report, Vainikainen's internal organs hadn't shown signs of long-term smoking. However, gum recession, one of the side effects of long-term snus usage, had been mentioned. I looked up Merja Vainikainen's number on my cell phone.

"Is there news?" she asked eagerly after a perfunctory hello.

"Not exactly, just a small question. Did Pentti use snus?"

Merja Vainikainen went silent for a moment. In the background I could hear the sound of traffic. Apparently she was walking on a busy street. "Why do you ask?"

"In a homicide investigation, everything is important." I heard the screeching of a streetcar and honking horns, and Merja Vainikainen must have had a difficult time hearing me, because she practically shouted her response.

"Yes, unfortunately Pentti did use snus occasionally. He learned the habit from his first wife, who was Swedish. I couldn't stand it, especially not what it did to his teeth. He promised to quit, but I think he may have continued doing it in secret sometimes, hiding it from me like a teenager hiding from his mom. At least I was able to convince him to get some veneers. His teeth were this horrible yellow, and it was completely unprofessional for a person of his stature in the sporting world. Is there anything else? I need to get on the tram, and I don't want to broadcast my personal business to the other passengers."

When I didn't reply immediately, Merja Vainikainen hung up. Koivu was on another call, apparently asking Vainikainen's coworkers about the snuff use. He received the same answer I had: Pentti Vainikainen occasionally used Swedish-style snus. He usually kept one or two pouches in a small metal container, which he carried in his breast pocket.

"So where did the pouch from his mouth end up? It wasn't mentioned in the autopsy report," Ursula said.

"He must have spat it into the trash, and now it's in the same place as all the other MobAbility garbage," Puupponen said. "Or his wife pulled it out of his mouth when she started CPR. Did she mention anything like that?"

"No." I pressed the callback button on my phone, but this time Merja Vainikainen didn't answer. The call went to voice mail, and I left a message asking her to get in touch with me as soon as possible.

"The spouse is always the first suspect," Ursula said, stating the obvious. "But why would Merja Vainikainen want to kill her husband? Or Ristiluoma or Jutta? I thought they were supposed to be a happy couple, although you never can know how it is behind closed doors. Vainikainen sent his wife sappy love e-mails, even though they worked in the same building. I almost tossed my cookies when I read them."

My phone rang, and the number was vaguely familiar. A bright but businesslike female voice greeted me.

"This is Kirsti Grotenfelt. You asked me to call you when I got back from vacation. What the heck are you doing back in the department? Isn't Anni Kuusimäki supposed to be running homicide investigations now?"

"Yes, she is. This is only temporary. But your timing is impeccable, because we were just wondering about a couple of things in Pentti Vainikainen's autopsy report. The mucous membranes in his mouth showed signs of chemical burns, presumably because he died of nicotine poisoning. Would it be possible for snus to cause that?"

I could hear Kirsti Grotenfelt tapping at her keyboard. She'd taken over a few years earlier from "Carcass" Kervinen, the previous medical examiner, after his suicide. I'd been elsewhere for most of that time, so I didn't know Grotenfelt or her approach very well. We'd only worked together on one homicide case, which I'd thought was the last of my police career.

"Wait, here are the details . . . The burns were concentrated on the roof of the palate and the right cheek. Yes, this does look like a snus lesion. I'll look over everything more closely and then get back to you. This is what happens when I leave for a couple of days—everything turns to chaos. I was only away for a long weekend in Venice. It's still full-on summer there."

Kirsti Grotenfelt's original training was as a physician, but now she was studying the dead rather than healing the living. I wondered whether I should ask her about my nausea symptoms. I'd checked my IUD the previous night, and it was right where it was supposed to be, so pregnancy couldn't be the cause. But my subordinates were listening, and asking Kirsti about my personal ailments while we were both on the clock wasn't appropriate anyway. I would go to the doctor once I'd wrapped up this investigation.

"Have you heard from Helsinki?" Puupponen asked, and I realized that I needed to inform Perävaara of the new turns the case had taken. That could wait until our meeting was done. Fortunately, the daily papers' news of the homicides had already shrunk to a couple of columns that basically said there was no new information.

"Did Vainikainen's files contain anything more interesting than love notes to Merja?" I asked Ursula.

"It was mostly business. But I have to point out that Koivu isn't the world's most competent computer user. There was one interesting folder named Finnish Field Sports Fund, which was password protected. What could that be? Google didn't have anything on it."

"It's just some coaching foundation. I found it too," Koivu said indignantly.

"That's the only file Vainikainen bothered to secure?"

"Yes. Should I check with someone at the Athletics Federation?" Ursula said.

"Call after the meeting," I said. Ursula continued her description of Vainikainen's files, but the rest of them weren't of much interest. He wouldn't have stored any big secrets on a work computer that was open to everyone, however, and Koivu had already done a superficial search of Vainikainen's home computer.

"The next step is to talk to Vainikainen's friends, relatives, and former teachers," I finally said in frustration. "But let's finish up what we've started first. Is there anything new on the threatening calls to Jutta?"

"Koskelo is the only hit. Are you going to end Särkikoski's protection?" Puupponen asked.

"Of course not. The bomb was in her car."

"So now all we have to do is find the person who wanted to get rid of both Vainikainen and Särkikoski. Maybe he thought that a smaller amount of poison would work on Jutta, since she didn't smoke or chew," Puupponen said. "Maybe he thought he could get rid of both of them at the campaign launch, where there were lots of people and—"

"Ville, come on. Are you saying he was willing to kill bystanders? There was a huge risk of someone besides Särkikoski eating one of those sandwiches," Ursula said, interrupting.

"We already know he's a risk-taker. A gambler. Isn't that what your profiling training said?"

"Usually a perpetrator like this is extremely arrogant and believes he can't fail," Ursula admitted. "Only two names come to mind, and they don't seem to fit the profile: Väärä and Koskelo. Koskelo did make that threatening call. But he wouldn't have put his own protégé in danger. We only have Väärä's word that he didn't agree to the biomedical training program Vainikainen offered. Could Jutta be protecting Väärä?"

That idea kept running through my mind as I closed myself in my office and tried to reach Perävaara. His cell phone went to voice mail, and when I tried to get in touch with him through the Helsinki Police Department switchboard, they said he was out of the building. So I sent him a text asking him to call me. It felt like most of my work was trying to contact people and failing. Then I checked in on Jutta at the hospital. The head nurse told me that she was ready to be released.

Before that could happen, I needed to find a safe place for Jutta to stay until we had the killer behind bars. I would prefer to keep her where she was, but Töölö Hospital needed the bed. Maintaining a guard at Jutta's home would be difficult, especially if the guard was a man, and it would also attract unwanted attention. The head nurse gave us until noon the next day to figure it out.

After hanging up, I e-mailed Taskinen about the issue. Finland didn't have as extensive a witness protection program as a bigger country like the United States, but we had a few safe houses, which we naturally didn't mention in the media. With Taskinen's unlimited budget, we might be able to get her a spot.

Just as I hit send, Perävaara called. I told him it looked like Vainikainen had been the intended victim of the first killing.

"Can we meet?" Perävaara said. "I can come out to Espoo for a change. We're still investigating the explosive, and we still aren't sure whether it was put together by an amateur or a professional. The terror-ism and explosives group has been pounding the pavement all weekend, but all the usual suspects have been quiet. Either no one knows any-thing, or we're dealing with someone everyone is afraid of. And I don't want anyone like that in my city."

I heard someone enter the conference room and my colleagues greet them enthusiastically. Then a knock came at the door.

"Enter," I said, and Visa Pihko walked in.

"What brought you here?" I stood up to shake Pihko's hand, and he pulled me into the conference room with him. I was a little surprised, but then he explained.

"I told you I was working on a big money-laundering case. We've made some progress, and it looks like our investigations overlap. The intersection is Pentti Vainikainen, or rather the Finnish Field Sports Fund, of which he was the chairman."

"I just spent two hours trying to crack the password on that file folder!" Ursula exclaimed. "I was about to give up and send it to IT. What is the Field Sports Fund?" She glared at Pihko, who had left our department before she came on board. They probably hadn't met before. She didn't seem to be testing her powers of attraction on him.

Pihko sat down in the free chair next to Ursula and took a moment to get comfortable. He paused for dramatic effect. I remained standing and stretched nonchalantly, though I was excited too.

"I'll give you a brief outline. One of our suspected money-laun-dering sites is a luxury fitness club called Fit & Fun, east of the Market Square in Helsinki. It's a private club, and to get in you have to have the recommendation of two members. The club has a gym and some aerobics classes, a couple of saunas, a swimming pool, hot tubs, and a bar and restaurant. The gym and the restaurant have great views of the sea. It's a pretty sweet place. The owners have previously been accused of pimping, but the charge was dropped for lack of evidence, and up until now the club has managed to pass all of its audits. The last time they were audited, however, the investigators looked a little more closely. It appears that Fit & Fun not only helps its members with their health and nutrition, it also helps them meet their sexual needs, as well as providing supplements and even drugs to the ones who want them."

"And Pentti Vainikainen was a member?" Ursula asked impatiently. Pihko glanced at her in irritation. He didn't want anyone to ruin his performance. "Yes, but that isn't the key. The important thing is that Fit & Fun donated significant sums of money, about three hundred thousand euros, to the Finnish Field Sports Fund four years ago when it was founded, and then that money was placed in fixed-term accounts to collect interest. This connection interested me, of course, and I looked up the charter documents in the register of associations. The founding members were Pentti Vainikainen, Juhani Linkosalo, who died a couple of years ago in the Swiss Alps in a skiing accident that appears to have been a genuine accident, and Kari Laakkonen, who is one of the principal shareholders in Fit & Fun. Pentti Vainikainen was the chairman of the fund's board since the beginning, and Merja Salminen was named the board secretary at the first annual meeting. The board also includes two other members, who are Fit & Fun customers. They've met once a year for a general meeting, and according to the bylaws, six members plus the chairman must be present in order to form a quorum. As we've investigated this case, however, it's become apparent that those other two board members didn't even know such an organization existed. Pentti Vainikainen also donated forty thousand euros to the fund when it was founded, which was money he'd inherited just prior. That's pretty strange, given that the very next year he took out a large mortgage with Merja Salminen, who is now his widow. According to the organization's charter and bylaws, the purpose of the fund is to distribute stipends to Finnish field athletes, but so far, they haven't awarded any, instead focusing first on growing their capital, and that's been going well, since at the beginning of the month they had nearly five hundred thousand euros in their accounts." Pihko paused, and then he smiled at me.

"The treasurer of the fund is named as Unto Lohi, who heard about the organization for the first time when I contacted him. He had no idea he was on the board of anything. But only one person has ever had the right to sign for the Finnish Field Sports Fund or access its account: Pentti Vainikainen."

"So the fund is a straw man?" Puupponen said. Koivu stood up to make coffee, apparently believing that a guest with such important news should be served something.

"That's how it looks," Pihko said. "I don't really know how cognizant Pentti Vainikainen was of any of this. It may be that he didn't connect the dots until recently. The fund's accounts were emptied on Sunday of last week, two days before his death. Almost half a million euros have disappeared like dust in the wind. Well, into a Swiss bank account we don't have any way to access."

"Did Vainikainen empty it?"

"It was emptied out online using Vainikainen's log-in. He had the only one."

I felt even more confused than before. If Vainikainen had been mixed up in a money-laundering scheme, then the use of explosives familiar to Afghan terrorists wasn't out of the question. But someone had blown up Jutta's car after Vainikainen was already dead. Could Jutta have known about the Field Sports Fund? Or did someone just think she knew about it? What the hell was going on?

"I only have one request," Pihko said. "I know that you want to solve your case as soon as possible, but I also want to nab Kari Laakkonen. He has links to many other money-laundering fronts, so this would be a really big score for us. I'd like to ask you not to interrogate him yet."

"What do you mean, 'yet'?"

"Maybe in a day or two. We're on the verge of breaking this thing wide open. That's why it's important that this doesn't leak, especially to the media. If Laakkonen finds out that we've figured out what Fit &

Fun is up to, he might start destroying evidence. When we're ready, you can have him on a silver platter. Agreed?"

I wondered if I should consult with Taskinen. Then again, I had the authority to make agreements with Pihko. And besides, he had gone out of his way to share his information with us, so why not return the favor?

"Has the name Tapani Ristiluoma come up in your investigation?" Koivu asked.

"No," Pihko said. "There's no Fit & Fun member named Ristiluoma."

I asked the same question about Jutta Särkikoski, and the answer was negative again, as it was for everyone else who had been at the MobAbility campaign launch after-party.

Were financial malfeasance and the connections between MobAbility and Fit & Fun Jutta's big scoop, the one she was protecting her source for?

"What about Merja Vainikainen?" I asked. "Have you interviewed her? If she's the board secretary, she must have been aware of what was going on. Did she sign the general meeting minutes?"

"I haven't seen any meeting minutes, just the incorporation documents sent to the register of associations and the bank statements I had to fight the Helsinki District Court to get. You violent-crime detectives have it easy. When you conduct interviews, you rarely have a truly intelligent person on the other side of the table. White-collar criminals are a lot more challenging to match wits with."

I guessed that meant Pihko wouldn't be too interested in filling in as commander of the Espoo Police Violent Crime Unit. Thankfully that wasn't my problem.

"Who wants more coffee?" Koivu asked. I definitely didn't. I called Merja Vainikainen's number, but she didn't answer. How much had Merja known about what Pentti was up to?

The conference room door opened again, and now Jyrki Taskinen entered. He was also happy to see Pihko but turned down the coffee and chocolate cookies Koivu tried to press on him.

"The safe house is all set up. I've arranged for transport tomorrow at twelve o'clock. Will you inform the subject? You know her better." Taskinen gave me a look that said I had little choice in the matter, but a quick stop by the hospital might do me good, so I had no reason to object. I wanted to clear my mind, and a little time alone would help. Did someone have a bicycle here at the station they could lend me? It was a clear fall day, and it would be wonderful to coast along the bay and watch the flocks of geese gathering in the sky.

But Pihko was headed to Pasila, and he volunteered to drop me off at the hospital if I could leave right away. I asked Ursula to take the Field Sports Fund files to the IT office and assigned some other quick tasks before rushing off with him.

"If you can get those files open, will you send me copies?" he asked as we climbed into his car.

"Of course. How connected is Fit & Fun to organized crime? Could they have a connection with someone from Russia with experience setting car bombs?"

"Some of the drugs and women come from Russia but not all of them. We've only been handling the financial side, but Narcotics is involved as well. It isn't easy to collaborate with them, since they always seem to be fighting amongst themselves about their procedures. I'm most interested in the fraud side, less so in how they got the money. We'll have to see whether there's enough evidence to prove the procurement charges. Why are you asking about Russian bomb makers? Do you think a professional took out Ristiluoma?"

"It's possible. Perävaara hasn't been able to get any tips on the bomber."

"If Perävaara is in the dark, then the situation must be bad. It takes a lot to stump him. How are you enjoying being back on the job?"

I replied with a weak smile. Pihko drove through Tapiola to the West Highway. I looked at the Waterfall Building on the right as we passed. Puupponen was on his way in the afternoon to interview Satu Häkkinen, the one who Anneli Vainio claimed had been infatuated with Tapani Ristiluoma. If we thought of the poisoning and the car bombing as two separate and unrelated crimes, then Häkkinen would have a spot on the list of suspects for Ristiluoma's murder. But would she have access to someone who knew how to build a bomb, or know how to build a bomb herself? That seemed unlikely, but we had to check every possibility. It was an established fact that 99 percent of police work was wasted effort, but we rarely knew ahead of time which 1 percent would turn out to be the right lead.

My phone rang just as we were crossing the final bridge into Helsinki.

It was Outi from my real job as domestic violence researcher. We'd agreed that she would check my e-mail and let me know if there was anything that I needed to respond to personally. She was calling to let me know that she'd forwarded a couple of e-mails to my personal account. I'd have to wait to read them until I got home or back to the station. It was hard to believe that I'd only been working this case for six days. It felt more like six weeks.

A terrier yapped as it frolicked in a pile of leaves in the yard of Töölö Hospital. I knew the guard on duty and said hello.

Jutta was already sitting up and reading one of the books Leena and I had taken from her apartment.

"Hi! I thought you were the nurse or an orderly. Lunch will be here soon. I'm starting to get my appetite back, and I could really go for some good pasta or some roasted vegetables. I must be recovering."

"Great! We've arranged you a place in a safe house—I can't promise you gourmet, but at least you can look forward to a change in diet. You're being moved tomorrow."

"A safe house? Where is it?"

"We'll find out tomorrow. Tell your parents you won't be able to contact them for a while. But don't worry, we're close to solving this. This is all just precaution. You may not be in danger anymore," I said, then filled Jutta in on what we'd discovered about the car accident.

"Miikka Harju! That can't be right! He's such a nice guy. So you're saying the crash wasn't intentional?" Jutta clutched her blanket.

"He swears it was an accident. The Lohja police are interviewing witnesses. Maybe someone will be able to back up Miikka's story. I haven't heard from them today."

"Is Miikka in jail?" Jutta looked bewildered. "I swore I would take revenge on whoever hurt me and stole more than half a year of my freelance wages. But now that I know it was Miikka, I can't even be angry. Strange."

"Miikka is still free."

"He isn't behind any of these other attacks, right?"

I decided to tell Jutta about Pentti Vainikainen and the snus. When she heard that Vainikainen had been the intended victim, Jutta went white. I'd expected her to be relieved, but she was anything but. Instead she began to shake.

"Have I messed everything up?" she said, seemingly to herself. "But Pentti didn't even know about the e-mail. Of course the sender didn't know that Pentti hadn't read the message, because it was probably deleted immediately . . . Would the sender have sent it again? Why didn't I think of that?"

"Jutta, what the hell are you talking about?" I said, interrupting her muttered monologue. "What e-mail? Does this have something to do with your source?"

Jutta let out a small cry and put her hand to her mouth. There was panic in her eyes. I continued pressing her.

"So your source wouldn't have hurt you, but he could have killed Pentti Vainikainen? Is that what you mean? Don't start blubbering. That isn't going to help!" I snapped like Ursula would when Jutta's eyes began to well up. "You're going to tell me who your source is right now, and then I'll decide if anyone else needs to know. If you really want to go to that safe house, the time to talk is now!"

Jutta went silent. I felt like standing up and walking out of the hospital and out of her life. How had I ever gotten mixed up in this case?

An orderly appeared with a food cart, but Jutta claimed she wasn't hungry. The young man left the tray anyway. When I saw the chicken fricassee and blancmange, I understood why she had no appetite.

"OK, Maria, I'll tell you," Jutta finally said. "But you can't get her in trouble. Or me either. The e-mail with the information about Sami Terävä and Eero Salo selling doping drugs at a gym in Helsinki—"

"Fit & Fun, right?"

"Apparently you've already gotten pretty far! Yes, that's correct. The e-mail was addressed to Pentti Vainikainen, sent from a member of the club. It was intended to warn him and the federation about Salo and Terävä's doping, in the hopes that Pentti would be able to intervene before another scandal erupted."

I didn't understand. Had Pentti Vainikainen been Jutta's source? No, that didn't make any sense. Why would he have wanted to burn his partners at Fit & Fun? Jutta must have noticed my confusion, because she continued.

"Pentti never received the e-mail. It was forwarded to me and then destroyed." Jutta grimaced painfully and then forced herself to continue. "You've met Merja's daughter, Mona, right? I did a story about her once, and we e-mailed every now and then. In the spring of last year, her eating disorder was getting out of control, and Merja and Pentti were trying to get her a bed in a treatment facility. Mona interpreted that as Pentti wanting to get rid of her so he could be alone with her mother. To get back at him, she went through his e-mail, looking for something that she could use to hurt him. She found the doping e-mail and forwarded it to me. I'm sure you understand why I was protecting my source. My source was Mona."

20

"Did Mona have a habit of using her stepfather's computer without his permission?" I asked Jutta, once I'd recovered from her startling admission. Jutta said she didn't know. Was it possible that Mona had figured out Pentti Vainikainen's log-in information for the Field Sports Fund accounts and transferred the money to Switzerland? Could she have somehow opened a bank account in a foreign country?

"Was the relationship between Mona and Pentti strained?" I asked. Merja Vainikainen had stressed that, given the circumstances, her daughter and her husband had gotten along well, but of course she would have said that if she wanted to protect Mona. Could Mona have poisoned Pentti to get rid of him before he could send her away? It would be easy for someone living in the same household to spike his snus with nicotine, but what about the sandwiches? As I understood it, eating disorders were often the internalization of anger or aggression, common among people who felt helpless or out of control in their lives. But someone being mentally ill didn't mean they were a murderer. I remembered Mona's withdrawn face and the bleakness of her black room.

"I don't know. Mona didn't tell me much about their relationship. After that one interview, Mona e-mailed me but not very often. Now I'm ashamed to admit it, but at the time I was annoyed by her e-mails.

I didn't know how I was supposed to react. I'm a reporter, not a mental health professional. But I did reply. I tried to be nice to her."

"Did you save the e-mails? What did she write to you about?" Jutta said she'd deleted the e-mails almost immediately after receiving them. After the accident, they'd stopped coming. From what she could remember, they'd just been typical teenage venting. Mona was bullied at school, and Jutta encouraged her to tell her teachers or her mother, but Mona refused.

"Maybe I was shirking my duty by not following up. I was shocked when I saw her later on at Adaptive Sports. She looked so . . . old, or something. It wasn't just the extra weight. It was that she seemed to have absolutely no desire, like she didn't even want to be alive. I don't believe that she would have wanted to hurt me, though. And anyway, she wouldn't have the strength for it."

That was all Jutta could tell me. I would have to see Mona and Merja Vainikainen immediately. Maybe we wouldn't need to move her to a safe house after all. Maybe none of this had been about her.

I told Jutta I had to leave, then ran outside while scrolling through my phone for Merja Vainikainen's number. I called her as soon as I passed through the hospital doors. The first call went straight to voice mail, so I redialed. The third time, I got through. Her voice was tense.

"You can't contact Mona right now. I finally got her into the hospital. I finally convinced them that this is a life-threatening situation, that she could very well gorge herself to death. Pentti's death has pushed her even further off balance."

"Where is Mona now?"

"At Lapinlahti Hospital in Helsinki, at the eating disorder clinic. Only her father and I can contact her. I beg you not to upset her. This is already hard enough!"

"Did Mona have a habit of using your husband's computer?"

Merja was silent for a long time. I tried to listen for sounds in the background, but all I could make out was a faint buzzing. Was she at work, or was she at home, finally able to mourn her husband now that others were caring for her sick child?

"I couldn't monitor Mona every moment," Merja eventually replied. "Theoretically she was going to school—it was her first year of high school—but I don't think she ever went. Hardly any of her old friends go to her new school, and I doubt she's made any new ones. I don't understand how a young person's life can go so wrong . . ." I heard tears in Merja's voice, but I continued anyway.

"Did Pentti ever mention that someone had broken into his computer?"

"Do you mean his home computer or at work? What is this about?"

Instead of sharing the details of our investigation, I asked whether she was at work. I could come to meet her. I had to talk to her about this Field Sports Fund thing, even at the risk of word making its way back to Kari Laakkonen.

"Yes, I'm here. Life must go on. You can come by anytime. I'll be here at least until five. By the way, when will Pentti's body be released? It would be a relief to know when we'll be able to bury him. People are asking."

"The lab tests aren't yet completed." As I said that, I remembered that Kirsti Grotenfelt hadn't called me back yet. I would go to Adaptive Sports, but before then I needed to stop by my real office in Helsinki to say hi and read the e-mails Outi had told me about. If we had to put our investigation on ice for a couple of days as Pihko had requested, I could use the time to start getting ready to return to normal life. I'd make sure I couldn't be forced to return to homicide investigation against my will again. Of course, I'd given in far too easily—or had some subconscious part of me wanted this assignment? Was it the need to help Jutta and Hillevi, whom I already knew?

I jumped on a tram to go across town. The colors of the leaves in the park at Finlandia Hall were at their peak, so the neighboring construction site for the Helsinki Music Center looked even uglier. Antti had attended a couple of rallies for the preservation of the nineteenth-century railway warehouses that had previously stood on the site. He'd jokingly dubbed himself the defender of hopeless causes.

I got off at the main train station and picked up a sandwich at the café, then went back outside to sit in the square and eat. Once the weather turned, the square would be converted into an ice rink. I'd promised Iida that this winter she could try to teach me a waltz jump.

At the office, Jarkko and I quickly caught up. I didn't get to chat with Outi, because she was in a meeting with a client.

I sat down at my desk and turned on the computer, but I didn't get a chance to open my e-mail before my police cell phone rang. It was the Espoo police station switchboard.

"Someone is trying to contact you from Afghanistan. The line is terrible. Should I patch you through anyway?"

"Yes." A call from Afghanistan? I barely had time to wonder what was going on before a terrible squealing static replaced the dispatcher's voice. Instinctively I moved the phone away from my ear, but thankfully the static faded, and I could hear a male voice.

"Hello, this is First Lieutenant Olli Salminen. Am I speaking with the detective investigating the deaths of Pentti Vainikainen and Tapani Ristiluoma?"

"Yes."

"Good. I just heard about the killings early this morning. We've been a little hemmed in, and it takes a while for us to get news of home. I'm a peacekeeper here in Afghanistan, working on bomb disposal."

The line started squealing again, and I didn't hear what Salminen said next. When the line finally cleared, I asked him to repeat himself.

"I'm Pentti Vainikainen's wife Merja's ex-husband," Salminen shouted into the phone. "Is it true that this Ristiluoma person died in an explosion?"

I answered in the affirmative, and then Salminen asked what explosive had been used. Detective Perävaara hadn't released that information.

I began wondering why Lieutenant Salminen had called me instead of Detective Perävaara. I received my answer when Salminen continued.

"Detective Perävaara asked me to call you. Can you tell me what explosive was used?"

When I didn't respond immediately, Salminen yelled again. "I'm an explosives expert, and Merja learned a lot from me. Too much. But when I realized what she's really like, it was already too late. I taught her how to make TATP—I've regretted it ever since. At the time, I was training a bomb dog to detect TATP at each of its stages of production, and he lived at home with us. I've been afraid that Merja would use it to hurt Mona. Some terrorists call TATP the 'Mother of Satan.' That's a fitting description of Merja. Such a cruel woman . . ."

Salminen's voice faded, and the call dropped. I called the Espoo switchboard and asked for the number. I tried to call back, but all I got was a recording in Farsi. From the number prefix, I could tell Salminen had called from a cell phone, so I sent him a text message asking him to contact me again as soon as possible. Then I decided to call Detective Perävaara.

As I was pulling his name up in my contacts, I opened my e-mail inbox. The third-most recent e-mail was from Hillevi Litmanen's Adaptive Sports account. What could she need now?

Perävaara answered, and I told him about Olli Salminen's call while also trying to read the e-mail, whose sender seemed to be someone other than Hillevi. The multitasking didn't work very well, and I looked away from the screen so I could concentrate on the conversation with Perävaara.

"It was definitely TATP," he was saying. "That stuff is easy to make at home but unpredictable, even in the hands of a professional. But apparently Mrs. Vainikainen received good training?"

"It looks that way."

"If TATP gets wet, it can delay the explosion. Maybe the car was supposed to explode immediately when started, but everything didn't go according to plan. Or Mrs. Vainikainen figured out a way to set the bomb in the Sports Building parking lot without anyone seeing her. That would be pretty risky, though."

"Which one of us is going to get the search warrant for the Vainikainen home? It's your jurisdiction, since technically the Ristiluoma case is Helsinki territory. Will a bomb dog be able to find traces of the explosive even if it's no longer in the house?"

"Maybe. What should we do about Mrs. Vainikainen?"

"I'm actually on my way to see her at her office. Get one of your patrol cars ready to back me up if I need it." Then I told Perävaara what I'd learned about the Vainikainens and the Field Sports Fund. Were whatever actions we took in the next few hours going to endanger Pihko's operation? That was mostly about money, however, and this was about human lives.

Finally, I got a chance to read the message from Hillevi's e-mail address. The subject was simply "Hello Detective Maria," but when I read the body of the message, it felt as if the whole world had lurched like a rudderless ship in a thirty-knot gale.

> Hi Detective Maria. I finally realized you're the same person I was writing to before. This is Mona Linnakangas, but I'm also the Snork Maiden. Maybe you'll believe me now since I've told you about the Groke and Hemulen before. But now Hemulen is dead, and I'm sure that the Groke, my mother, Merja Vainikainen, killed him. I'm writing this from Hillevi's computer, and hopefully the Groke won't interrupt me. She isn't a mother, she's a monster, and Hemulen finally realized it too. My former step-dad Olli was smarter, and in the beginning things were good with him. He made the Groke treat me better and wouldn't let her hit me. The Groke told

Hemulen that I won't listen otherwise and that Hemulen couldn't understand because he didn't have any children of his own. I'm lazy, stupid, fat, ugly, evil, bad, and I don't know how to do anything right, and that's why it's OK to hit me. And sometimes I believe that too, and then the only thing that helps me feel better is to eat and eat and eat.

But you never know about the Groke. Sometimes she slips me a twenty and tells me to buy whatever I want. You can get a lot of chocolate for twenty euros. Sometimes she makes me food, healthy things like carrot soup, and says that I have to eat. But I don't want the Groke's food anymore, because I think she puts sleeping medicine in it. After I binge, I usually fall asleep, but there shouldn't be anything in carrot soup to make me pass out.

They fought about me, the Groke and Hemulen. It started in August when it was so hot, and one day I was just wearing a T-shirt and Hemulen saw the burns on my arm. He asked if I was burning myself, and I said no. Where did the scars come from? he demanded. I said I didn't know. He brought the scars up with the Groke and said that they had to take me to a doctor. I was supposed to visit my dad that summer, but the Groke said she didn't want me in Lapland and that my dad had never cared about me, and that he hates ugly women.

The Groke thought Hemulen wasn't coming home until late that night, and she burned me again with the iron, but Hemulen was in the garage and heard me screaming. The Groke said it was just an accident, because I was so clumsy, and that she wasn't going to let me use the iron anymore. Hemulen asked if that was true. I said it was because the Groke was standing right there. After that the Groke never let me be alone with Hemulen, and now Hemulen is gone. The Groke says he ate poison.

I don't remember much from these past few days. The Groke must be slipping me something again. She says we have to go to the doctor now. She told Miikka that I'm going to finally get treatment and that she's so relieved. I don't know where she's taking me. The Groke says all you can eat there is carrot soup and sauerkraut, and that every day you have to walk ten kilometers and go to the gym, and that there are beautiful thin anorexics there too but that they won't see me because they're afraid of fatsos like me, that they'd rather die than be like me.

I'm afraid of the Groke. The Groke didn't just shout at Hemulen about me. She also yelled about money and trips and stuff. I don't want to be the next one to die, so it's good that I get to go to the hospital. Maybe I can tell them where the scars are from. Maybe we can iron all that fat away, the Groke said once. Can you help . . .

I looked at the timestamp on the e-mail. It was sent the previous day at 1:25 p.m. Mona had written the message while we'd been interviewing her mother in the conference room a few feet away.

Was Mona telling the truth? Merja claimed that her daughter had spent two weeks with her father over the summer and had come back even more disturbed. What was Mona's father's first name? All of my interview notes were at the police station, and I couldn't access the police databases from this office. I closed my eyes and tried to remember.

Jari. That was it. A common Finnish name. I called Information and asked for a phone number for Jari Linnakangas, and was soon connected. A female voice with a Russian accent answered.

"Jari meditating. I not bother him now."

"This is important! Who are you?"

"Tatyana Morozov, member of the Crystal Commune. Who can I ask Jari call once he finished in about half hour?"

"Do you live there permanently?"

"Yes, this my third year. I already know good Finnish . . ."

"Did Jari's daughter, Mona Linnakangas, visit there in August?"

"No, no, no! That woman not let her, Jari old wife. Won't let Jari see daughter at all. He very sad. Who I talking to?"

I told her who I was and asked her to have Linnakangas call me, even though what she'd told me was enough. What else had Merja been lying about? Had Mona really gone to a treatment facility? I had to find out right away.

While I was on hold at the hospital, I tried to organize my thoughts. It was easy to understand why Merja Vainikainen had killed Pentti. She had both motive and opportunity. Merja had probably been the one who'd moved the Field Sports Fund money to Switzerland. But why would Merja want to kill Jutta or Ristiluoma?

The voice of the receptionist at Lapinlahti Hospital interrupted my thoughts. At first, she refused to divulge any patient information, because I wasn't family. And I didn't want to reveal any more details about an ongoing investigation than I absolutely had to. Finally, the switchboard operator agreed to connect me to the charge nurse.

"This is Detective Maria Kallio from the Espoo police. I'm investigating two homicides, and I need information about a patient who was admitted yesterday, Mona Linnakangas."

"My, the police . . . Well, I can tell you right now that we didn't admit any new patients yesterday. All of our beds are full."

"So you don't have a young woman named Mona Linnakangas there? She's sixteen years old and suffers from compulsive overeating."

"No. Try the Children's Hospital. Maybe she's been admitted there."

I searched in vain for Mona in the region's hospitals. As I finished my last call, I looked out the window to the other side of the square. There were plenty of taxis lined up in front of the train station.

Without checking whether Merja Vainikainen was in her office, I ran down the stairs and across the square to the nearest waiting car. I asked the driver to take me to the Sports Building. On the way I tried to find Mona's cell phone number, but there was none listed under her name. That was strange. What kind of sixteen-year-old doesn't have a phone?

Mona didn't, as Jari Linnakangas confirmed when he returned my call during the taxi ride.

"Mona lost her phone in the spring, and Merja thought her punishment should be six months without one. I don't care much for material things, but that seemed awfully harsh. How was she supposed to keep in touch with her friends? According to Merja, I don't have any right to interfere in my daughter's life because I don't pay child support. It's not that I don't want to, it's just that I haven't had any income in the past couple of years. Here at the Crystal Commune, we try to get by on as little as possible."

"When did you last see your daughter?"

"The summer before last, when I was in Helsinki. I know Merja bashes me to Mona, so it's no wonder she doesn't care for me. My relationship with Merja was a mistake from the start. I was attracted by her lack of fear, her ski jumping and speed skiing . . . And there was plenty of fast living with her. Too much, really."

"Was Merja violent toward you or Mona?" I saw the taxi driver's eyes flash in the rearview mirror. Hopefully he wasn't in the habit of tipping off reporters. The driver was an average-looking young guy, and I'd guessed he was an emigrant from Estonia, based on the way he'd pronounced his Finnish.

"As far as I know, she treated Mona fine. I wouldn't have let her have full custody otherwise! She slapped me a couple of times, but I didn't think it was a big deal. Back then . . . Well, now I think differently. Our community eschews all violence. Why are you asking?"

"Don't you watch the news at your commune?"

Jari Linnakangas laughed, his voice ringing like a little boy's.

"We aren't completely backward, even if we live somewhat off the grid. We get the newspaper, and we listen to the radio. What happened? Is Mona OK?"

"I don't know. Her stepfather was murdered a week ago, and now I can't find her. Apparently Merja has been abusing Mona for some time. Have you ever noticed burns or other scars or bruises on her?"

"No! But . . ." Linnakangas paused to think. "It's been a few years since I've seen her in anything but very modest, sack-like clothing. She's ashamed of her body. I tried to get her to go swimming with me in the sea when I was with her last time. It was that really hot summer, but she wouldn't do it. You don't suspect Mona of killing Vainikainen, do you?"

Jari Linnakangas wasn't laughing anymore. He said something but not into the receiver. It seemed there were other people in the room. The taxi driver braked to let a gaggle of first graders pass on the crosswalk, and the sudden movement made nausea rise in my throat again. The children were just as small and delicate as Taneli, but together in their little pack they were safe. I wanted to believe that mothers couldn't burn their own flesh and blood with irons, but I knew all too well that wasn't the case.

I asked Linnakangas to contact me if he heard anything from Mona. I'd managed to unsettle him enough for him to say he was leaving for Helsinki as soon as possible. I realized I didn't know anything about Mona's grandparents. Had Merja isolated her from them too? Hadn't anyone noticed what was happening?

Mona had turned to me, and I hadn't done anything to help her. And now here we were.

The taxi dropped me off in front of the Sports Building. I looked out across the now-familiar parking lot. Workers were repairing the damage to the wall of the building left by the blast, and the broken window had already been replaced. Just as I finished paying the taxi, Koivu called.

"Hi, Maria. Where are you?"

"At the Sports Building, on my way to Adaptive Sports to see Merja Vainikainen. I have some questions for her."

"A new witness volunteered. Jutta Särkikoski's neighbor's father, who was at his daughter's apartment last week watching her cat. I just interviewed him. He's seventy-six and half deaf, but he's still sharp enough. He used to work as an auto mechanic. At first, he didn't realize what he saw. He says that last Thursday he hadn't been able to sleep, so he went out for a little walk. He claims to have seen a 'blond girl' messing with the bottom of a car and asked if she needed help. He remembered the exact model of the car and the license plate number except the last letter. It was Jutta's."

"What do you mean . . . did Jutta set the bomb under her own car?" A man walking by glanced at me curiously, and I realized I was speaking louder than I'd meant to. I was only fifteen feet from the place where Tapani Ristiluoma had been blown to smithereens, and now the area was covered with flowers and candles. Some of the grave candles had already gone out, and their white plastic shells looked somehow

290

obscene. Had Jutta lost her mind and decided to take out Ristiluoma? But no—the explosive pointed to Merja.

"We showed this new witness Jutta Särkikoski's picture. He didn't get a close look at the woman's face, but he said that she was thin and blond and definitely didn't have any crutches."

"Merja Vainikainen is thin and blond, and she knows how to make TATP." I briefly filled Koivu in on the conversations I'd had during the day.

"Have the team meet at the station at five. I intend to arrest Vainikainen, assuming she's in her office as planned."

The guard was still in the lobby of the Sports Building, and today he had a German shepherd with him, who stared at me with altogether too much interest. In the elevator an acquaintance greeted me—she was one of the head coaches for my children's figure-skating club—but I had a difficult time conversing with her even for the short ride. I practically ran to the hall that led to the Adaptive Sports offices.

I knocked on the door that said "Vainikainen." No one answered. I tried the handle, which moved but was locked. I poked my head into the conference room, but there was no sign of Merja Vainikainen there either. Hillevi Litmanen's office was empty. When I closed that door, Miikka Harju peeked out of his own.

"Are you looking for Merja? I haven't seen her all day. She left to take Mona to the doctor yesterday and hasn't been back since. She isn't answering her phone either. Maybe she's finally taking some time off."

"Do you have a key to her office?"

"No. I only have keys to the downstairs door, my office, and the conference room. But I'm sure the janitor can get it open. He's unlocked other doors when people forgot their keys. Should I call him?"

"Yes, thank you." While he did that, I went into the conference room and tried Merja's number with no luck. I called Koivu back and asked him to issue a travel ban on Merja Vainikainen, and to get the others to help him determine whether Merja had booked any tickets.

"And get a trace on her cell phone location. We have probable cause. Why the hell did I think she'd just be waiting here for me? Tell me the second you hear anything!"

My next call was to Detective Perävaara. "It's Maria again. Do you have that search warrant yet? No? OK, send a patrol car over to the Vainikainen home anyway. I'm issuing an arrest warrant for Merja. If the girl is there, take her in too and bring them both to me. We already have the borders closed. We have to find her!"

Possible scenarios raced through my head. Merja had already escaped—how could I have known where she'd been today when I spoke with her? She could have flown halfway across the world by now. And Mona? Was she lying unconscious or even dead in her mother's house? Could Merja have killed her own daughter?

"You're in luck." I jumped at Miikka Harju's voice. I hadn't seen him come into the conference room. "The janitor was fixing something downstairs, and he's coming right up. He has a key for Merja's door, so we don't have to call a locksmith." Harju tried to smile. "By the way, I got a call from the Lohja police today. They told me to come in on Friday for questioning. They don't seem to be in a hurry."

"Do you know any of Merja Vainikainen's friends? Who does she spend her free time with? Is there anyone in the building she goes to lunch with?"

Harju hadn't been interested in his boss's private life and couldn't help, other than to tell me to ask at the Athletics Federation since Merja had worked there before. The janitor came just then and, after a little fumbling, found the right key and opened Merja Vainikainen's office.

Harju followed behind me. I asked him to turn on Merja's computer while I went through the drawers. In the top drawer, I found a powder compact, pens, a Fit & Fun diamond-level membership card, and two unopened packages of pantyhose. The second and third drawers were full of ordinary paperwork. The binders on the shelves seemed just as mundane. There were no pictures of Mona or Pentti in the office, just posters for the MobAbility/ASA campaign, one with Toni Väärä showing off his lumbar spine belt and another with two middle-aged women playing wheelchair basketball.

"I don't know Merja's password, so I can't get past the log-in screen," Harju said. "What are you looking for?"

I didn't quite know what to tell him. Maybe flight reservations, or receipts for the transfer of half a million euros from Finland to Switzerland? How could a bank have allowed that much money to be transferred all at once? Had Merja killed Pentti for the money? In my mind's eye, I saw the endless interviews ahead of us, all the time we'd have to spend with every person who knew the Vainikainens. We would have to contact Mona's school.

Helsinki patrol car 525 reported that the Vainikainen house looked empty. The officers had gone to ask the neighbors about a spare key, but no one had been home. I asked them to have a look through Mona's window, but they didn't have a ladder with them. I ordered them to break a downstairs window and go inside. Only after they'd searched the house from the dining room to the shed in the back yard would I be satisfied.

I sat down for a moment in Merja's desk chair and stared at the computer screen. I tried passwords. *Pentti. Mona. Linnakangas. Ikonen*, which was Merja's maiden name. No luck. *Skijump, speedski . . .* nothing. Ursula would have been much better at this. Harju stalked the room like a dog searching for its own tail, opening binders as if he were a cop too.

In the corner of the room was a steel wardrobe. I walked over to it and peeked inside. The familiar smell of sweaty workout clothes wafted from the top shelf, and there were gym shoes on the bottom. On a hanger was a delicate pink blazer with cherry-red flowers embroidered on the collar. I riffled through the pockets and found a car key.

"Opel Astra Cosmo. Do you know if these are Merja's car keys?"

Harju glanced at it. "No, Merja has a Volkswagen. This must be for Pentti's car. He left it here the day of the campaign. Merja and Hillevi drove to MobAbility in Merja's car, and me, Jutta, and Pentti went in

Jutta's car. Pentti's car is probably still in his spot in the parking lot. Should we go have a look? I drove Pentti home a couple of times after he'd had a few too many drinks during a negotiation."

I was ready to grasp at any potential clue, so I followed Harju to the employee parking lot on the north side of the building. Outside, it was drizzling. Pentti Vainikainen's luxury-model Opel was parked near the stairs. Harju opened the car door for me. I hesitated for a second but then decided that any remaining fingerprints didn't matter anymore. I opened the glove box. Inside I found the car's registration, a flashlight, an ice scraper, and a couple of CDs. Vainikainen was a fan of the band Yö.

"The cabin," Harju suddenly said. "The Vainikainens rent a cabin on the Porkkala Peninsula. They were there the weekend before Pentti's death."

"Porkkala? Where? Out on the tip?"

"No, it's on the bay, on the west side. The road turns off just before that little café. Merja threw a sauna night for us there in August, but it wasn't a very fun party. I had to listen to her abusing Hillevi while Jutta was in the sauna. Maybe Merja is there?"

I didn't wait around wondering whether I could trust Miikka Harju, or whether it was legal to use a suspect as an assistant. When I inserted the modern folding key into the ignition, the engine sprang to life. The gas tank was nearly full, and I noticed the parking pass glittering on the dashboard. Vainikainen had had a reserved space. I scooted over to the passenger seat.

"You drive, and don't worry about the speed limit. This is an emergency. I'm going to have to make some calls on the way."

Harju got in and took off, tires squealing. At the gate he waved the parking pass in front of the sensor, then hit the gas before the boom was fully up. I tried to forget that I was sitting next to a reckless driver who had run a car off the road and nearly taken two people's lives a year earlier, even as I wished I had a siren and light in my bag. On second thought, I added one more item to my wish list: a gun.

Not that I wanted to use one.

—————————◆—————————

21

Miikka Harju didn't hold back, getting us up to eighty miles an hour on the West Highway, and when the speed limit went from eighty to one hundred, he redlined the engine. Harju didn't know the exact address or the owner of the cabin, so I had to rely on his memory of the route. I was on the phone, trying to get at least one patrol car to meet us. I was reluctant to launch a large-scale assault when we didn't even know whether Merja Vainikainen was at the place. I was more concerned about Mona than her mother.

"Why is finding Merja so important?" Harju asked as we reached the edge of the city. "Are you afraid she might harm herself?"

I thought for a second. Harju was a civilian, but every citizen was obligated to assist the police if asked. In his former employment, Harju must have worked with police officials frequently. But if I wanted his help, I had to tell him the truth.

"It appears that Merja poisoned her husband and blew up Jutta Särkikoski's car." Harju's hands trembled, and the car momentarily drifted toward the median, but Harju quickly corrected his path.

"Is that so? So the poison wasn't meant for Jutta Särkikoski?"

"I don't know yet. The Ristiluoma murder still doesn't make sense. Unless Merja wanted to create a diversion by shifting attention from Pentti to Jutta."

If Merja had been the one making death threats to Jutta, that meant she'd been planning this crime for a long time. Did the idea come to her when she hired Jutta for the MobAbility campaign, or was it earlier than that?

"Was Merja behind Jutta's death threats?" Harju asked, rage in his voice.

"Not all of them." I didn't bother telling him about Ilpo Koskelo, though the whole mess would eventually come out in the dozens or even hundreds of articles that would be written about the case. I couldn't think about that now.

"What if I had confessed a year ago that I was to blame for that accident? Would any of this have happened?" Harju's face was colorless, and his knuckles clenched the steering wheel, making the veins on the backs of his hands stand out.

"What-ifs aren't going to help now. Merja was the one who decided to start killing people."

When the road narrowed to two lanes, Harju started passing the other cars so recklessly that I had to tell him to slow down. And besides, we were coming up on a caravan of Russian vehicle-transport trucks headed for the port, so we would just have to join the queue. Espoo car 56 was near the turnoff for the Porkkala Peninsula area and promised to come as soon as they wrapped up their traffic stop. The line of semi-trucks stopped at a red light, and it seemed to take an eternity for it to start moving again. The smell of diesel filled the car, and Harju tried to adjust the ventilation.

The main road down to the peninsula was empty, and Harju drifted between lanes to take the corners faster, completely ignoring the occasional twenty-five-miles-per-hour signs. I was feeling nauseated again and turned down the heat. Sweat began to run down my neck and between my breasts, so I put my hair up in a bun and wiped my forehead. I wasn't usually prone to motion sickness.

"Can you remember what the view of the road is like from the cabin?"

"I don't think it's very good. The lot is forested. I've only been there once, so I hope I can even find the place. The turnoff should be coming soon." Harju finally braked. We drove through a small settlement, and then I could see the sea glimmering beyond the bridge in front of us. Harju made a right-hand turn, sharp enough that we skidded, and he had to course-correct in order to keep us out of the ditch.

"This car is pretty nimble compared to a fire truck," he said. "I didn't usually drive, but I was trained for it. One more skill that went to waste." There was bitterness in his voice, but I didn't have time to remind him he'd been the one who drank himself out of a job, because just then a cow moose appeared in front of the car. Harju slammed on the brakes, and my seat belt jerked me hard enough that I thought I might have broken some ribs. At least we didn't hit the moose, and the airbags didn't go off. She casually sauntered across the road, followed by her two calves.

"How far is it from here?" I asked Harju once the moose family was gone.

"A couple of kilometers. It's a one-way lane for the last eight hundred meters."

"We'll go slowly and park the car a few hundred meters away from the cabin." I couldn't think of anything in my handbag that could serve as a weapon. I asked Harju if he had something, and he said he always carried a Swiss Army knife.

"But the blade is only seven centimeters, so it doesn't look very threatening."

"It's still enough to kill someone," I replied, and Harju gave me a funny look. A Swiss Army knife wasn't going to be enough if Merja had TATP.

"Do the Vainikainens hunt? Do you know if there are weapons at the cabin?"

Harju didn't know. At the top of a small rise, we turned left onto a narrow road full of potholes. After a few hundred yards, there was a wide spot where the road forked.

"Best to leave the car here. Should I turn it around?" Harju asked.

"Yes. Leave enough space for the patrol car to get through. Is this the last turnaround?"

"If I remember right, the yard has room for a couple of cars. Is there a flashlight in the glove box?"

"Yes, but it won't be dark for a couple of hours."

"It's also a weapon," Harju said dryly.

Suddenly I was happy that Miikka Harju was with me. With his help we could play for time. I told him my plan: if Merja Vainikainen was in the cabin, Harju would be the one to approach. He would say that he was worried about her and had come to see if she was alright. I would stay in the background until the first patrol car arrived.

"In that case, I should drive all the way up," Harju said.

"In Pentti Vainikainen's car? Bad idea. Say you took a taxi. Also say that you're afraid for Merja's mental health now that Mona is in the hospital."

"Is she?"

"I couldn't find Mona at Lapinlahti or any of the other facilities. And yesterday she sent me an e-mail telling me she suspects that Merja killed Pentti."

"Holy fuck, what a mess!"

We got out of the car, and Harju started walking down the dirt road, bordered on either side by dense pine forest. We were on some sort of narrow peninsula, heading in the direction of the sea. A two-story vacation home built of dark logs stood on the top of the small hill at the end of the road. Calling it a cabin would have been inaccurate, given its size and the attached observation tower on the shore side of the building.

I began circling around the right side of the house. Harju walked down the path through the front yard, and I heard him ring the doorbell. After a while he rang again. I reached the end of the peninsula and looked back. A blue Volkswagen sat parked under the carport. Merja Vainikainen's car.

"Merja? It's Miikka. Are you here? You weren't answering your phone, so I came to see if you're alright!" Harju yelled in a loud, commanding voice. He walked around the side of the house, peering into the downstairs windows and trying to find a way in. Then I saw him pull out his cell phone, presumably trying to call Merja. I strained to hear ringing inside or out, but I only heard the screeching of gulls out to sea. A spider had spun a web nearly half a yard across between two saplings, and on it, beads of precipitation shimmered in the narrow strip of light shining from the sea. I saw chanterelles growing in the moss, but they would have to stay where they were.

Harju walked over to the carport and turned on the lights. He tried the car doors without success. Then he examined the wall, apparently looking for a key. When the door to the house opened, he jumped. There stood Merja Vainikainen. She was dressed in an oversize dark-brown bathrobe. She yawned.

"Miikka! What are you doing here?" There was no wind, so I was able to hear Merja even though I was a few dozen yards away. Harju bent down to hug her. Oh hell, had I walked into a trap? Was Miikka Harju working with Merja? Had I been lured to a secluded cabin, where it would be easy to get rid of me?

But then Merja refused to let Harju into the house.

"I just need to rest. I haven't slept much since Pentti died. Now that Mona is in treatment, I can focus on myself for a while. The police haven't told me when they'll be able to release Pentti's body, so I can't start arranging the funeral yet."

Merja's claims sounded plausible, though she continued to stand on the threshold, blocking Harju's way.

"How did you get here? I didn't hear a car."

"I took a taxi. It dropped me off up the road. I wanted to walk a little. What hospital is Mona in, by the way?"

"Lapinlahti. How do you intend to get home? There are only a couple of buses a day."

Carefully I edged toward the house. I hoped that I wouldn't be easy to see among the pine saplings. Now I couldn't hear what they were saying, but whatever Harju had said managed to convince Merja to let him into the house.

The west side of the house only had small, narrow windows, but the windows on the south end took up nearly the entire wall. When the door closed behind Merja, I circled back to the west side. The patrol car had been less than twenty miles away. Where was it?

Above me I heard a bang and glanced up. The tower window was open, and Mona was trying to push her shoulders through the narrow space. A wave of relief washed over me. She was alive! I tried to motion to her to keep quiet, but I was too late.

"Detective Maria!" she screamed urgently. "Here I am! You have to help. The Groke is holding me captive!"

A huge cracking sound came from inside. I rushed to the door. It was locked. I ran to the carport, searching for something I could use to smash a window. There was an iron digging bar, which I grabbed, then ran toward the large windows on the south side. Then I raised the bar.

I stopped midmotion when I saw Merja and Miikka Harju standing in the large living room. Harju was facing me, but he didn't seem to see me. I could see him well enough to see the terror in his expression. Merja had her back to me. Her left hand hung against her side, but I couldn't see the right. Was she holding a knife or a pistol? Would I have time to break the window and take her down before she hurt Harju?

"Maria!" Mona shouted again. Harju had seen me—he shook his head. That was the wrong move.

Merja turned toward the window, and I saw what was in her hand. I was no explosives expert, but I could guess what the metal object that she held was: a TATP bomb ready to detonate. Merja took a step toward me, and I saw that one of the windows was a sliding glass door. She opened it.

"It seems we have more visitors," she said. Her voice was surprisingly calm. "What brings you here, Detective Kallio?"

"You're under arrest."

Merja laughed, but it sounded forced. At some point she'd taken off the bathrobe. She was dressed in a pink cotton track suit and running shoes.

"Why would you arrest me?" she asked. Then Mona shouted again.

"I'm up here, Maria! Please, unlock the door!"

"Why are you holding your daughter prisoner?"

"The doctors told me to. They can't admit her until the day after tomorrow, but they promised us a bed for her. At Lapinlahti Hospital. I just have to keep her locked up for now, so she can't binge before then. It's part of the treatment program. Could you please put that digging bar away before you come inside?"

I didn't put the digging bar down or make any other move. I just stared at Merja. How did she think she was going to get out of this situation?

I had to play for time. I didn't know how dangerous the explosive was, or how easy it might be to detonate it. At least there wasn't a visible fuse.

"I'll come in, but just to get Mona," I said, my voice shaking. Merja backed up a few steps, allowing her to see both me and Harju. His mouth was a tense line. In this situation, a familiar colleague, someone like Koivu, would have been better company. We would be able to predict each other's reactions and calculate accordingly. Harju was a wild card, though I assumed that, as a former firefighter, he knew how to respond under pressure.

There was the sound of a car driving up the drive. I heard a knock at the door, and then someone shouted my name. Once, twice.

"So there are more of you," Merja stated. "How many?"

"One patrol now, but more are on their way," I lied.

"Detective Kallio!" They were now using a megaphone. I heard Mona shrieking from the window. The patrol officers wouldn't shoot her, would they? I'd told them we were trying to arrest a woman suspected of murder, and from a distance Mona could be taken for an adult.

"They'll break down the door if you don't open it. They have the tools. Give that"—I pointed to the bomb—"to me. There's no reason to harm anyone else."

"Come off it!" Merja laughed again. "Fine, let's go open the door. You two walk in front. Miikka, has Detective Kallio told you what I'm holding in my hands? Or maybe the police haven't figured out what blew up Jutta's car. This contains TATP, which can be set off by a hard impact. If I turn this little knob the other way and shake, it explodes. You saw what kind of damage it did in the parking lot of the Sports Building. And this contains a double dose."

My mouth went dry, and I saw stars in front of my eyes. Not again. Taskinen would be sorry if I died. But I couldn't die. I couldn't.

"Kallio goes first, then you follow her, Miikka. You'll do as I say or get this bomb tossed your way. Kallio will open the door."

The door was about ten yards from the living room, which felt like a long way. When I opened the door, I saw two faces I didn't recognize. One of the officers was a young woman with dark hair, and the other was a slender man in his sixties.

"Hello, I'm Senior Officer Väh—" the man said before a rough shove sent me flying out toward the young woman. I dropped the digging bar. The door slammed behind me.

"What the hell—" the officer said. I urgently waved the two of them away from the door and the blast radius. Both were armed, but their pistols were holstered, and they didn't have bulletproof vests or helmets. Their vehicle was a sedan rather than a van. I couldn't see Mona in the tower window anymore.

"There is—" I began, but my phone interrupted me. As I fumbled in my pockets, I realized that my hands were shaking.

"It's Miikka." His voice was so tense he could barely speak. "Merja has some requests."

I turned my phone on speaker so my colleagues could hear, and Merja began talking.

"You're going to order any other police coming this way to turn back. The ones who are here can stay. Then you're going to let me leave. I'll be taking Miikka with me."

"Agreed." I didn't remind Merja about Mona, hoping she would leave her daughter behind.

"Tell your colleagues what I have. Tell the others too. How do they say it in the movies? She's armed and dangerous."

"I'll tell them. Are you coming out?"

"First I need to make some preparations and say good-bye to my beloved daughter. Although I doubt any tears will be shed. But be ready. This won't take long."

Then Merja hung up. Quickly I briefed the patrol officers. The male officer introduced himself as Matti Vähämaa and his partner as Junior Officer Jonna Otala. He lived in the area and knew that, at the moment, there was only one road off the peninsula because a key bridge was temporarily closed on the other route. So Merja was trapped.

"We should set up a roadblock at Eestinkylä, at the intersection there. Should I handle it?"

"Yes! Tell them this is a very serious situation, and that the suspect has a hostage. She won't get far, since I've already issued a travel ban. The most important thing is that no more lives are lost." I decided to try to get Harju out of there, but I wasn't going to offer myself in his place. What would I do if Merja tried to switch prisoners? A police officer was always more valuable than a civilian, so why had she pushed me out of the house instead of him?

Otala inspected the surroundings as if preparing for an attack. I could read in her eyes that this was also the first truly dangerous situation she'd been in in her career.

The weather had cleared as evening approached, and sunlight filtered through the trees from the west, illuminating the door as it opened. Miikka Harju came out first, followed by Merja wheeling a carry-on bag and wearing a quilted jacket with a fur collar. The coat was too heavy for the relatively warm fall day. In her other hand she carried the bomb. Harju climbed into the car first, and Merja watched as he backed it out of the carport. The officers and I retreated as the car approached. I guessed the range of the shrapnel would be at least twenty yards. I remembered Jutta's mangled face and was barely able to keep myself from running away as fast as I could.

"I'm a pretty good shot, but this revolver isn't a precision weapon," Vähämaa whispered.

"Keep your pistols holstered," I whispered. Our exchange caught Merja's attention. She still held the bomb as a queen might her scepter. She set the suitcase in the back seat of the car and then sat down next to Harju. I held my breath as the car began moving across the yard. Soon it would be gone, along with the bomb, and we could save Mona . . .

But then the car stopped as close to us as it could, and Harju rolled down his window.

"Merja says you have to come over here right now," he said to me. "Or she'll blow me up."

Of course, Merja would die in the explosion too, as would I once I got close to the car. Still, I forced my legs to move. With each step I felt as though I had lead weights around my ankles.

"Walk around the front of the car to Merja's window," Harju said. I did as instructed. She rolled down her window. Sunlight shone from behind her, turning her hair into a golden halo around her shadowed face.

"Detective, tell me one thing." Merja's voice was almost cheerful. "How did you figure it all out?"

"It was easy," I said, though it was probably unwise to provoke her. "Fraud investigators were already on the trail of the Field Sports Fund, and your ex-husband Olli Salminen told me that you had a knack for explosives. And Mona helped us too," I continued vengefully. I hadn't heard any sounds of violence from inside, and I thought that Miikka Harju would have said something if Merja had harmed Mona. He probably would have risked his life to prevent it.

"Olli Salminen! What a bastard! Tell me why I always have such horrible luck with men. Jari was a daydreamer I fell in love with due to naïveté and inexperience, and despite his profession, Olli was a tenderhearted idiot who always took Mona's side. And then Pentti—God damn him! Instead of letting us enjoy life with his inheritance, he invested it in some semicriminal foundation! I married him because of that money! His monkey business with Laakkonen was so clumsy that I knew they'd get caught, and I didn't want to be left out in the cold. I was so stupid! I didn't ask for a prenup, and Pentti invested his inheritance without asking me, and then all my savings went into that blasted house! Pentti was just like Jari. He could never hold on to money. He always tried to live the way his wealthy CEO friends did, serving expensive cognac to every government minister and the other clowns who came around."

I didn't have a tape recorder, and there was no way to discreetly start the voice recorder on my phone. Merja must have deduced from my use of the digging bar that I wasn't carrying a gun. Because she seemed to be in a talkative mood, I asked her a question.

"I understand why you'd want to get rid of Pentti, but why Jutta?" Merja laughed like a character in a horror movie.

"Jutta was such a useful idiot! She was already afraid. I knew that Pentti and his buddies had hired a couple of small-time gangsters to call and send her letters before her accident. I contacted one of them and wrote a few letters myself. Jutta ran straight to the police, just like I thought she would. It didn't matter to me who or how many people died along with Pentti. And it still doesn't. Remember that," Merja said and suddenly turned toward Harju. I went to put Merja in a stranglehold, but she turned back and hit my wrist.

"Drive!" she yelled at Harju, who stepped on the gas, leaving deep tire marks in the dirt road. The car disappeared around a corner, and I sat down on the grass. The danger had passed for now. Vähämaa and Otala ran over to me.

"Are you alright?" Otala asked. I nodded, unable to speak. I had to get inside and drink some water. I had to save Mona. I heard her voice again, but I couldn't make out the words.

Then I smelled smoke. I looked toward the south side of the house and saw fire through the windows on the first floor. Suddenly I was in motion again, running toward the house. Mona pushed her head through the window.

"Help! I can't get out! There's a fire!"

Just then the house's fire alarm went off. Otala, who had run after me, pulled out her phone and called the fire department. The nearest fire station was in Kirkkonummi, back on the highway, and the fire trucks would be slowed by our roadblock. It would probably take fifteen to twenty minutes for them to get here. I left Vähämaa and Otala to handle those arrangements and rushed toward the house.

"Mona, don't worry! Help is coming! Can you tell where the fire is?"

"On the stairs. I can't get the door open. Mom locked it from the outside!"

"Keep the door closed. It's protecting you! Are there any fire extinguishers in the house?"

Mona didn't answer. She kept trying to force herself through the small window, which would have been too narrow even for Iida. There was another, bigger window, but the drop from it to the ground was more than twenty feet. I looked around for a fire ladder but didn't see anything on the front of the house or the water side. Under the carport I found a ten-foot ladder, but that would barely reach to the lower level of the roof.

"We need a ladder!" I yelled to Otala.

"We have a rope. And a fire extinguisher."

"OK, let's try to locate the fire through the windows." I hadn't had a chance to really look around when I'd been inside the house, but I recalled that there had been stairs to the second floor right under the tower. Through a window, and I could see flames leaping distressingly high. They might not reach Mona before the fire department arrived, but how would she avoid breathing in the smoke? I ran back to stand below the tower window.

"Mona, are there any towels or sheets in the room?"

"There's a shawl . . . and a tablecloth."

"Stuff them in the crack under the door! Be brave. Help is coming!" Only the thought of my own children prevented me from charging into the house.

"Do you have water?" I yelled when Mona returned to the window. Thank God Merja hadn't drugged her! But maybe her not doing so was worse. Had she thought that her daughter didn't even deserve to die of smoke inhalation peacefully, in her sleep?

"Yes, one bottle!"

"Get your hair wet! If you have a handkerchief, get it wet too and breath through it. Or use a pillowcase!" *Oh, let the fire department come now,* I prayed. I remembered how winding and narrow the road was, and that a fire truck wouldn't be nearly as agile as our car had been.

"Hold the ladder. I'll climb onto the second-story roof," said a male voice suddenly from behind me. I turned and saw Miikka Harju. There was a scrape on his right cheek, and his pant leg was shredded. An open wound was visible through the hole in the fabric. He was breathing heavily—he must have been running.

"Miikka! How did you . . . ?"

"Merja said you'd need a firefighter and threw me out of the car. I didn't see that she'd started . . . The tower's fire escape is on the west side. You get to it through the roof. It's a shitty design, which is why I noticed it when I was here with Pentti. Cops carry rope, yeah?"

This last question was directed at Vähämaa, who hoofed it back to their car to get the rope.

"And you have that digging bar, right, Maria? Go get it and bring it here. I can use it to break the window if I can't find anything else." I took off running as Mona screamed above. The flames had spread throughout the downstairs now as well. The roof must be hot as hell already, and Harju didn't have his firefighting gear.

"Bring that tarp from the carport too!" He yelled. "You'll use it to catch Mona!" I got what he'd asked for and ran back to the tower.

"Are you sure we shouldn't wait for the fire truck?" I said as Vähämaa, Otala, and I supported the ladder so Miikka could climb onto the roof. He'd tied the rope around his waist.

"No time! And if I hadn't been such a coward, none of this would have happened. OK, are you ready?"

Vähämaa bent under the ladder so that part of the weight rested on his shoulders, and Otala and I strained to hold it steady. Harju weighed nearly two hundred pounds, and it took all the strength the three of us could muster to help him onto the roof.

"Go under Mona's window and fold the tarp over four times, then get ready to catch her."

Harju had already managed to climb onto the roof of the tower and seemed to be looking for a place to tie the other end of the rope. It was already getting dark outside. The flames illuminated the area around the house, but the electricity had gone out inside. What if there were more explosives in the house? If the fire reached them, we would all be goners.

Harju had secured the rope, and he was using it to lower himself down, until his feet reached the windowsill of the tower room. Otala prepared the tarp. I hadn't practiced catching a jumper since my time at the police academy twenty years earlier.

"Mona, can you break the window?" Harju shouted. "Look, there's a metal chair. Throw it through the window! I'll get out of the way. Look out below!"

There was an enormous crash, and then a heavy office chair flew out, accompanied by a hail of glittering shards. Otala grabbed the chair and tossed it aside. Harju returned to the window and brushed the worst of the glass fragments out of the way. His face was wet with sweat, and the heat made me sweat too. The house was fully ablaze now. It would be pointless to try to use the fire extinguisher.

"Mona, you have to be brave now." Miikka's voice was kind. "Take my hand and slide down the roof a little. Then you can jump onto the tarp. Come, get onto the windowsill."

"I can't. I'm too heavy!"

"Yes, you can! I'm coming to help you." Harju jumped into the room, and after a moment he assisted Mona onto the windowsill and then climbed up after her. The windowsill shook under their combined weight. We stretched the tarp tight. Hopefully it would hold.

"I'll hold the rope in place. Slide now!" Harju ordered.

Mona howled like an injured animal as the rough rope burned her hands. Her grip failed almost immediately, but we got the tarp under her and kept her from hitting the ground. I pulled the weeping girl into my arms and walked her away from the fire. She was breathing heavily. I heard a siren and couldn't remember a time when that sound had ever been sweeter.

Miikka Harju had climbed out the window and now hung by the rope around his waist. The flames were coming out of the downstairs windows toward him. I shouted a warning, but the flames had already caught Miikka's pant leg. He screamed and tried without success to put out the flames. Then he pulled a knife out of his pocket, cut the rope, and dropped to the ground, where the tarp no longer waited to catch his fall.

———————◆———————

22

Miikka Harju was still alive when the police and firefighters arrived. He'd been knocked out on impact, and I'd used my jacket to put out the flames on his jeans, then put him in the rescue position and covered him with the tarp to keep him warm. Thankfully he'd only received second-degree burns.

The firefighters had begun the daunting work of putting out the blaze. I warned them of the possibility of explosives. They'd reached Porkkala Road just as the roadblock was being set up and so had almost certainly passed Merja Vainikainen driving the other way.

The other police officers were taking care of Harju, so I could turn my attention to Mona, though there wasn't much I could do for her beyond giving her something to drink and wrapping her in a blanket from the fire truck. She seemed slightly drugged, though that could have been the shock.

About twenty minutes after the fire truck arrived, my phone rang. The caller was Liisa Rasilainen.

"I'm on my way, in the ambulance. It's taking a while, because the ambulance arrived at the roadblock at the same time as Merja Vainikainen. We'll be there in five minutes."

"What about Vainikainen?" I walked away from Mona, though I doubted she was listening.

"She's on her way to Holding. I'll fill you in when I get there. The paramedics want me to ask about injuries there."

I told her, and after a few minutes, the ambulance pulled up. Liisa Rasilainen jumped out after the paramedic team. They'd been followed by another fire truck, which had a hard time fitting in the yard and didn't hesitate to drive over the berry bushes. When the paramedics began working on Harju and Officer Otala took charge of Mona, I took Liisa by the hand and led her far enough away so that I could hear her over the crackling of the flames and the blasting water.

"Did Merja Vainikainen hurt anyone else? Did the bomb go off?"

"The whole thing was a farce. I was one of the first ones to start setting up the roadblock, since I happened to be out this way inspecting some graffiti. We had five patrol cars on site and SWAT on the way when Vainikainen drove right over our spike strip. She got out of her car, swearing and waving that round bomb, seemingly unconcerned about all the guns pointing at her. She wasn't afraid; we were. My heart rate had to have been a hundred and fifty. Vainikainen claimed the bomb was so powerful that if she detonated it, everything within a square kilometer would be vaporized, leaving nothing but a hole in the ground. Of course, we had bomb experts with us, and they said that was bullshit. Vainikainen freaked out because we didn't believe her and threw the bomb in the air. I took off running like everyone else, but I stopped short when nothing happened and Vainikainen started to laugh like a maniac. The bomb was just a metal part to a washing machine. Is she the one you've been after for those murders?"

I nodded. Liisa looked at me for a moment and then wrapped her arms around me. For a moment we held on to each other as if our lives depended on it, and we didn't let go until my phone rang.

The incident commander at the roadblock confirmed that Merja Vainikainen had been arrested and taken to the Espoo police station. As far as I was concerned, she could spend the night in a cell alone. I sent my team a text message notifying them that Vainikainen had been captured and that we were taking the rest of the night off. We would meet as normal at nine a.m.

Rasilainen and I caught a ride home in car 56. My kids were still awake, and my mother-in-law was with them, because Antti had gone to a concert he'd bought the tickets for weeks earlier. Iida asked about the smell of smoke that clung to my hair and clothes, and Taneli asked if I had time to continue reading Pippi Longstocking to him. We'd left off at a cliff-hanger: Pippi was leaving Tommy and Annika to go to the South Seas. Even though Iida knew how the story went, her lip trembled during the good-bye scene, and Taneli looked terribly serious. I didn't burst into tears until the part where Pippi decides to stay with her beloved friends.

My blubbering irritated the kids. I didn't want to explain that I was weeping more for the events of the past week than the happy ending of the book. After they fell asleep, I stood outside their doors for a long time, just listening. Then I went to wash my hair and hang my clothes to air out.

We'd tried to find a home where we could see the stars. Venjamin slipped outside after me, and I let him go. He wouldn't be gone long, because he was afraid of dogs and cars. I waved to the woman next door and her two-year-old daughter, Norppa, who was Venjamin's greatest admirer. We talked about homeowner's association business. Thinking about when to hold the last neighborhood cleanup day of the year was relaxing. This was the normal life I wanted to return to.

I was still awake when Antti got home. He'd gone out with a couple of friends to analyze the concert over a beer. I'd considered drinking some whiskey, but after a sniff I'd decided that it smelled too smoky for this night. I sat in the kitchen with a cup of rooibos tea in front of me, along with a couple of cinnamon sweet rolls thawed out from the freezer. I offered one of them to Antti.

"Was it a good concert?" I asked. Antti's answer flowed right past me. He could just as easily have been speaking Croatian or Swahili.

I was suddenly starving and thought about making myself a cheese sandwich.

"How early do you have to get up?" Antti asked after completing his rundown of the concert.

"Just the usual. I'm almost done. We had a breakthrough, and the perpetrator confessed. She's in jail now."

"You should have told me! That's fantastic!" Antti hugged me, which was a little awkward because he was standing up. I felt his abs through his black cotton shirt. Thankfully I wasn't feeling weepy anymore.

"So no danger this time?" Antti continued. I didn't elaborate, because I wasn't in the mood for a sermon. But if Harju and I hadn't sped out to Porkkala, Mona might be dead now, and Merja might have tried to frame her for the murders. Antti held me tight, and he muttered words of relief into my hair. He had been worried about how I would cope, but he'd still let me make my own choice. I appreciated that immensely.

Despite the grandiose admissions Merja Vainikainen had made at the vacation home in Porkkala, by the next morning she'd changed her tune. I went to see her with Koivu, and she claimed the whole thing had been a big misunderstanding and that she'd just been distraught because the clinic wouldn't take Mona. She continued this charade for three days.

There was enough circumstantial evidence for the district court to remand her for trial. Merja refused to breathe a word without her lawyer, and at first, I handled all the interrogations during business hours, with Koivu as my partner. Ursula and Puupponen worked half days on the Vainikainen-Ristiluoma pretrial investigation, spending the rest of their time on the Violent Crime Unit's other cases. Soon I began to tire of dealing with arrogant and tight-lipped Merja Vainikainen, in part because she brought out the worst in me. When she claimed that Mona had set fire to the cabin in Porkkala, I had to leave the interrogation room to stop myself from hitting her. Detective Perävaara came to a couple of interrogations, and during those Merja pretended to be completely ignorant about explosives. Pihko interviewed her as well, and to him Merja claimed that she hadn't heard anything about the Field Sports Fund and only knew Fit & Fun by name.

"We're in a tough spot with that one," Pihko said. "But Kari Laakkonen will talk once we soften him up a little, and maybe he'll testify against Vainikainen."

Merja had been arrested on a Tuesday. On Wednesday, Taskinen was in Tampere at the Police University College, lecturing future squad leaders on leadership skills. On Thursday morning I tried again to get Merja to talk, and when I got sick of it I returned to my office. I found Taskinen hanging around in our conference room.

"Maria! Congratulations! You caught your woman in record time."

Koivu, who'd been just behind me, thought it best to make himself scarce. Ursula and Puupponen had gone to Helsinki to interview Perävaara's bomb expert, so we had the room to ourselves. Taskinen pulled over a chair for me, and I sat down, waiting for what he had to say. Taskinen hadn't shaved that morning, and the stubble on his cheeks and jaw was a mixture of gold and silver. There were dark circles under his eyes, and his skin was the color of yeast, as it always was when he hadn't been sleeping.

"It turned out to be so simple," Taskinen said and sat down next to me. "The killer was the next of kin. I feel sorry for Pentti. We were in the same marathoner group in the early nineties. I think you'll get the silver cross of merit for this. I'm going to file the nomination."

"I don't need medals. I just want to get back to my life."

Taskinen put one hand on my shoulder and brought his face so close to mine that I could no longer distinguish between the gold and the gray in his beard.

"Think carefully, Maria. You're good at this. Don't waste your skills."

"Good at what? This was all luck. The information just fell in my lap. Anyone could have come to the same conclusion. Someone quicker could have done it before Ristiluoma died."

"Don't underestimate yourself. We're getting praise from a lot of important people. Pentti Vainikainen was a nice guy, but his methods were a little quaint. No one would have wished him such an unpleasant end, but had they known, people wouldn't have approved of his actions."

I remembered all the praise of Pentti Vainikainen I'd heard during the investigation. The acclaim would dissolve quickly when it came out that he hadn't been playing fair.

"How many of the people who are complimenting me knew about what was going on at Fit & Fun?"

"How should I know?" Taskinen replied all too quickly. "Anyway, it's good everything is now coming to light. Visa Pihko has turned into a top-notch white-collar crime investigator. That boy's going to go far. By the way, have you eaten? They're serving pesto chicken downstairs. It's the best thing this kitchen puts out."

I was hungry. For appearance's sake I called Koivu to be our third, and in the end his wife, Anu, joined us, as well as Puupponen when he returned from Helsinki. He was in such a boisterous mood that the rest of us didn't have to do any talking. I did like these people, and I enjoyed working with them. But the work itself wasn't what I wanted.

I took the weekend off. I'd purposefully kept my work phone turned off, but on Sunday morning, the officer on duty in Holding called our landline.

"Hi, Detective Kallio. Merja Vainikainen is demanding to see you. She says she wants to talk."

"Let her wait till tomorrow. I'm taking the day off."

"She's screaming and beating on the door."

"I think the door can handle it. I'm going mushrooming with my family."

On Monday morning there were messages on my phone from Merja and her lawyer. I never figured out what convinced her to confess. I suspected it might have been as simple as a desire for attention. Detective Perävaara and I had issued a terse statement to the media, saying that one person had been arrested for the murder of Vainikainen and Ristiluoma. Most of the reporters were able to draw their own conclusions when they found they couldn't reach Merja Vainikainen, and the owner of the vacation home in Porkkala was only too happy to accept payment for revealing who his renters had been.

Because Merja had requested the meeting, I'd assumed that she'd reached her breaking point, but I really didn't know what to expect. Her hair helmet was backcombed as high as it could be without the hairspray to hold it in place. Her eyes beneath were just as hostile as before, and the faded, oversize prison jumpsuit didn't make her look the least bit cowed.

"I asked you here because I finally intend to tell the truth . . ." She paused. ". . . the truth about Pentti, my third husband. I've truly never had luck with men. The first was a good-for-nothing dreamer, the second was a bomb-obsessed mercenary, and the third was a complete idiot with money. He invested the wealth I'd worked so hard for in an illegal scam, while I slaved away to pay our mortgage. You can't imagine what it's like to work in the sports world, or maybe you can. Is it the same in the police? In speeches the bigwigs always say they want more women in leadership, but in practice we jump from one short-term gig to the next, and we get paid eighty cents for every man's euro. And, even if you manage to do something important, the men take all the glory. I left the Athletics Federation because if I'd stayed, I would have ended up doing all of Pentti's work, even as he played the great leader. At Adaptive Sports I could at least try to build my own career, but then Pentti had to ruin it all by getting mixed up in this shady business."

That was the beginning of Merja's three-hour monologue, which I occasionally tried to interrupt with a question. It was pointless—Merja told what she wanted to tell. She was trying to earn my sympathy by blaming Pentti and the patriarchal sports world, but that didn't account for the fact that she had abused her child and then tried to burn her to death. Or that she'd spiked her husband's snus with nicotine, as well as added it to the garlic mayonnaise, which just so happened to have been one of Pentti's favorite foods. She'd pulled the snus out of his mouth while pretending to attempt to revive him. She'd also been the one to suggest that he'd had a heart attack, though she'd known otherwise.

"Where did the snus pouch from Pentti's mouth end up?" I was finally able to ask during our third interview the following Tuesday evening.

"I put it in a napkin in my pocket, then threw it in a trash can on the street," she said. "I always hated Pentti's snus habit. That bulging lip was so not sexy, and his teeth were disgusting before he got those veneers. I always said that using snus would cause him trouble, and I was right, wasn't I?"

These meetings with Merja Vainikainen were exhausting. She didn't regret what she'd done. She believed she was entirely justified, and so clever, because she'd thought to grab Jutta's car keys ahead of time and make a copy. That was why the car alarm didn't go off when Merja installed the bomb. For Merja it was personally mortifying that the heavy rain had gotten water on the TATP, which delayed the explosion and killed the wrong person. Ristiluoma had weighed sixty pounds more than Jutta, which may have played a role in the late detonation.

"It was Olli's fault. He didn't tell me the stuff isn't always reliable. If Jutta had died, I never would have been caught. How can I have such fucking bad luck?"

I tried to understand what had made Merja so vengeful, and I was startled to realize that it was easy for me to label men who behaved the same way simply as psychopaths with no logical reason for their actions, but when it was a woman, I went looking for an external explanation. I decided that I didn't need to understand Merja. Still I was sure that her lawyer would request a psychological evaluation.

So far, the Field Sports Fund money was nowhere to be found, and Pihko doubted it would ever be recovered, but the Fit & Fun money launderers had been arrested and would drown under a deluge of charges. Once she'd started talking, Merja Vainikainen seemed happy to tell Pihko everything she knew about their activities. Pihko said that, at first, he'd thought she was being so talkative to lighten her own sentence, but soon he realized that she just enjoyed creating trouble for others. Gradually it also became clear that Merja's main motivation had been money.

"Everything I've ever had came from hard work. I never inherited anything, and I lost in each divorce," she said during an interview with me and Pihko. "Pentti thought I didn't know about the Field Sports Fund money. He left his log-in and password right out in the open. Who will get the money now? It's mine, do you hear me?"

Merja had been plotting for a long time. Hiring Jutta Särkikoski at Adaptive Sports had been part of it, and Merja had been the one to restart the death threats. She'd bought several prepaid SIM cards for that purpose. And she'd planned for the death threats to end with Jutta's death.

"I don't have anything against Jutta. Actually, I quite like her. We've both been oppressed by stupid men," Merja said when I questioned her for the last time. "But she happened to fit my plan. She should have been a martyr to Finnish free speech, which would have been an honorable death. Just like I'm a martyr to inequality."

"No, you aren't," I said. Koivu looked up from the voice recorder. I went on, "If you think that equality means acting like the cowardly men who oppress you, then you have a lot to learn." For a moment I felt that I'd found my inner Ursula, and it felt good.

Mona was the only thing Merja wouldn't talk about, other than to maintain that the girl had set the fire herself. But the fire investigators proved otherwise: The tower room had been locked from the outside, and rags and paper soaked in heating oil had been piled in the hall in front of the door.

Mona was finally in the eating disorder clinic at Lapinlahti Hospital. Jari Linnakangas had left the Crystal Commune for the time being and was living in an apartment hotel so he could visit her every day. Her recovery would take a long time, years perhaps. Merja had encouraged her daughter's compulsive eating, to justify her contempt and, ultimately, the abuse. According to Olli Salminen, Merja needed a sense of control and superiority in order to feel powerful. Still it was hard for me to understand what she'd done.

"Women can be just as cruel as men," Ursula said. We were sitting in the conference room drinking coffee. "Take me, for example. About once I week I want to kill someone, and I entertain myself by planning how to do it. Thankfully I'm a cop and know there is no such thing as a perfect crime. I'm a pretty smart chick, but even I would get caught in the end. So all the rat bastards in this building are safe."

Many times I'd felt like asking Ursula what she intended to do about Puupponen, but so far I'd managed to keep my mouth shut. Maybe Ursula needed to want someone unattainable, and oddly enough that person was our scrawny, red-haired corny joke slinger. Kristian seemed to have disappeared from Ursula's life, and he faded from my thoughts as well.

Three weeks after the explosion, I was sitting with Leena and Jutta at Tapani Ristiluoma's memorial at the Haukilahti Water Tower restaurant. The sea stretched out below us, looking silver-blue and cold. The day was sunny, with some red blazing in the trees. Raking had become part of my nightly routine, serving to get the blood moving in my arms and legs after a day in front of a computer.

Ristiluoma wasn't a member of any church, so he'd been cremated in the presence of his nearest relatives. I'd hesitated to come to the memorial service, but Ristiluoma's sister had asked that I attend. There was no priest to preside, but at least there would be a police officer, albeit one soon to leave the force. The pretrial investigation was nearly complete, and soon I would be able to return to my office in downtown Helsinki. But first I intended to demand some change in protocol for the project.

"We need to have the authority to track down anonymous sources like the Snork Maiden, like Mona. We can't treat these people like guinea pigs. Pentti Vainikainen and Tapani Ristiluoma would be alive today if we'd figured out who Mona was and put a stop to Merja Vainikainen," I'd told Leena as I drove to the memorial.

"You and Miikka Harju are both so eager to take the blame, you idiots. Merja Vainikainen killed her husband and Ristiluoma. No one made her do it. And people have a right to anonymity. Maybe there could be an exception for minors, but do you really want Big Brother keeping tabs on everyone all the time?" Leena asked. "Sociologists aren't any more responsible for the lives of the people they study than lawyers are the people they defend. Are you sure you can approach your research objectively?"

"Probably not," I admitted. "But don't start with me. I have no intention of filling in for Anni while she's on maternity leave, not even if Taskinen comes begging on his knees. I'm going to finish this project and then see what comes up next. I may be able to find some international work through the Police University College. I forgot to tell you—I met with Merja Vainikainen's second husband, Olli Salminen, when he was on leave. He came to give a statement about Merja's explosives knowledge. He said that they really need female police officers in Afghanistan, and that means women to train them."

Leena knew without me saying it that my family would limit my options. I hadn't told her about the nausea I'd experienced during the investigation. I had gone to a doctor, and she thought that the symptoms might be psychosomatic, caused by my fear of being hurt again. "It's perfectly normal," she'd said. I wouldn't tell anyone about this weakness, but it allowed me to justify not applying for Anni's position. Not that I needed justification. I would miss working with Koivu and Puupponen, and Ursula too. I'd promised to treat them to dinner once the final reports were filed with the prosecutor.

Ristiluoma's portrait stared at us from between two candles. He'd lost his life because he'd tried to help Jutta. Anneli Vainio and Satu Häkkinen from MobAbility delivered a brief eulogy, though the latter mostly just sobbed. Hillevi was there, along with Leena, who had found herself as acting director of Adaptive Sports after Merja's imprisonment.

Miikka Harju remained in the hospital, but the doctors had told me that he would be back to normal before long. I'd stopped by as soon as he was able to receive visitors. One of his legs had been badly burned, and he had some scrapes and a few minor fractures. He'd have to face responsibility for the car accident eventually, but I believed he would get off with a fine. I'd replayed his fall in my mind and still wasn't sure whether he'd intended to end his life when he cut the rope. Maybe I'd ask him if we met again.

Jutta Särkikoski had made a full recovery from the explosion, and she needed only one crutch these days. By Christmas she might not even need that. Now that no one was threatening her, she seemed to have a new lease on life. She'd been offered a permanent position on the Aamulehti sports desk in Tampere. A change of scenery would do her good, since Espoo held too many painful memories. She promised to move into an apartment that Leena could access in her wheelchair, and then we could come visit. Jutta had announced that she didn't intend to press charges against Ilpo Koskelo.

"But I'm going to rake Ilpo and Toni over the coals if they don't start putting up some better times," she said. "I'm not afraid anymore. Even if someone threatens my life, I'm going to write exactly what I want to write. In the Finnish sports world there are still taboos and good-old-boys' clubs that need shaking up, to say nothing of international sports politics. Can you believe they gave the summer Olympics to Beijing? Then they play pious about human rights, after selling out to the highest bidder."

"It's just a show. The Olympics, I mean," Leena said. "Athletes are the gladiators of this age, and they're still entertaining us by risking their lives. And the crowds go wild."

I wasn't as excited about the Olympics as I'd been as a child. Back then it had been easy to believe the speeches about peace and goodwill. I still had a good dose of the armchair athlete in me, and I hoped Toni Väärä would achieve his dream. He and his coach were headed to the south of Spain right after Ristiluoma's memorial. The camp would last three months, although Koskelo would return to Finland occasionally and spend Christmas with his family. But Väärä would spend the whole three months in Spain.

"We're going to live in a small mountain town with hardly any other Finns," he told me as we were exchanging news after the formal portion of the memorial. "Actually, I wanted to ask you something. Would you mind stepping out onto the balcony with me?"

I grabbed my coat, and we went outside. The wind was bracing that high up, and I saw a lone sailboat disappear behind the shelter of the islands. I vaguely remembered a sailing trip ten years ago, in a boat that wasn't my own, with the entirely wrong man, and I realized that the memory wasn't painful anymore. I was able to leave behind more than just the Espoo Police Department.

"When we were talking . . . When you were at my apartment in Turku . . ." Väärä tripped over his words, so I knew this had something to do with his sexual orientation. "You said you knew a family with four kids and two sets of parents, two men and two women. Is that true?"

"Yes. I can give you their phone number, if you want. They're nice people and active in the Rainbow Families movement."

"I told the girl my parents chose for me that I can't get engaged to her. I've thought about it a lot, because I really do want kids of my own. But marrying her would be cruel, because I could never have the same feelings for her as I did for Janne."

"Have you seen him again?"

"No. I'm not ready for dating and all the talk it would cause. For the next few years, I'm going to concentrate on running." Väärä smiled shyly, and I patted him on the shoulder.

"In Turku you said that if we'd lived forty years ago, you would have been considered a criminal, and it would have been my job to arrest you. In some ways the world is moving in a better direction."

"Maybe. If only I could get my parents to understand. Ilpo promised to talk to them, but I'm not ready for that either. Maybe they'll accept me once I've won a Euro Championship medal or something."

"A lot of people have different ideas about God and his requirements than your parents do, Toni." I wanted to tell him that he had every right to expect his parents to love him exactly as he was, without having to achieve something big or deny his own sexuality, but I'd be wasting my breath. He would have to realize that for himself.

As Leena and I were leaving the memorial, Hillevi asked if she could catch a ride. We waited in the parking lot while she had a cigarette. She was happy, because Jouni Litmanen had violated his restraining order on his very first furlough, and that meant he wouldn't automatically qualify for parole after serving half of his sentence. Hillevi talked a lot about Miikka Harju, and I got the impression she was visiting him nearly every day. She liked taking care of people, and now she seemed to think she could help Harju recover and keep him sober. Maybe it would work. He needed forgiveness, and Hillevi was prepared to offer it.

"My last name is Karjula now, by the way. I took back my maiden name," she said as we were dropping her off.

That night I went to the Flatfeet band practice. We had gigs lined up for the Espoo Police Violent Crime Unit Christmas party and the Helsinki

Narcotics Unit Christmas party. Söderholm thought we should add a couple of new covers to our repertoire, because he and Montonen hadn't had time to write any new material. Our bassist, Pasi Ropponen, never commented on set list choices. He just played whatever he was told to.

"We should at least do Juice's "Police Academy," Söderholm said. "I can sing it. But let's do some classical music too."

"What the hell?" Montonen exclaimed, but I guessed that Söderholm only meant an album called *Classical Music* by the Rehtorit. I was right.

"'I Know Everything,' isn't as obvious a choice as that one from Juice, I know. I think it will work for us, though, since we know everything too. Let's listen to it." Söderholm put the album on. He put a match in his mouth to chew, since smoking wasn't allowed in our practice space.

"That's fine, but do you even have the sheet music?" Montonen asked after the song was done.

"What, can't you play by ear?" Söderholm passed handwritten words and chords to Montonen and me. "But as you may have noticed, this is for a female vocalist. Maria should sing it."

I stared dumbfounded at my bandmates. I'd sung backup vocal before, but I wasn't a soloist, and I never would be. We'd agreed on that from the start.

"Good idea! At least try," Ropponen said when he saw my expression.

"Don't worry, we'll tell you to shut up if it sounds terrible! Come one, let's go through the rhythm and melody a few times and then add the words."

Even though I was among friends, singing still made me nervous. It wasn't horrible, though. I started to get a feel for it by the third round with the words and the guitar solo. When we reached the chorus, I belted with gusto, reminding us that you never leave a friend, and all you have to know is who loves you and what record is playing.

The most important things were just that simple.

ABOUT THE AUTHOR

Photo © 2011 Tomas Whitehouse

Leena Lehtolainen was born in Vesanto, Finland, to parents who taught language and literature. At the age of ten, she began her first book—a young adult novel—and published it two years later, followed by a second book at the age of seventeen. The author of the long-running bestselling Maria Kallio Mystery series, Leena has received numerous awards, including the 1997 Vuoden Johtolanka (Clue) Award for the best Finnish crime novel and the Great Finnish Book Club prize in 2000. Her work has been published in twenty-nine languages. Besides writing, Leena enjoys classical singing, her beloved cats, and—her greatest passion—figure skating. Her nonfiction book about the sport, *The Enchantment of Figure Skating*, was chosen as the Sport Book of the Year 2011 in Finland. Leena lives in Finland with her husband and two sons.

ABOUT THE TRANSLATOR

Photo © 2015 Aaron Turley

Owen F. Witesman is a professional literary translator with a master's in Finnish and Estonian-area studies and a PhD in public affairs from Indiana University. He has translated dozens of Finnish books into English, including novels, children's books, poetry, plays, graphic novels, and nonfiction. His recent translations include the first nine novels in the Maria Kallio series, the dark family drama *Norma* by Sofi Oksanen, and *Oneiron* by Laura Lindstedt, 2015 winner of the Finlandia Prize for Literature. He currently resides in Springville, Utah, with his wife, three daughters, one son, two dogs, a cat, five chickens, and twenty-nine fruit trees.